Praise for SAVANNAH ROYALS

"Barrett's sexy feminist novel takes readers on a twisty, dark, and delicious ride through the glittering highs and gritty lows of 1919 Savannah. Kat is a perfectly imperfect heroine, who will steal readers' hearts as easily as she'd lift their jewels, having them on the edge of their seats rooting for her page after thrilling page. This novel had me in its thrall from the first sentence and has not let me go, even after the last."
—Jess Armstrong, *USA Today* bestselling author of the Ruby Vaughn Mysteries

"An intoxicating blend of passion, survival, and instinct, with an unforgettably ambitious heroine. *Savannah Royals* takes you on a sultry journey from the Georgia bayou, with a cast of masterfully flawed characters living on the fringes, to the decadent Jekyll Island ballrooms of old-money privilege. Like a Prohibition-era Becky Sharpe, sly and cunning Kat navigates—and manipulates—both worlds with ease. I could not put this novel down."
—Paulette Kennedy, bestselling author of *The Artist of Blackberry Grange*

"In *Savannah Royals*, Lindsay Barrett has created a sexy and suspenseful thrill ride of a historical romance. From the breezy glitz of southern high society to the roiling tumult of the Catacombs, I

couldn't turn these pages fast enough. There's so much to love: Kat's greedy, striving heart, Matthew's delectable swoon and gut-wrenching goodness, and a whole host of well-drawn, morally gray thieves who kept me guessing until the *very* end. Barrett seamlessly weaves both glorious romance and walloping suspense. An absolutely refreshing, delicious read from start to finish."
—Erin Langston, *New York Times* celebrated author of *Forever Your Rogue*

"Barrett has delivered a steamy and high-stakes romp through jazz-age Savannah, with a perfectly imperfect conwoman, her gang of thieves, and their irresistible mark. The perfect blend of romance, intrigue, and historical detail. SAVANNAH ROYALS is an absolute delight."
—Jenny Adams, author of *A Deadly Endeavor*

SAVANNAH ROYALS

A Savannah Wolves Heist Novel

LINDSAY BARRETT

Cover design by Austin Drake | Bottle Cap Creative

Edited by Rachel Shipp

Paperback ISBN: 979-8-9925012-0-9

E-book ISBN: 979-8-9925012-1-6

To the eighteen-year-old girl who wanted to be a writer but wasn't yet brave enough to fight for that dream.

To that girl who always believed. Who never stopped writing.

Fifteen years later—

We did it.

PROLOGUE

Savannah, 1904

WHEN I WAS SIX years old, I became a wolf.

It happened when I found my mom on the concrete floor of our tiny slice of privacy in the Catacombs. We'd discovered the crevice between the walls almost six months prior and had held our ground there ever since. The Catacombs were full of twisting paths and secret inlets like ours, but they were also full of people. Desperate people.

And there was always someone waiting to take what was yours.

You see, beneath the bustling commercial streets of Savannah lay a secret. A dirty one. A place where dreams came to die, dampened and smothered by labyrinthine limestone walls. Walls that once bore witness to the hidden underdealings of the Savannah slave trade and now, some fifty years later, still hid a battered people. Battered by falling dust motes from trundling overhead streetcars. Battered by rumbling bellies and arthritic backs, hardened by nights curled on stone floors. Battered and buried beneath a lifetime of futile choices.

Because what glittered aboveground could rot below.

Savannah was rotting.

That morning began like any other. My mother had been gone—off on one of her benders—for almost two days, and I was returning from scavenging for food in the alleys of the riverside bayou district. It was time-consuming work, sneaking and creeping through pebbled offshoots and crevices in the Catacombs, doubling back to ensure I wasn't followed.

This was the life of a gutter rat. A life where the most valuable things I owned were the breath in my lungs and the blood in my veins. Unfortunately, blood was spilled daily beneath the streets of Savannah.

My mother's voice echoed in my mind. *Children shouldn't be seen in the Catacombs, Kat. If they can't see you, they'll never catch you.*

When I finally returned home...well, that was when I found my mom. She was face down on the concrete, her matted red hair fanned out around her.

"Mom." I shook her bony shoulder, hoping she was alert enough to help me flip her over this time. "Mama," I whined again, shaking harder. She was very stiff. I stepped back, biting my lip and reaching for her arm. It was ice cold beneath my fingers.

My eyes widened as I backed away, all the way until my spine hit limestone. I sank to my knees and wrapped my arms around my legs.

It was there that Paul found me—minutes, hours, possibly days later.

"Kat!" He grabbed my arm with his slender fingers, his boyish voice cracking with fear. "Kat, we gotta go. There's a raid." He tried to pull me to my feet, casting a sidelong glance at my mom on the floor.

I reared back. "Leave me alone, Paul."

"Kat, you can't stay here. We have to move!"

I could hear footsteps now, pounding in the tunnel just beyond our crevice. I looked at my mom, then back at Paul, afraid. "I'm not leaving my mom."

Paul let out a string of expletives rather impressive for a nine-year-old before letting me go. I narrowed my eyes in annoyance; I always reminded him gentlemen don't curse. He always told me it was a damn good thing he wasn't a gentleman then.

Paul stepped over to my mom and turned her head to the side. His sharp eyes tracked the powder beneath her nose, the empty snuffboxes and tonic bottles on the ground. His fingers gently probed the side of her neck, searching.

"Kat..." His gaze was kind when it landed on me.

I put my fingers in my ears. I didn't want to hear him say it, and I certainly didn't want his kindness. Not right now.

"What's this?" a voice called from the alleyway. "Stop! I found something."

There was rustling at the entry crevice now. A smattering of loose pebbles and dust cascaded from the ceiling where the man was probing. Even in the dim light, I could see the tips of his fingers reaching into our space.

Into our *home*.

Paul crossed the floor on silent feet and grabbed my hand. He pulled me up so fast and hard, my shoulder wrenched in its socket. Pressing a finger to my lips, Paul shook his head. He dragged me across the tiny space to another crack in the wall, a tiny, dead-end hollow. Just narrow enough to conceal two cowering, malnourished kids. Paul pushed me in first, then followed. I was smaller, so I crouched down silently, peering around Paul's legs. That's when I noticed the pocketknife clutched in his hand.

I held my breath as two sets of feet strode into our lair.

"Aw hell, what's this?" A foot kicked my mom, nudging her.

"She dead?"

"As a doornail," the first man confirmed.

My stomach lurched, a howl strangling in my throat. Paul grabbed a tuft of my hair, winding his fist in tight to keep me silent. With every breath, sulfuric damp and grit filled my nose. Like rotten eggs.

"Fucking waste of a woman. She's young and look at that hair—we could've made a fortune off her."

"Fellas don't pay shit for dope-fiends. You know that. Check the snuffboxes, see if there's any powder left."

"Empty. Figures." One set of footsteps started walking away. "Look, there's something in the corner." He bent down and picked up Mr. Wiggles. I'd left the toy bear by the wall where I'd sunk down so many hours earlier. Paul's grip tightened again.

"Think she had a brat?"

"I don't see one."

"If the kid has half a brain, they've scampered. Orphanage has too many mouths, and everyone knows it."

"If she's got that red hair, she'll be better off at the orphanage than down here."

"True." The man dropped Mr. Wiggles, and I let out a quiet breath. They were leaving.

We waited in silence for almost ten minutes before Paul released his grip on me.

"I don't want to go to the orphanage, Paul," I whispered. "I don't have to go, right? I don't have Mama's red hair. I'll be safe here."

"You don't have to go anywhere, Kitty-Kat. You can come with me."

"Can Mr. Wiggles come too?"

"Sure." Paul walked over to pick up the bear. "But we need to go now, before another round of raids comes. Can you be quiet and brave? Can you be a wolf, Kitty-Kat?"

"Yes," I said proudly. Playing wolves was one of our favorite games.

Paul's hideout wasn't far from the entrance to the Combs, but it was hard to reach. You had to crawl upward to a side alcove, then through a crack in the ceiling. Paul had been there for as long as I'd known him.

"Home sweet home," he crowed, dragging me into his den.

I was surprised to see two boys, dirty and displaced, huddled together inside.

"Mierda! Who the hell is this, Paul?" one of them asked, jumping to his feet. He spoke with an accent, but it was hard to say where from. You could find all sorts in the Combs.

"Tony, this is Katarina," Paul said. "She needs a place to stay."

"Kat," I corrected.

"She sure as hell ain't staying here." Tony crossed his golden-brown arms. "No girls allowed in the pack."

"My pack, my rules," Paul said. "You don't like it, you can leave."

"I ain't leavin'. I was here first," Tony argued. "Come on Paul, she's a *girl*...and a gringa, to boot! She'll be useless. Deadweight."

"You're so dumb, Tony." High color rose in Paul's pale cheeks as he stormed over to the boy and poked him in the chest. Hard. "In a couple of years, she's gonna be worth fifty of you."

"We'll see about that." Tony slumped back to the ground. With narrowed eyes, he nodded sharply and pointed at me. "You can share Paul's corner. Don't come anywhere near mine."

"Four corners, four people," I told him, proud of myself for counting. "I'll take my own, thank you very much."

And with as much dignity as I could muster, I clutched my bear to my chest, tipped my nose in the air, and pranced over to the empty spot.

Paul stifled a laugh. "She's something, ain't she?"

"Yeah. She's...something," Tony muttered.

"I think she's a wolf." The third boy finally spoke. He was lanky with black skin and big, hollow eyes. Deep shadows were etched in the somber lines of his face. "Look at her dark hair. She's a wolf," he continued. "Just like us."

"Welcome to the Wolfpack, Kitty-Kat." Paul tossed me a bruised apple.

"Whoa." I snatched the fruit out of the air. "Where'd you get this?"

The boys all laughed.

"We get whatever we want, whenever we want," Tony said. "We're *reyes*—kings. Royals."

"We'll teach you how to get whatever you want too," Paul promised.

I smiled at the three dark-haired boys, liking the sound of that very much. I took a big bite of the apple, licking the juice from my fingers, not wanting to waste a drop.

That's the moment I became a wolf.

Wolves, you see, are always hungry, and even at just six years old, I was *famished*.

CHAPTER ONE

Savannah, 1919

THE TINKLING OF CHINA teacups and high-pitched peals of girlish laughter are almost more than I can bear. My head is positively pounding. The morning sunlight streaming through thick glass windows has pushed me into a seat at a corner table, deep in shadow.

Which—who am I jesting?—is where I prefer to be at these trivial events. I sag slightly in the corset under my morning gown, but Headmistress Helena's hawk eyes land on me. I right myself, crossing my legs at the ankle beneath the table. For good measure, I paste on a soft, bland smile. The headmistress gives a curt nod before moving on.

I sigh and relax my posture again. I'm coming off another long night with the Royals—publicly known and feared as the Wolfpack—casing Astor Manor for the umpteenth time.

How many more nights we gonna do this, Paul? Tony asked, flipping his dark hair.

As long as it takes. We'll only get one shot.

My eyes track my classmates as they mingle through the brightly lit tearoom. They swarm the visiting young men like bees to a honeycomb, their buzz a bit louder than usual because the entire trifecta is here—the eligible sons of the Morgan, Astor, and DaMolin families. Three American dynasties under one roof.

It's a feeding frenzy here today, I muse, fanning myself in my corner. Lionesses on the hunt.

But with just under a year left at Telfair Academy, a premier boarding and collegiate finishing school for young ladies of the American South, I suppose I understand why.

I absentmindedly drum my fingers as Florence Vanderbilt, head bitch in our class, gabs at the blond guy. They're a perfect pair, both yellow-haired and blue-eyed. A matching set of Anglo porcelain dolls. She laughs coquettishly at something he says and rests her hand on his forearm. His gaze flickers briefly to her hand, then away. I chuckle to myself, amused by both her transparency and his disinterest.

"Miss Quinn." Headmistress Helena is back. "Why don't you talk to some of the young men? It's one of the first open houses of the season, and—"

"I shall. I'm just taking a short respite," I reply, trying to shut her lecture down before she can really pick up steam.

"I understand you're very fulfilled by your apprenticeship with Raymond," she begins carefully, tucking a lock of salt-and-pepper hair behind her ear.

"Yes, ma'am." I lift my hand to examine the many rings on my fingers, all but one crafted by my own hands in the back room of Ray's jewelry shop.

"But you should take advantage of *every* opportunity the Academy offers," she says, undeterred.

"Perchance not every opportunity is right for every lady." I narrow my eyes.

She laughs. "Pray tell, Katarina, how would you even know, sitting here, sulking in the corner?"

I don't deign to respond. After all, I can hardly tell her I already have someone waiting for me. Someone I sneak out to see half the nights of the week while the other girls sleep in their feathery beds, virginal and blissfully unaware. Dreams of sugarplums and fairy dust and rich boys have never been my own. It's the adrenaline-filled rush of a good con and a stolen moment in the dead of the night I crave.

With Paul.

"You might be surprised, Katarina. You think you have it all figured out, that you already know where you're headed, but you shouldn't ignore the opportunities around you for the sake of stubbornness."

With that, the headmistress takes her leave.

I try to hide my annoyance. It's not like I always *sulk in the corner*. I've been plenty sociable in the past. My position here is invaluable. I've met dozens of marks at these parties, relayed countless inside tips to Paul. It's why he planted me here in the first place, finagling my interview with his silver tongue three years ago.

Infiltrate their ranks, Kat, he told me. *You become one of them, then we become one of them. Just think what we can do, working from the inside.*

He was right. Paul's tenacity and cunning nature have combined with my newfound status and skills to open doors ushering the Wolfpack into a golden era. Today, my Royals are the premier, most feared gang ever to transcend the bayou. The first to reach the upper crest of Savannah society. Everyone knows the Wolfpack now.

We keep our operation small, just the four of us. No leaks. No loose lips. As our leader, Paul's reputation is relatively well known, but very, very few know his face. Even fewer know mine—the notorious Cat Burglar—or Abe's or Tony's. We stay invisible, secretly and obsessively controlling every aspect of every job. It's quality over quantity that sets us apart. The quality of the heist itself, the quality of the loot. Selectivity is the name of the game.

It is, oddly enough, the same principle many of my classmates apply to screening their future prospects. The bigger the fish, the better. I admire the irony as my fellow fourth-years continue swarming the trifecta.

I brush cool fingers across my pounding head. I'm just not up for it. Not today, when we're less than a month away from hitting our biggest mark yet. Not today, when I'm so exhausted I can hardly—

"You look like you could use this almost as much as I can," a voice interrupts my thoughts.

I drop my hand to my lap and snap my eyes up. Big fish.

It's one of the trifecta. The blond guy Florence was just gabbing up. I furtively slide my gaze across the room, and sure enough, she's watching him closely.

"I'll make you a deal," the man continues. "I'll give you this"—he waves a china teacup under my nose—"if you let me hide here with you for ten minutes."

"I don't particularly like tea."

"It's not tea."

He smiles, and despite myself, I'm intrigued. It's a world-class smile. The kind that stops traffic.

"It's French espresso."

"Where'd you get *that*?" I lean forward, doubly intrigued now.

"The kitchens. They've been sneaking me treats since I learned where to get them two decades ago. Just don't rat me out to my mom, okay?"

I follow his head bob to our benefactress, Lady Genevieve DaMolin. She and Headmistress Helena are thick as thieves, but Lady Genevieve calls the shots. It's *her* name that's ultimately synonymous with Telfair.

"I see." I nod. "So you're from...the DaMolin family, then?"

A strange flicker crosses his face, but he nods. I continue running my gaze over him, my brow furrowing as I try to remember his name. The two other members of the trifecta I know quite well.

Target: Daniel Dufour, age twenty-two. Grandson of the late, great, interminably wealthy financier J.P. Morgan. Undergraduate business studies degree from Harvard. Founding family of the elite Jekyll Island Club, the most exclusive society for millionaires in the world, just off the coast of Georgia. Marriage status: eligible, highly eligible.

Target: Harrison "Harry" Astor, age twenty-six. Recent West Point graduate, risen to the rank of major in the Great War. Nephew of the tragically deceased John Jacob Astor, lost to us just a few years ago in the sinking of the RMS Titanic. Family are real estate tycoons with holdings up and down the East Coast, including the pertinently noteworthy Astor Manor at 447 Bull Street, Savannah, Georgia. Marriage status: eligible, highly eligible.

But this one, this DaMolin fella, isn't here often. He looks a little different too. His hair is slightly longer than most men wear theirs, waving over his ears to the nape of his neck. Not perfectly tamed and manicured.

I cast around the back of my mind for his name. I'm certain I've talked to him before. I must have. Once or twice. Probably.

"I'm Matthew," he finally offers, putting me out of my misery. "Matthew DaMolin."

"Katarina Quinn," I reply. And because I do want that espresso, I kick out a chair with my foot. "Sit, I'll hide you."

"Thanks." He slides one of his two teacups to me before taking a big gulp from his own. After he swallows, he leans back to rest his head against the wall. He closes his eyes, his lashes casting dark shadows in the hollows beneath his lids.

I know why I'm so tired, but why is he?

I bite my tongue. Asking a question would invite conversation. And inviting conversation could lead to banter. And from banter, it's on to flirting...and that's just not a journey I'm interested in taking this morning.

"I beg your pardon." He lifts his head and turns guiltily. "I'm being terribly rude, aren't I? Where are you from, Miss Katarina?"

"You're not rude." I almost laugh at him. Almost. "You're tired, I'm tired. We can just sit together." *Quietly.*

"Why are you tired?"

"I don't know, Mr. DaMolin." I slip the tiniest bit of suggestion into my tone, just enough to, hopefully, do the trick. "Why are you?"

"Because I worked last night at the hospital. I'm a physician. So for the record, it's either Matthew or Dr. DaMolin. Preferably Matthew, but you may take your pick."

"Oh." That clams me right up.

Being a physician is a good job, but it's notoriously brutal. Not only do you have to be smart, but the hours are long. Sometimes excruciatingly so. They do decently well for their families, but it's hard work. And it's certainly not the usual position men who visit the Academy strive for. The majority label themselves as businessmen, entrepreneurs, or for the truly elite, philanthropists. All of which is code for "my family is rich, and I am too."

Well, not *everyone*. Perhaps I'm being harsh. Plenty of middle-class gentlemen mingle with us, but they aren't big fish. Not like this guy.

"I told you mine, now let's hear yours." He smiles faintly, waiting.

"I suppose you won't believe me if I say I was training to be a nurse and also worked the night shift?"

"Mmm, not quite. My mother makes sure I know which women apprentice at the hospital. Just in case I magically decide to show interest."

I can't help myself. "If you're not interested," I say, taking a demure sip of coffee, "what are you doing here?"

"I make an effort to attend events when I can because it's important to my mother."

"I see." I narrow my eyes at him, trying to ascertain his real motive.

"You don't believe me?" He laughs and leans closer, like a confidant. "Just watch. In approximately five seconds, her eyes are going to slip over here, tracking me down."

I wait, shifting discreetly to look at Lady Genevieve.

"Three...two..."

Her gaze lands on us. It flickers between Matthew and me, close together in our private corner. She offers her son a hopeful little smile, then a tiny wave.

I let out a sound halfway between "oh" and "aw" at the naked optimism in her eyes.

"You think that's good, shall we give her the thrill of the century? Take a turn outside with me." He pushes back from the table and offers me his arm.

He's been a nice distraction, quite unexpected, but Florence is still watching. Not only her scornful eyes but also the hopeful ones of Headmistress Helena and Lady Genevieve are on me. I hesitate, weighing my options.

I don't make a habit of poking the bear that is Florence Vanderbilt—I understand the game, and I'm far from stupid—but I've been disappointing the headmistress every other day lately. And relationships are all about currency exchange.

Without further ado, I grace him with a sparkling smile and slide my arm through his. "Lead the way."

IF I THOUGHT THE sunlight streaming through the tearoom windows had been abusive, I'm wholly unprepared for the onslaught of the real thing as we promenade outside. I close my eyes momentarily. My free hand strays to my twinging head.

Matthew guides me to the edge of the brick terrace. "I've always loved the gardens at the Academy."

"Yes, they're beautiful," I murmur.

When we reach the wrought iron railing, he releases my arm and leans forward. We're quiet for a few moments, gazing over the sunken courtyard. It's ringed by blue and purple hydrangea bushes and shaded beneath a cluster of ageless oaks, dripping with Spanish moss.

My muscles unkink as we listen to the bubbling fountain, a trinity of dancing cherubs with water spouting from their mouths and fingers. Sunshine warms my face. Impulsively, I lean on the railing next to Matthew, sagging into the bones of my corset.

He glances at me but doesn't say anything.

"The sun feels good," I admit, extending my hands over the open air, stretching and letting light leach into my pores.

His gaze lingers, taking stock of my many rings.

"Curiouser and curiouser." He turns around, resting elbows and forearms on the railing, his long legs comfortably stretched out. A sliver of suspenders comes into view as his jacket falls open. "The questions are mounting up, Miss Katarina."

"What questions?"

"Where are you from? What were you doing last night? Are you a pirate?" He nods toward my bejeweled fingers as he asks the last one.

I don't want to acknowledge the first question, and I certainly don't want to answer the second, so I settle for the third. "Would you be intrigued if I were? Is that your type—bohemian? Infidel? Nomad, perhaps?"

"Not even a little bit." He raises his eyebrows in amusement and smiles. "But then again, renegades and grifters aren't part of my standard social circle."

Hmm, then you really wouldn't like my answer to your second question.

In lieu of addressing the irony, I turn the tables. "What about you then?"

"What about me?"

I slip into the mundanely predictable shoptalk. "Where were you educated?"

"Vanderbilt. I graduated from their medical school three years past."

Ah, there it is.

All the old money families are connected. No doubt it's how he knows Florence. I bet her father personally stamped his acceptance to medical school.

I must not hide my distaste because Matthew's follow-up is prompt. "Do you dislike Vanderbilt? I mean, it's no Harvard, but—"

"Vanderbilt is lovely." I offer nothing more. Brevity is truly the most excellent bait.

"But...?" Matthew looks at me.

"But nothing. Harvard is overrated. Harvard men are a dime a dozen, are they not?"

He tips his head back and laughs, the sound ringing through the empty garden. A weeping cluster of Spanish moss billows softly, perhaps on the breath of his laugh. "Now there's an independent thought if ever I've heard one. Please, tell me more."

A quick shiver runs up my spine. *Challenge accepted.*

"Let me see...the DaMolin family." I tap a finger against my lip in mock scrutiny. "Distant relations to Queen Victoria, but close enough to have been gifted heirloom treasures...rubies, I believe? Crafted into a necklace?" A spectacular necklace, to be precise, worth more than the sum of everything I've ever stolen in my life. The very thought has my sticky fingers tingling. "What were you, first cousins?"

"Second," he grunts. "But that was lifetimes ago. That necklace is on its third generation now."

"Fascinating. Old English turned new American in the 1800s. Subsequent fortune made in the news and publishing industries, supported by aggressive investments. And yet you—a newly minted *physician*—forsake the hallowed Harvard...not interested in the hotsy-totsy cleavage parade inside—"

"Hotsy-totsy cleavage parade?" He chortles again.

"You have a better name for them?"

"I merely find the reference to be of prescient irony." He nods at my corset-enhanced bustline.

Hook, line, sinker. "So you *are* interested? Or at least noticing?"

"Come on." He shakes his head. "That's not fair."

I smile deviously. "Who said I play fair?"

"You're a piece of work, aren't you?" He finally looks away from me, but he's grinning. "So that's it? You think you've got me all figured out?"

"Oh, bless your heart." I toss more chum in the water. "I'm just getting started."

He looks back to me. "Very well, enlighten me."

"You work long hours at a thankless job you don't need, so either you have a savior complex or you're compensating for something. Youngest child—"

"I never told you that," he interrupts.

"No, but I remember it now." I tap my lip again. "Youngest child, second born son...successful older brother groomed to take over the family business...yes...definitely a compensation complex, no doubt about it. Did Mommy and Daddy not love you enough?"

"Okay, Freud. I think we'll call it there." He rises from the railing, no longer amused.

I mock pout. "Is our game over? It's just turning dilly."

"It really is. Perhaps it's my turn now?"

A challenge in his eyes grabs my attention. It's wholly unexpected, a deviation from the usual song and dance.

I chew the inside of my cheek. Part of me wonders what he'll say; another part doesn't want to care.

Curiosity wins out. "Sure."

"Well, let's see..." He begins to tick off his fingers. "You didn't know who I was when I came to your table, which is unusual, to say the least. You've successfully dodged nearly every question I've asked. And you're a fourth-year like the others in there, right?"

I nod.

"So together, that means you've got your ducks in a row. You've got some poor sap in your sights, and by year-end, you'll have a big sparkling diamond on your finger. Then you'll move to a sprawling house in the country and make lots of pretty babies. Am I right?"

"Actually, you couldn't possibly be more wrong," I answer, annoyed by his shallow appraisal.

"Shocking! A superficial assessment based on assumptions and stereotypes is *wrong*?" He looks deliberately at me.

I smile, only a little contrite. "You're clever. It's fun."

"Yeah, it's been a gas." He runs a hand through his blond hair as he takes a step back.

But because I understand people—especially men—all too well, I step forward to close the distance between us.

"You liked it," I tell him.

"Maybe I did." His smile is coming back, mirth brewing in his blue eyes. "But only a little."

"You can't check off the standard boxes with me, like you do with the others." I jerk my head toward the tearoom. "And it kills you to not have me all figured out. It's part of your complex, remember?"

He's silent, listening, watching me closely. Riveted.

Predictable.

"I'm bored," I say. "I'm going inside. You can watch my backside as I walk away, I won't mind."

I hear his surprised laughter, but I don't look back. I don't need to.

He calls out just before I slip inside. "For what it's worth, my mom and dad loved me plenty growing up. And my 'successful' older brother is a piece of work. Just like you."

Eating from the palm of my hand.

CHAPTER TWO

THE FOURTH-YEAR OPEN HOUSE concludes just before noon, leaving my afternoon free. I trot back to my bedroom suite after the last guest departs, seeking to exchange the stifling, antiquated morning gown for something more comfortable. When I reach the door, my roommate Melinda is at my heels.

"What're you gonna do with the rest of the day, Kat?" She's practically breathing down my neck.

"Going, Mellie. What am I *going* to do with the rest of the day," I tirelessly correct her, just like I always do. "Christ, Mellie, we're *fourth-years*."

"Sorry." Her cheeks turn pink. "What are you going to do this afternoon, Kat?"

I open the door and walk away as I answer. "First, I'm going to get out of this corset—"

"Swell idea. Me too."

"Then I'll likely swing by Raymond's to do some work," I conclude, as if she hadn't interrupted. My fingers itch at the thought of my latest project, dreamed up by my own mind for a change, not Ray's or Paul's.

"You work too much," Melinda mutters. "Seriously, Kat. We've got an afternoon off. Let's do something *fun*."

"Your job at the bakery isn't fun?" I slip halfway out of my gown, reach behind my back, and with a flick of my wrist, I send the laces of my corset tumbling. It's a trick I learned long before coming to the Academy from many a quick-change with the Royals.

It's one Mellie, however, has yet to master. She's got her hands behind her waist, contorting every which way to reach the laces. Her cheeks puff pink with exertion. I wait, somewhat impatiently, until she caves and exposes the bindings to me. I cross the room to undo them.

"Thanks," she mumbles.

I return to my side and pull out a chemise and one of the Academy-sanctioned uniforms, a maroon sheath dress with a Peter Pan collar. I tug them over my head, one after the other, as my morning gown drops from my waist to the floor. Silk charmeuse pools around my feet. After a cursory glance in the mirror, I head for the door.

"Wait!"

I look back to see Mellie still working her way out of her corset. Her taffeta gown sits in a tangled heap around her ankles.

I stifle a laugh. "Goodbye, Mellie."

As I close the door behind me, she shouts, "If you think I'm gonna hang up your morning gown, you got another think coming, sister."

Going to, Mellie. Going.

I'd make excuses for her, but we're fourth-years now, like I told her. I don't care if she was raised on a plantation farm in the boondocks of Georgia—I was raised in the Catacombs, for Christ's sake! Elocution and grammar lessons began on day one, and by now, it should really be second nature.

I step into the sunshine and make my habitual strides to the streetcar stop. My job at Raymond's is less than a ten-minute ride to downtown Savannah.

Or a twenty-minute walk. I look up at the shining September sun, deliberating.

Most days, I'm rushing from class or lessons to my Academy-sponsored apprenticeship. I rarely have the luxury of walking. Today, the entire afternoon stretches out before me, and Ray isn't expecting me. I redirect my legs, heading for the brick sidewalk.

I'm about halfway to Raymond's when someone falls into step beside me. I don't need to look to know who. Our strides naturally synchronize, coaxing a secret smile to my lips.

"Hey, Kitty-Kat."

The timbre of his voice washes over me. I fight a shiver.

"Hey," I whisper back.

"You're walking today."

"I am. Which, clearly, you anticipated." I shouldn't be surprised. Paul always knows exactly where to find me. He's magic like that. Fairy-born, we call him. Appeared in the dark of the night as a baby on the orphanage's steps and vanished just the same a few years later, straight into life as an urchin in the Catacombs. Where he met me.

Paul tips his head to the sky and smiles. Black, whiskered scruff dusts his upper neck and cheeks. I can just make out the edge of a tattoo, the barest hint peeking out from beneath the collar of his shirt.

"It's a beautiful day," he observes. "And what do beautiful girls do on beautiful days? Well, one particular beautiful girl, that is."

"Slick. You woo all the ladies with that mouth?"

"Just one." Quick as lightning, he grabs my hand and yanks, pulling me into an alley.

"Paul," I whisper-hiss, "be careful. I'm in my Academy uniform." I glance back to the street, checking for onlookers.

"I'm always careful, you know that."

He pins me against a soot-speckled brick wall and presses his lips to mine. My resistance melts.

Nobody in the whole world kisses like Paul. Women could spend their entire lives searching, and they'd never find a kiss like his. Pure, undiluted molten fire.

"It's been four days," Paul rumbles, pressing his hard crotch into me.

"Maybe it wouldn't"—I move my lips over his—"have been four days"—more kisses—"if you didn't have us running stakeouts...every other night."

"Stay with me tonight."

"I can't."

"Yes. You can." He moves his lips to the hollow spot on my neck, just beneath my ear.

"Paul," I murmur, "I'm worn slap out. I'm *sleeping* tonight."

"With me. You're sleeping *with me* tonight."

I lean back and laugh, resting my head on the warm bricks. "You're incorrigible."

His grin is wolfish and endearing. "Would you really have me any other way?"

"No," I admit.

Because I love how impulsive he is. How he always finds me. How he sees what he wants, whatever he wants, and he takes it. No second thoughts. No hesitation.

"I need to go to work," I tell him. "You know, so I can move *your* contraband."

"It's a dirty job, doll." He sneaks in one more kiss at the side of my mouth as I drift toward the street. "But somebody's gotta do it."

When I glance back, he's already gone.

"RAY?"

I bang open the back door of the shop. My gaze sweeps the workroom, passing over Ray's empty station and mine. The desk and overhead lights are off.

He must be out on the floor.

Moving from the back room to the front is like crossing worlds through a magic portal. The lighting turns brilliant, the walls stark, crisp white. Glass cases run the length of the room, surfaces warm from the heat of overhead spotlights. Black velvet abounds. Gemstones sparkle.

When I poke my head out, Ray is with a customer. He waves me over. "Perfect timing, kid."

I hate working the floor, but I answer his summons. The buyer, a brunette in her late forties, ogles my uniform with delight. "Oh, you're an Academy girl? My Mabel just started there last month."

I smile politely.

"Is this your apprenticeship?" She needs no encouragement and looks around the jewelry shop with interest. "Certainly a prestigious one."

"Yes, I'm very lucky. Raymond's work is truly a cut above the rest."

"Oh, indeed. He's simply premier, in a league of his own." She positively trills with excitement. "I can only hope to see Mabel doing something like this in a few years."

"I'm sure she will," I murmur, glancing down at the glass case. I blink twice when I notice the marquise-cut emerald earrings laid out before us.

Ray meets my eyes, a knowing flicker passing between us.

"Well now, aren't these divine?" I gesture at the earrings.

"Do you think so?" The woman considers them. "I simply can't make up my mind between these two pairs."

There's a second set of earrings on the counter, but I'm zeroed in on the first.

Target acquired.

"The marquise cut is so unique and elegant," I say to her. "They're a standout piece. The only one like it in the whole store."

"Really?"

"Would you like to try them on?" I bend over to pull out a mirror.

"May I?" She looks to Ray.

"Of course, madam."

We let her tinker in front of the mirror for a few moments before I pounce, hungry for the kill.

"Stunning," I pronounce. "Simply stunning. They bring out the hazel in your eyes."

"Hmm...yes...they really do. You know, my Mabel has bright green eyes, like yours...don't know where she got them...but you're right, these are stunning. One day, they'll likely be hers." She grins in the mirror. "I'll take them."

"Wonderful." Ray is all smiles as he rings her up.

I wait until she leaves before releasing a nervous laugh.

"Well done, kid." Ray claps me on the shoulder. "You're getting a bump in your cut for that. You closed the deal like a pro."

"I can't believe how quickly you moved those. I only finished them last week."

"I never have trouble selling your stuff, Kat. Your work is meticulous, as flawless as the real McCoy. *I* can barely tell the difference between an original and one of your copies, and I've been in the business over forty years."

"Thanks, Ray." I push through the swinging door to the workroom.

My work with Ray is a myriad of things. He holds real estate on a corner lot in the busiest shopping district of downtown Savannah. It's all very hoity-toity; the who's who of high society are all logged customers in his black register book. Anyone who's anyone gets engaged with one of Ray's rings. And anyone who's anyone wears his latest pieces to galas and parties. His front-of-shop reputation is pristine, but he also does a roaring black-market trade out of his back room. Jewelry and other desirables. For those in the know, of course.

Ray has never apprenticed an Academy student before, but Paul was using him as a fence when I enrolled. A little introduction here, a slip to Headmistress Helena about my jewelry interests there...and *boom*, I landed myself in his shop at the start of my second year. It's a cushy arrangement, as far as apprenticeships go. Ray and I have no secrets between us. At first, I was merely a well-placed middleman, passing items from the Royals to Ray, moving cash from Ray back to the Royals. As long as we kept our black-market supply lines open, Ray signed my Academy supervision logs without batting an eye.

But it turned out, I have a lot of empty hours to fill at his shop. Under Ray's tutelage, I discovered I have quite an eye for detail. A superb eye, really. My duties gradually expanded from middleman to shopgirl to jewelry forger.

Our fleecing enterprise had not always been so remote and high profile. During my youngest years with the Royals, the game was, in fact, to simply be invisible. I learned how to walk with a tread lighter than air. How to lift a watch from an unassuming pocket or dangling from a wrist at the produce stalls. How to melt into evening shadows, to stand in plain sight on the busiest of afternoons in the city market...but have no one's eyes land on me at all.

If they can't see you, they'll never catch you...

There's an art to invisibility, so an artist—a *virtuoso*—I became. The memories burn technicolor bright.

"The Kat Burglar strikes again," Paul cawed the memorable day I came home with my first diamond necklace.

I was nine.

"Unbelievable," Tony breathed.

"How're we gonna move *that*?" Abe's eyes were wide.

"Leave it to me." With a smile, Paul snatched up the gems and was gone.

Yes, at first the game was to be invisible, and I was a natural. But then, much to my chagrin, the game started to change. Paul, of course, was the one who told me.

"Kitty-Kat, you're starting to get older now. People are gonna start looking."

"I'm good, Paul. Nobody ever sees me. You know that."

"Kitty-Kat, trust me. Soon you're gonna be impossible to miss." He pulled a strand of my inky hair through his fingers and looked at me. "You're *already* nearly impossible to miss."

That was the first day Paul kissed me.

I was thirteen.

After that day, the game became something else entirely. The game is being *seen*. Seen exactly how and when I want. Seen until the pivotal moment when I decide to disappear. All three boys can do parlor tricks and sleight of hand, but I'm the only one who can sweet talk us into the big leagues.

Don't worry, Mama, I think as I head to my workstation. *They'll still never catch me.*

"I almost forgot to tell you." Ray follows me. "I unloaded something for Paul the other night. Here's the cut."

"Golly, that's a lot of bills." I furrow my brow as I peek inside the envelope. "What did you move? We haven't run a job in weeks."

"Er, just some old odds and ends he had lying around."

"Really?" I lean against my desk, knowing full well Ray is lying. "Must have been some expensive odds and ends."

"I reckon he's been trying to make some extra scratch lately. You only have a few months left at the Academy. Pretty soon, you'll probably need to clear a space on one of your fingers." He nods suggestively at my rings.

I raise my eyebrows and rub my thumb over the signet on my right hand. "Paul already gave me a ring."

He makes a face, looking at me like I'm an idiot.

After a moment, I realize I am.

"Oh!" I glance down at my fingers, specifically the fourth one on my left hand. "Nah. That's not really Paul's style. He's far from the marrying type."

Ray shrugs and walks away. "You know better than me, I suppose. Pass along the cut, will ya?"

When he returns to the floor, I pull out my latest obsession piece for an afternoon of tinkering. It started as a wild daydream, born from a trip to the pictures with Paul to see Theda Bara in *Cleopatra*.

Spellbound. Captivated. That's how I felt watching her sashay about the elaborate set, dripping in gemstones from head to toe, turning the eye of every person in the theater, man and woman alike.

The idea for a multilayered gold, obsidian, and emerald collar showpiece percolated for nearly a year before I began crafting it with my fingers. Inspiration for a matching cobra statement ring struck soon after, an ode to the legend of Cleopatra's grief-stricken suicide by snakebite after the death of her lover, Mark Antony.

The utter deliciousness of an unscheduled afternoon stretches before me, endless time to indulge my wildest artistic fantasies. It's exceedingly rare to not have a project for either Ray or Paul take center stage on my desk, but our only upcoming job is the one at Astor Manor. And I can hardly make a forgery of the solid gold ballerina figurine we're after.

Titled *The Dancer*, the statuette is an Astor family treasure dating to the Italian Renaissance. As reclusive as it is renowned, we have only one grainy black-and-white film negative of the figurine atop a fireplace mantel somewhere in the manor. Paul got his hands on the photograph from a bayou contractor who had recently done interior work at the estate, but the rest of our information is sparse at best.

There are six fireplaces throughout the mansion, not including the massive hearth in the kitchen. Six possible locations the ballerina could be, the most challenging of which is the flue emptying into the master bedroom. All of this assumes, of course, *The Dancer* hasn't been moved since Paul's man captured the photograph several weeks ago.

It's a big job, the biggest we've ever undertaken, but we didn't earn our reputation by playing it safe. We've taken calculated risks before and always cashed them in for sizable payouts. And this would be a huge payout, one that could keep us living in high cotton for a lifetime. Not to mention the prestige from pulling off a heist against the Astor family. Some things, some *institutions*, are considered sacred. Untouchable.

But our mission has always been to prove nothing is untouchable. Not for us.

CHAPTER THREE

I RETURN TO THE Academy in the evening and sit quietly through dinner with Mellie. Our nightly routine is enduring—she chatters, I chew. When we walk back to our room, I notice, with mild amusement, my morning gown is no longer on the floor. Much like her mindless yammering, Mellie's predictability knows no bounds.

We're preparing for bed—me quiet, Mellie loud—when a familiar tapping begins at the window. One glance at my roommate reveals she heard it too. She has ears like a bat, this farmgirl.

"Nuh-uh, no way." Mellie gives me a cross look, then strides to the window as a second shower of pebbles hits the glass. She yanks the frame up and leans out to hiss, "She's not here. Go away!"

I rush across the room and stick my head out the window. Paul's grinning face looks up at me. I shove Mellie aside, hoping she didn't see him clearly. "What are you doing here?"

"You're not going to come over." He's matter-of-fact.

"No. I'm not."

"I knew you weren't. So I came to you. Come outside."

Mellie snorts. I turn to her and bite my lip.

"Oh no." She shakes her head. "Don't even think about it."

"I won't be long," I whisper, hitching a leg over the sill.

"Katarina, no." She grabs my arm and tries to pull me back.

"Mellie, let go."

"You're going to get us both in frightful trouble, Kat. You can't keep doing this. I'm going to tell. I mean it this time."

"You've not said a word for three years," I tell her, stone-faced. "You're certainly not going to say anything now."

She drops my arm. "You're so stupid, Kat. So, so, *so* stupid."

"Leave the sash open. I'll be back soon." I swing my other leg over the edge and find my usual toe holds in the weathered brick wall.

"And if I don't?" Mellie whispers. "Leave it open?"

If you don't, I'll still be able to get in, but I'll be out for your blood.

"Just leave it open, Mellie."

After scampering down the wall, I follow Paul away from the Academy, rounding a corner and crossing the street to the deserted, moonlit Forsyth Park. We seek shelter within a thick grove of moss-draped oak trees before I turn on him.

"What are you doing here?"

"I told you." He sticks his hands in his pockets. "I miss you."

"We were together last night." I fold my arms. "All of us."

He frowns and says, "That's not what I mean, Kat."

I point to the Academy. "Mellie might have *seen* you."

"So what?" He shrugs. "She has no clue who I am."

"We agreed. If you need me, you send Abe. Always Abe."

"I couldn't send Abe to do this." He reaches for me and brushes a lock of hair off my face. His fingers move over my cheeks, ghosting down to tickle my collarbone. Then he reaches behind my neck, slides his hands down my back and over my butt, pulling me in. He's already hard.

"You're thinking with your lower half," I tell him, slightly annoyed, slightly thrilled.

I can't help my body's response to him. It's been this way between us for years. No matter what my mouth says, my brain swirls with secret pleasure in knowing he came here, took this risk, purely for me.

"Maybe," he admits, grinning. "I know you're worn slap out, but let's spend an hour together. Please. I really have missed you, Kat."

It's the earnest look on his face that undoes me. Paul never begs; this is as close as it gets.

"One hour," I finally agree. "I trust you'll make it worth my while?"

"Don't I always?"

Paul's hands work the buttons on the collar of my dress as his lips meet mine. His kisses are strong, hungry. The center of my gut clenches as my gaze sweeps the park for voyeurs.

"Paul," I whisper his name, a familiar rush rising. The bottomlessly heady will-we-get-caught. The thrill from publicly doing something forbidden and reckless.

With *him*.

He inches up my dress and teases his fingers across my thigh before placing them right where I want them.

"Oh." I press against him.

He stays there for a few minutes, then pulls hard, ripping through my step-in chemise. My hands move feverishly to unclip his suspenders. I've never been a very patient person, and neither is Paul. Not where this is concerned. We are two bodies with one mind. Moving through the steps of a choreographed dance, a quickstep every time.

He lifts me onto his hips and presses my back into the nearest tree. Low-hanging Spanish moss surrounds us on four sides. I dip my fingers under his shirt, over his tattoo, tracing the swiping paw of the wolf tracking forward over his shoulder onto his right pectoral. Paul shivers.

Remotely, I hear the telltale tear of a paper condom wrapper.

"Kat." He sinks into me.

I return my fingers to the ink of the massive wolf coating his back, holding on.

There is so much hunger between us.

I tug his bottom lip with my teeth. He growls, increasing the pace. I press my lips to the paw on his shoulder. My panting breath heats the tattooed marks on his chest. We move together, murmured cries floating into the canopy of greenery overhead...

———◄◆►———

"Only twenty minutes gone, Kitty-Kat. Forty still to go."

Laughing, I give Paul a playful shove. He flops to the grass beneath the starry sky and reaches for me. I rest my chin on his chest, looking at his face as he closes his eyes.

"Wake me in forty minutes," he mumbles.

"How romantic." I sniff but snuggle into him.

His fingers brush through my long black hair.

"Did you have a good day, doll?" he murmurs, his chest rumbling beneath my ear.

"It was okay. There was an open house this morning."

"I know."

Of course you do. "I met someone interesting."

"Oh?"

"Don't you already know?"

"No." He laughs. "Who?"

"His name is Matthew. Matthew DaMolin."

"Matthew *DaMolin*?" Paul shifts beneath me.

"Yeah." My gaze flicks to his face. "You know him?"

"I know *of* him," Paul clarifies, settling back down. "And his family. Publishing titans, generational wealth. He's the younger son, works at the hospital, lives alone downtown...physician."

"Uh-huh." Paul's endless stream of knowledge never ceases to amaze me. I decide to bait him. "He's handsome."

"Is he now?" Paul angles my head in the crook of his arm so he can see me better. "Do I need to worry?"

There's no concern in his gaze. His dark irises laugh at me, knowing.

"Smug bastard." I roll my eyes.

"Wily wench."

After a few more laughs, we settle again. When Paul's breathing evens out and my eyes grow heavy, I force myself to stir.

"I should get back."

As I rise, I feel a lump weighing my skirt pocket. "Oh, I have something for you." I pull out Ray's payment. "I nearly forgot."

The envelope smacks him in the chest as he sits up. He opens it and quickly counts.

"What did you sell, Paul?"

He doesn't answer right away. When he's satisfied with the tally, he rolls over and rises.

"Paul?" I try again. "We haven't worked a job for weeks. What did you ask Ray to move?"

"You know I don't yank you outta here for every job we pull, Kitty-Kat."

"That doesn't answer my question."

"I didn't realize I have to answer to you." He flicks his hair before stretching to brush stray grass out of mine.

"Hmm." I reach up to snag his hand. I pull it down, straighten out his fingers, and trace the small king of diamonds symbol tattooed on his right ring finger. It's done in black ink, just like his wolf.

"I forgot. You're the king, right?" I raise my eyes to his.

He frowns, and I lift my own hand, sliding the thick, silver ring he gave me off my right ring finger. I've worn it every day since my sixteenth birthday. I flick my red queen of diamonds tattoo toward him.

"Maybe you forgot who you're talking to."

He smiles and kisses the mark on my finger. "I didn't forget, Kat. Is it really that important to you?"

"Your behavior, like you're hiding something, makes me think perchance it is."

"I'm not. It wasn't anything important, doll. Just some tribute I took from the Condor and Magpie gangs ages ago. Oil, gunpowder. The usual. Plus a few watches Tony lifted last week. You know he likes to have his fun."

I slide the ring back on my finger. "Okay."

"Okay?" He's incredulous. "That's it?"

"Yeah. You told me. That's all I wanted."

"Next time cut the theatrics, Kat." He looks disgruntled.

"It got your attention."

"It did, but I'd never forget." He slides his ring up slightly and reaches for my hand, placing our paired tattoos side by side.

Everyone in the Wolfpack is marked. Paul has the wolf across his back and shoulder. Abe and Tony each have pawprints and swipes tracking up their sides. The three boys had them done when I was fifteen, then they badgered me for a year about getting inked too. I refused.

But on my sixteenth birthday, after bringing in a particularly successful haul of stolen diamonds, Paul brought me to the tattoo parlor himself. He went in first, and I watched him get the king of diamonds tattoo. Then he handed me his silver signet ring, the one I'd seen on his finger since before I could remember. It's thick and old with an engraved crest weaving its way across the band. His only memento from the family who dropped him on the orphanage steps as an infant.

"I'm the king and you're the queen," he told me as he handed the ring over. "This is yours now. It'll cover your finger. No one has to know but us."

This was a very different ask than before, and I knew it. I carefully took the ring and sat down in the chair.

"Queen of diamonds, please," I whispered, handing over my finger.

That night I realized, ink or not, Paul marked me years ago. I was his, his queen of diamonds.

The boys put out a rumor of the Cat Burglar's mark a few weeks later, said I had a tiny silhouette of wolf ears on my wrist. Dainty. Feminine. The papers ran with it.

"Misdirection, Kitty-Kat," Paul told me. "It's the oldest trick in the book."

Snapping back to the present, I slowly follow Paul out of the arboretum.

"We'll do another night at Astor Manor tomorrow," he says, "and the boys want to go out on Saturday. Think you can get away?"

"Reckon I can. Where?"

"Tony wants to hit Carousel."

"Sounds dilly. Carousel is the cat's meow."

"Until tomorrow, doll. I love you." He kisses my hand farewell, then steals into the shadows of the park.

I take off in the opposite direction, back to the Academy.

Son of a bitch, Melinda.

Our room is dark, the window closed.

Resigned, I latch my fingers and toes into grooves between bricks and begin to climb, tapping into a skillset I've had since I was young. When I reach the window, I apply pressure with my hands to slide it up.

It doesn't budge; she must have locked it. What a killjoy.

I'm reaching to slide a dagger-like hairpin from my dark locks when a remorseful Melinda opens the window. I thrust my leg inside before she can change her mind.

"Sorry, Kat," she whispers. "I was mad."

"It's fine."

And it is.

Mellie and I aren't friends, not really, so she doesn't owe me anything. We tolerate each other, and we live well enough together. At this point, I've been sneaking out for so long, if the news came out, we'd both go down hard. She's complicit, and she knows it.

I land inside on silent feet and head to the bathroom for a quick wash.

She follows me, her brow furrowed. "Why are you covered in moss and grass?"

That's a gross exaggeration. "I'm not *covered* in grass."

"Who was that tonight?" she tries again.

"Hmm?" I play dumb.

"The fella who picked you up."

"Goodnight, Mellie." I make to close the bathroom door, but she sticks out her slippered foot.

"I saw him, Kat. It wasn't the dark-skinned guy. Are you stepping out on your beau?"

Mellie has no idea where I go or what I do when I sneak out. She only knows I do. Frequently. And she knows Abe from his occasional visits. In her simple mind, Abe is my taboo paramour from back home, the reason I'm not interested in any of the men who visit the Academy. I gladly let her think it; it's fairly harmless and only half-wrong.

Misdirection.

"Of course not," I tell her, narrowing my eyes. "I love him. You know that."

"Then who—"

"He was just a friend, Mellie. Geez. I left a lot of people behind when I came here. It's not easy, staying connected to both worlds."

She looks at her slippers, momentarily abashed.

"I'm not stepping out on my fella," I say firmly.

"I know you aren't," she whispers. "But I'm not sure you should be trying so hard to stay connected, Kat. You left the Catacombs behind for a reason. Same as me with the farm. Maybe it's time to move on."

And with that, she pulls her foot back and softly closes the door.

CHAPTER FOUR

MUCH TO OUR DISMAY, Florence Vanderbilt graces Mellie and me with her company at breakfast. A pious smile plays on her lips as she plunks down her plated egg-white omelet across from me.

"Did you enjoy the open house yesterday, Katarina?"

"Yes, it was lovely." I focus on stirring my Cream of Wheat.

"It certainly was. These opportunities are *so* important in our final year, don't you think?"

I merely nod, waiting for the shoe to drop. Florence is woefully predictable.

"Making a good match—it's positively crucial," she continues. "Having the right pedigree, being on similar paths...there's so much we need to consider. Don't you agree?"

I finally look at her, the insinuation crystal clear. I have a poor pedigree; I'm certainly not on the same path as the trifecta.

When I interviewed for admission to the Academy, there were a lot of reservations. People just like Florence on the panel, from donor families with long ancestries. People conditioned to turn up their noses at those beneath them on the social ladder. But Paul had prepared me well. I pilfered an exquisitely refined dress for the interview and pinned my hair in a conservative chignon. I walked straight in demure heels, saying "yes, ma'am" and "no, sir." Being a con artist and a Royal paid off in dividends that day, because Lady Genevieve agreed to let me in, tuition deferred.

Unlike Florence, whose family foots the bill upfront for her education, a select few girls, like Mellie and me, will have a small pile of loans to our names when we graduate. Loans I'll either slowly pay back with earned wages at Raymond's, or better yet, loans my wealthy, Academy-sanctioned husband will repay when we marry. The Academy doesn't take on charity cases out of the goodness of its heart, make no mistake, but once you're in, they protect their own. It's just smart business, after all, to protect one's investment.

"Katarina?" Florence's eyes are wide. "Don't you agree?"

Something deep inside of me—the wolf, no doubt—snarls, but I tamp it down. Instead, I give Florence the response she's after: submission.

I make a slight huff of agreement and lower my eyes as though sufficiently chastised. It costs little to do it, really. Only my dignity...and if I'm being honest, I surrendered that years ago. Buried it deep in the tunnels of the Catacombs. Dignity doesn't feed hungry mouths. Doesn't pay bills or buy new shoes.

Dignity, it turns out, is shockingly expensive.

Satisfied, Florence turns to her next victim. She nods at my roommate's plate, piled high with two buttered biscuits, eggs, and potato-sausage hash. "Smelly Mellie, you're never going to lose five pounds that way."

The nickname is unfortunate. It started in our first year when some of the girls found out Melinda came from a working plantation family. That she'd hauled manure and cleaned out chicken coops in her past life.

I come to Mellie's defense. "Who says she needs to lose five pounds?"

"She does." Florence points her fork at Mellie. "She whines about it to anyone who will listen."

It's true, but it's beside the point. "Mellie's waistline is fine. Far better a goal to lose five pounds than to pine for the ironclad shackles of marriage with every breath." I raise an eyebrow. "Don't you think?"

"I always tell myself the diet starts tomorrow." Mellie laughs nervously as Florence's cheeks burn rouge. "But somehow, tomorrow never seems to come."

I snort, amused, as a flash of silver-streaked hair enters my periphery. Headmistress Helena walks from table to table, dropping a piece of paper on each.

"Another social next week?" I ask, reading the notice.

"Gracious, back-to-back events?" Mellie sighs. "Talk about double duty."

"You should be grateful." Florence winds up for another swing. "It's not like you have any prospects, Melinda."

Mellie's cheeks blotch. "Well, there's still another year."

"Not everyone is looking for a husband, Florence," I chime in.

"Don't even get me started on you." Florence turns to me. "As if anyone would want to water down their lineage with Catacomb blood."

A few girls at the table titter uneasily, and something inside me snaps. Florence is so narrow-minded, never looking outside the small, satin-lined box in which she lives.

Target: Florence Vanderbilt.

"You know, Florence," I begin, "some of us have future prospects that enable us to support ourselves and not rely on a husband to repay our tuition. Marriage is a long-term commitment. I'm certainly not looking to blindly hitch my wagon to the richest fella who looks my way."

"Well, you don't have to worry then. Because none of them *are* looking your way."

"Matthew DaMolin was." I widen my eyes, playing innocent. "Yesterday."

Florence gapes, silenced at long last.

With the taste of victory on my tongue, I rise from the table. "Excuse me, ladies. I have a piano lesson this morning. Chat soon."

———◄○►———

IN THE STILL OF the night, Beethoven's Moonlight Sonata is far from my fingers but playing on loop in my brain. It's three hours to midnight, and I'm dressed in black from head to toe—a silk blouse that cuffs at my wrists, men's trousers clinging to my thighs.

"Three guards are inside the office in the carriage house, per usual. Next patrol is in thirty minutes." Tony steamrolls through his report. "A food delivery truck arrived an hour ago and is parked near the east kitchen, right on schedule. Her Ladyship and darling Harry are inside." He glances at his stolen watch of the week, a pocket timepiece with a gaudy, embossed lid and heavy chain. He absentmindedly flicks it open and closed. "They ate late tonight because Major Harry had a meeting at city hall."

Paul moves toward the iron gate. "Let's get closer."

Astor Manor is surrounded by an eight-foot wrought iron fence topped with barbed finials. There are no breaches around the perimeter, but ornamental fences only keep honest folks out.

When Paul locks his fingers together, I plant my foot to vault over. I graze the top before dropping down the other side. Abe springs up next, but he balances between spikes. One by one, the boys haul each other over the wall.

We move east around the manor, keeping to the shadows. When we reach the rear, we drop to our bellies and crawl to hide within the opulent landscaping of the sunken neo-Roman garden. From this vantage, we can clearly see into the house. The entire posterior is lined with panels of mullioned floor-to-ceiling windows. Grandiose Roman pillars stand sentinel on the outside portico. At three stories tall and twenty-six thousand square feet with thirteen bedrooms, six fireplaces, nineteen baths, and eight sitting rooms—plus the attached carriage house—Astor Manor is a monstrosity of marble-glazed brick in the heart of Savannah.

Like clockwork, it's lights-out for Lady Astor in the master bedroom a half hour after dinner, but Harry stays up, working in his third-floor office until almost midnight. When the lamp is finally extinguished, we wait for his bedroom light to flick on, but it never does. Instead, a door on the first floor opens. Light spills into the gardens.

"Fuck," Paul hisses, dragging us deeper into the brush.

Two gentlemen stride across the portico, pausing to lean against a pillar. One is most certainly Harry. The second is tall with a lanky build and sharp jawline. His suit, even in the dark, appears immaculately tailored. His face is in shadow, but there's something familiar about him.

"A little late for visitors, don't you think?" Abe whispers.

"I know him," I breathe, furrowing my brow as the two gentlemen light a cigarette to share. They're standing so close, their shoulders brush. "I'm certain I've seen him before. At the Academy."

Harry takes a deep drag on the cigarette, then passes it to his friend.

Tony wrinkles his nose in distaste. "How 'bout you spring for a second light, gentlemen? Honestly."

The two men finish their smoke, then disappear back inside. Less than ten minutes later, Harry's bedroom light turns on briefly, then off. Abed at long last.

"Harry is the problem," Abe says once the house is dark. "Lady Astor is regimented and predictable. She never deviates from her routine, but Harry..."

"Sometimes he's home for dinner, sometimes he's not. Some nights he's in bed by ten, other times he's up half the night," I say.

Tony gestures to the portico. "And apparently, some nights he invites mysterious gringos over for bedtime smokes. There's no pattern."

We've hashed this out a hundred times, and it always comes down to the same thing.

Harry.

It's almost impossible to pin down a night to run the job with him in the picture. There are certain constants, of course. Dinner is served at seven o'clock sharp. If Harry has a late meeting, it's pushed back by an hour. Lady Astor is always in bed by nine thirty p.m. and rises promptly at six in the morning. Staff members receive food deliveries on Tuesday and Thursday nights. A donation truck swings by on Monday mornings. The fireplaces are cleaned Monday evenings, and the windows are washed on Friday mornings. The list goes on and on.

"There's a military patron gala downtown the first Sunday of October," Tony says. "They'll both be gone all night for it."

"That's over two weeks away," Abe points out.

"And the fireplaces will be filthy on a Sunday." I wrinkle my nose in distaste. "Which is less than optimal."

"It's almost one." Tony consults his watch, and we return to silently casing the house. At 1:03, a soft light flicks on in the master suite. Moments later, a second one goes on in the bathroom.

"She's unbelievable." Tony shakes his head as he pulls out his small book to note the time. "Even pisses on schedule."

Every night we've watched, Lady Astor has arisen between 12:55 and 1:18 a.m. for a nighttime bathroom break. On average, it takes her seventy-three seconds, start to finish.

"This is our window," Paul muses. "Ten o'clock p.m. to one thirty a.m."

I shake my head. "But Harry—"

"We'll have to get him out," Paul says, stopping me short. "Either that or neutralize him."

Tony yawns, and it travels around our circle. I sink into Paul's side.

"Close your eyes, Kitty-Kat," he whispers, kissing my temple. "I'll wake you up if anything happens."

It's tempting, and he's so warm. Hard and soft in all the right places too. Knowing I won't miss much, I let my eyelids drift to half mast, then fully closed.

It's a safe bet because after two a.m., we enter what Abe calls the witching hours. The time when creation falls quiet. All is still, everyone in the world sound asleep. Everyone except ghosts and demons and witches.

And thieves.

CHAPTER FIVE

SATURDAY NIGHT, I MEET Paul and the guys at his loft on the outskirts of the bayou. He bought it just as I turned seventeen, when we'd been running steady jobs for two years. After our reputations—and the name of the Wolfpack—catapulted us into the stratosphere.

It was early summer of 1913 when we started running side jobs for Damien Keller, the leader of a bayou gang called the Magpies. I was fifteen.

"Why we doin' work for somebody else, Paul?" Abe asked, grunting as he lugged our assigned barrels down the street. "Especially after he stiffed us on payment last time."

"We're not just running jobs. We're learning. Like we learned about the Condors when Kat was seducing what's-his-name...lover boy."

"I didn't seduce him," I said sharply, dropping my barrel.

Abe snickered. Tony paused to wipe sweat from his brow. Even after midnight, the Savannah humidity didn't sleep. It merely exhaled. Tendrils of early morning mist, steam rising from perhaps hell itself, crept alongside us through the streets.

"I didn't!" I protested again. "Whatever he assumed was gonna happen...well, it didn't. Boys are dumb."

"And girls are brutal," Tony said, giving me his infamous side-eye.

Paul wouldn't be distracted. "Don't you see? All these bayou gangs...they're small fish. Stealing scraps from each other, staying downstream. They're like hyenas, all picking at the same carcass. We're better than that. We're gonna be bigger than that. We're gonna be the kingpin, the one they all bring their scraps to."

"Seems to me that's what we're doing for the Magpies, giving them our scraps," Abe muttered.

"Just wait," Paul told him. "They aren't gonna see us coming, but we're *Royals*. They'll know it soon enough."

Just before sunrise, we trudged, sweaty and exhausted, into Damien's lair. He and two underlings were still awake, playing cards and tossing coins on the table.

"It's done," Paul announced, crossing his arms over his chest. "We moved the barrels. All forty-eight."

"In one night?" Damien looked at Paul with a surveying brow. "Good work."

Then he went back to his cards. I exchanged an anxious look with Tony. Paul cleared his throat.

"Was there something you wanted?" Damien asked, dragging his eyes away from the game.

"You owe us money. For tonight's job, and the one last week."

Damien laughed. "It's a privilege to work for the Magpies, kid. Run a few more jobs, then we'll talk payment and moving up the ranks. You haven't done shit yet."

"We're not looking to move up the ranks. We're independent contractors." Paul stayed firm. "And we deserve to be paid for our work. No one in your little band of misfits could've done what we did tonight, and you know it."

Paul! I inhaled sharply, my heart jumping into my throat.

Damien dropped his cards on the table and rose. His form was lithe, his fingers long. I didn't like the hungry gleam in his eye. I reached my right hand out subtly, twining my fingers into the back of Paul's shirt, cautioning him.

"You're what? Eighteen, kid?" Damien took a slinking step closer to us. "Have some respect, pay your dues."

"With all *due* respect," Paul said, "we're not leaving until we've been paid. You stiffed us once already, and we don't work for free. It's time to pay up."

Damien's two henchmen rose from their seats, flanking their leader.

"Kid, you ain't gettin' shit from me. And you're starting to piss me off."

"That makes two of us." Paul's jaw ticked.

He snorted. "You got balls of steel, boy, I'll give you that. But it takes a hell of a lot more than balls to make it in the bayou. Should I give you a little lesson, a little financial advice perhaps? Prices and costs...they can be tricky when you get into the big leagues."

The henchman on the right flashed a leering smile and slowly cracked his knuckles.

Suddenly, Damien latched his glinting eyes on me. "What's your name, sweetheart?"

My mouth ran dry. Paul immediately stepped in front of me. Abe and Tony closed ranks.

Damien laughed and raised his hands. "We're learning here, right? She's a pretty little thing, isn't she, kid?"

Paul remained silent. Tony's hand grazed my wrist. When I looked down, three of his fingers lay flush on my skin.

Three.

"How much?" Damien probed.

"She's not for sale." Paul was quick.

"Everything is for sale, everyone has a price. Is she yours?"

One of Tony's fingers disappeared.

Two.

Damien laughed again. "You need to learn how to hide your hand better. It's written all over your face. She's valuable to you. Therefore, she's valuable to *me*. See how that works? She's the price tonight."

Tony removed another finger.

One.

"Take the girl."

Damien's muscle lunged, but Paul was faster. As he ducked beneath them, the steel of his knife flashed. I screamed. Tony and Abe collided with the henchmen.

"Paul!"

My heart sank as he rammed Damien. They crashed to the floor. In one quick slide, the knife went in and out of the Magpie's stomach. Paul sprang to his feet to help Abe subdue his attacker.

I moved to aid Tony, lunging to land a strong punch across the bridge of the henchman's bulbous nose. Tony followed with a blow to the back of his head that dropped him like a stone. When I looked across the room, Paul and Abe had their attacker on his knees, his hands behind his head. Abe stood menacingly over him. Paul backed away.

Damien was gasping like a fish on the floor. Sticky red blood oozed out of the hole from Paul's knife. I wanted to look away, but Paul strode over and wrenched Damien's head back by his hair. His mouth was inches from the Magpie's face.

"You want her life? I charge *double* for it. Nonrefundable." Paul rose and walked to where Tony and I stood. Damien's eyes were leaking, but they followed Paul's every move. Quick as lightning, Paul slid the knife across the unconscious Magpie's throat. I tried to control my expression as blood spurted out, spraying Tony's pant leg. I stepped back.

"Fool me once," Paul muttered, striding back to Damien, "shame on you. Fool me twice..." He considered before plunging the knife into

Damien's stomach. "Nobody fools me twice." He withdrew the knife as Damien's eyes shuttered.

I held my breath as Paul turned to the remaining Magpie. The man began to shake his head. "Please...I won't...please..."

Without responding, Paul dipped his fingers into the pool of Damien's blood. With a sweep of his free hand, he cleared the cards and coins from the rickety table, then began to paint the surface. His movements were short and brusque, tracing the shadowy, crude outline of a howling wolf's head in blood on the tabletop.

He turned, wiping his stained hand on his pants, taking his time. The Magpie watched him prowl across the room and grunted when Paul's fist sunk into his gut.

"Paul," I started, finally finding my voice and stepping toward him.

He held an arm up, signaling me to stop. A ravenous glimmer shone in his eyes. A hunger. I held his gaze. Against all odds, I *understood*. I understood the feeling all too well. I cocked one corner of my mouth in a small smile.

"Consider this an object lesson." Paul turned back to our captive, sliding down to his haunches to whisper in the Magpie's ear. "You want one of us, I take *two* of you. My price is *double* whatever you lowlifes charge."

The man nodded vigorously.

"What's your name?" Paul asked.

"Craig."

"Swell. Tell them, Craig." Paul rose to his feet and turned to us. "Let's go."

"Wait," the man choked out. "Who...?"

"The Wolfpack." Paul tossed his bloody knife on the table. "Tell them. Tell them all."

THAT NIGHT MARKED THE beginning of our new dawn, that run-in and cutdown of the Magpie gang. The Wolfpack burst onto the scene of Savannah's underworld, leaving an unapologetic trail of blood and lore in its wake. Paul wrangled my interview at the Academy just after my eighteenth birthday, and the marks, capers, and infamy continued to grow.

When Paul first told me he was ready to buy a flat and move out of the Catacombs, I asked him why he wanted a hideout in the bayou when he could afford something nicer. Something closer to the city center.

"This is where we're from, Katarina," he said, using my full name for emphasis. "And this is where we work. We need to be here. I *want* to be here."

At the time, I admired his principles and dedication to the bayou. Most people want to escape the place, but not Paul. He's always been proud of where we come from. At least, that's what I thought. But last year, he splurged and bought a glossy apartment in downtown Savannah.

To be closer to his *new* work, he told me.

Both homes are nice, but the bayou loft will always be my favorite. It's the first place we could call our own. The first place I ever truly felt safe. And Paul was right; this hideout is authentic to who we are—the colorful draped silks, stolen Persian rugs, scattered wicker crates, eclectic furniture, a tiny fire escape overlooking the swampy streets of the bayou...

This is the life—the empire—we built together. This place reeks of our early years, of both the struggles and the victories.

I let myself into the loft and call out a greeting to Paul and the boys. As I cross the living room, I pause to adjust a Parisian silk over an antique Turkish floor lamp, casting a hundred hues of red across the room. When I'm satisfied with the effect, I move to the Victrola phonograph. The cabinet doors whine when I tug them open. I place an old Billy Murray record on the turntable and set the needle. As the opening score swells, I slip inside the master bedroom to change for our night out. Paul is already there, dressed in tailored pants and a half-unbuttoned, herringbone vest. A matching newsboy cap and pocket chain complete his look.

"What should I wear tonight?" I ask, sliding open the doors to an overflowing closet. I absentmindedly sway to the bluesy notes from the phonograph as I peruse my options.

"Something hotsy-totsy."

"Well, that's a given." I pull out a whimsically draped confection of crimson chiffon. It's a Lucile creation, one of Lady Duff-Gordon's more risqué blends of lingerie and evening wear. I hold the dress up to my body and spin for Paul. When his eyes spark, I'm sold. I turn to examine my extensive collection of wigs.

"Blonde." Paul reaches around me and pulls out a blunt-cut, chin-length, platinum bob.

"Hmm...short? Really?"

"Yeah. And a red lip." He leans in and kisses me hard.

"Aces." I step into the dress, turning for Paul to do up the hooked buttons. While his fingers work, my own fly through my hair, weaving two French braids. I secure them in a crown with pins. Paul hands me the wig, and I put it on. Next comes a long strand of plumply exquisite pearls, stolen several years ago from a Savannah socialite. I loop the plunder twice around my neck so the first strand fits choker tight, the second dangling low over my décolletage.

A knock sounds at the door. "Hey, lovebirds, let's get a wiggle on!"

"Kat's not ready yet." Paul opens the door as I begin pawing through my makeup products.

Tony peeks inside, eyeing my ensemble. "Mierda, Kat. You shopping for a replacement beau tonight, gringa?"

I frown at his reflection in the mirror and begin painting my face. "No, and I need five more minutes." Ten to fix up the finger waves in my wig.

Tony ambles into the room and lounges on the bed. He has three buttons undone on his dress shirt, exposing a smattering of dark chest hair. He takes a deep swig from a bottle of gin, then passes it to Paul. Abe hovers in the doorway, Tony's foil in naught but an informal white sleeveless shirt and workman's pants. He strikes an impressive figure with his dark, round shoulders on full display, straining a pair of worn suspenders.

"You still want to hit Carousel, right?" Paul asks, taking his own gulp from the bottle. He hands it off to me, placing it on my vanity with a *thud*.

"Absolutely," Tony replies. "The jazz will be hot tonight."

It's a new sound, jazz, and it's taking Savannah by storm this year. Tony and I can't get enough. I swipe the mascara wand over my lashes, then pick up the bottle of gin. It's an expensive label, one from Paul's not-so-secret stash. I tip my head back to take a big gulp, then a second.

"Easy, killer." Paul reaches for the bottle.

"I think she's a hellraiser." I point to my reflection in the mirror and grin wickedly. "I can feel it. Must be the hair."

"Oh boy!" Tony slaps his hands together and rubs. "She's getting into character. Look out, ladies and gents."

I pick up red lipstick, meeting Paul's heated gaze in the mirror as I sweep it on.

"Bella, Katarina," Tony pronounces. "Now can we go?"

"Yeah, yeah," I mutter, and Tony breezes from the room.

"You look real swell, doll," Paul whispers. His hand quickly caresses my backside before he departs.

I pause to give myself a final once-over in the mirror. Alcohol thrums through my veins, excitement flushing my cheeks. When I turn, Abe is the only one remaining, hovering in the doorway.

"How do I look?" I cock out a hip.

"Like the cat's meow. As always." Abe has the gin, and he takes a deep swallow, eyes locked on me. Electricity crackles in his gaze. Lingering.

My blood simmers, and I bask in his attention, the way a kitten licks up every last drop of cream.

"You like?" I step close to him and loop my fingers through his suspenders, leaning my hips dangerously close to his.

Nine days out of ten, Abe is like my brother, but sometimes, on that tenth day, when temptation burns in those dark eyes of his...it's fun to play. I flutter my lashes as a throaty laugh bubbles out.

Hellraiser indeed.

"Christ, Kat." He fidgets, then steps back, glancing nervously over his shoulder. "We should go."

"One more sip." I steal the gin from him and take another swig, a little smaller this time.

Abe watches me swallow, wary but riveted. "You're going to be a handful this evening, aren't you?"

"Your favorite kind of handful." I eye him knowingly as I pass the bottle back. "Your turn."

He watches me again. Smiles slowly.

Then he chugs.

CHAPTER SIX

When we reach Carousel, the outdoor saloon is lit up spectacularly. There are more than twenty public squares throughout the city of Savannah, and the old-time carousel that gives the bar its name is central to this one. An intrepid entrepreneur saw potential in the children's ride, long since abandoned and rusted out, restoring and converting it into an after-hours money-making machine.

Paul takes my hand as we amble to the nearest bar. There are two of them, carved into opposite sides of the carousel itself. Traditional mirrors and big white bulb lights twinkle overhead, moths fluttering lazily in their wake. Gold trim is everywhere, flaking slightly from direct and constant exposure to the bayou's humidity. Several adventurous patrons swing themselves up on wooden horses as they sip their drinks. Others dance to the beat of live jazz music streaming from a pair of dueling trumpet and saxophone players in the square. Their instrument cases, open at their feet, swim with bills.

"Kat?" Tony leans over Paul's shoulder. "Kat, what do you want?"

"A martini."

"Rockefeller's drink?" Paul murmurs, nuzzling me. "You have expensive taste tonight, m'lady."

I shrug and point at my reflection above the bar. "She's making the decisions, not me."

Abe shoulders around us to distribute drinks. He gives Paul his signature old-fashioned, then passes over my martini. His gaze lingers on me as he hands off the glass. Tony pulls back from the bar with two beers, one for himself and one for Abe.

"Cheers, Royals." Paul tips his drink in.

Two martinis later, I start to dance in the square with the other revelers. I take turns pulling in Paul, Abe, and Tony, one by one. Each boy humors me for a few minutes before returning to the bar. Tony is by far the best dancer, but even he doesn't linger tonight. He departs as soon as the final notes of our tango fade, off to chase a skirt on the opposite side of the bar. In his absence, I assess my prospects. Paul leans casually on the counter with Abe, watching for my next move. It doesn't take long to attract a groping pair of hands on my hips.

"What are you drinking?" a deep voice murmurs in my ear.

"A martini," I tell my stranger.

Two minutes later, one magically appears in my hand. Such spectacular service.

I subtly tip the glass and wink in Paul and Abe's direction, eliciting laughs as I continue dancing with my mystery man. After a few minutes, however, his hands start wandering, and I decide to take my leave. If it's not Paul, Abe, or Tony, I'm quick to bore. Besides, Paul's eyebrows are lowering with each passing moment. Abe's too.

I turn to smile politely at my new friend, gripping his wrists to hold them still. "Thanks for the drink," I tell him, "but I need to take a dance break."

"Wanna go somewhere?" he murmurs, sliding his right hand behind my neck.

Really, really no. "Thanks for the drink," I repeat and pull away.

He makes one more attempt, reaching out to grab my wrist. Possessive.

Abe rises from the bar, and I fight the urge to roll my eyes. He of all people knows I can handle myself. It's why Paul hasn't moved from his perch.

"Come on now. I bought you a drink," the fella protests.

The Academy-bred lady inside me shrinks, but the wolf never does. And the wolf always wins.

"Yes, you bought a drink. You didn't buy *me*." I narrow my eyes, pointedly, dangerously, before twisting my wrist to break free. "Enjoy your night."

I trot back to the guys as Paul signals the bartender. "Another martini?"

While I wait, I reach over and take a sip of Abe's beer. I hand it back and lick my lips as he swallows the dregs. He holds his fingers up for the barmaid. She's wildly popular tonight—it's quite a rarity to see a woman tending bar—but she swoops over swiftly to take Abe's order. Paul blazes up a cigarette with his silver lighter and offers me a drag.

Tony rejoins us soon after, bringing with him two tittering bayou brunettes—one for him and one, presumably, for Abe. One of the women is smoking a hash joint. She offers us all a hit. Paul and I decline, but Abe and Tony accept. Paul smokes the occasional cigarette, but he never messes with street drugs. Not ever. Says he's seen more than enough of that in the Catacombs. It's something of a silent agreement between the two of us, a blood pact sworn the day he found me beside my mother's body. We don't use; we don't deal. The Wolfpack will never feed that particular appetite of Savannah's black market.

We chat as a group for a short while before Tony decides he wants to go underground.

In the center of the merry-go-round, there's a trapdoor, a portal to the dark side of Carousel—a hidden speakeasy. Whispers run rampant through the streets of Savannah about the looming threat of the temperance movement. The amendment has been ratified. Prohibition is coming, sure as the tide of 1920, and make no mistake, the city saloons are preparing for war. Already cellars are being quietly converted, expanded, and trialed as liquor dens and dance halls. For those in the know, of course...and for those willing to look the other way. If there's anything my upbringing has taught me, it's that the black market will always find a way to keep turning. And those bluenoses who run the American Congress are fools if they expect anything less.

The temperature in Carousel's cellar is a refreshing ten degrees cooler than aboveground. The Savannah humidity becomes a distant memory, but the air down here is heavily laden with smoke. There's a dark, velveteen bar along one wall. Faint echoes of the live music percolate from above.

It's nearly wall-to-wall bodies down here tonight, either gyrating to the beat or crowding the lone bartender for his finest hooch. Tony jumps into the fray with the two brunettes. I lose them in the smoky haze within minutes.

"It's packed like a can o' sardines down here tonight. You wanna dance? Or should we go back out?" Paul speaks the words directly into my ear.

"Tony's in there." I point to the mob.

Paul shrugs. "He's a big boy."

True enough.

I look at Abe, but he also shrugs. *Whatever you want,* his lazy drawl whispers in my mind, though his lips don't move. He smiles languidly because he knows.

Emboldened, I reach for both fellas' hands and plunge into the pit. We weave between swinging hips and stomping heels, carving out our own space in the crowd. Paul slips behind me, and Abe takes my front. The three of us move to the beat, dancing, sweating the alcohol from our systems.

Abe and I attract more than a few judgmental stares, but I resolutely ignore them. Even here in the bayou, where the lines of propriety are fluid, the stigma of the Jim Crow South is a red-hot brand. As inherent to the community as our beloved Spanish moss, an epiphyte canopy of prejudice hangs over Savannah, casting shadows so deep, all sunlight is blocked. Growth made impossible.

Paul's hands move over me unchecked as my heart pounds in rhythm with the trumpet. Abe is far more conservative with his touch, but his eyes pool into mine. My entire body thrums, a live wire sparking.

I feel daring tonight, so I step forward and grind my hips into Abe's. I wait breathlessly for his reaction, wondering if he'll pull away. I stay close, swinging with him. He swallows and looks over my shoulder at Paul. I hold my breath, but he must get what he needs, because his hands hook onto me seconds later. He lowers his forehead to mine, closer than close. When I exhale, he inhales.

Paul's deep chuckle rumbles in my ear several minutes later. "Let's go back outside."

His words raise shivers of promise on my neck. I give a cursory glance for Tony, but I don't see him. We emerge from the trapdoor to find the outdoor crowd has died down. I understand why when the first breath of humid air hits.

Abe slinks to the bar, and I follow him with my eyes. Paul slides his arms around my waist from behind and nuzzles my neck.

"You want Abe tonight, doll?" he asks. "It's okay—you know I don't mind sharing with him."

I don't reply right away. My eyes narrow as the barmaid flutters over to Abe like he conjured her out of thin air. He orders a drink, and she stays near, chatting him up, laughing as she pops his bottle cap. My hackles rise.

"Go get him." Paul gently slaps my ass, urging me forward.

I hold Paul's attention as I sashay to the bar. I love it. My veins sing with adrenaline. I sidle up to Abe, wiggling myself between him and the counter. He takes a sip of beer and looks at me with interest, waiting.

"What're you gonna do, hellraiser?" His voice is deep and teasing. He knows perfectly well what I'm going to do, but I plow forward anyway.

Barreling ahead like a runaway train, I slide my arms around Abe's neck. His eyes flicker with anticipation as I rise on tiptoes to kiss him. He puts his beer down and presses both hands to the bar, pinning me in. I slip my tongue in his mouth and suck gently. When I pull away, we both look at Paul, who jerks his head.

"Let's go home." I take Abe's hand.

We follow Paul as he cuts a path through the square. I lift his billfold from his pocket and toss some scratch into the musicians' cases. Paul chuckles when he realizes what I've done.

"Dirty little thief," he teases, swiping for the wallet.

I spin away in jest, furtively passing the contraband from my right hand to my left. I very much enjoy the look on Paul's face when he snatches my right arm and comes up with an empty palm, fooled by my sleight of hand.

"Looking for something?" I lift my left hand, his billfold dangling between two fingers.

His lighthearted snort becomes a deep, throaty laugh. "Smooth move, Kitty-Kat. Who taught you to turn tricks like that?" His eyes glimmer knowingly for a fleeting second before he turns on a dime and takes off running. "Bet I can beat you home," he says over his shoulder. "*Both* of you."

The three of us tear through moonlit streets, yipping and laughing like the wolves we are. I can't tell if I'm breathless with exertion or anticipation. As Paul unlocks the door to our loft, Abe leans me against the wall. He closes his lips over mine. The door swings open, and he drags me inside, backing me right into Paul's waiting arms.

Someone kicks the door shut, but I barely notice. There's one set of lips on mine, another moves over my neck. Paul's fingers work the buttons at my back while Abe pulls off my wig. He drops it to the floor as I push back his suspenders and rip off his white shirt. The fingers of my left hand slide up his ribs, darting across his pawprint tattoos. I reach my right hand behind me and wrap it around Paul's neck, leaning back to kiss him.

The three of us slowly make our way to the master bedroom. Once inside, I step out of my dress. Abe sits on the bed to unstrap my heels and pull down my stockings. He presses fluttering kisses to my knees and thighs while he works. Paul finds the bottle of gin and falls back on the bed, waiting.

Power rushes through my veins, the power of holding both men like liquid mercury in my palm. Hot and fluid and languid and *mine*. When my shoes and stockings are gone, Abe's kisses move from my thighs to my center. My head tips back, my jaw slack.

"Kat," he murmurs, breath hot between my legs.

Paul pulls a swig of gin, then crawls to us. I push Abe onto his back, and he pulls me with him, straight onto his lap, breath hitching. Paul tosses him a condom. With little hesitation, Abe positions me, then slides in with a satisfied groan. Paul moves behind me and grabs my hips, changing the angle for himself. I cry out once they're both inside, filling me, front and back.

"Kat?" Paul asks, waiting for my go-ahead.

I give it.

It's not the first time we've done this, and the guys have their rhythm well sorted. They know when I'm close, and their pace quickens. They thrust together, twice. I implode, falling onto Abe's chest. I'm completely oblivious as they both finish, one after the other, a few thrusts later. I'm inhabiting another planet. Floating on the ceiling.

Paul collapses on the bed, the motion gently bouncing Abe and me up and down. Abe, whose strong arms are still wrapped tightly around me, holding on like I'm a buoy in a storm. I stay there with him, breathless. Paul kisses me lazily, amused. Abe runs his fingers up and down my arm.

I sigh and close my eyes, drifting into oblivion with these two men—wolves—beside me.

———◄O►———

"HEY." IT'S PAUL WHO wakes me at dawn, gently shaking my shoulder. "We have to get you back to the Academy. The sun will rise soon."

Abe snores softly, blissfully unaware. I dress quickly but pause before leaving the room. I don't want to wake him, but...

"Don't worry, I'll tell him for you," Paul says.

"What, exactly, will you tell him?" Because I'm wondering what to say myself.

His eyes are understanding as he shrugs. "That you love him."

"Yes," I admit, "but not like I love you." It's important to me that Paul knows.

He reaches out to tweak one of my bedraggled braids. "I know, Kitty-Kat. You don't have to worry. Not with me. Not with any of us."

CHAPTER SEVEN

"That's what you're wearing tonight?" Melinda looks incredulous.

"What? Emerald is a great color on me. Matches my eyes." I know full well that's not her complaint. I turn to the mirror in our bedroom and fluff my hair.

"It has *pants*. And nearly bare shoulders."

"It's a pair of Paul Poiret's jupe-culottes, Mellie."

She stares blankly.

"Harem pants, Mellie," I explain, trying to keep condescension out of my tone. "Inspired by the Parisian ballet performance of Scheherazade. Ring any bells?"

She only continues to stare.

I sigh. "Well, they're in style. Here's a wild thought—maybe in all your free time, you pick up a fashion magazine every once in a while. *Vogue* is a good place to start."

"I just..." She finally finds her voice, shaking her head in disbelief. "I can't believe you're going to wear that tonight."

"Don't worry, I'm still wearing heels and a brassiere," I assure her. "I'm not a total heathen."

"*Those* heels?" She points to the gold, winged, T-strap heels on the floor.

"Yes," I say tiredly, whirling to face her. "Do you have a problem with those too?"

"No. It's just…" She meets my eyes, curious, perhaps a little envious. "Where do you get all this chic stuff?"

Oh.

"I do a lot of secondhand shopping."

The lie comes easily because it's born from truth. Other people's closets are a great place to shop. The bottomless stolen cashflow from my thief boyfriend doesn't hurt either.

"You always look so smart." She's wistful now, examining her own closet.

I can't argue with her. The emerald green pantaloons interwoven with gold filigree and pearlescent beads that shimmer as I walk *are* pretty smart.

"Do you…do you want to borrow something?" I ask, rather uncertain. This is uncharted water.

Mellie leans over, peering into my closet.

"It might be fun to do something a little different tonight," she finally squeaks.

I zero in on her pink cheeks. "Why tonight?"

"No reason." Her response comes quickly. Too quickly.

I stare her down, knowing she'll crack.

"It's only…"

"Only what?"

"Only…Bobby said he might stop by?" She phrases it like a question.

"Bobby Marino? The baker's son?" I stifle a laugh.

"We've been spending time together at work. Since this event is in the evening, he said he might be able to drop by. Maybe."

I nod and magnanimously gesture toward my closet. "You can take whatever you want. I have another pair of pantaloons, if you'd like. They're on the right."

"I'm not wearing those," she screeches, her pitch increasing tenfold. "Heavens to Betsy, Kat—perchance I walk before I run?"

"Okay. Well, the dresses are on this side." I point to the left, stifling another laugh. She walks over and homes in on the heavily skirted, robe de style gowns, staying well within her comfort zone.

"You know," I begin, "you don't always have to wear a ballgown to these events. This is a mixer in the billiard rooms, Mellie. It's supposed to be *fun*."

"Ballgowns are fun."

I ignore this unhinged remark. "What about this one?" I pull out a narrow, translucently layered, pastel evening dress with just a hint of silver shimmer. It's a Jacques Doucet original, highly reminiscent of one of Monet's watercolors. For my tastes, it's a bit conservative and overly feminine with its beaded cap sleeves and empire waist. But for Mellie...

"Oh." She's drawn to the glittering romanticism like a magpie.

"Consider it yours."

We arrive in the Academy billiard room promptly. I make my rounds, saying hello to a few fellas who are regulars and sharing performative air kisses with my classmates, the usual dog and pony show. I settle in beside the shuffleboard table, observing the few girls bold enough to play.

"You always look so desperately in need of a beverage at these events."

I turn toward the familiar voice and focus on Matthew DaMolin's sparkling blue eyes. He hands me a glass of white wine.

"Matthew. I didn't realize you were here," I lie smoothly.

Please. I knew the precise minute he walked in behind Daniel Dufour and Harry Astor. Harry is tonight's target, after all.

"Indeed." He takes a sip from his own drink. "Present and accounted for."

"What is this, two events in one week?" I tease. "Is that a record for you?"

"Not in one week." He looks a bit uncomfortable.

"You were at the open house seven days ago. Last I checked, there are seven days in one week."

His eyes twinkle. "So you've been counting the days since you last saw me?"

I suppose he's got me there. I want to scowl, but I instead flash a dazzling fake smile. "Thanks for the drink," I say, casting around my brain for an excuse to take my leave.

"Do you play?" He gestures to the shuffleboard table.

"Uh...well, the table looks rather full right now," I answer faintly, still plotting my escape. I spot Daniel and Harry across the room, talking to Florence.

"What about pool?" He moves slowly toward an empty table. Against my better judgment, I fall into step beside him. "Want to give it a try? I can teach you."

"Sure, why not?" I mentally pause my Harry plan. It can wait until after I've wiped the floor with Matthew. Shouldn't take long. I do love to mix pleasure with business.

A few stray balls are scattered across the table. Matthew grabs a pool cue and bends over the green felt. A lock of blond hair falls over his right eye as he focuses, but he doesn't flinch. He fires off a clean shot across the length of the table, sinking a ball. It's an impressive strike, actually. I give him a sidelong glance, recalibrating.

"You're aiming to get the balls in the pockets," he explains, handing the stick to me. "On your first turn, you can aim for either stripes or solids...any ball except the black eight. That goes in last."

I accept the pool cue and place my wineglass down. He moves behind me, showing me how to hold it. His fingers dart skillfully over mine, but there's nothing lingering or inappropriate in his touch, which surprises me. It's kind of sexy actually, watching his fingers move so quickly, barely brushing mine.

Wondering what will happen next, I bend over to line up a shot. He follows, but only halfway, gently placing one hand on the outermost edge of my waist. Light as a feather. He murmurs something in my ear about angles, but I'm not really listening. I focus on the shot I want, not the easy one he recommends. I've always had a flair for the dramatic.

"Like this?" I fire off the cue ball, sending it forward in a clear strike. It collides between two striped balls, splitting them into either direction. I smile with satisfaction as they drop into opposite corner pockets. It's a fantastic shot, one that definitely overestimates my abilities, but it has the effect I want.

Matthew blinks twice, surprised. "You already know how to play?"

"I never said I didn't." I lean on the pool cue. "You assumed, so I let you have your little moment. Are you disappointed?"

"Not in the slightest." His eyes flicker with excitement. "This just got a lot more interesting. Care to raise the stakes?"

"What, like strip pool?" I glance around the crowded room, confused. "I hardly think that's wise. Too many spectators."

When I look back, however, his eyes are wide, bursting with shock. Suddenly, I realize I've jumped to the wrong conclusion. The *very* wrong conclusion. I'm not in the slums of the bayou with the Royals; I'm at the Academy. With the son of our benefactress. For the first time in recent history, I fight a blush.

"Um. No," he finally manages. "My intentions were not nearly so bold."

"Indeed not. I was merely jesting. Perchance you'll enlighten me?" I tilt my chin up, trying to salvage whatever dignity I have left. Per usual, it seems buried deep in the Catacombs, exactly where I left it.

"For every ball I sink, you have to answer a question. And you *have* to answer. Honestly. No more of the dodging nonsense you pulled the other day."

"And if *I* sink a ball?"

"You get to ask *me* something. Tit for tat."

I bite my lip. There's not an awful lot for me to gain in this game.

"What's the matter? Scared you'll lose?" Matthew baits.

It's stupid. I know exactly what he's doing, but he's awfully cute when he smiles like that. And he's awfully clever as well.

I pick up my wineglass and drain the whole thing. "You've got yourself a deal."

After racking the balls, I accept the pool cue to break, and I get off a decent shot. Two-thirds of the balls scatter, only a few remaining stubbornly clustered in the middle.

"Stripes or solids, stripes or solids..." Matthew murmurs, drumming his fingers on the table as he peruses the field. He accepts the stick from me and walks around the table. "Eh, I like solids." Quick as lightning, he bends over and fires off a shot to sink his first ball.

"Dammit," I mutter under my breath.

"Oh, I think..." He props his chin in his right hand on the table. "I *think* that means I get a question. Don't worry, we'll start off easy. When's your birthday? And I'm talking month, day, and year. No skimping."

This isn't bad, all things considered. "December 2, 1897."

"So you're twenty-one?"

"You're fast," I drawl.

Then I have the privilege of watching him line up and nail his next shot. I snort, already frustrated.

"Where are you from, Katarina?"

I consider lying, but half the people in this room know where I'm from—his mother included—so what's the point?

Better yet, why should I care?

"I'm from the Catacombs," I answer, jutting out my chin, daring him to say something. I've heard it all before.

He blinks and lowers the cue.

"Not what you expected, huh?"

"Not quite," he admits. "Your parents?"

"My mom died when I was six. I never met my father." My voice is hard now. "That was a freebie."

I wait for the inevitable "I'm so sorry" to begin. I'm already prepared to hate him for it, just like I do when everyone else says the empty words. But to my surprise, he doesn't respond at all. Instead, he bends over to line up another shot. He has two options on the table—one straight shot into the corner pocket and a more challenging side-pocket option. He aims for the latter and chips it, missing.

"Your turn." His fingers brush mine as he quietly hands off the stick.

My heart stutters as I recognize his subtle kindness. He's giving me a temporary reprieve.

"I hope you're not going easy on me," I warn, accepting the pool cue.

"I wouldn't dream of it. It was a tough shot."

"Hooey," I mutter, but I'm secretly pleased. Moments later, I drop my first stripe, and I turn to consider him. "When's *your* birthday?"

He flashes his dimples. "September 1, 1894. I just turned twenty-five."

"Oh." I'm surprised to realize he's only a few months older than Paul. I wrinkle my nose, because for some reason, Matthew and Paul do not coexist well in my brain.

I lean over the table again, my mind swimming. Paul floats to the forefront as my stomach churns with an unfamiliar sensation: guilt. It unsettles me. Matthew is far from the first simp I've fed lines to. It's harmless, always is. But I'm woefully distracted nonetheless, and I miss my next ball.

"My turn." Matthew lines up his shot and another solid slides into the pocket. He rises slowly, victorious. "Where is your apprenticeship?"

"At Raymond's in downtown Savannah."

"The jeweler? *That* Raymond?"

I've surprised him again. "Yes. Are you familiar with him?"

"Of course. My mom's engagement and wedding bands are Raymond's. Along with half her jewelry collection. It's a very prestigious place to apprentice."

"Well, I work mostly in the back," I admit. "Examining shipments, tracking inventory, and...making things."

"You've made pieces that have sold at Raymond's?"

"Yes."

He shakes his head, hair flopping over his eyes again as he bends over. "That's impressive, Katarina. Raymond's standards are incredibly high."

Matthew stands right beside me as he aims. I let my gaze wander over his grip on the pool cue and the angle of his jaw. Fresh blond stubble coats his chin and cheeks. I splay my fingers on the table as he shoots. Unsurprisingly, it's another strike.

He thinks hard before he speaks. I tap my fingers on the table, waiting not-so-patiently for his question. He looks down, then points to my fingers. All ten are bejeweled, as usual.

"Did you make your rings?"

"All but this one," I admit, pointing to Paul's thick silver band on my right hand. Thank goodness the tattoo is fully hidden because he examines my fingers closely. Each one. It feels like an eternity when he stares at Paul's ring.

Matthew misses his next shot. I sink mine.

I don't have a question prepared, but I trace my eyes over the blond scruff on his face again. He didn't have that when we met last week.

"When did you last bathe?"

"What?" He bursts out laughing. "What kind of a question is that?"

"And *shave*," I add, revealing my real interest. I mime rubbing a hand on my chin. "You're all...scruffy."

"If you must know, I haven't bathed since yesterday morning, some thirty-six hours ago. I worked yesterday, stayed on overnight call at the hospital, then worked another full shift today. I came straight here after getting off."

"You worked thirty-six hours at the hospital, then came *here*?" My jaw drops. "Why?"

"That's a new question, I believe." He puts his hands on the table, challenging.

I bend over and take the shot. When another stripe bites the dust, I rise, triumphant. "Why did you work thirty-six hours straight and come here, of all places?"

"Because I wanted to see you again," he answers, shrugging. "I wanted to see if you're as good as I remember."

"And?" My palms are sweating slightly. I adjust my grip on the pool stick.

"And you haven't disappointed me," he admits with a chuckle.

After that disclosure, I miss my next shot, but Matthew proceeds to sink two more. First, he asks me what my favorite color is.

"Today? Green." I pluck at my emerald pantsuit to illustrate.

While I'm waiting for his sixth question, he buffs the tip of the cue with chalk.

"Any day now," I remind him, but he continues to take his time, fingers moving around and around. He examines the head closely when he's done, blowing lightly to scatter the excess.

"Do you have a fella? Someone courting you?" His cheeks tinge adorably pink after he asks.

I bite my lip, Paul looming once more. I'm not wholly sure what he would want me to say. On the one hand, I absolutely know. On the other...Paul trusts me to make the right decisions for myself and for the Wolfpack. To do what I need to do so we build the strongest circle of contacts. He encourages it.

"Perhaps." I stick partially to the truth. "There's a fella back home...it's rather complicated." Matthew listens patiently as I waffle. "You know, I mean...we've known each other forever. And just...well, you know how it is."

"Not quite." He smiles. "Is it a yes or a no?"

"I've made him no promises, nor him to me." Yes, this feels true; this I can say. "So I suppose...no? No, I'm not being 'courted.' It's not like that."

I swallow reflexively. He's standing very close, and I'm simply fascinated by his stubble. It's different from Paul's and Abe's. Theirs grows dark and full, thick sandpaper. Matthew's blond is intriguing, and I really want to touch it. For investigative purposes, of course.

Matthew looks closely at me, and I wonder, for the briefest flicker, if he's going to kiss me. The thought makes me terribly anxious. I hold my breath, waiting, but he steps back.

"That," he says, pointing at me, "is the most nervous I've ever seen you. And the fastest I've ever heard you talk."

Unnerved, I walk around the table to put some distance between us. "It's still your shot," I remind him. The table is quite lopsided with his one remaining ball and my five.

The way the field is aligned, he can attempt an angled chip into one of the side pockets. But it's a steep angle. His eyes are focused, and he exhales gently as he shoots.

"This is absolute malarkey," I announce after the ball rolls into the pocket.

He smiles and positions himself to take a chip at the eight ball.

"What, no question for that one? You don't want to know what I plan to name my firstborn son? Or what I do at night during the full moon?"

"I can't think of one right now, so I'm banking it for later."

"I'm not sure I'll be good for it later," I tell him, narrowing my eyes.

"Eight ball, side pocket."

"Horsefeathers!" I examine the trick shot he's going to attempt.

He concentrates, gnawing on his lower lip. My eyes widen, following the trajectory after he shoots. Mercifully, the ball bounces just to the side of the pocket, granting me a final reprieve.

The state of the table is downright embarrassing, and I'm desperate to rectify the situation. I pick my angle, bending down slowly.

All of a sudden, Matthew is behind me. He leans over as I line up my shot. His hand goes to my hip, more confidently than last time, with far more contact than when he thought he was teaching me how to shoot. His lips are less than an inch from my ear when he whispers to me.

"You sure you know what you're doing?"

"Yes, thank you. I know exactly what I'm doing," I snap. "And so do you, ya scoundrel. Shoo!"

"But I finally thought of my question."

I ignore him to concentrate on my shot. Just as I'm preparing to flick my wrist, he plays his trump card.

"Who did you play strip pool with, Katarina?" His whispering breath is hot against my ear.

His shocking question more than does its job. I miss my target disgracefully.

"No fair," I whine, turning to him.

"If you don't play fair, *I* certainly won't." He smiles wickedly. "I'm waiting on your answer, by the way."

"I am *not* answering."

"You most certainly are."

"I most certainly am not. It's none of your beeswax!"

"Was it a guy? *The* guy?"

These are dangerous waters, but I was made to swim there. And he's had me on my heels for far too long in this game. *You get what you ask for, Matthew.*

"Not guy. Guys," I stipulate boldly. "Plural." Three of them, to be exact. He whistles and steps back.

"Again, not that it's any of your beeswax."

"Guess I deserve that."

"So what do you think?" I challenge. "Am I still living up to your expectations?"

I'm determined to show him I'm not ashamed of who I am. Because I'm not. Paul, Abe, and Tony are nothing to be ashamed of.

"You, Katarina, exceed expectations. Every time." With that, he sinks the eight ball, and the game is finished.

"You don't get a question for that one," I say. "It's game over."

"Oh, I certainly do." He chuckles. "But I'll save it for later."

As our game breaks up, so does the larger gathering. I glance sidelong at Matthew's wristwatch as people trickle outside. It's already after ten p.m.

"Heavens to Betsy!" I grab Matthew's arm. "Is your friend Daniel still here? I need to talk to him."

Matthew's expression is puzzled, but he scans the room and points. "He's over there, with Harry."

Target acquired.

On the periphery of my focus, my wolf has been tracking Harry all evening—cataloging his interactions—and Daniel hasn't left his side. The best route of attack is indirect, and tonight, my route is Daniel.

Also, rather conveniently, Matthew.

I grab my leverage's arm and steer him toward the other gentlemen. As we move, I release an under-the-breath murmur. "Time to reunite the trifecta."

"The what?"

"Oh gosh." I didn't mean to say that out loud. "Gracious, Matthew, why can't I control my mouth around you tonight?"

"I wish you wouldn't try." He laughs. "I'm learning all sorts of interesting things. What in tarnation is the *trifecta*?"

"It's..." I shrug hopelessly. "It's what some of the gals call you. You and Daniel and Harry—the trifecta."

Matthew's eyebrows shoot up.

"Because you're all young and handsome and not married and...you know, your families all are really..." *Wealthy, Matthew. Really fucking wealthy.*

His eyebrows rise higher and higher into his hairline as I talk. That's when I decide it's time to clam up. In fact, I probably should have clammed up hours ago.

"Matthew." Daniel leans in for a handshake.

"And Katarina." Harry greets me with a shifty smile. "This is unexpected."

"Saw you two running the pool table," Daniel says. "It's been forever since we've played. You'll have to have me over one night for a game at your place, Matt."

"Certainly, we'll set something up."

"And we'll have to invite Katarina too," Daniel adds. "Who knew you could shoot pool?"

I flash a coy smile. "Oh, I'm full of surprises."

"It's that Catacomb upbringing," Harry replies. "She's not nearly as buttoned-up as most of these girls. I bet you learned all kinds of tricks down there." His tone is pleasant, but there's a suggestive glint in his eye I don't altogether like.

Matthew frowns but doesn't say anything.

"Hey, Matt?" Daniel claps his shoulder. "I was going to find you before you left. We're throwing an impromptu stag party for Johnnie Rockefeller tomorrow and are headed out to Jekyll Island. It's still offseason, but they're opening the clubhouse for the party."

Harry gives me a light glance before adding his two cents. "It'll be total debauchery, Matt. You know Johnnie doesn't do anything halfway. We're staying on the island. His family is having the bedrooms at Indian Mound aired out."

Staying over? Could it really be so simple?

My jaw drops, my mind racing to the job at Astor Manor. To cover, I squeak out a question. "Indian Mound?"

"The Rockefeller family's cottage at the Jekyll Island Club," Daniel explains. "So what do you say, Matt? Can you make it?"

"I can't, unfortunately," he replies. "I have to work at the hospital tomorrow. I start a twenty-four-hour shift in the morning."

I turn to him in surprise. "Another twenty-four-hour shift? When do you sleep?" I frown when he laughs.

"Matt works all the time," Harry says. "You'll learn that soon enough, Katarina—haven't you noticed he's not usually at these events?"

"Right." Matthew fidgets uncomfortably before turning to me. "Didn't you have something to tell Daniel?"

I stall. "Well, it's a bit of a secret actually. I reckon I shan't say it in front of everyone."

"I love secrets!" Daniel's brown eyes light up. "You have to tell us. Come on, out with it."

"Okay..." I draw out the word as I think. I've got something prepared, of course, but I'd hoped it wouldn't come to this.

All three men are expectant.

"My friend Florence thinks you're plumb swell!" I blurt. Daniel and Harry both start heckling.

"Florence *Vanderbilt*?" Harry repeats. "She thinks anyone with money in the bank is *plumb swell*. Me, Daniel, Matthew..."

"Yeah, that secret doesn't amount to a hill of beans," Daniel says once his laughter subsides. "Flo and I have been on the make—and then some—for years." He winks. "But thanks, Katarina. I'll take it under advisement. If she's interested in coming back for seconds, who am I to refuse?"

I fight the urge to roll my eyes. It's undoubtedly time to depart.

"Matthew?" I tighten my grip on his arm. "Shall we step outside?"

He nods. "Have fun tomorrow, fellas. Good seeing you."

"You mentioned last week you like the gardens, right?" I prattle as we exit the billiard room. "Have you seen them at night before?"

"Yes, loads of times. My mom works here, remember?"

"Oh, that's right." I sigh dramatically. "Never mind. It's getting late, and apparently you have to work another absurd shift tomorrow, so…"

"So…?"

"So I should say goodnight to you."

"But I still have one question."

I lean against him in exasperation. "Haven't you tortured me enough this evening?"

He laughs. "You did fine. Exceeded expectations, remember?"

"Yes, and embarrassed myself all over the place."

"You didn't embarrass yourself. Honesty isn't embarrassing. It's refreshing."

"I was talking about our game of pool."

"Oh, well…" He pulls a face. "I suppose it *was* a tad humiliating."

"Humiliating?" I repeat, appalled.

"Just a tad, I said."

"Indeed." I turn to face him. "So you see, Matthew, I've had quite a trying evening. Unless you're offering a very stiff drink before asking me yet *another* potentially scandalous question, I'm going to take my leave."

"I can get you a stiff drink."

"Where?" I cross my arms, calling his bluff.

"My mom's office. She keeps a bottle of whiskey in the bottom drawer of her desk."

"Lady Genevieve?" I gasp. "Surely not."

"It's mostly for my dad when he visits, but it's in there." His mischievous smile is back, tugging at something deep in my stomach.

"We shouldn't..." I say.

"Probably not," he agrees.

"But you could...you could get in?"

"Of course."

My heartbeat races, just like it always does at the thought of breaking the rules, of doing something I shouldn't.

"Show me."

CHAPTER EIGHT

"Well, I do declare, who would have thought?" I drag my fingers across Lady Genevieve's mahogany desk. "Straitlaced Matthew DaMolin...breaking all kinds of rules?"

"Who said I'm straitlaced?" He pulls a crystal decanter from the bottom drawer, then plunks down two glass tumblers. "I got you down here with me, didn't I?"

"You did," I admit. I can only imagine the repercussions if we're caught here, alone, but I shiver with pleasure at the illicit thrill.

Matthew pours two thimble-sized drinks, clinks his glass to mine, and throws back. My stomach clenches deliciously as his stubbled throat bobs, the whiskey sliding down in a single gulp. He places the empty tumbler down with a soft *clink*, his eyes lifting to mine.

I toss my own shot back. It burns as it glides down...burns so good. I lick my lips, then extend my glass for a refill. "Another."

Matthew's second pour is heftier than the first.

"M'lady," he murmurs as he hands the glass over. There's a wry, challenging smile in his eyes as I accept the drink.

"Careful, pretty boy." I sit on the wooden desk. "You might find you're punching beyond your weight."

He looks at me sitting, casual and irreverent, on his mother's desk. "I think I am."

I swing my tumbler, gesturing. "This is every fella's fantasy, isn't it? Alone at night with a pretty girl in his mother's office, sipping whiskey. Wow—I'm such a cliché. Wait a minute, we've come full circle. We're back to Freud...and your Mommy and Daddy issues." I open my mouth and place a mock-shocked hand over it.

"You're a real trip." His eyes glitter as he takes a slow sip of whiskey.

I hold his gaze and take a deep pull of my own. "Clearly, you enjoy the ride."

"I do," he admits, walking over to stand between my legs. He looks intently at me, his face inches from mine. "You were right. It drives me absolutely crazy that I can't figure you out. I never know what's going to come out of your mouth next." His gaze drops to my lips, his voice now a whisper. "Who are you?"

I swallow the rest of my drink before answering. My sight lowers to a framed black-and-white photograph on the desk. It's a wedding portrait, Lady Genevieve and her husband. The infamous DaMolin ruby necklace hangs around her neck in all its glory. I forcibly withhold a whistle, my fingertips tingling. Itching.

When I raise my lashes, the question still hangs on Matthew's lips, his eyes brimming with it.

"Is that your final question?" I ask. "Who am I?"

"That one is going to take months to riddle out. So no, it's not the question tonight."

"What is it then? You gave me my drink, so I'll give you your answer."

He's quiet for a minute. In the dim light, his sapphire eyes are ablaze.

"Katarina..." he breathes. He tucks a lock of dark hair behind my ear. "Katarina, can I kiss you?"

My heart stutters at his vulnerability, but I'm disappointed. It's the first time all night he's disappointed me. I consider for a moment before answering.

"No," I tell him, placing my empty glass on the desk.

"Why not?"

"Because you asked," I reply. "If you want to kiss me, I expect you to just do it. I don't want to be *asked*. I want to be *kissed*."

"I come from a world where people ask first."

"And I come from a world where people *take*."

"I'm not going to take advantage of you, Katarina." He shakes his head. "That's not who I am."

I shrug one shoulder, unmoved. "I guess that leaves us in a bit of a predicament."

"You like games, don't you?" He nods, understanding. "I like games too. Maybe we'll play by your rules next time, but tonight we're sticking to mine."

And with that, he takes my hands and slides me off the desk.

"Meaning what?"

"Meaning we're going to put the whiskey away, and I'm going to lock up this office, then I'll walk you to the front staircase to say goodnight. Like a gentleman."

I pout. "That doesn't sound like a particularly fun game."

"It's not the one you're used to, I'm sure."

It most certainly is not. "Your game, your rules."

He takes my hand again and pulls me out of the office, locking the door behind us. He keeps ahold of me until we reach the main staircase.

"Goodnight, Katarina." He lifts my hand to kiss the knuckles. Prim and excruciatingly proper. "Sleep well."

"Wait," I call out as he turns to go. I feel supremely dissatisfied, and that's very annoying, but now two of these Academy events have been a heck of a lot more fun since he's been around. Against my better judgment, I swallow my pride. "Will you be at the annual picnic next weekend?"

"I usually am. My parents are the hosts."

Right. *Very smooth, Kat.*

"But I may have to work this year." He watches me closely. "My older brother, Ethan, will certainly be there though, and he's still a bachelor. A charming officer, fresh from the ranks of the Great War. You needn't worry. The trifecta will stay intact."

I smile, amused by his quick wit.

"Besides, Ethan is a much better catch than me—a war hero set to inherit the family publishing empire." Matthew's smile is self-deprecating. "I'm sure the sharks will be out in full force."

"Is that really how you see us? Sharks?"

"Yes. *You* are most definitely a shark."

"Moi?" I place a hand to my breastbone in playful astonishment.

"Yes, you. Don't act surprised."

"I'll take it as a compliment. Goodnight, Matthew."

"You should. Goodnight, Katarina."

A shark. Hmm...I mull it over as I traipse upstairs alone. That's certainly a new one.

And then it hits me clear in the face. Sharks are scavengers and carnivores, just like wolves.

Maybe Matthew DaMolin really does have me all figured out.

———◦○◦———

WHEN I REACH MY bedroom, I'm confronted with a new problem. A quite pressing problem that somehow took a backseat to drinking whiskey tonight with Matthew.

Melinda is inside our room, already asleep—thank goodness—but I need to contact the Royals to tell them about Harry. We need to move on Astor Manor *tomorrow.*

I go to the window and quietly open it, peering into the darkness. Usually after evening events at the Academy, Abe waits in Forsyth Park in case I have any inside tips to pass along. But it's late tonight—much later than usual—and there's a very good chance Abe has already returned to the bayou. I can hardly expect him to wait around all night while I'm busy drinking whiskey in glorified closets with cute rich boys.

Which, by the way, *never* happens.

I swing a leg over the windowsill, then push off the wall, flying down to earth instead of climbing. I land nimbly on my toes with bent knees, gold heels slamming with a *clack* on the cobblestones. I exhale in a huff and point my feet in the direction of the tiny arboretum that marks our rendezvous point. The park looks deserted.

There's nothing for it, I realize. I'll either have to find a running streetcar or hoof it all the way to the bayou on foot. I groan, bracing myself for yet another long night, when I see the slightest rustling at the edge of the trees ahead. My breath catches.

A dark silhouette steps forward, just enough for moonlight to flash across his face.

"Abe!" I fly into his arms, hard and fast. He grunts at the impact. "I'm so happy to see you."

"Hi, Kat," he rumbles.

"I can't believe you're still here. Thank god." I release him and step back.

"Where have you been?" He sticks his hands in his pockets as though it doesn't matter, but I can tell he's a little miffed.

"I was with someone," I say slowly. "I'm really sorry."

"How was your night? You look grand."

I swallow my guilt about Matthew. "It was good—I have hot news. Harry Astor is going to be out tomorrow. All night."

"Tomorrow?" Abe's face falls. "That barely gives us any time to prepare."

"But, Abe, it's perfect." I rush to explain. "It's a Thursday night, which means the food delivery folks will be there, and Lady Astor will be alone in the house. Harry will be at a stag party on Jekyll Island."

"Hold your horses, Kat. A stag party? Who in tarnation has a stag party on a Thursday?"

I wave the question away. "Unemployed rich boys, that's who."

"Are you sure you heard correctly?"

"Yes. Daniel Dufour and Harry Astor talked about it. They said..." I try to remember exactly. "They said it's an impromptu stag party for Johnnie Rockefeller, they're opening the clubhouse early, and airing out one of the cottages on the island for an overnight. I was standing right there when Harry said it. Right beside him. He was inviting Matthew, and—"

"Matthew DaMolin?" Abe raises an eyebrow.

"Yes," I whisper, suddenly nervous.

"Is that who you were with tonight?"

"Not that it matters, but yes. He's who I was with."

"Paul told me you met him last week," Abe offers. "He had me shadow him for a few days."

"Oh my god, he didn't." I groan.

"He's pretty boring." Abe shrugs. "Just works a lot, down at the hospital. He's either there or his apartment in the city."

"Good to know." It's hard to keep annoyance out of my voice.

"Don't be mad, Kat. You know how Paul is."

I do know, always keeping his tabs. I wrap my arms around my ribs, because suddenly, I feel like crying.

Abe's face softens. "You okay?"

I blink a few times. It came out of nowhere, but I'm overwhelmed. Rode hard and put up wet.

I'm exhausted from the insane schedule I've been pulling lately. I'm sexually frustrated from the abrupt end to my game with Matthew tonight.

I'm emotionally drained from having to compartmentalize so many twisted relationships, clutching secrets to my chest like daggers.

I shouldn't have to justify anything to anyone. Not who I'm seeing or what I'm doing. None of it.

And because that's how I feel right now—impulsive and vulnerable and positively aching with need—I stand on my tiptoes and press my lips very forcefully to Abe's. Trying to prove I can have whatever I want, whenever I want it.

"Kat, no." He pulls away. "You're upset about something. I don't know what, but this is not the solution."

"It could be a very good solution, actually." I give him my best puppy-dog eyes.

"Cute, but I don't think so."

I drop my arms and step back, rejected and dejected all over again. It's worse the second time around.

"Hey." He tips my chin up with his hand. "What's going on with you tonight?"

"Nothing."

"Kat, you haven't kissed me twice in the same week...ever. What happened on Saturday should tide us over for months. That's just how we operate. You know I love you, but you're head over heels for my best friend. He would cut off my dick if I—"

"I know. I'm sorry." My voice cracks. "I'm just frustrated from my evening, and I'm projecting it on you. I'm sorry," I repeat.

"*Sexually* frustrated?" Abe cocks an eyebrow. Once again, he's too quick for his own good. "From DaMolin?"

I roll my eyes. "I didn't say that. You did."

"Are you telling me you made a pass at him tonight, and he said *no*?" Abe laughs incredulously. "Wow, I must be losing my touch. I missed the fact he was queer during my two days of surveillance."

"He's not queer," I say. "He's a gentleman. And I didn't make a pass at him. Please."

"Sure." Abe smiles, and I don't miss the lines of hidden laughter etched onto his face.

"Can we just drop it?"

"Works for me." He's still smiling. Presumptuous.

"Just tell Paul and Tony about the job. I'll see you tomorrow."

CHAPTER NINE

In the pitch dark of night, a crescent moon is our only light. Astor Manor looms before us, cloaked in shadow. A most tantalizing temptation indeed.

"Kat, everything set? You remember the floorplan?" Paul asks.

"Yes, I'm ready." I bounce on my toes.

"Time check." He thrusts his tarnished gold pocket watch into the center of our circle. Abe, Tony, and I follow suit with our own timepieces, synchronizing down to the second. Tony, facetious as always, wears a watch on each arm.

When Paul is satisfied, he nods. "All right, it's 10:14 p.m. now. In sixty seconds, Tony and I will move on the carriage house."

"Stay safe," I murmur.

Paul nods again, his eyes never leaving his watch.

"Three, two, one...get a wiggle on!"

We divide into two groups, moving in opposite directions through the shadows of Astor Manor's neo-Roman garden. Paul and Tony head east to the carriage house, disappearing behind a curtain of Spanish moss. Abe and I, both clad in our trademark black, slink around a corner to huddle against the manor's west wall, hearts pounding.

We chose the western perimeter as my takeoff point for one specific reason—the three-story stone fireplace flue. The exterior of the mansion is made of polished marble bricks, too expensively smooth for even my adroit feet to find purchase. But the home's multiple fireplace flues are made of deep-cut, angular stones. Several of the chimneys jut out solely at the rooftop level, but this one very conveniently runs up the entirety of the manor's exterior, ground to roof.

Abe glides, phantomlike, across the west lawn. When we reach the stone chimney, he locks his fingers together to give me a boost. Unnecessary but kind. As I establish my grip, I wonder if our quarry—that beautiful gold ballerina—is perhaps just on the other side of the stone walls beneath my fingers. My mouth drips with molten honey, tasting her nearness.

As Abe melts back into the cover of darkness, I scamper upward.

It's a very slim flue, but toeholds are easy to find in the grooves between rough-hewn stones. I'm a vertical trapeze artist—stretching, pulling, flying. I reach the roof in about sixty seconds. The breeze lifts the end of my ponytail as I peer at the carriage house. A ground-level light is on near the guards' quarters, but I can't see inside. I have no way of knowing if the three watchmen are still locked, safe and snug, in their office, bartering responsibilities for patrols with throws of their dice. No way of knowing if Paul and Tony have moved to disable them. No way of knowing if an alarm has been sounded.

Anxious, I glance at my watch. It's 10:18, the precise minute Paul planned to breach. I exhale slowly, blowing down my concern.

I have to trust him—*them*—to get their job done. Same as they're trusting me to do mine.

I creep along the roof's edge, keeping as close to the gutter as I can to avoid slipping on sloped tile. I'm a tightrope walker now, arms out and legs steady as I traverse all the way to the eastern perimeter of the house. The side where the scullery and delivery truck are.

There's another chimney over here, this time a double-wide flue for the main kitchen. After another quick glimpse at my watch, I cup my gloved hands around my lips and let out a melodic bird whistle, designed to mimic the three-part coo of Savannah's ever-present mourning doves. This is Abe's ten-minute warning. The only one I'll give before disappearing into the belly of the beast.

Arms trembling with adrenaline, I haul myself atop the flue. Before I start my descent, I pause for a steadying breath.

Chimneys are death traps. There are a dozen different ways to get stuck inside. They've been the downfall of hundreds of thieves throughout history. But I'm no ordinary thief. And the flue of this chimney is bigger than most because it ends at the massive hearth of the ground floor kitchen. It's nearly two feet all around.

Slowly, slowly, slowly I lower myself. I keep my body straight and tall, flexing my feet, locking in stability with my toes on the wall. My core is tight as a spring. The real work, however, falls to my arms. I bend them at a ninety-degree angle so my hands are near my ears. I press my gloved palms against the wall, ensuring I won't slip. Then, little by little, like an inchworm, I begin to descend.

It's excruciating work. I'm panting at the halfway point; I'm sooty and sweaty near the bottom. The interior stones of the flue radiate heat at me, every breath tinged with woodsmoke. And all the while, my watch ticks away beside my ear, clocking every second like the pound of a funeral drum.

When the concrete base of the hearth is in sight, my body nearly spasms with relief. At this height, I could safely drop and relieve the terrible ache in my shoulders and arms, but I pause, listening closely. I need to be sure.

I grin when I hear it, the sound of raucous laughter and clinking glasses.

At first, we couldn't figure out why the delivery truck loitered outside the manor on Thursday evenings. Two weeks ago, Tony "borrowed" a uniform from one of the delivery men and slipped aboard the truck in his stead. That's when we learned about the gambling.

On Thursdays, after all the food is unloaded, the delivery workers and kitchen staff run a weekly card game in the servants' hall. Chores stay largely unfinished until morning, limiting after-hours foot traffic through the kitchen and manor.

Satisfied with the recon, I take a deep breath and let go. I land in a crouch on the balls of my feet and pull a cloth from my pocket to wipe soot from my gloves and shoes. Then I crawl out of the fireplace and around the corner, scampering like a rat. I check my watch again. Sixty-seven seconds until I'm due to meet Abe.

The house is silent and dark as I sneak to the back terrace. When I arrive, I unlock multiple deadbolts on the glass-paneled garden door.

"Long time no see, Kitty-Kat." Smirking, Abe slides out from behind a column and strides into the manor.

"Abe." I quickly turn all three locks on the door. *Just as you were.* "Any news on Paul and Tony?"

"About three minutes ago, they flicked the carriage house lights in the five-beat signal we practiced."

I sigh with relief, lowering my eyes. As Abe checks his timepiece, my nimble, sticky fingers drift idly to a nearby table. It houses a set of tiny crystal animals. A glass menagerie. The collection must have cost a fortune.

I whistle, plucking an animal from the outer ring. "Look, Abe. Is this what I think it is?" I hold the glass wolf up.

"Ironic." He chuckles.

"It's beautiful." I put the wolf down. "Ready to divide and conquer?"

"Meet you at the stairwell in five."

We depart to hunt down the fireplaces scattered throughout the home, splitting up to check the first four; Abe takes the bottom floor while I take the middle. My heart roars in my ears, my breath swelling like a tornado in my chest as I prowl up the stairs. I slip into an interior sitting room featuring a beautiful marble fireplace. The lighting is dim, so I cross the room to check the mantel, sweeping my hand across the cool marble.

No dancer.

My second target is a few paces down the hall. This mantel is made of intricately carved mahogany. A lethal pair of crossed swords is mounted above, and two portraits of eighteenth-century gentlemen in full finery and wigs hang astride. Like sentinels, their eyes seem to follow my every step as I approach, then bore into my back as I depart, empty-handed and breathless, moments later. I shiver as I click the door shut.

Hoping Abe had better luck, I tiptoe toward our rendezvous point at the main stairwell. Every creak and groan of the house sends a dizzying wave of anxiety across my vision. I freeze before rounding the final corner, hearing a dangerous whisper of footsteps. I stuff a fist over my mouth to muffle my ragged breath, leaning my head around for a peek.

Abe.

I exhale in a *whoosh* and reveal myself. Abe eyes my empty hands, then shakes his head. His search, like mine, turned up nothing.

I raise my eyes to the swirling staircase, apprehensive. Looks like we're headed for the third floor, the private living quarters. Abe points upward, silently asking if I'm ready.

We're a well-oiled machine. Abe and I slink up the stairs and down the hall in perfect tandem. The plush carpeting muffles any hint of footfalls as we head to our first checkpoint, Harry's office. The door is locked, but that won't keep us out.

On bended knee, Abe slips a slender flathead from his waistline and jimmies the door. A few soft *clicks* later, we're in. I close the heavy door behind us while Abe heads for the fireplace.

"Dammit," he mutters, turning to me.

Five fireplaces searched, five empty. The ballerina is either safely ensconced in the master bedroom or it's nowhere to be found, and the entire job will have been for naught.

"We're going to have to wait it out, Kat. Like we talked about," Abe says.

"What time is it?"

"Eleven fifteen."

"We need to hide for almost *two hours*?"

"Yes. There's a linen closet right outside the master," Abe reminds me. "That's Plan B."

"Can't we just stay here?" I offer weakly. "The door is locked. The staff probably won't come in here to clean..."

Abe shakes his head. "That's not the plan, Kat. This room is a hot zone. If Harry returns, this is the first place he'll come. We have no extraction plan."

"He's not coming home."

"Plan B, Kat." Abe stonewalls me. "We don't go rogue mid-mission, we always follow the plan. We wait directly outside the master bedroom, and when the time is right, we make our move."

"And if she doesn't wake up for her usual pee, Abe? What then?"

"We'll tackle that if we come to it. That's why I'm here with you."

I look at my partner with unease, understanding now why Paul was so insistent I have back-up inside the house.

Lady Astor is Abe's assignment, I realize.

If it comes to that.

"Let's go." Abe heads for the hallway. I wait patiently while he crouches, clicking tumblers back in place to lock the door.

"Like we were never here," I murmur when he rises.

When we reach the closet, Abe chivalrously swings the door open. I squeeze myself inside, wiggling like a fish on a hook as I try to maximize space. Abe takes one look at my fidgeting and shakes his head. He pulls me by the arm and switches our positions. Once inside, he sits on the floor and leans against the wall, stretching his legs the length of the closet.

He holds his arms out to me and lowers his voice. "Come here, Kat."

"You want me to sit on you? For two hours?"

"You weigh ten pounds. I'll be fine."

I stare at him, unconvinced.

"Come here, Kat," he urges again.

Reluctantly, I step inside. I straddle him, still standing, and pull the closet door shut, plunging us into darkness. I sink onto his lap and wrap my arms and legs around Abe's middle like a monkey. He grunts softly as I jockey my position.

"Kat, watch where you're...distributing your weight."

"This was your brilliant idea."

"I know. I just want to make sure I still have the ability to procreate after this."

"I'd be doing the world a favor if you couldn't," I mumble, nestling my chin on his shoulder.

"Hilarious."

My eyes slowly begin to adjust, making out the angular planes of Abe's face and eyes. "Now what?"

"What do you mean, *now what*?"

"I mean, what are we going to do in here for nearly two hours, Abe?"

"I don't know what *you're* going to do, but I'm going to catch some sleep."

"You're gonna *sleep*?" I ask, disbelieving. "In the middle of a job?"

"Yup." He yawns mightily and tightens his arms around me. "I'm tired, you're warm. Wake me in ninety minutes."

I huff in annoyance but say nothing more. I try to sit still, but after only five minutes, my legs are already stiff. My adrenaline is pumping, endorphins running full throttle. How can Abe possibly sleep at a time like this? I could climb back up the chimney and dance on the rooftop naked.

"Abe?"

"Ya?"

"I'm bored."

"Christ, Kat." He opens his eyes.

"Play with me?"

"*Play* with you? We're in a fucking closet," he hisses. "What could you possibly have in mind?"

"We could try...three times in one week?"

"You wanna start necking?" He's dubious.

"I wanna do *something*."

"Like make Paul's ears bleed? Because, again, I'd like to retain my ability to procreate, and if Paul heard you ask that, he'd have my hide. And my front."

"Paul doesn't mind sharing me with you."

"Paul only shares when he's around to supervise."

"Is that a no?"

He groans, shifting beneath me. "It's not a good idea, Kat."

"Okay. We can do something else then."

"Like sleep?"

I shake my head. "I can't sleep. You shouldn't either."

"All right," he sighs. "You win."

"I do?"

"Yes. Come here." He reaches for my face.

"Really?"

"Yeah. If you won't let me sleep, I may as well get something out of it."

"So romantic," I grumble.

"Watch yourself." His tone is sharp. "If you want romance, go to Paul. Now clam up, Kat." His fingers lightly graze my cheeks before he presses his lips to mine.

Hunger, fast and stabbing, flares. We are a tangle of demanding lips and groping fingers. All impulse, no thought. Hips pressing into groin.

My endorphins sigh. Adrenaline sings.

When my lips become swollen from his kisses, I move to the base of his neck, sucking and tugging. Little nips. Hard pulls. Abe groans.

His hands slide up and down my waist. Time blurs, the whispering ticks of our synchronized watches urging us on. We're feverish at first, then slow and thorough. No nerve ending left untouched. Every knot languidly unkinked.

I've never kissed Abe like this before, and now I know what a mistake that's been. Romance or not, I taste love on his lips.

"Kat." He pulls back. "It's almost time."

"Is it?" I mumble, dazed.

"We should get into position."

On shaky legs, I rise. Blood rushes painfully in. I cling to the wall as Abe wiggles to stand beside me.

"Fucking Christ," he groans. He kicks out his long legs, hands sneaking to adjust the tented crotch of his pants.

"Sorry," I whisper.

"You're not sorry," he grumbles, still rearranging.

I don't reply because he's right. I'm not sorry.

In the hallway, we stare at our watches, bated breaths coming in time with the tick of every second. We press our ears against the master bedroom door, listening.

One o'clock comes and goes.

Then 1:05.

1:10.

At 1:15, I start hyperventilating.

"What if she doesn't get up tonight?" I whisper. "What then?"

"She will."

"What if she *doesn't*?"

Suddenly, light streams into the hallway from beneath the door. Abe steps back, and my heart stutters. He points expectantly.

I put my hand on the doorknob. If I believed in God, this would be the moment to pray.

But I don't. God doesn't live in the dark corners of the Catacombs. God doesn't breathe at the point of our knives. God didn't turn water to wine, not for us. Only *we* have ever done that. For ourselves and for each other.

Emboldened, I raise my eyelids and crack open the door. The bed is on my immediate right, the blankets pulled back, an empty indentation in the sheets. The fireplace is across the room, and...

There she is.

The Dancer.

Bathroom light trickles into the bedroom. Lady Astor left the door wide open, but I don't hesitate. There simply isn't time.

Fortune favors the bold, I remind myself. Then that whispering, ubiquitous voice speaks. *If they can't see you, they'll never catch you, Kat.*

I sneak ahead, darting on light feet past the door and to the mantel. I reach up to seize the glimmering ballerina. She's much heavier than anticipated. Solid. Easily the weight of a full gold bar, perhaps two.

Holding my breath, I dart back across the room. The toilet flushes when I reach the door, the bathroom light extinguishes.

I slip through the crack into the hallway and catch Abe finishing up his work. He's painted our wolf mark across the white wood of the bedroom door. The now universally-understood sign the Wolfpack was here.

Abe takes my hand and pulls me down the hall, all the way to a corner room at the opposite end. It's a bedroom, probably a spare if the lack of personal items and clutter indicate anything. He clicks the door shut and reaches for the figurine.

He whistles softly. "Wow. She's the real McCoy, huh, Kat? What a beaut."

"She is," I admit, admiring the heftiness of the gold in my grip, the way the ballerina shines, her eyes twinkling in the moonlight.

"Let's get the heck outta here." Abe strides over to the window and unlocks it. It glides up without a sound. "Ladies first."

I swing my legs out and reach for the metal drainpipe to my right, dangling off the side of the house.

"Remember to close the window behind you," I tell Abe. "See you at the bottom."

I slide down, keeping the ballerina tucked securely in my arm as I plummet to the ground. Overhead, Abe swings his feet out and grabs the pipe, shifting his weight. I hold my breath. The pipe is solid, made of metal, and we're trusting blindly it will hold him.

Once he has a good grip, Abe palms the windowpane with his gloved hand, sliding the glass down. Moments later, he drops down the pipe to join me. I don't release my breath until he's safely on the ground.

In a giddy daze, we traipse to the carriage house and give a coded knock, a familiar four-beat rhythm to signal Paul and Tony. The door swings open, and there they are, the other half of our pack. A little rumpled and ruffled, but none the worse for the wear. There's a good bit of blood on the floor. Spatters on their shirts and arms. Peeking over Paul's shoulder, I see the three guards piled in a corner.

They aren't breathing.

"Did you really have to kill them?" I ask, looking at Paul. He has a small laceration above his left eyebrow, but it's long since clotted over.

"When it turned into a three-hour job, yes," he replies. "We couldn't ensure they'd stay unconscious. Or that they wouldn't wake and alert the authorities before we got away. You know the motto, Kat—fool me once..."

"Shame on you," I finish the first part. "Fool me twice—"

"Nobody fools me," he concludes. "We don't allow that to happen."

I nod. Risk management. I glance at the pile one more time. Remorse, a most unsettling mistress, tightens around my neck like a noose. It was nothing more than misfortune that cut these lives short tonight, leaving countless loose strings—family, loved ones—to dangle evermore in the wind.

The hot metal of our plunder grows warm in my hand, branding me.

"Can I see her?" Paul asks, reaching his hand out.

I pass *The Dancer* over.

"You're unbelievable, Kat." He examines the gold figurine, rapture in his eyes. "We really pulled it off."

"We really did."

Paul drifts to the window to admire the gilded loot in the moonlight.

"Plan B, huh?" Tony strides over. "Everything go smoothly on your end, guys? Enjoy your two hours of closet time?"

"We survived." I'm evasive.

"I bet." Tony leans in close, his eyes crinkling with amusement before he whispers in my ear. "You might wanna tell Abe to cover his hickey before Paul sees it. Just a suggestion."

"What?"

"The vamp bite...on his neck." He raises an eyebrow. "I mean, *I* don't care what you two got up to in the closet, but I bet Paul will."

I glance at Abe, and sure enough, he's sporting a tiny red bruise where his neck joins his shoulder. I give his black shirt a quick tug to hide the evidence. Abe looks down and sees what I'm doing, his eyes wide and accusing. I smile apologetically.

Looks like Plan B was slightly more dangerous than either of us realized.

<hr/>

BY NOON THE NEXT day, pandemonium reigns. The news is everywhere. It's all anyone can talk about. I can't take two steps in the Academy corridors without hearing someone whispering about the heist.

"Did you hear?"

"The Wolfpack!"

"They hit Astor Manor."

"Astor Manor?"

"Was Harry home? Is he okay?"

"They're menaces."

"They're vigilantes!"

"They're extraordinary."

"They're *dangerous*."

CHAPTER TEN

"PAUL?" I SLAM THE door of his city flat.

"In the kitchen, doll."

"What are you doing?" I'm taken aback as I enter the room. "It smells amazing in here."

Paul pauses over a saucepan. "I'm trying something new—cooking."

"What? I didn't even know you *could* cook." I lean around him. Two small chicken breasts sizzle in a pan, smothered in a simmering, deliciously creamy sauce. There's an uncorked bottle of wine on the counter, flanked by two glasses.

"I don't usually bother," Paul begins, "but Abe mentioned something about you needing some good romancing..."

Sensing danger, I cross my arms. My green eyes flick to his. "What exactly did the traitor say?"

"Relax, Kat." He laughs. "I'm not mad. Abe didn't tattle. I saw the hickey."

"Oh." I gnaw on my lip. "I'm sorry, it was my fault. He wanted to rest, and I...I told him I was bored."

Paul turns to dice an onion, light glinting off the blade of his chef's knife. His eyes are downcast when he finally speaks. "Doll." He sighs, the endearment punctuated by a heavy, thudding slice of the knife. "We've never talked about exclusivity, have we? I understand you—who you are, what you need. And sometimes, where Abe is concerned, you just can't seem to help yourself."

I look closely at Paul before I reply. His tone is neutral, but his grip on the knife is tight, white-knuckled.

Paul and I have never laid down any formal rules where our relationship is concerned. After nearly ten years together, founded and grounded in hell itself, there's a certain level of implicit understanding. The door may be open, but at the end of the day, we always come home to each other. We've both had our share of fleeting flirtations and dalliances with marks, but they mean very little when two people are bonded the way Paul and I are. Abe is the rare exception, and our trust with him is absolute, forged in the same fire that welded Paul and me together.

"Would you prefer I try though?" I finally ask. Abe has been a rotating player in our bedroom for years, but I'd be lying if I said he came without strings. I'm not opposed to exclusivity with Paul, but I want to hear the words from him. For him to ask.

Paul shrugs and turns back to mind the stove. "I love the way you are, Kat. You're impulsive and passionate, and you chase adventures. It's why we're so good together...because I'm built exactly the same way. Abe doesn't bother me."

"Would it bother you if it was someone else though?"

As he considers this, Paul grabs the knife again. He scrapes the blade to sweep the diced onion into the pan. Steam rises, filling the air with cloying humidity. "That's a difficult question to answer, Kat. I won't ask for anything you aren't willing to give."

You're not asking, but are you expecting it nonetheless? I swallow the words, uncertain how they'll be received. My gaze falls on a copy of the evening newspaper. The front page is open, headlines screaming.

"Ah." Paul slides the paper down the counter. "Picked this up on my walk home. Reckon it's wise to keep abreast of these dangerous times we live in."

I crack a smile. It feels like only yesterday we were just a misfit crew of kids in the Combs, teaching each other how to read from scrounged newspapers. Tony's family taught him the alphabet and phonics before he undertook his infamous stowaway journey from Cuba to America, but Spanish was his comfort language. Paul knew the alphabet as well; it proved one of few lessons that stuck after his brief stint in the orphanage. Working in tandem, they cobbled together an understanding solid enough to bring Abe and me up to speed.

I always hated the dry newspaper scraps, littered as they were with complex rhetoric and political propaganda, but the day Paul came home with a filched copy of a newly released storybook, *Peter and Wendy*...that was when the tide turned. For the first time, I truly lost myself in the pages of a book. We all did. And we played pretend as Peter's—really Paul's—Lost Boys for weeks, flying down alleys in the Catacomb tunnels, hiding in alcoves to escape Hook. I didn't pick up a news circular for nearly a month, just turned the pages of Peter's story until they began pulling loose from the binding. Such is the power of an imaginative tale in the hands of a child, particularly a story that resonates as more fact than fiction.

But the centerfold tale in tonight's evening edition is not nearly so whimsical. The entire cover features a full-page story about us, the Wolf-pack. Much of the text is focused on the heist at Astor Manor, but there's also a dedicated section on identifying us.

Three men and one woman...dark-haired...early twenties...wolf tattoos on the males' backs, left wrist tattoo on the female...Paul, surname un-known...highly dangerous...

"It continues on pages three and four." Paul nods coolly to the notation on the corner.

"The information on our tattoos is wrong." I point to the relevant section. The boys are tattooed on their sides, and mine is on my finger. "Except for yours, I guess."

"Luckily, you're the only one who gets to see me without my shirt, so I think we're safe."

"This doesn't make you nervous?"

"Not really. It's malarkey, pure speculation. It's no different from after we pulled our last big job."

"I suppose you're right…"

But I chew uncertainly on the inside of my cheek as we sit down to eat. Paul pours two glasses of wine, then slides a plate in front of me, the tantalizing smell of garlic and oregano hitting me full in the face.

"Speaking of news, I've been meaning to ask…" Paul sinks into the adjacent chair and tosses the newspaper aside. "Have you heard anything else from the DaMolin fella? You know, the one whose family *owns* this paper?"

I smile, but my response is careful. I bring a delicate bite of chicken to my lips before answering. "Why so interested?"

"I think he might be valuable."

"In what way?" I put my fork down.

"If we ever want to pull off another high-profile job. Perhaps at…say, Jekyll Island."

"And *why* would we want to do that?"

"Oh, I dunno, Kat." He places a teasing finger to his chin, mock speculating. "Jekyll Island hosts one-sixth of the world's total wealth during the winter. It's where the Federal Reserve was created, the first transcontinental phone call too. The wealth there is staggering, not to mention the prestige of pulling off a job like that. It's the Holy Grail of heists, the pièce de résistance! If I had my druthers—"

"Is your memory so short you've already forgotten the job we *just* pulled?"

"Doll, I'm looking ahead to what's next. What options we have going forward. The DaMolins are just that—an option. They've been members of the club for two decades, even built their own cottage on the grounds. A cottage where—rumor has it—the infamous DaMolin rubies are locked away. I know you've heard of those." His smile turns impish.

"Of course I've heard of them." I snort, then sip my wine, pondering this. Pondering him.

The Holy Grail of heists...

Paul stands from his chair. His fingers glide over my collarbone as he bends down behind me. His breath tickles my ear as he whispers, "Those rubies would look stunning around your neck."

Shivers rise.

"Absolutely stunning. So," he continues, his tone mesmerizing, "has he come around again, the DaMolin fella?"

The spell breaks. The legs of my chair screech as I push back. "He may have." I grab my wineglass and head for the bedroom, hoping against hope Paul won't follow.

"*May* have?" To my chagrin, he's right on my heels. "Why are you being coy?"

"I'm not being coy." I sit on the bed. "He *may* have come around on Wednesday. You *may* have had Abe tail him for two days last week. It's all very mysterious, isn't it?"

"You and Abe talk too much."

"We talk because we know when your wheels are turning, Paul, and I'm not sure I like where they're headed. I need a break for a little while. Please."

"Okay." He raises his hands. "We'll take a break. I'm just saying, in the meantime—"

"Do my job?" I narrow my eyes.

He snorts. "Come on, Kat. I'm making the same suggestion I've made a dozen times before. Why're you getting so defensive about it today? Is he interested or not?"

I place my wineglass on the bedside table with a decisive *thud*. A dollop of liquid sloshes onto the wood.

"He's interested." Frankly, I wish it would bother Paul a little more.

"Good. Keep him that way."

I forcibly withhold an eye roll as I yank open the drawer, searching for something to mop up the spill. As the drawer slides out, however, it's not napkins I see first. It's a revolver.

I freeze.

Paul *hates* guns. He enforces a strict no-gun policy among the gangs in the bayou. At least, he tries to. He says real men don't fight with guns, only cowards do. In the Wolfpack, we only brandish knives. The other gangs know the rules, but there are always heaters floating around the bayou. Much like the threat of Prohibition, nothing stops the black market. But if Paul catches one of the underlings with the weapon, he'll flay them alive.

"Paul." I find my voice. "Why do you have a gun?"

He's quick with a response, almost rehearsed. "For protection."

"You never had a gun in the bayou loft, and it's far less safe than here. I think this"—I pull the revolver out, feeling its deadly weight in my hands—"makes you a hypocrite."

"It doesn't make me a hypocrite." He takes the gun and tucks it back inside the drawer.

"I think it might," I reply. "It certainly might make you a hypocrite."

He sighs again and sinks onto the bed beside me. "No, it makes me just like everybody else."

"Since when have we aimed to be like everybody else?"

"Kat, I decide what risks I'm willing to take. At this apartment, I'm usually alone or with only you. So yes, I keep a gun here. To protect me...and to protect you. It's not like I'm out trolling the streets of the bayou, packing heat."

I listen patiently as he explains.

"I'm a wanted man, remember? Everyone in Savannah is hunting wolves these days. We have to be smart."

"I don't like it."

"You don't have to like it, doll." He rises from the bed and crosses the room, then hovers uncertainly in the doorway. "Are you mad at me?"

"I'm not mad at you, Paul," I whisper, wrapping my arms around myself. "It just worries me you think you need a gun. It tells me—even more emphatically—we should lay low for a while. The Astor Manor job is the stuff of legend. We need to let it breathe. Take a break."

Paul doesn't reply, and I look carefully at him, closing the distance between us. My gaze glides over every inch of his achingly familiar face, stuttering over a new mark.

"Speaking of Astor Manor, seems the guards put up quite the fight." I brush my finger across the cut above his eyebrow. "How'd this happen?"

"One of 'em had a switchblade."

"I worry about you," I admit, staring at the wound, "on jobs when we're not together."

He looks away. "Doesn't seem like you were too worried while you were in the closet with Abe."

"You said you weren't mad about that." I swat his arm.

"You're right, that wasn't fair." He tosses me a sheepish grin. "I worry too." He reaches for my right hand. Slowly, he traces my queen of diamonds tattoo. "A king is nothing without his queen, you know. You're not ducking out on me, right?"

"Never." Because I love him the way I breathe, since the beginning, without thought. The way the Spanish moss hangs from the trees, organically, inseparable. The way starry-eyed Wendy loved Peter.

Completely.

And that's when I finally kiss him, kiss him long and sweet. And I don't stop for hours. Not until after the lights go down and the sun sets. Not until we stumble into his bed and shed our clothes. Not until his eyes drift shut and his breathing slackens as he wraps me from behind. Not even then, really. Because then I slide his right hand off my shoulder and drag it to my lips, gently kissing his king of diamonds tattoo.

And that's how I finally fall asleep, with my lips resting softly on his finger...and the tantalizing imagined weight of heirloom rubies around my neck.

CHAPTER ELEVEN

THE COLOR OF THE day is white.

White clouds in the sky.

White pebbles, white sand beneath my feet.

White dress.

White shoes.

White. White. White.

As my gaze scans the crowd at the annual Academy picnic, I tell myself I'm not looking for anyone in particular. The gathering is on one of the sandy beaches of Jekyll Island—not at the renowned clubhouse itself, but close enough to sense wealth in the air by mere proximity. It smells of crisp cotton linens and fresh lemons, of biting sea salt tears of privilege.

There are plenty of potential marks here today, rich fellas with empty brains and deep pockets, but I skulk through the throng almost perfunctorily, searching for a hint of familiar blond hair.

At some point during my not-so-surreptitious hunt, I spot Lady Genevieve. She's with her husband and another tall man, hard at work hoisting watermelons onto a banquet table. The man's jawline is reminiscent of Matthew's, but his head is topped with stylishly manicured dark hair, his posture ramrod straight. A flash of disillusionment hits when I realize it's Ethan, Matthew's older brother. West Point cadet, raised to captain during the Great War. Known for exquisitely tailored suits and a booming laugh, a laugh I can nearly hear when he tips his head back. I recognize him from former Academy events.

And perhaps somewhere else...a more recent connection tugs my memory, sliding back and forth at the edges of my mind, like the roiling tide of the Atlantic.

Despite myself, I watch the family for a few minutes. It seems Matthew had to work after all, because he's nowhere in sight. The three DaMolins move in tandem, quiet and efficient, preparing the watermelon.

There's a faint *thump* behind me, but my attention is focused on the tiny group. They're so in tune with one another. It's like me with the Royals...or perhaps not? This is a *real* family, united by blood. I'm trying to discern whether there's something different about them, something to set them apart from my own.

I tilt my head, pondering, and give a soft yelp when a hand squeezes my shoulder from behind.

"Why are you spying on my family, Katarina?" a deep voice whispers in my ear.

His breath is warm. I fight a shiver.

"Matthew." I laugh nervously, a little embarrassed but entirely glad to find he's here.

"Are you looking for someone?" He moves his lips to my cheek, softly pressing them to my skin. A small shock *zings* through my body at his unexpected familiarity. I give a guilty start, then cast a sweeping look around the picnic for voyeurs. I turn to see Matthew in a white linen shirt, his grin brighter than the sun.

I blink twice, rendered mute.

"Wow, *speechless*, Katarina? I don't think I've met this woman yet. Hi, I'm Matthew DaMolin."

He sticks out his hand for a formal shake. I take it with a chuckle.

"You're in an awfully good mood today."

"Why shouldn't I be? I have the whole weekend off, the sun is shining, I slept a full ten hours, bathed and shaved this morning—just for you." He winks, and I laugh again. "And here you are, looking for *me* out of the hundreds of people here today."

"Who says I was looking for you?"

"Please! You've been found out, Katarina."

And suddenly, I'm laughing again, grinning from ear to ear like a complete idiot.

"So are you happy to see me?" he asks. "It sure seems like it."

I strive for a modicum of composure. "I am, actually. I hoped you would introduce me to your brother." I point at Ethan and smile mischievously.

"Bullshit."

"Language, Matthew. There are ladies and gentlemen nearby," I admonish, nodding toward his parents. "Is this going to be our game today?"

"It can be. I call you on your bullshit, that could certainly be fun. It'll keep me pretty busy, 'cause every other word out of your mouth is full of it."

"Hey!" I swat him, but he grabs my hand mid-flight.

"So would you like to meet my family? You were looking at them like they hold the meaning of life. I'll introduce you, then you'll realize the acclaimed DaMolin clan is just as dysfunctional and ordinary as the rest of the serfs."

"Serfs?" I chortle, but when he reaches for my hand again, I pull back, uncertain.

The tiniest crease appears between Matthew's eyebrows. "Is something wrong?"

I lick my lips. Standing here with him, with this man who's so very luminous and whole, his all-American family ten yards away…I feel my own story, my otherness, acutely. I wrap my arms around my core. My words come out slowly, stilted and drawn. "Your family…it's rather different from mine, Matthew." I nod toward his parents again. "It must have been nice growing up."

"No family is perfect, Kat. Certainly not mine." Matthew sighs, frown lines deepening. "Being a DaMolin is a privilege, but it doesn't magically make things easy. I'm sure you heard the rumors. We make our living publishing news, and my father's fall from grace was quite a headline."

I shake my hair away from my face before replying. I *have* heard the rumors, but I'm surprised he's bringing them up. Headlines rarely reflect reality. How many times has the tale of the Wolfpack been sensationalized to sell copies?

"Rumors are whispers in the wind, Matthew," I say. "Loud today, forgotten tomorrow. Not to malign your family's business, but newspapers exist to sell themselves. They very rarely tell the full story."

"Well, in the case of my father, they had it right. He fell in line thirty years ago to make a proper marriage, one befitting the DaMolin name, but he considered himself married in theory only. His vows meant next to nothing. He sought companionship outside the bonds of his marriage with courtesans—one of whom was my mother."

I nod.

"Ethan and I are technically half-brothers," Matthew continues. "His mom died during childbirth, and my dad married my mother—my mother the *courtesan*, less than six months later. A marriage of honest love this time, but certainly not one recognized by polite society. It was, so I'm told, the height of scandal.

"The irony of all this"—he waves his hand at the picnic around us—"is that, in those early years, my mother had little business teaching anyone how to be a lady. She needed the lessons Telfair provided as much as the few girls who enrolled. Her life's work, turning out premier ladies of high society, was her own veiled barb against the institution at large. I quite love that about her, actually." He smiles wryly. "She found a way to have the last laugh—the women who once looked down their noses at her now quietly send their daughters to Telfair to be educated."

"I was right," I reply, "the full story is far better than the rumors. I absolutely adore your mother after hearing this. The gumption—can you just imagine?"

"I don't have to imagine." He pulls a face. "I lived it, Katarina."

I wince softly. "I'm sorry, Matthew. I wasn't assuming—"

"I know you weren't." He stops me. "It's okay. You're right. Scandal or not, I was luckier than most, and I love my family. They're wonderful. Not perfect, but forged in fire and all the better for it. My dad looks at my mom like she walks on water, so what does it really matter what other people sometimes say?"

"And Ethan?" I ask.

Matthew shrugs. "He wasn't even six months old when my mother married our father. He's called her 'Mom' since he learned how to talk, and he views her as nothing less. Beneath his banter and bluster, Ethan is fiercely loyal. He has a big heart, with great capacity for compassion and empathy. We all do. How could we not after what we went through together?"

"How did you put it...forged in fire?" It's the way I describe my relationship with the Royals. I quite like that he views his own family similarly.

"I did. Our family name has been restored, but it took a lifetime to do it. Along the way, I've been called every name in the book, and 'bastard' is perhaps the kindest. My parents raised us to be progressive in a world still clinging to the skirts of pomp and circumstance. I'm not interested in the bread-and-circus show. I want to be in the trenches, helping people who need it, not looking down my nose at them. Because trust me, I know what it feels like to be both."

"I suppose I owe you an apology," I say, surprising myself. "I misjudged you."

"You're hardly the first to do so, and you certainly won't be the last. I hope you're taking a second look now though." His eyes pool so deep into my own, the world tilts beneath my feet.

Dangerous, dangerous.

For my own safety, I pull away. And because I'm a coward, I lighten my tone, desperate for levity. "Well, from one serf to another then, I suppose I'm prepared for an introduction."

Matthew smiles, full white teeth and dimples. "You'll be brilliant. There's nothing to be nervous about, they don't bite…well, sometimes my brother does," he admits, "but he's mostly harmless."

Without waiting for my reply, Matthew stoops to pick up a box of watermelons by his feet. He shifts the weight to his hip so he can manage it with one arm, then he grabs my hand, towing me forward.

His mother tracks our approach with sharp eyes. "Matthew, dear," she calls, "right here." She points beside her feet for the box, her gaze lingering on our joined hands. "Miss Quinn, wonderful to see you. How are you, dearest?"

"Good afternoon, Lady Genevieve. It's nice to see you too." I slip into my Academy training. "Everything is quite well, thank you."

"Andrew." She swats her husband's arm. "Andrew!"

The patriarch of the DaMolin family glances up from the melon he's slicing.

"Andrew, darling, this is Katarina Quinn." She looks hard at her husband, trying to convey significance. "She's in her final year at the Academy."

"Good afternoon, sir." I sink into a brief curtsy, but he holds out a hand to stop me. In the corner of my eye, Ethan smirks.

"That's not necessary, I assure you." Andrew turns to his wife. "Are you really still teaching them to curtsy at the Academy? That's quite antiquated, darling. Do we need to overhaul the curriculum?"

As his father speaks, Ethan's eyes flicker between his brother and me, assessing. He steps forward. "Hello, Katarina. I'm confident my reputation precedes me—Captain Ethan DaMolin, infamous heir to the DaMolin empire." He smiles impishly. "Do I get a curtsy too?"

"Ethan!" his mother hisses.

"Only jesting." He extends his palm. "I'm Ethan, Matt's older, infinitely more dilly brother."

"I'm Katarina." I take his hand. "Matthew's younger but still infinitely more dilly friend."

Ethan graces me with a sultry laugh. He knocks his brother on the arm, but his eyes stay zeroed in on me. "Shall we take a promenade, Katarina? Matt, buzz off for a tick to help Mom and Dad."

"Not a chance," Matthew says.

"Did he tell you I'm nice?" Ethan suddenly turns to me. "I'm perfectly nice. I'll bring you right back to him so you can do more of that adorable hand-holding in just a few minutes."

Matthew glowers at his brother.

"Actually, he told me you bite," I reply. "But that's hardly a problem. So do I."

Ethan throws his head back and guffaws, then punches Matthew's arm again. "Where in tarnation did you find a dame like her?" he chides his brother. "Are you a masochist? I don't pull your leg enough?"

"I guess not." Matthew's response is dry.

"All right, you know what? I'll let it slide this time. All three of us can go. This will be simply grand."

CHAPTER TWELVE

As our promenade begins, I'm bundled in the center, flanked by Ethan and Matthew. Strolling as a unit, we head down to the pebbly beach.

"So, Katarina, my brother doesn't have many *friends*." Ethan emphasizes the last word. "Are you aware he works all the time? Literally, all the time. Since he was eighteen."

I shrug. "His work ethic, the thing he's most passionate about? That's where you're hitting him? Try again."

Ethan smiles. "Passionate, huh? Tell me, Miss Katarina, what exactly do you know of my brother's passions? Could you, perchance, be speaking from personal experience?"

"Ethan," Matthew warns. "Out of bounds."

"No, it's fine." I put a hand on Matthew's arm. "Actually, Ethan, your brother is a perfect gentleman. To a fault."

"Is he now?"

"Yes...except perhaps at the pool table."

"Mmm." Ethan's smile is knowing. "He wiped the floor with you there, huh? Don't worry, he does it to everyone. He has a table in his apartment and zero social life."

"I'm certain a rematch would bring a different outcome." I stick my chin out.

Matthew grins. "Doubtful."

"You know...I like you ten times less when we're playing pool."

"Bullshit," Matthew whispers to me. "You loved it. I think losing is good for you."

Ethan rubs his chin, continuing to watch us with interest. After a brief pause, he fires again. "Tell me more about yourself, Katarina. Something stimulating." He gives me a playful wink before sliding a gilded antique pocket watch from his trousers. Faint grooves of engraving catch the light as he flicks the lid open. "You have sixty seconds to impress me. Go."

For the first time, I falter. I don't like talking about myself. Too many lies, too many pitfalls. Too many secrets I shouldn't tell.

"Fifty seconds." Ethan taps the watch.

But just because I *shouldn't* tell them, doesn't mean I can't *show* them. Something simple but effective. And most definitely stimulating...

Target: Ethan DaMolin.

We're still walking, so I "accidentally" give a soft kick to Ethan's shoe. He looks down briefly. It's all I need.

Misdirection.

I stumble forward, as though the impact threw me off. Matthew reaches for my elbow. I grab onto him.

"You okay?" he asks.

"I'm fine. Sorry, Ethan, how much time do I have left?"

He glances down, noticing his now empty hand. "What the—"

"Oh, bless your heart. I'll just check myself, shall I?" I lift his pilfered pocket watch, cataloging the wink of tiny rubies at the end of the clock hands. "Looks like only twenty-two seconds left."

When he turns his shocked gaze on me, I go for the knockout punch.

"Good heavens, this feels like the longest minute of my life. Perhaps I should just confirm..." I lift up Matthew's wristwatch in my other hand, comparing the two timepieces.

Matthew grabs his forearm, but it's bare. "How did you do that?"

"Magic," I answer, smiling sweetly. "You might want to check your pants while you're at it. It seems your fly is unbuttoned. Yours too, Ethan."

The brothers exchange mortified looks while I laugh.

Ethan recovers first. "Congratulations, Katarina—that's the most action my brother's had in years."

I shrug before, regrettably, handing back his ruby-encrusted timepiece. "Being a gentleman will do that to you."

"Where did you learn to do that?"

"Well, Matthew already knows this, but..." I take a deep breath. "I grew up in the Catacombs. I have certain...proclivities other Academy girls don't. Survival skills, if you will."

"Proclivities, huh? Well, aren't you just the cat's meow, Katarina? All the Academy events I've suffered through over the years...how on earth did I miss you?"

"Easily. I've never been one of the floozies in your doting harem."

"Whyever not? What exactly is it about a workaholic, uptight doctor that holds your very valuable attention?"

Matthew gives me a sidelong, curious glance.

"I'm not precisely certain yet," I answer honestly. I flick my eyes to Matthew's face, then back to his brother. "When I figure it out, I'll let you know."

"Well played, Katarina. I see your time at the Academy isn't lost on you."

"Thank you, sir." I mock curtsy, and Ethan's face lights up.

"That earns you a bonus point." He nods at my curtsy. "It's not nearly as nice as the one you gave my father, but now that I know you better, I don't think you drop to your knees for just anyone."

"Unlike you, huh, Ethan?" Matthew teases, smiling wickedly.

"Oho! That's below the belt, Matt," Ethan declares. "For that, I'm going to ask your *friend* Katarina one final question. Don't worry, it will be highly embarrassing...and confidential." He drags me away before Matthew can protest.

I swallow when Ethan leans in close. I know it's going to be bad before he opens his mouth. I can just feel it.

"So, Katarina, tell me just one more thing, sweetheart." His breath tickles my ear. "Have you dropped to your knees with your pert little mouth open for my brother yet?"

My jaw drops. Matthew shifts nervously from foot to foot, watching us.

"No," I finally manage. "Perfect gentleman, remember?"

I'm blushing scarlet; I can't help it.

"Trust me, Katarina. He's not. None of us are." He reaches into his pocket to pull out a cigarette and lighter. "Lucky for him, I don't think you're a perfect little lady either. So make it good for him when you do. God knows, it's been a while."

As he walks away, I move my mouth mechanically, searching for something...anything. I don't let anyone get the last word on me, but for once, I have no comeback. Ethan thumbs his lighter until it sparks, cupping his free hand around the cigarette between his teeth. He pulls a deep drag and blows out a fluid stream of smoke. As he exhales, something in my brain clicks.

Expensive suit. Coiffed hair. A burning light.

It was Ethan DaMolin I saw last week at Astor Manor, sharing a midnight smoke with Harry. I'm sure of it. What dastardly backroom business were those two up to so late at night?

"Ah, the harem awaits." Ethan puffs. His cigarette dangles from his lips as he gestures up the beach toward a pack of giggling girls. He gives me another wink, this time conspiratorial. In spite of myself, I let out a small laugh.

"You're a swell dame, Katarina," he tells me, nodding approval. "I apologize for being forward, but we DaMolins protect our own. We have to.

Should you stick around, you'll find my bark is far worse than my bite."
Ethan claps his brother on the shoulder as he departs.

Matthew is openly wary as he walks over to me. "What did he say to you?"

"Nothing," I mutter.

"Do I really need to call bullshit again?"

"It's honestly not worth repeating. Trust me."

"I want to know—"

"He asked if I'd sucked your dick," I announce stiffly. "And then, when I told him no, he insinuated I would. Soon."

"Oh. Mercy." His face pales, and he looks over his shoulder at his brother's departing back. "I'm going to murder him. Katarina, I'm so sorry. Ethan has never concerned himself with boundaries."

"Honestly, Matthew, it's fine. I'm a big girl. Big enough to decide whose dick I suck. And how and when it happens. Because it *has* happened. Unlike my classmates, the Academy's ivory cage means very little to me."

Matthew's eyes widen, surprised at my outburst. "I can't believe I'm going to say this..." He runs his fingers through his hair, rumpling it rather adorably. "Do you really think you're the only gal at the Academy who's sucked someone's dick, Katarina? You're not. One of those girls offers to suck off mine at almost every event. Ethan's too."

I blink and digest this. Who—

"The real reason you're not like those ladies over there"—he jerks his head—"is that you *haven't* offered. You don't give a flying fuck who my parents are or how much money I do or don't have. That is why you're different."

"Matthew?"

"*What?*" He shoves his hands in his pockets, agitated.

I pause, considering the words I'm about to say. I roll them around in my head, tasting their curious flavor. Trying to decide whether I'm hungry enough to set them free. I've never said anything like this to any other mark, never had the thought or barest whiff of desire cross my mind. I wonder, faintly, if this makes me a traitor to Paul, but I push the thought deep down, shelving it for introspection when I'm alone.

"What would you say to me right now if I offered?" I hold his eyes with my own.

"Offered what?"

I look meaningfully at him.

"Christ, Katarina." He shakes his head. "No."

I see straight through him. *"Bull. Shit."*

He meets my gaze head-on, but he doesn't say anything. The silence stretches for an eternity. We've traversed quite far along the beach, out of sight of the picnickers, which suits nicely.

"Do you..." He rubs his mouth nervously. "Katarina, we're at a family picnic. Outside."

"I understand. It's not a deterrent for me."

"Are you serious?"

"Yes."

"Why?"

"Does it really matter?" I ask, surprised.

"Yes. It does. It matters to me, very much."

"Because..." I grasp for the words, trying to explain to myself as much as him. There's a certain calculation here, there always is. But also...

Because I'm curious what it's like to touch the sun.

"Don't think about it. Don't bullshit me. Just tell me why." A muscle ticks in his jaw.

"Because you make me want to," I reply simply. "You. Not Ethan or your family or your money. Just you."

He's still silent, evaluating me.

"You make me laugh," I add. "A lot. Which doesn't hurt."

Finally, he cracks a smile. "You make me laugh too. I wish we could just...wind back the clock and return to that."

"You'd rather laugh with me than sneak off down the beach?" I'm incredulous.

"Katarina, I'll take whatever you're willing to give, but we have plenty of time."

"Kat," I correct. "My friends call me Kat."

"Hi, Kat. I'm Matt." He moves in toward me, a single slow step. "Nice to meet you. Again."

"Hi, Matt."

"Hi, Kat," he repeats, whispering now.

I hold my breath. He's standing close. Very close.

Slowly, so very slowly, his hand reaches up to cup my cheek. His blue eyes are startlingly clear—like I can see straight through them into his mind—and I wonder, briefly, what he sees in my green ones. If he can see straight through me too.

Before I can wonder further, he kisses me. Softly, tentatively. A question not voiced, but asked nonetheless. It's sweetness and light and sunshine and butterflies...everything I've always thought I didn't want, but somehow, coming from him, it feels exactly right.

Because *he* is sweetness and light and sunshine and butterflies. And maybe I didn't want it before, but I suddenly realize I sure as hell want it now. Maybe, just like losing to him at pool, this is good for me. Maybe *he* could be good for me.

If he were Paul or Abe, I'd drag him down the beach without a second thought. But he isn't a wolf. He's Matthew. So, of course, he politely pulls away from my lips after only a few seconds. Pulls away, takes my hand, and together we rejoin the party.

And honestly, it's a little disappointing, but for once in my life, it also feels like enough. Because I know what hunger is. I know what it's like to be positively ravenous. Insatiable even.

But today, after the smallest of bites, I'm full.

———————

WHEN THE SUN REACHES its apex over Jekyll Island, I've returned to the shore with Matt. We're seated side by side in the white, pebbly sand. The waves roll in just beyond our feet, the natural tideline ebbing and flowing with as much ease as the words streaming from our lips. Never having left Savannah, I'm enraptured by Matthew's tales of travel, particularly his time at Vanderbilt.

"Nashville sounds simply grand," I breathe, captivated. "Whatever persuaded you to return to Savannah after medical school?"

He smiles. "My family is here, Kat. My community. Where else would I want to practice medicine?"

I blink twice, disarmed by a shadowy undercurrent of Paul in Matthew's explanation.

"Where at the hospital do you work?" I ask, barreling forward. "Are there specialties?"

"A few, principally medical and surgical. I work on the medical side, but since the war ended, there's been research and publications on emergency medical techniques, the kind they used on the battlefield. A friend of mine from Vanderbilt deployed to the Western Front, and we exchanged letters. His firsthand accounts were...well, at times, they were difficult to read, but so very important all the same."

"Oh." The corners of my mouth turn down, mimicking his own. "This friend...was he drafted?"

"No." In profile, I notice the barest tightening of Matthew's jaw. His fingers clench into the sand. "He enlisted. They came recruiting at Vanderbilt, offered an accelerated education if we enlisted and deployed as battlefield physicians. William took the deal."

"I see. Quite brave of him." I look away, straight over the horizon line. I want to ask, so many men on the frontlines were lost. But I don't dare. I hold my breath, waiting.

"Yes, quite. All the men who deployed, whether drafted or enlisted, were brave. That's partly why I let Ethan get away with so much." The corner of Matthew's lip curls in a wry smile. "He deserves a good laugh. There was precious little to laugh about for so many years...certainly not while he was in France."

I put a hand on his arm.

"But the past is meant to be learned from," Matthew continues, nodding. "I've referenced William's letters often. His lens as a physician was intrepid, and the techniques they developed during the war are applicable to the home front as well. I'm in talks with the hospital now, developing our own modified field medicine program to respond to trauma throughout Savannah."

"That sounds like rather important work. I'd like to see this bravehearted battlefield Matthew in action. Perhaps I'll stop by during one of your night shifts for a tour," I tease.

"Absolutely not. The hospital after midnight is no place you want to be, Kat. The streets aren't safe at that time either. I would know. It's how I make my living. These gangs in the bayou...things are only getting worse."

And because I can't think of a safe response, I bend forward and slip off my shoes, one after the other. Then I jump ahead and kick my toes in the water, spraying droplets, shooting off a hundred ripples.

I turn to face Matt and smile. "Look out!"

I slowly draw my leg back, giving him plenty of time to evade, but he only sits there, grinning. Daring me. Unsaid words oscillate between us, swelling bigger and stronger than the ripples in the water.

Will you or won't you?

Will you—

I kick, spraying him with water. On reflex, he lifts a hand, but it's ineffective against the onslaught.

Much to my surprise, he laughs and bends over to roll up his trousers, his shoes coming off. He charges into the shallows after me and starts kicking back, showing no mercy.

"Matt, I'm wearing *white*," I squeal after a particularly big spray.

"You should have thought of that before you started a fight you can't finish."

"Oh, I can finish it."

"Can you, pipsqueak?"

And because he asked for it, I deliver.

Target: Matthew DaMolin.

In one quick move, I dart forward and grab his arm. I spin around and duck, yanking him forward over my shoulder. He flips and lands on his butt in the water. I straighten and brush off my hands. "I think that finishes it rather effectively."

With a shocked laugh, he hauls himself out of the water. His pants are soaked.

"Guess I shouldn't have worried about you holding your own in the hospital after midnight. You're the thug who lands my patients in there in the first place."

He's teasing, but he's so close to the truth I bite my lip. I've given away far too much. Again.

"You're lucky you wore white today," he adds, eyeing me for payback.

"Such a gentleman." I follow behind as he heads for the beach.

"Perhaps," he says. "Or perhaps I just don't want anyone else seeing what I've decided is mine." The grin he tosses over his shoulder is downright sinful.

"Hmm, possessive already?" My heart jumps into my throat.

"Yes. Yes, I think I am. In fact, I'm so possessive, I'm going to go to my mother and ask her for a date with you straightaway. Which is the pinnacle of embarrassment because it's my mom."

"Chaperoned Academy dates are no fun. I'll meet you wherever you want, whenever you want."

"So it's a yes then? To a date?"

Paul's face flashes through my mind.

He told me he's okay with this. He told *me to do this.*

"Yes," I answer, my heart thudding wildly.

"I'll talk to my mother tomorrow. We'll do it the right way. At first."

"Oho! Well, aren't you confident now? You're already convinced you're getting a second date?"

"Yes, I am. And a third and fourth too...uh-oh, I think the Ethan in me is showing."

I tilt my head back to laugh, deep and full. It's an honest laugh, which surprises me as much as him.

"I ought to walk you back," he murmurs, perhaps a bit regretfully. "The sun is setting, and they've brought the motorcars around." He nods up the beach to where my classmates are gathered.

I extend my arm to him, and Matthew walks me to where my fellow fourth-years congregate. Surprisingly, I notice Daniel hovering nearby with Florence, whose cheeks are flushed and lifted by a grin. Mellie's eyes bug out of her head when I arrive with Matthew. And because it's Mellie—she literally can't help herself—she attaches to my side, practically hyperventilating in my ear.

Matthew gives her a brief questioning glance, but I'm not interested in an introduction. Not today. I forcibly separate from her, dragging Matthew a few steps away.

"I'll see you soon for that date, Kat," he whispers.

And then, in front of all the girls still standing on the grass and all the ones inside the motorcars with their noses pressed to glass, Matthew DaMolin—in soaking wet pants—leans in and presses his lips to mine.

It's about as big a statement as he could possibly make, and the whispers begin immediately.

CHAPTER THIRTEEN

THE MONTH OF OCTOBER passes in a blur. I see Matthew usually once a week. We go on chaperoned dates throughout the city and spend time together at social events on Academy grounds. An afternoon stroll in the gardens, or perhaps Forsyth Park, a tour through a downtown museum, a few dinners at corner restaurants. It could be fun, but we're always accompanied by an Academy-sanctioned babysitter. They do their best to be unobtrusive, they really try. But unfortunately, for someone like me, who's never had a parental presence in her life, it's a tough pill to swallow.

So everything stays sweet and innocent between Matthew and me. Adorable, right?

Except I don't do adorable. Not even a little bit. My inner adrenaline addict is in the throes of full-blown withdrawal.

Until one heart-stopping conversation at an Academy evening social.

I'm clustered in a group with the trifecta and Florence. She's plastered to Daniel's side, putting Harry through his paces with gossip about the Astor Manor caper.

"Harry, were you home when it happened?" she asks, drawing a hand to her breast. "When they were *in* the house?"

"No, I was out that night." He crosses his arms. "My mother was alone."

Florence shudders. "Thank goodness they didn't hurt her."

"She's lucky they didn't," Matthew says. "The violence downtown is getting worse. I stitch people up almost every night."

Despite myself, I can't remain silent. "Surely, not all of those people are victims of the Wolfpack?"

"No, but some of 'em are. And that's only counting the ones who stay alive long enough to get to me. The morgue is busier than the hospital these days."

"It's not going to change anytime soon, Matt," Daniel says, shaking his head. "This Wolfpack and some of the other gangs, they're smart. And they're getting bolder. Crime isn't relegated to the bayou and the Catacombs anymore. If they can get into Astor Manor, they can get in anywhere."

"How *did* they get in?" Florence asks.

"No idea." Harry shrugs. "It was the middle of the night. There were no witnesses. The doors to the house were all locked from the inside, so it's quite the mystery. We did find one unsecured window on the third story, but it's over twenty feet up. Perhaps that was the entry and exit point, but if so, I sure as hell don't know how they managed it."

"The Cat Burglar," Florence offers. "They say she can do just about anything."

I fidget, shifting my weight from foot to foot.

"The walls under that window are sheer marble over twenty feet high," he repeats. "If she scaled up and down that without breaking her neck, my hat's off to her. I'm just grateful they left my mother sleeping in her bed. She didn't notice anything was wrong until morning when she saw the mark painted on the door..."

Moments like this remind me just how tenuous my footing here truly is. How close I'm dancing to the sun with Matthew.

And I ask myself, over and over, *is this worth it?*

Paul would say *yes*, but he's a greedy idiot. Matthew is blithely unaware, an idiot of a different kind. I'm perhaps the most objective person here, but I'm becoming less and less so by the day. For the first time in my life, I'm paralyzed with indecision. How can I justify a relationship under the guise of "business as usual" when the rapidly ratcheting rate of my pulse tells a different story?

Little by little, Matthew and I are getting to know each other. Since we're always watched, there's not much to fill the time but talking. It's treacherous because, usually, I intentionally keep an emotional distance from my marks.

But Matthew is a brilliant conversationalist. He draws me in and keeps me laughing until my cheeks are sore. I learn about his family and his work. He tells me stories from growing up, and I offer a few of my own. I hint at the personalities of Paul, Abe, and Tony. I desperately want him to know where I come from, so I share as much as I can, and believe it or not, he does start to understand me. On one or two occasions, he tries to ask about Paul, but I'm tight-lipped. Our relationship is hard to explain these days, even to myself.

During this time, the Royals remain relatively silent. Paul stays true to his word and doesn't harass me about any jobs, giving me the break I desperately need. Ray continues handing off large chunks of bills to me every two weeks or so. I dutifully pass them to Paul, privately wondering what he's moving in the bayou to bring in such consistent profit. The one time I ask, he tells me he's been selling tribute from Craig and the Magpies.

It's plausible, I suppose. Craig is his squeeze, the main contact point for the Magpie gang since Damien's death. But something in my gut tells me there's more. That, for the first time in our lives, neither Paul nor I are being entirely honest with the other.

Much to Mellie's dismay, I continue to sneak out of the Academy once a week to meet up with the Royals or to spend a night alone with Paul. He doesn't ask about Matthew again, and I don't tell him anything, but I caught a flash of Abe's dark hair around a corner on our museum date. Paul is keeping his tabs.

We come to our first confrontational head over the issue in the final week of the month. On Wednesday night, I sneak out to the bayou loft. Tony is out, but Paul and Abe are both there. Paul is less than amused when I ask him to change our Hallows' Eve plans from Saturday to Friday.

"Why?"

I don't answer right away. The conflict boils within me.

"Because her new beau probably invited her to do something Saturday," Abe says with a laugh, head buried in a bowl of cereal.

That's right. Ten o'clock at night and the boy is slurping down cereal. With a rolled-up joint on the table beside him.

"Is that why?" Paul's eyes dart to me.

I take a deep breath. "Yes."

Without looking up from his bowl, Abe triumphantly flicks his spoon.

"His parents host an annual Hallows' Eve party at their cottage on Jekyll Island to open the club's season. It's on Saturday, and yes, he invited me. To Jekyll Island."

Paul studies my face, but I keep it blank. It doesn't matter what he says. I've already made up my mind to go, but I don't want him to know that. The mark of a good queen is letting her king think he's the one holding the cards.

"He invited you..." Paul repeats slowly. "To the Jekyll Island Club?"

"Yes."

Nothing else needs to be said. The promise of opportunity hanging in the air is more than enough bait.

"Fine," he grumbles. "We'll go out Friday instead. And you're gonna look around that house very closely while you're there. Every nook, every cranny. The whole damn club if you can manage it. Get your little boyfriend to give you a grand tour."

I nod.

"And Friday night, when we're together," he continues, "I'm going to screw your brains out. So you don't forget who you actually belong to."

Abe snorts into his bowl.

"Hey, peanut gallery," Paul warns, "I've heard just about enough outta you."

"I know who I belong to, Paul." I sidle over and press my lips to his.

His kiss is as fierce and powerful as ever; it feels good and achingly familiar. The usual fire ignites. I let him pull me into the bedroom and kick the door closed.

I stay with him for two hours, being enjoyed by him and enjoying being his. Because it's true: I am his, and he is mine.

But deep down, I know that I don't belong to anyone but myself.

I choose who I give myself to. And tonight, I choose him.

CHAPTER FOURTEEN

MELLIE'S EYES ARE FULL of longing as I get ready for the party on Saturday.

"I wish I was invited." She sighs wistfully from a stretched-out position on her bed.

I don't deign to reply. I finish fastening a pair of square, French-cut diamond studs in my ears—a little gift from Raymond. One he doesn't realize he's lending me for the party. I wonder, faintly, if I should consider a matching pair of emerald and obsidian earrings to complement the Cleopatra collar and ring...but I've barely had any time to work on my pet project. Best finish what I've started before adding more to my plate.

I dig through my closet until I find my black high heels, then reach for the final touch—a black-velvet cat-ear headband. I slip it on and turn to face Mellie. "Well, what do you think?"

"Do you want my honest opinion? Or the sugarcoated one?"

"Oh, Mellie." I laugh softly. "I think you'll give me the honest one whether I want to hear it or not."

"It's a lot, Kat," she says, eyeing me from head to toe. "I mean, you look quite hotsy-totsy, and it's certainly...progressive."

"Coming from you, that's almost a compliment."

"Matthew will like it."

"Why do you say that?"

"Because I can see your gams," she points out.

I spin around to the mirror, checking myself. I fluff the tulle around my waist speculatively.

"I mean, don't get me wrong, if my legs looked like that"—she gestures at me—"maybe I'd wear an outfit like that too. But probably not."

"There's a skirt over my legs, Mellie." A beautiful cascade of shimmering black tulle over charcoal silk stockings, to be precise.

"A *sheer* skirt."

"There's no skin showing," I maintain. "I'm a black cat, a Kat-arina, if you will." I've always loved irony.

Mellie snorts. "I get the costume. Subtle as it is."

"All right, well, this has been a gas," I say, clapping my hands, "but I best be going."

"Have fun." She follows me to the door. "And for heaven's sake, tell him to keep his hands to himself."

"Goodnight, Mellie." I close the door in her face and sigh.

Florence, whose own family is made up of Jekyll Island regulars, is waiting for me in the Academy's entry hall. She's styled herself in a blush pink ballerina costume, complete with a scooped neckline and tapered skirt to showcase dainty heels with ribbons trailing up her calves. The heavy and exquisitely detailed beadwork along her bust and shoulders suggest the gown is a House of Worth original. When I inquire politely, Florence confirms with a rather pleased simper that it was, indeed, shipped straight from the Parisian fashion house.

Outside, a black motorcar and driver await, ready to escort us to Jekyll Island. We pass most of the drive in silence, perfect for me to take copious mental notes as we near our destination. There's a one-lane bridge marking the sole entrance and exit to the island, followed by an iron archway complete with gatehouse and guard. Unlike in downtown Savannah, there are no streetlamps—neither gas nor electric—on the island. The only illumination comes from our car's flickering headlights. We drive under a shadowy canopy of trees, winding our way deeper and deeper to the heart of the island.

When we round the final bend, the majestic Jekyll Island Club rises before us like the moon. The turreted Queen Anne clubhouse is lit up spectacularly, the famed northwestern tower beaming brilliance into the dark night. The hedges and flowerbeds are perfectly manicured, not a blade out of place on the grand front lawn. A wraparound drive deposits at the foot of a double-wide staircase, which leads to a sweeping veranda. Three men sit in rocking chairs, puffing cigars and sipping drinks in the moonlight. Behind them and through glass doors, an elaborate, crystal chandelier dangles, filigree glinting amidst flickers of soft candlelight.

Regrettably, our driver bypasses the main building before I can glean much more. We begin wending our way through private residences. Florence is kind—or perhaps arrogant—enough to narrate.

"That's Crane Cottage," she murmurs, pointing. "Finished construction only two years ago. It's an Italianate Renaissance work of art, the biggest and most expensive cottage on the island."

"Wow," I murmur.

"And here's Indian Mound"—she gestures again—"the Rockefeller property. Oh, look, that's Moss Cottage, where the Macys stay. Theirs was the first home here to be wired for electricity. It was quite innovative near the turn of the century, you know, but of course they all have it now."

"Of course." I play along.

She continues to provide a delightfully comprehensive guided tour—one I plan to regurgitate, word for word, back to Paul—until our car pulls to a halt.

"And this," she sighs dreamily, "is Cherokee Cottage, the DaMolins' property. Their view of the East River is simply divine."

If I could pick my jaw up, I'd agree. The "cottage" is sweepingly majestic with an adobe tiled roof and white stucco walls. The architecture is pointedly symmetric, the north and south wings pristine mirror images. Palm trees flank the front of the estate, fronds blowing gently in the riverside breeze.

Florence and I walk up to the home together, and the paired front doors sweep open to welcome us. My gaze peruses the high ceiling of the entryway, then the countless gilded mirrors hanging over paneled walls and crown moldings. Beneath my heels, the Bocote wood floor gleams. I'm so captivated by the opulence, I almost miss the creeping, servile attendant in our midst.

"Good evening, Charlie," Florence says.

"Miss Vanderbilt, a pleasure to welcome your return," he replies. "Shall we?"

I must not merit a greeting because Charlie turns on his heel to depart. Faint party chatter echoes as we step deeper into the home. I reach my fingers out, phantomlike, to brush the ivory banister as we pass the grand staircase. It's double-wide and covered with plush carpet, curling and sweeping up to the second floor. The grandeur calls to me, the thief inside salivating.

What must it have been like to grow up here?

I think, almost automatically, of Peter's den with Wendy and his Lost Boys. Of sleeping on stone floors in the Catacombs with Paul, Abe, and Tony...a completely different world. An insidious feeling of insecurity—a rising suspicion that perhaps I'm out of my depth—creeps into my stomach. I should hate this excess, should decry its very existence when there are starving people in the Catacombs of Savannah right now. People like me.

I should.

But I don't.

Instead, I'm possessed with the most primal, single-minded *want* I've ever felt in my life. A hunger so deep, it lives and breathes in my very core, a snake rising from slumber with a rattling tail. Hissing its way through every fiber of my being until I'm poisoned and electrified from the inside out. It actually frightens me, how sharp and crystalline this festering desire is, how my fingers burn with it.

Trailing insidiously in desire's wake is fear. Fear that I couldn't possibly measure up here. Fear that all this—the deepest desires of my avaricious heart—will never be mine. That I, the starving and abandoned girl from the Catacombs, am simply not worthy.

Charlie guides us to the revelry, depositing us at the edge of the party before melting away. Predictably, Florence is gone seconds later, off to curry Daniel's favor. I'm left alone.

In this area of the house, a series of drawing rooms and lounges spill into each other, overflowing with mingling costumed guests. There's a milled-hardwood phonograph with gold finish nearby, spinning notes of classical music throughout the soirée. Waiters circulate with trays of bubbling champagne. I absentmindedly snag a glass, fingers registering the delicate composition of the crystal stem. As I glance around the room, I suddenly worry my fashion-forward cat costume will read gauche in a scene overflowing with such old money.

I take a swig of champagne. As the drink glides down, my mind crystallizes, categorizing several important things at once.

Principally, no one here is looking twice at me. The fear of inadequacy is on the inside, not the out, and that simply won't do. In a single sweep, I note the gait and posture of the guests in the room. I listen to the lilt of their voices, observe the genteel flourishes of their gestures and polite head tilts. I become a chameleon and melt seamlessly into my surroundings. I roll my shoulders back and glide into the room with renewed confidence. My steps are unhurried and smooth, my eyes bright, a vague smile playing at my lips. I *become*.

As I weave through the crowd, a woman compliments my costume. I give her a closed-lip smile and delicate murmur of thanks before continuing on my way. As I stride deeper into the room, curiously appreciative eyes flick to me, then away. In this highly exclusive club that sees the same faces year after year, I am a black-clad enigma. Hopefully, a beautiful one at that.

Beauty may be only skin deep, but it opens many locked doors.

It's not long before I locate my target. Matthew wears a pair of tan breeches, a tattered white shirt, and a leather vest. A lopsided sash is knotted haphazardly around his head. He appears, even from a distance, distinctly disheveled.

As I approach, Matthew's gaze catches mine, and his smile lights up. He quickly excuses himself from his companions. My heart upticks as he comes closer. There's at least two days of blond scruff on his face.

"Kat, you're here." He leans in to brush a quick kiss on my cheek, drawing eyeballs our way. "And you're...a cat?"

"Yup," I confirm happily. "Kat the cat. Clever, right?"

"It's perfect." His eyes dip briefly to my corset-enhanced cleavage. He runs his hands down my black velvet sleeves, thumb brushing my bare wrist at the end. "I like this."

"Quite. And you're..." I pull back to study him, still puzzling it over. "What are you?"

"I'm a pirate," he says with a shifty grin. "Arg, matey! Can't you tell?"

I laugh and reach out to tweak the sash around his head. "I can actually. It's quite good."

"It's fun, I suppose. This is kind of stupid though." He reaches up to pull the sash off and stuffs it in his back pocket.

"How did you come up with this?"

"It's a family thing. We dress up every year with a different theme. This year we're a pirate crew. See my dad over there? He's the captain, in that long coat. Ethan is the first mate, naturally." He points to his brother, chatting in a small group with Harry Astor and a pretty woman dressed as a cowgirl.

"And my mom—over there—well, I think she's a wench?" Matthew laughs. "She's calling herself 'the Lady of the Ship,' or something ridiculous like that, but I'm pretty sure she's just a plain old sea wench."

I throw my head back and laugh. "I love it even more knowing you're all doing it together. How fun!"

"Some years are more fun than others." He wrinkles his nose. "One time, my mom picked a circus theme, and Ethan made me be a clown. I had a red nose and everything. He came up to me a thousand times during the night to squeeze it and demand I tell jokes."

I nod toward the first mate and his cowgirl companion. "Who's the gal he's with tonight?" I ask. "Did he bring a date?"

Matthew snorts. "Ethan? Never. Ethan doesn't date. He just messes girls around. His latest was a prima from the Paris Ballet. She was touring the East Coast this past summer and gave Ethan a few 'private lessons' in her free time." He snickers.

"And what about you?"

"I was at medical school, then indentured to the hospital for the last six years, Kat. I don't really date either."

"But you've 'messed girls around?'" I borrow his term, trying to be blasé. "Like your brother?"

His smile is roguish, so handsome I nearly forget myself. "If I have—and wouldn't you like to know—I've been far more discreet than him. If you catch my mother looking at you like you're an apparition, that's why. She's never seen me with a woman before. Ever."

"Really? Wow." I digest this news.

"Surprised?" He shrugs. "I haven't lived at home since I was eighteen. My parents don't need to know everything about my life, and neither does my brother."

"Hmm...what about me? Do I get to know?"

"I'll tell you mine if you tell me yours." His shifty grin is back, but I ignore it.

I'm so not telling him mine. How would I even begin to explain Paul and Abe?

"So where do you live downtown?" I ask instead.

"On Jones Street."

It's a very fancy reference, lots of old money townhomes. Near Raymond's, actually.

"Maybe I'll have the pleasure of stopping by sometime," I say casually. "Since, apparently, there's a revolving door policy."

He laughs. "Definitely not a revolving door, Kat. One woman over the course of a year. And one before that in medical school."

And just like that, he shares. So simple. So easy. So Matthew.

"Would you let me beat you at pool if I came over?" I ask.

"What?"

"You have a table, right? Ethan mentioned it at the picnic."

"You have a good memory."

"I always remember the things that interest me." I try to inject some suggestion because we've been talking for a while, and *talk* is not what I came here for tonight. Unchaperoned at long last. He doesn't seem sure how to respond though, so I take the plunge and try again. "Will you show me around? I'd love to see more of the house."

"Certainly." He takes my arm.

The temperature is cooler in the hallway, but when he moves toward another room full of partygoers, I stop him.

"Matt. This house is full of empty rooms, but you want to keep me in the three that are full of other people?" I raise an eyebrow.

He glances over his shoulder, back into the room with his parents. "I don't want to take advantage, Katarina. You're a girl from the Academy. A lady. My parents would kill me."

"I'm giving you the advantage, Matt. Trust me, you can take it."

He takes a deep breath. "Would you like to see the library?"

"I'd love to. I'm a *voracious* reader."

As we walk down the corridor, away from the guests, I inspect the wall paintings with interest. I'm hardly an art critic, but I'm certain I spot a Rembrandt and a Degas hanging side by side. An ornate, mahogany end table displays a collection of antique snuffboxes beneath the dome of a stained-glass Tiffany lamp, and—good heavens!—is that a Fabergé egg in a gold stand? I momentarily close my eyes against the onslaught. This degree of wealth is staggering, and the man on my arm holds the keys to the kingdom owning it all.

How on earth, I wonder, is he so very unaffected?

In contrast, I feel rather faint.

When we pass the dimly lit, mirrored-wall foyer, I reach my hand out for another brush of the ivory banister, seeking the grounding of something tactile. It really is exquisite.

Matthew stops. "Ethan and I used to slide down that when we were kids."

I look at it with renewed interest. "Seems like a dilly good time."

"It was. Until once..." He takes my hand and drags me around to the base. "I rammed into Ethan, here at the end, and we crashed. I knocked my jaw into the molding. See how this wood is stained lighter than the rest?"

I do.

"They had to replace it. Somehow, it chipped when I landed. My mother was madder than a wet hen."

"Ouch, sounds painful."

"I knocked out two baby teeth and scratched up my jaw pretty good," he declares proudly, "but no lasting damage."

"I'll be the judge of that." I graze my fingers across his chin and cheek, finally having an excuse to revel in the feel of his stubble. It's absolutely delicious. "I really like this," I tell him, fingering the scruff. Magnetized.

"I thought you liked me clean-shaven?" he whispers. "You asked about it once at the Academy."

"I was asking because I liked it."

His lips are soft and sweet when he lowers them to mine. I'm patient for a few minutes while we kiss. It's longer than he's ever held and moved with me before, but there's nothing behind it but innocence. No fire. No racing heart, no fumbling fingers. No urgency or desire. I'm so disappointed, I could cry. His hands wrap around me, but they stay firmly on my back and shoulders. He's being gentle, and I can't stand it.

I *know* there's chemistry. I feel it every time he looks at me. When he smiles, my gut clenches. Heart in my throat. But the minute he presses his lips to mine, the connection seems to shrivel up and die.

I realize, abruptly, we're at a crossroads. I'm not interested in a relationship that's comfortable and familiar, doomed to end in exploitation and heartbreak. If that's where this is headed, then it's better to end things now, before Paul gets his hooks in deeper. Before he makes *me* get my hooks in deeper. I don't want to hurt Matthew or his family, not in such a personal way. He's either worth the risk or he's not. And right now, I need to conduct a risk assessment.

"Matt." I stop him with a frustrated groan. "I'm going to be honest with you, and it's only because you're absolutely killing me."

"Okay." He swallows nervously.

"It's been rather lovely, spending all this time with you over the last month. But this"—I gesture between us—"polite, respectful kisses...it doesn't do it for me. Not even close. If we're going to keep seeing each other, I need to know you can give me a lot more."

"Katarina—" he begins.

I can hear the excuse before he even strings it together.

"So either you stop treating me like a porcelain doll, or I go home right now." My tone is final. Nonnegotiable.

"I'm not trying to treat you like a doll," he answers. "I'm trying to be respectful. To treat you like a lady. The way you deserve to be treated."

"Not all women want to be treated like a lady, Matthew. I certainly don't."

He looks closely at me. I'm locked in on his blue eyes. I see temptation burning there, and it gives me the tiniest of thrills. He just needs one more push.

"What's it going to be?" I whisper, raising my eyebrows. Daring him.

The moment stretches between us, interminable. The hallway is silent, but it's a silence so loud, it roars in my ears like a crescendo. I'm deafened with desire. Combusting with it.

Matthew lets out a soft groan before slamming me into the mirrored wall, his lips crashing over mine. His tongue dips into my mouth. Fingers rake through my hair. My body ignites, sparks finally roaring to life.

Yes. This. I press my hips into his, craving the closeness. *Just like this.*

His kisses are confident and demanding now. Unforgiving. Openly wanting.

I yield, surrendering my mouth to him. I moan into his lips and run my hands through his soft blond hair. His fingers tangle in my curls, then pull, forcing my head back to expose my neck. When his lips press into the hollow space below my ear, I exhale sharply. He slides one hand to cup my cheek and presses the other, palm flat, onto the mirror behind us.

"Katarina," he whispers, his nose brushing mine. Foreheads touching.

I slide my fingers over his chest. Down, down, down. I pause for a moment at his waistband, then plummet further. He's straining against his costume breeches, almost too much for my hand. I give him a gentle squeeze, and his answering moan nearly takes me out at the knees.

I'm feverish with wanting. Coming undone all too fast for him, yet slow enough to hurt.

When my fingers move to work the buttons of his fly, Matthew's eyes pop open.

"Not here," he hisses, grabbing my hand. "Charlie could be around."

"Charlie?"

"The club caretaker. He's like a ghost. He's ancient, and he's everywhere."

I'm panting with desire when he grabs my hand, leaving a smudged, sweaty palmprint on the gilded mirror. He pulls me down another hallway, into a dark room. He closes the door behind us with a soft *click*.

We pick up exactly where we left off. My hands go to his pants, and I sink to my knees in anticipation. But Matt's fingers encircle my wrists, yanking me upward and pressing me back against the door.

"You drive me wild, Kat," he murmurs into my lips. "Let me show you how much."

With an astounding degree of confidence, his hand slides between my legs. Slides to a place I've only ever let Paul and Abe touch. He rubs me gently, and it feels so good, I actually grind myself into him, wanting more pressure. So much more pressure. His fingers move, digging through layers and layers of tulle. He's searching for a break in the fabric of my costume, but he won't find one. And beneath the traitorous tulle are my heavy silk stockings to contend with. There's simply no way he's getting me out of this monstrosity of a costume. It's an impractical nightmare.

Betrayed by my exquisite fashion sense. It's certainly a fitting way for me to perish.

"Kat?" he finally asks. "I have no idea what you're wearing, and don't get me wrong, I like it, but—"

I shake my head and moan. "It's...it's not coming off. Not easily. Just..." I trail off, hoping he can read my mind.

"That's okay," he says. "I know what you need." His hand goes back down, moving between my legs with measured assurance.

I cry out, eyelids slamming shut.

"Shh," he murmurs into my neck.

His hand starts working me over my clothes. I haven't had anyone touch me like this in years, having graduated to—what I thought were—bigger and better things. But Matthew is never afraid to prove me wrong. Exquisitely wrong. Wrong in a way that sets my mind tumbling and reeling. Bringing me to the brink, pushing me straight over the edge. He presses his lips to mine, swallowing my whimpers. I melt.

When I collapse into him, he continues brushing me with kisses. I shudder on the comedown, opening my eyes to brilliant, steady blue.

Breath by breath, I return to myself. I cannot remember the last time someone made me come from outside my pants. Maybe never. Not like this. Certainly not without the expectation of something in return.

I tip my head onto his shoulder, stuporous. "I have no idea what you just did or how you did it but consider me sufficiently impressed."

"So you're not going home?"

"I'm not going anywhere, Matt."

CHAPTER FIFTEEN

THE NIGHT AFTER THE Hallows' Eve party, I have an unexpected visitor. I'm brushing my teeth when Mellie shrieks in our bedroom, dithering by the window.

"Kat," she groans, throwing her hands up in frustration. "It's one of your boyfriends. I can't keep them straight anymore."

My heart hammers. I cross the room and pull the curtains.

It's Abe, standing outside, giving me a shy wave. Since Mellie's peeking over my shoulder, he waves to her too. A small salute.

"Oh my god!" She trips over herself and topples backward, landing gracelessly on her butt.

"He doesn't bite." I laugh at her and swing a leg out. "Just let me see what he wants. I'll be right back."

"Kaaaat," she whines. "You know I hate it when you do this."

"Right back," I repeat, disappearing down the wall. I traipse after Abe to our copse of trees in the park.

"Hi, Kat."

"Hi, Abe." I cross my arms and wait. He usually only comes to pass along a message from Paul or to pick up intel after an event.

"So..." He sticks his hands in his pockets.

"So?"

"How was your party last night?"

"It was grand, thanks. Is everything okay with the Royals?"

"It is."

"So...?" I draw out the word. "What brought you here tonight?"

"I'm just...checking in with you."

"Checking in about what?"

"Come on, Kat." He rolls his eyes. "Paul wants to know how last night went. If you learned anything."

"Couldn't it wait until we meet at Farley's later in the week?"

Farley's is one of our frequent haunts in the bayou, a tavern where we go for drinks several times a month. The owner is a longtime personal friend, and in a similar manner to Ray, he allows us to use the back room of his establishment as a pitstop in our black-market trade.

"Well...I'm supposed to feel you out about something else too." Abe looks embarrassed, and it's then I realize why he's really here.

"About Matthew?" My eyes narrow. "Did Paul have someone at the party? Were *you* there?"

"No!" He raises his palms in protest. "But Paul has more than just me for eyes and ears, you know."

I'm silent. And my silence likely damns me.

"I see. I won't tell him," Abe decides with a nod.

"Tell him what, exactly?"

"You don't have to do that, Kat. Not with me. It's written all over your face."

"What is?"

"You let him touch you." Abe shrugs. "It's fine."

Anger flares. "Then why are you here, 'checking up,' if it's fine?"

"*I* said it was fine. I don't care if you have the hots for the doctor. I'm not here right now to serve my own interests."

"Well, if Paul has a problem with it, maybe he should drag his ass out of the bayou and come talk to me himself," I say. "Better yet, maybe he shouldn't be so quick to pimp me out for his next dream job."

"Whew." Abe exhales. "The two of you have a lot to talk about."

"I just don't understand why he's suddenly so interested. Or why he thinks he has the right. He's never cared about my Academy dates before."

"Well, they've all been meaningless before. Or am I wrong?" Abe's eyes are pensive, searching.

"I don't know," I mumble.

"If you let him touch you—which I can tell you did—I know I'm right. You've always cut it off before that point. You've saved that for only Paul and me."

"Are you upset with me?"

"Of course not, Kat. You've never been mine. And you'd be bored with me within a week if you were. I'm honestly surprised the doctor has lasted this long. It means Paul's probably right to keep an eye on him."

ON TUESDAY, PAUL STOPS by at the end of my work hours at Ray's. When he arrives, I'm busy inlaying emerald snake eyes into the obsidian head of Cleopatra's cobra ring. The elaborate collar has just recently been completed, after weeks spent troubleshooting a finicky box clasp.

While I work, Paul disappears into the stockroom with Ray. As he emerges, he slips another cash envelope into the interior pocket of his jacket. After Ray leaves, I reluctantly put my project away for the day.

I take a deep breath as we head outside together. "Abe stopped by on Sunday. On your orders, I presume?"

"I just sent him to check in." He already sounds guarded; Abe clearly warned him.

"Right. About that." I take another deep breath. "In the future, if you're 'checking in' about my relationship with Matthew, maybe you should do it yourself. Abe is not the one with the problem. Abe is used to seeing me with someone else, and he's fine with it. Apparently, you are not."

"It's not that I'm not fine with it, Kat." He sighs. "I'm trying to understand. He's just another mark...right?"

"You wanted me to get to know him, to find out about him and his family. You *told* me to do this, Paul. You don't get to be irritated if I decide I like what I've found."

"And do you?" he asks. "Do you like what you've found?"

"If you trusted me, if *we* were secure, you wouldn't have to ask. Or send Abe to spy on me."

"Kat, I've never asked you to be exclusive with me. Is that what you want? Are you testing me?"

"No, I'm not testing you. You know me better than that." But he can't have it both ways either—expecting me to blindly follow his orders, demanding all of me without giving all of himself in return.

"I can't figure out if you want me to be jealous, or if you want me to ignore what's happening altogether. What *is* happening, Kat?"

"I could ask you the same question," I say, narrowing my eyes.

"What are you talking about?"

I tweak his jacket, right where the damning cash sits against his chest. "More Magpie tribute?"

"Yes, Magpie tribute from Craig. And from the Condors. The usual," he lies smoothly.

I sniff and stare straight ahead. "You know what? Maybe I'll be honest with you when you decide to be honest with me."

"I *am* being honest with you. What do you think I'm doing in the bayou all week while you're prancing around the school or off on dates with your new beau?"

"I don't know what you're doing, Paul, but it's certainly more than the usual tribute payments and fleeces. Much more."

"I've raised prices. And they're getting antsy with firearms again. I didn't want you to worry, but I confiscated three guns off the Magpies this week and moved them through Ray."

"On the black market? Where they'll just trickle right back into the Magpies' hands in another week?"

"Ray only unloads the guns to well-vetted customers."

"Or so he tells you."

"He knows what I expect."

"He's a *businessman*, Paul. He answers to the highest bidder."

"We're just gonna have to agree to disagree on multiple points today. I'm willing to shelve it if you are."

"Fine."

When we reach Farley's, Paul asks me, carefully, about the Jekyll Island Club and Cherokee Cottage. We slip into familiar territory as I tell him the things I noticed about the structure, layout, valuables, and security.

"It's not much," I admit. "I wasn't exactly able to give myself a grand tour."

"It's a good start."

His response settles uneasily in my stomach, burrowing like a slithering snake.

NOVEMBER BRINGS COLD NIGHTS and crisp falling leaves. Matthew and I alternate chaperoned and unchaperoned dates. We continue the charade through the school channels every two weeks, but in between, I meet him all over the city. We get dinner after his shift or take long walks. Sometimes we go into Marino's Bakery and sample whatever Mellie's recommendation of the week is. We can usually find a secluded space to be alone for a while too. He doesn't invite me to his apartment, and I don't push for it. I'm still seeing Paul on the weekends, even though I feel more and more conflicted by the day. It's getting harder to keep these two parts of my life separate.

One day blurs contentedly into the next until, suddenly, December and Christmas are looming. The day before my birthday, I'm busy soldering the metal bases for a series of earring fakes in the back room at Ray's. Cleopatra's near-complete cobra ring sits abandoned on a corner of my desk. As I work, its accusatory emerald eyes burn into me, jealous with neglect.

"Kat." Ray's head pops in from the front floor. "Can you come out here? I need your help with a customer."

"Sure." I blow away the smoky residue surrounding my desk. Ray rarely pulls me onto the floor; I wonder what he needs my help with.

I wipe my hands on a discarded polishing cloth and push through the swinging door. Ray is bent over a far counter, talking to a male customer with blond hair. The man's back is to me, blocking the counter. They're in the diamond section. I walk over to see what they're examining.

"Ah, Katarina," Ray says. "Perfect. We need you to settle a dispute for us. This young man believes you'd prefer this pair of Old Mine-cut diamond earrings while I'm betting on the French-cut pair over here."

"What?" I round the final corner in shock and look at the customer. I do a double take. "Matthew?"

"Surprise," he says with a small wave. "Happy birthday, Kat."

"What are you doing here?"

"Picking out your birthday gift. Well, really, you're about to pick it."

I immediately shake my head. "You're not buying me diamonds, Matthew. It's excessive."

"Don't worry, Kat. I'm giving him a friendly discount," Ray chimes in, winking at me. "Since it's for a special cause."

I look back and forth between the two men, utterly mystified.

Matthew reaches over the counter to grab my hand, tugging me close. "You can have anything you want, but Ray pulled some options to get you started."

Trancelike, I examine the velveteen board. There are five pairs of diamond earrings. As usual, Ray's taste is flawless, but I shake my head again.

Matthew looks me in the eyes. "Kat, I thought for a really long time about what to give you for your birthday. I know it seems like a lot, but the thing you talk about loving the most is your work here, your jewelry. So pick something and don't feel guilty. I chose earrings because, heaven knows, you seem to already have enough rings." He reaches for my hand, gently rubbing his thumb over my bedazzled fingers. "But you can have whatever you want."

"Earrings are good," I whisper.

"Yeah?" He gives me a small smile, and as I offer one back, his grin grows and grows. Soon, I have the full blast of Matthew DaMolin sunshine hitting me in the face. It warms me from head to toe.

"Which pair do you like?" He slides the black velvet tray toward me.

I pick up the French-cut studs Ray mentioned. They're classic and beautiful and...familiar? I blink twice, recognizing them as the very same earrings I "borrowed" for the Jekyll Island Hallows' Eve party. My eyes dart, there and gone, to Ray. The corner of his mouth is upturned in a knowing smirk.

"Are those the ones?" Matthew prods.

When I say yes, Ray preens.

"I knew it," he crows. "I know ya like I know the back of my hand, kid."

I turn to Matthew. "I don't even know what to say. Thank you—they're the nicest thing anyone has ever given me. And they'll be the fanciest thing I've ever owned." Aside from a few things I've stolen.

"You're welcome. Happy one-day-early birthday, Kat."

"Kat?" Ray is writing down the sale in his little black book. "You're done for the day. Why don't you pack up and enjoy the evening with your young man?"

"Are you sure? I'm not quite done with the bases for those earrings—"

"I'm sure." He waves me off. "Go out and celebrate."

Gratified, I walk back through the swinging door and start cleaning my tools. Cleopatra's cobra ring winks at me, emeralds twinkling to mirror my raised spirits. I'm almost done when Ray pops into the workroom.

"That fella out there"—he jerks his head conspiratorially—"he's one of the good ones, Katarina. Where in tarnation did you find him? He's a long step up from the gutters of the bayou, and he talks about you like you hung the moon and the stars in the sky."

"You like him, huh? I'm not surprised." I smile. "Everyone does."

"Everyone except Paul, I bet." His smile is knowing.

I nod slowly, chewing on my cheek.

"I'm going to tell you something, Katarina, and I'm only going to say it once because it's not my place. You know I love both you and Paul, very much. You're like the kids I never had. But very, very rarely is our first love our final love. Or even our truest love. Maybe it will be for you, I don't know. But when you choose a partner, you're choosing an entire life and family. Take your time and don't rush it. At the end of the day, I want you to make the choice that's best for you. I want you to be able to say you chose your life, you didn't settle for it."

"Thank you, Ray," I whisper.

———◦◦◦———

I CELEBRATE MY BIRTHDAY with the Royals over the weekend. We have an ongoing birthday tradition amongst the four of us—stolen gifts only. It started when we were broke and couldn't afford much, and it's evolved into who can present the most outrageous pilfered gift. The current trump item was stolen by Paul for Tony's last birthday. He swiped a street sign from downtown Savannah that matches the name of Tony's favorite jazz club, Abercorn Street. The sign now hangs in a place of honor above Tony's bed.

One by one, the boys emerge from their rooms, each concealing his pillage behind his back. Abe starts us off with a doozy. He hands me a tiny, crystal wolf. "It's from—"

"I know exactly where it's from," I cut him off, aghast. My eyes are full of awe. "Astor Manor. When did you take it?"

"Immediately after you put it down. Swiped it." He shrugs. "It's small enough, I knew they'd never notice it's missing."

"Wow." I examine the beautiful wolf for another moment before leaning in to hug him. "It's perfect. I love it."

Tony nudges Paul. "You go next."

"No. I'm going last," Paul says.

"I don't wanna follow that." Tony gestures to the wolf.

I laugh. "Just give it to me, Tony."

Somewhat dejectedly, he presents me with a watch.

"Is this a signature Tony special?" I squeal. Lifting watches is Tony's forte. He loves it. Every week, he has a new bauble on his wrist and two more in his pocket. There's no less than twenty timepieces ticking away in his bedroom at any given time.

"It is," he says happily. "I canvased the streets for two days, watching for exactly the right one."

"Aw." I ruffle his hair. "You're such a thoughtful thief."

"Okay, you're up, Paul," Abe announces.

"All right, so I don't know if it technically counts as stolen..." Paul slowly pulls his hands out from behind his back to reveal a ratty old stuffed bear. "It was more like a search-and-rescue mission than theft, but here you go."

"Is that..." I pucker my brows. "Mr. Wiggles?"

"Sure is."

Something pulls, deep in my gut. Love and pain and hope and sadness, all swirling at once. "No way. Where did you find him?"

"I went down to our old hole in the Catacombs. We left a bunch of stuff there, remember? It doesn't look like anyone has found or used the place since we've been gone."

"And Mr. Wiggles was there?" I'd forgotten all about the little bear but holding him in my hand brings forth a huge resurgence of memories.

"He sure was, tucked away in your corner."

When Paul smiles, everything inside me melts into a gooey puddle. It's an incredibly thoughtful gift, and I know what it must have cost him to go back to that place to find this. My heart stutters at his vulnerability. Worlds collide inside of me in the blink of an eye. The before and the after. The then and the now.

Very rarely is our first love our final love. Or even our truest, Ray said.

But what if it is, I wonder? Wouldn't it feel exactly like this?

I was fifteen years old when I first told Paul I was in love with him. It was so many things that made me fall, a kaleidoscope of moments. A lifetime of running through moonlit streets, shared glimpses as thieving fingers darted in and out of pockets, stolen kisses behind limestone corners in the Catacombs, watching each other's backs during the day, holding on tight during cold nights on stone floors...

But most of all, it was the moment our eyes locked during that first red night in Damien's lair. The first time we ever spilled blood to protect each other. It was the look of pure, ravenous, insatiable hunger that overtook Paul's face. He was my mirror, reflecting the same hunger that had burned low and slow in my bones my entire life. Kindred spirits, twin fires—that's what we were. Paul pulled the pin on the grenade to my heart that night, when my soul recognized the darkest, most voracious parts of myself in him. That is when I truly fell in love.

I think back to a handsome man with blue eyes and a sharp tongue, buying me diamonds; it's every girl's dream come true. But then there's the faces of the three boys—the three *men*—in front of me. These men, who searched the city of Savannah with their hearts in their eyes, willing to beg, borrow, and steal the whole world for me. It's fathomless, the kind of love that can never be bought or measured.

I swallow. "These are the best gifts you three have ever given me."

"Mission accomplished," Tony cheers. And then they're all wishing me another chorusing round of *happy birthday* before Tony announces he's off to bed.

"I have one more gift for you," Paul whispers in my ear. Abe crosses the floor to stand in front of me. His eyes snap, crackle, and pop when they meet mine.

"Oh, yeah? What's that?" The corners of my mouth lift in a secret smile.

"We both do." He nods to Abe, who reaches out to brush my hair back from my face.

"I'm intrigued."

Paul lifts me from behind, directly into Abe's waiting arms. And together, the three of us disappear into the master bedroom.

CHAPTER SIXTEEN

THE ROYALS AND I plan a rendezvous at Farley's the week after my birthday. I'm careful to suggest an evening when Matthew is working. If Paul is bothered by my subterfuge, he doesn't say so. He's been on his best behavior as of late.

When we arrive, Paul heads to the back room to check on our cache and exchange some stashed scratch. Abe follows him while Tony and I walk up to the bar. A few patrons perch on stools at the far end of the counter, but overall, the place is quiet.

"Hey, Farls," Tony greets our friend, reaching over the counter to clasp the bartender's hand.

"Good to see y'all." Farley bobs his head, his crinkled eyes teasing a smile. "What'll it be tonight?"

"What do you think, Kat?" Tony turns to me. "A cask of wine and a handle of whiskey?"

"Comin' right up." Farley winks before turning around.

Abe joins us at the counter just as Farley is handing over our bottles. He reaches for his billfold, but the bartender stops him.

"You know your scratch is no good here, Abe. I'll put it on your tab."

"Thanks, Farley," Abe answers.

"Hey, when's he gonna move that powder out?" Farley jerks his head toward the stockroom, where Paul is still puttering around. "Makes me nervous, having that stuff back there."

I assume he's talking about bootlegged gunpowder, a frequently passed and traded commodity through the back of the tavern. I examine the shoddy wooden roof and walls of the pub, silently agreeing with Farley. This place could go up in flames with barely a spark, and the gunpowder will more than finish the job.

"Not sure, boss," Abe admits.

Farley shakes his head. "I don't like it. It's risky, that is."

We take our bottles to a table in the middle of the room. Eventually, Paul emerges to join us. His eyes are shaded by a fedora, shirtsleeves rolled to his elbows. His chest strains beneath a pair of brown suspenders. He looks a little loose, a little dangerous, a whole lot tempting. Too illicit for his own good.

"Everything jake?" Tony asks, lighting up a cigarette.

"Yeah."

"Farley wants the powder out," Abe says.

The barback's watchful eyes snap to attention as he listens.

"Okay." Paul glances sidelong at me, then away. "I'll move it when we leave tonight."

Abe nods at Farley, who returns to mopping his counter.

Tony pulls a deck of cards from his pocket and starts dealing. The pack is well-worn from many nights of use. I couldn't even begin to estimate how many hours we've spent playing poker here. Far too many to count.

I accept my first hand from Tony and settle in. Abe takes a swig from the whiskey and passes the bottle around.

Tony and Abe make absolute fools of Paul and me in the initial rounds, but as the night progresses, I rally. Paul continues to take a walloping though. His hands get worse and worse as the moon rises.

"Lady Luck is not on my side tonight," he says, dropping his cards after his umpteenth fold of the evening.

Sometime around midnight, the tavern empties out, but we stay to play a few more hands. Farley putzes around behind the bar, going through his closing routine. I'm busy laughing at something Tony just said, so I don't immediately notice the door kicking open. What I do notice is Paul's body as it snaps to attention beside me, his posture tight.

"Sorry, fellas," Farley calls to the newcomers, stepping out from behind the counter. "We're closing."

A gun goes off, and I scream. Farley falls to the floor. Eyes shut, a bullet wound blooming in his chest.

Six men rush in.

Abe jumps up from our table, headbutting the nearest intruder's gut. Two assailants swarm him. Together, they wrestle Abe to the floor. The other three men line up in front of Tony, Paul, and me. Tony rises to his feet, but the *click* of a cocking revolver in his face forces him back into his seat. I glance under the table and see Paul's knife in his hand, but it's useless. Instead of fighting back, he ducks his head, hiding his face under the brim of his hat. With a quick move, he pops his collar around his cheeks as well.

"Gentlemen, m'lady. Put your hands where I can see them," the man with the gun drawls.

Heart racing, I comply. I place my palms flat on the table and glance at Abe on the floor. There's just one man standing over him now, but he's got his boot resting on Abe's ribs and a gun pointed at his head. Abe is pinned on his side, a trickle of blood dripping from his lip.

"Once we get what we came for, we'll be on our way. Just sit there politely and nobody else needs to get hurt." The gunman spits at Abe while two henchmen crack the register open.

Silently, I wonder if these men know Farley's is one of our safe houses. They haven't made any move toward the back room, so hopefully, this is just a terrible coincidence. These things happen in the bayou. So many gangs, fighting for scraps...

Just empty the register and leave, I silently plead.

Paul nudges my foot beneath the table, but he keeps his head down.

"Magpies," he whispers, barely releasing his breath. He tilts his head toward the gunman in front of Tony. "Craig."

My heart stutters.

I recognize the name. Paul gets his Magpie tribute from Craig—he's the survivor, the one we let escape the night we took down Damien Keller. The years have worn him down, weathered and hardened his face and body. I can only hope the same is true of us. The gang doesn't seem to know who they're holding, but if Craig recognizes Paul...

I fidget nervously in my seat. Only two of the Magpies have guns, the one trained on Abe and the one in Craig's hand. The rest are only packing knives.

"Sit still, princess." Craig's attention shifts to me. Paul presses down hard on my foot.

"S-s-sorry," I mutter, quickly looking down.

Interested now, Craig walks over to me. He sweeps my dark hair back from my face and runs his grimy fingers down my cheek. I grit my teeth but don't move. Paul's head is still down, but his fingers fist on the tabletop, knuckles turning white.

"What'sa matter, fella? You don't like me touching her?" Craig's focus shifts to Paul for the first time. He bends down for a better look and inhales sharply. "Holy shit!"

Paul rises to lunge, but Craig is quick. He swings the revolver directly against Paul's forehead. With a sharp flick of the barrel, he knocks the fedora off Paul's head. It tumbles back and flutters to the ground.

"Sit the fuck down, *Paul,*" he hisses. His gaze sweeps the room, looking at me, then Tony, then Abe. Slowly. Calculating.

"No guns in my bayou, Craig," Paul says, trying to distract him. "You know that."

Craig ignores him, continuing to stare at Abe. "Four people. Four...wolves?" Disbelief is etched on his face. He has the attention of his whole band of thieves.

"Check 'em," Craig calls out. "Him." He points to Abe, pinned on the floor.

Keeping the gun trained on his head, the Magpie looming over Abe bends down. Slowly, he lifts the side of his shirt, revealing the wolf tracks inking their way over Abe's ribs.

"I'll be goddamned," Craig hoots, rubbing his jaw. "We caught ourselves some *wolves* tonight, boys. Pat 'em down. All of them. Can't be too careful."

One by one, each of us is searched. They pull knives from Abe and Tony, one each. And three off Paul. They toss the contraband on the bar, saving me for last.

"Stand up." Craig swings the gun from Paul to me. I rise slowly and step away from our table as two men descend. Their hands rove all over, lingering in places where they know damn well I'm not packing anything.

I stiffen at their touch. "I don't have anything on me, Craig. Call your dogs off."

"Patience, patience, little wolf. Can't be too careful."

His men continue groping, and Paul snarls from the table. Craig watches Paul's rapidly darkening face with delight.

"Isn't this fascinating, fellas?" he calls out. "I think we've discovered a little game."

The men pause.

"You *really* don't like it when we touch her, do you?"

Paul. I stare hard, warning him. He's going to get us in much deeper trouble if he doesn't ramp up his poker face.

"Is she your bitch, Paul?" Craig walks over and presses the cold barrel of the gun to my temple. I hold my breath, but I don't close my eyes. I keep them pinned on Paul, willing him not to give the game away.

"Yes..." Craig breathes. He takes my jaw in his hand, turning it from side to side. "You're the real prize, aren't you? Paul's infamous Cat Burglar."

He's so quick I don't see it coming. He backhands me across the face. Hard. My cheek and jaw sting, then burn. Branded in the shape of his foul fingers.

"Don't fucking touch her," Paul whispers from his seat. His tone is calm, but it promises murder.

"You're not really in a position to make demands, Paul, but I can see you're getting upset. I don't want that. We're all friends here, right? Old friends from the bayou. You don't want me to hit her? Fine. I don't have to hit her. What do you think about this instead?" He tugs me close, pressing his hips into mine. His hand skates up the side of my ribs, reaching. Teasing.

I school my expression into a mask of calm. I don't want Paul to see me getting upset, and I certainly don't want to give this cretin even a second of satisfaction.

"Is this better?" Craig asks. His hand settles on my backside.

"Enough!" Paul slams his fist on the table.

Paul...I inwardly groan. Tony closes his eyes and exhales slowly.

We're well and truly fucked now.

"Enough," Paul repeats, more quietly this time. His gaze is locked on Craig. "I'm the one you really want. We both know it. I'm the kingpin, and I'm sitting right here. Either take your shot, or put the gun down so we can sort this out like civilized men."

"Unbelievable." Craig cackles. "Merciless Paul. Cold, ruthless Paul. Everyone says you're bulletproof, but it looks like there's a heart under there after all."

Panicking, I look at Abe, still helpless and pinned on the floor. His dark eyes are wide with fear.

"The real question is..." Craig's attention moves back to me. He removes the gun from my temple, and—I can't help it—I exhale mightily. "How does she feel about you?"

A new kind of fear blooms when Craig slides the gun from my face to Paul's, removing all rationality, all logic, from my mind.

"Whaddya think, little wolf?" he asks me. "Should I shoot him?"

I swallow mechanically.

"Take the heater," he tells one of his men.

A bearded Magpie grabs the weapon, keeping it trained on Paul.

Craig flexes his fists once, then lands a brutal punch to Paul's right eye. He winds up quickly and swings again, hitting the exact same spot. Paul releases a small grunt at the second impact, and that's all it takes to completely undo me.

"Stop," I implore. "Just...stop."

I'll do anything, give anything. There is no price I won't pay to make it stop.

Craig pulls back, victory glinting in his eyes. "Just like I thought," he whispers. "Come here, little wolf."

I walk slowly, like a sleepwalker.

When Craig reaches for my hips, his grip is sharp enough to leave marks. He nods to his friend, and the bearded man presses the revolver directly to the center of Paul's forehead.

"You're gonna watch this," Craig says to Paul. "You're gonna watch, and you're gonna enjoy it." He grabs the back of my head and forces his lips on mine. It's pure instinct to resist—I wiggle and try to pull away—but his claws are wound tight into my hair. Welding me in place.

A thudding of fists erupts from the corner, followed by a groan.

Abe.

Gasping, I wrench away with enough vigor that hair rips from my scalp. I pull in a second desperate breath as I lean around Craig.

Abe is struggling again, trying to rise and fight. He's quickly pushed to the ground, this time with a blooming black eye to match Paul's. The man above him rears back and lands a harsh kick to his ribs. Abe curls around his gut. The brute steps back for another go, and I turn to Craig.

"Call him off," I rasp.

Another grunt from Abe.

Craig yanks my hair, tugging my head back. "What's it worth to you?"

"You know exactly what it's worth." I narrow my eyes but play along, sliding my arms around his neck. Abe takes a third kick as I do.

"Call. Him. Off." I hold Craig's eyes.

He waves his hand, and the man abusing Abe stands down. Craig pushes me back, then forces me onto the low counter of the bar.

I scan the room. The four men without guns aren't really threats. They're clustered loosely around the room, leering at me with interest. Two of them sit on the tables, completely at ease. The man guarding Abe is similarly lecherous, and his gun hangs limply by his side.

Unfortunately, Abe is on the floor with his eyes squeezed shut, his breaths coming in shallow pants. The other problem—the most pressing problem, really—is the man guarding Paul. The revolver is still trained firmly on his forehead, and that trigger can be pulled in an instant.

"Are you watching, Paul?" Craig taunts.

When he climbs on top of me, I realize we're not getting out of this alive. Not any of us. I'm collateral damage, useful to hurt Paul, but once Craig is finished, he'll kill us. One by one. Letting him have his way bought us time, but I haven't changed the outcome.

Not yet.

I've accomplished my first job though. Craig thinks I'm submissive and helpless.

But he's wrong. I am neither.

I am a wolf.

I turn my head to Paul, and he meets my gaze. We've never needed words. His dark eyes flick to my right. All the knives, the ones they stripped from the guys, lie behind me on the counter. Ripe for the taking. One of Paul's is closest. A corner of my mouth lifts, liking the irony.

"I'm going to fuck you so hard," Craig murmurs. His lips move sloppily across my neck. "I'm going to fuck you harder than he's ever fucked you in his miserable life."

Target acquired.

I burn my eyes into Tony's now, making sure he's ready. He tightens his mouth and crosses his arms. Three fingers appear on his shirtsleeve. I try to bend my neck to spot Abe, but there's no way to warn him. I can only hope his eyes are open. Or at least his ears. He'll need to move quickly.

Tony drops a finger. *Two.*

I wait.

One.

When his last finger falls, my hand darts overhead, grip closing around Paul's knife.

"Abe!" I scream as I swing my arm around and plunge the blade deep into Craig's back. It's a clean stick, angled under his ribs on the left side. One and done, exactly the way Paul taught me long ago.

You gotta come at them quick and hard, Kitty-Kat, because they're always gonna be bigger than you.

Craig slumps on top of me. I kick him off, rolling his carcass to the floor.

Across the room, my wolves move in synchronicity. Paul ducks in his seat as Tony grabs a glass whiskey bottle. He swings hard, shattering it into a million shards against the bearded man's face. The gun goes off, but it fires wide before clattering to the floor.

On the ground, Abe kicks out with his right leg, sweeping the feet from under his attacker. I move to his aid, but a stray Magpie with a knife rushes me. I duck his wild swing and plunge my blade into his gut. He drops to the floor.

Abe is still on the ground, but so is his attacker. The gun lies several feet away, forgotten. They're tussling for position on the floor, but Abe quickly loses and gets pinned. He's wheezing, badly hurt. I'm behind the Magpie in a flash, and with a flick of my wrists, I snap his neck. Shoving him aside with a grunt, I crouch over Abe.

"Savage," he pants, eyes flicking to the dead man beside us.

"Abe." My hands fly everywhere, all over him. Checking.

"My ribs." He closes his eyes again.

Across the room, there's one man still standing. Tony and Paul have him cornered. They have their knives now, and it's over quickly. I stay with Abe, scanning the floor for movement from the downed attackers.

"Check them all," Paul roars. He plunges his knife into the temple of the nearest Magpie. Tony thunders to the next and does the same. I inhale sharply at their brutality.

"They saw our faces, Kat," Abe whispers between pants. He's wiggling, trying to rise. "We have to make sure."

He's right. We do.

When it's finally done, Paul crosses the room.

"Kat." He crushes me to his chest. "Oh, Kat."

He doesn't say anything more, but I feel his fear and his regret—his apology—nonetheless. Feel it in the tremoring grip of his arms, impossibly tight around me.

I bury my face in his shirt to hide my tears. There's nothing I hate more than showing weakness in front of the guys, but the memory of Craig—the slimy feel of his hand on the back of my head, moving up and down my body—is too real, too fresh. My cheek burns where he slapped me. I sniff loudly.

"Kat." Paul's arms flex around me. Abe and Tony are there too, forming a cocoon.

"I'm fine." The words come automatic. A reflex.

"It's okay to not be fine," Abe murmurs. "Just for a minute. It's just us."

It's just us.

I exhale shakily, drawing inexplicable comfort simply from their nearness. Their protection, their love. After one final hiccup, I turn to look at the fellas. "What are we gonna do now?" I whisper, peeking at Farley, cold and still beside his beloved bar.

Paul releases me. "Now we have to..." He surveys the room with clinical precision, but his hands tremble. "We have to make it look like *we* hit this place."

"Like *we* hit it?" Tony repeats.

"You got a better idea?" Paul whirls on him. "We've got seven bodies in here and a shit ton of blood. We'll never be able to clean it up. It's a slaughter."

Abe slumps against the wall and nods.

"We'll finish emptying the register, move our stuff out of the back," Paul continues. "Then we'll put our mark on the wall. No one will ever know different."

"The other Magpies will know." I point to the men. "They'll know different."

"I'll deal with them. I'll *annihilate* them." Venom, pure and undiluted, blazes in Paul's eyes, from his lips. It's a promise, and I know he's good for it.

Silently, we enact the plan. Cleaning house.

Before we depart, Tony walks behind the bar. He pulls a coin-sized tub of paint from his pocket and dips his finger. Slowly, he paints our black wolf on the wall. It feels sacrilegious.

"Lo siento, mi amigo," he whispers to Farley as he finishes. He crouches over our friend, resting his paint-stained hand on the man's chest before ducking his head. "Padre nuestro, que estás en el cielo. Santificado sea tu nombre..."

I blink furiously and whisper my own quick prayer to the heavens, more for Farley's sake than mine. Like always, I'm filled with the frustrating sensation that no one is listening, that no one cares. That Paul and Abe and Tony and I are walking out of this pub by the tenacity of our own hands, not by the grace of any god.

Paul takes the paint from Tony. He crosses to the wall, blackens his finger, and slowly scratches one line below our wolf symbol. Not a prayer, but a message. Not for God, but for the Magpies.

He writes slowly. Deliberately. Anger bleeds from his fingers into the dripping black paint on the wall.

No guns in my bayou.

CHAPTER SEVENTEEN

THE DAY AFTER THE Farley's incident, the papers have a field day with us again. The headlines are jarring.

Brutal Slaying of Seven by Wolves

Bayou Brutality in the time of the Wolf

Wolfpack Slaughterhouse

Knowing the real story is gut-wrenchingly painful. Like getting sucker punched over and over, no end in sight. I'm running on zero sleep, too afraid to close my eyes in the darkness of my bedroom during the short hours before dawn.

And then there's my face to contend with. For the next several days, I slink into the bathroom before Mellie wakes to paint over the purple bruise, faintly handprint-shaped, on my right cheek. The dark bags beneath my eyes, as well. Not even my dreams are safe...

"Kat, wake up! Kat, you're dreaming."

My eyes fly open, darting around the bedroom. My paranoia is high—it's the second time in one night Mellie has roused me from the grips of a nightmare. She plucks worriedly at the sweat-soaked bedsheets tangled around me.

"Kat, are you okay? Are you ill?" She bends low and brushes the back of her hand to my sweaty cheek, checking my temperature. I flinch from the contact, the ghost of Craig's slap rising from the dead.

"What...?" Mellie leans closer, eyes narrowing. "What's that on your cheek?"

I roll onto my right side to hide the evidence. There are smears of face paint on my pillow.

"Kat, is that—"

"It's nothing." The tenor of my voice tells her the discussion is over. "I'm sorry I woke you. I'm fine now. Let's go back to sleep."

Only faintly reassured, she slips away. Once her breathing evens out, I steal from my bed to clean my face, then carefully reapply paint to conceal the bruise once more, blending carefully.

It's a good thing, because when Mellie rises in the morning, her sharp eyes go straight to my face. I feign sleep, right cheek deliberately exposed, the barest crack between my lid and lashes. The worried lines on her face disappear, ready to believe it was a trick of the light. Nothing more than shadows.

People are primed to see only what they want.

But the newspapers...those are a different story. Far more difficult to ignore and certainly unable to be muted. Sensation sells, the darker the better. Circulars fly off newsstands at unprecedented rates, eyeballs hungrily devouring every word on streetcorners, at dining tables, on the streetcar, everywhere. Paul says the newspapers should give us a cut for all the issues we sell.

"Maybe you should make that your next great business venture," I tell him bitterly.

"Maybe I will," he answers. "Doesn't your little boyfriend's family own the paper? Could be fun."

But it's not the press consuming Paul. It's revenge. He's single-minded, possessed by fury. All of it directed at the Magpies. He begins plotting their imminent downfall, but we'll have to wait before striking. Abe is out of commission with his bruised ribs. It will be a long recovery before he's back to full strength.

Almost a week after the attack, I'm out with Matthew when we stroll by a shoddy, hastily erected newspaper stand. They've been cropping up out of the woodwork to meet the rise in demand.

Matthew pauses to scan the graphic headlines, almost all of which are still focused on bayou crime and the infamous Wolfpack. He shakes his head.

I loop my arm through his and shift my weight, feeling the reassuring, cold steel of the dagger in my boot. I've not left home without the weapon since the incident at Farley's. I will never be caught unprotected again.

Eventually, if only to get Matthew to stop reading the cruel recounts, I speak up. "What do you know about them?" I ask. "The Wolves."

"More than you'd think."

My heart stutters as I turn to him. For one terrifying moment, I half expect him to say he knows. About me. About Paul. About everything. Matthew is so quick; it really wouldn't take much for him to put it together. I'm dancing very close to the sun indeed.

"I know they're like ghosts," he says. "They broke into Astor Manor, which should have been impossible."

I let out a subtle *whoosh* of breath.

"I know they're ruthless. That I've stitched up more people than I can count who ran afoul of their knives. That I haven't been able to save them all."

I fight to keep my expression neutral. "You don't really know them, Matthew. No one does. I'm sure they have their reasons."

"It's hard to think of reasons for why seven people are dead, Kat. And countless others too. I don't have any reasons to offer family members when I can't save their loved one. It's just...it's hard, you know? It's hard all around."

"I can't even imagine," I tell him. "I can't imagine doing what you do." Because I can't.

We're silent for a moment before I offer one more piece of wisdom. One more disguised piece of my puzzle.

"They're from the Catacombs, Matthew. Like me. It's different there. You can't imagine the choices you have to make every day, just to survive."

We stroll onward without another word, my mind soothed only by the press of the dagger-tip, soft as a lover's kiss, into my skin with every step.

CHAPTER EIGHTEEN

THE WEEK BEFORE CHRISTMAS, the Academy hosts a holiday party in the upstairs billiard room. Matthew shows up early for the event, and we stake out the corner table where we played pool so many months ago. We're racking up balls for our first game when he turns to me.

"I have a question for you."

"Oh no." I stand upright. "I'm not playing that game again. We're shooting pool for bragging rights, not deep dark secrets."

"It's not about a deep dark secret," he replies, amused. "It's about New Year's Eve. There's an annual party at the Jekyll Island Club, one of the biggest of the year. My family always attends."

"Oh." I lean on the table and wait.

"I'm allowed to bring a date."

"Huh." I go back to racking up the balls, playing nonchalant. "That's nice."

"It is. It would be even nicer if you go with me. You can stay overnight at our cottage after the party."

I freeze. "Spend New Year's with you?" I've never rung in the New Year with anyone but the Royals.

With *Paul*.

"Yes." Matthew's gaze is earnest but piercing. "I already spoke with my parents about it."

I laugh. "Oh, did you now?"

"Yes. It will be an overnight together, but so long as I'm on my gentlemanly best behavior, they agreed to let you come."

"I'm not sure I'm interested then," I tease.

He smiles. "They won't be around the whole time, Kat. It's New Year's, the club's biggest party of the season. Plenty of distraction afoot." He steps closer and slowly slides his hands over my hips. "So what do you reckon?"

This is big. New Year's together. With Matthew's family. Overnight.

Paul will kill me.

But a New Year's Eve party on Jekyll Island...I would die to be there. To be there as an invited guest, not as a thief slinking in the shadows. Always on the outside looking in.

And New Year's with Matthew? My traitorous heart skips a beat.

"Okay," I hear myself say.

"Yeah?" His grin stabs with its sincerity.

"Yes, I would love to go with you."

Wider still, that smile. Bright enough to eclipse any doubt. "Great! We'll have a guest room aired out for you."

I bend over to break while Matthew chatters on about logistics. Blood rushes in my ears, muffling my attention as though my head is stuffed with cotton.

New Year's with Matthew, New Year's with Matthew...

New Year's *without* Paul.

I can scarcely fathom it.

We're just finishing our first game when Mellie stumbles over with Bobby Marino in tow. From underwater, I hear Matthew suggest something that sounds like "doubles" for the next game. I mechanically begin to rerack, but Mellie latches onto my arm. Her fingernails dig into my skin.

"Kaaat," she hisses, fluttering anxiously.

"What?"

She widens her eyes and starts convulsing her neck to the right. Her nails are still embedded in my forearm.

"Mellie, what's gotten into you?" She's like a cat on a hot tin roof.

"Kat!" she hisses again and jerks her head, more directly this time. Straight toward the billiard room door.

When I follow her eyes, the floor drops beneath me.

There, silhouetted in the doorway, stands Abe.

"Kat, what is he doing here?" Mellie whispers.

At this point, we've attracted the attention of the gentlemen.

"Um," I breathe, "I'm not sure."

"Kat?" Matthew's tone is uncertain.

It's easy enough for him to follow my gaze. Abe's dark skin stands out in the lily-white room, branding him an outsider. But his chin is high, his three-piece suit immaculate. Even still, a number of scornful eyes are turned his way. My heart contracts painfully. The upper lip of my wolf curls, instinctive. Protective.

"Beg pardon." I shake my head, clearing it. "I must excuse myself. I'll be right back." I give Matthew's cheek a quick, reassuring kiss.

"Kat!" My roommate's hiss is downright deadly this time.

"Right back." I look at her. *Please, Mellie,* I internally beg. *Help me out here. Just once. Please.*

I cross the room to Abe in seconds and grab him by the arm. I squeeze harder than strictly necessary as I pull him aside.

"What are you doing here?" I demand. My gaze darts, unconsciously, back to Matthew. When I see him staring, I drop Abe's arm, as though burned.

"Pleasure to see you too, Katarina." Abe's nod is formal as he plays the gentleman.

"Don't toy with me. Paul or Tony had better be in a ditch *dying* right now."

"Not quite," he admits.

"Then what. Are you. Doing here?" I punctuate the words. "And where in the world did you find this suit?"

"You're not the only one who can play dress-up, Kat."

I stare at him. Wait. All too aware of the unforgiving attention of half the room still on us, on the black man daring to talk to a white Academy girl. Centuries of racial divide run deep in Savannah, webbing their way into the very foundation of society, like the vine-like, underground tunnels of the Catacombs themselves. The lines may blur in the blue-collar bayou, but not here. Not in polite Savannah society. By walking into this room tonight, Abe has made himself immensely vulnerable.

"Why would you risk showing up here, Abe?"

Eventually, he sighs. His eyes flick over my shoulder toward Matthew.

"Are you joking?" I'm flabbergasted. "He sent you to spy on me? *Here?*"

Abe shrugs. "You know how Paul is, Kat."

"I think you should go."

"No, unfortunately, I'm here to stay." He looks over my shoulder again. "Your friends are giving me the evil eye."

"Well, let's see." I tap my finger against my lip. "Mellie thinks you're my secret beau from the Catacombs, and Matthew..."

"Also thinks I'm your secret beau. Dilly." Abe sticks his hands in his pockets, annoyed. "Well, I'm not here for a pissing contest or to start a race riot, so let's go set the record straight, shall we?" He shoulders around me and heads for the pool table. Shocked, I hurry to catch up.

"Good evening." Abe extends a hand to Matthew and flashes a big smile. "I'm Abe."

I almost hit the deck when he gives his real name. Mellie's jaw is on the floor.

"I'm Matthew." He does Abe a credit just by returning the shake. The collective crowd in the billiard room is watching him—Matthew

DaMolin—closely. They'll take their cue from him. "How do you know Katarina?"

"Oh, Kat and I go way back," Abe drawls. Matthew's eyes register his casual use of my nickname. "We grew up together. Old friends."

Mellie starts fanning herself. Her histrionics catch Abe's attention, so he turns to her.

"Abe." He offers his name and hand again. His eyes slide over her figure from head to toe, lingering ever so slightly on her soft curves, her flushed face.

Don't you dare be a dog, Abe, I warn him with a look. I know what he likes, but my roommate is absolutely off limits.

Mellie gives the barest of return shakes, likely trying to avoid his highly contagious Catacomb-itis. "Melinda. I'm Kat's roommate," she says weakly.

"Pleasure to finally meet you, Melinda. Kat has told me much about you."

"Indeed?" The tenor of her voice skyrockets, and her cheeks, if possible, blush even deeper.

Abe smiles, biting his lip and giving her one final appreciative glance before turning to Bobby. When the last introduction is complete, all eyes in the group turn to me.

Unexpectedly, it's Matthew who steps in for the save. "We were about to start a game. Would you care to join us?" he asks Abe, polite beyond reproach.

"Sure. Kat and I used to play pool together all the time," Abe answers, grinning like the imp he is. "It's been a while though."

Oh, sweet lord. The strip pool...

Matthew's head whips to me, a question and an accusation burning in his eyes.

I sway on the spot. Mellie reaches to grab me, but I lean into Matthew's ear instead. Damage control, the swifter the better.

"He's just a friend, I swear," I whisper to him. "I will tell you everything later tonight." Well, almost everything.

Vaguely reassured, he reaches for the pool stick. Then Mellie does what she does best—throws me to the wolves.

"You know, I'm honestly quite terrible at this game," she declares, backing away. "I'll sit this round out. You can take my spot, Abe. I was partnering with Matthew."

"I'm not sure that will be fair." I try to keep my tone light. Abe and Matthew on the same team? They'll destroy us. Only with Matthew tied to a Mellie-sized anchor did Bobby and I stand a chance.

"Who said anything about fair?" Matthew's grin is devilish. "Remember when we decided losing was good for you?"

Abe smiles lazily, very much liking the sound of that. He looks at Matthew, an alliance forming. That's when I know I'm in real trouble.

"You got a good break?" Matthew asks, tossing his pool cue to Abe.

Abe smirks and bends over the table, a quiet groan slipping between his teeth. The barest of grimaces crosses his face as he exhales. It's pure instinct to reach for him. I brush my fingers over his injured ribs, concerned.

Abe coughs pointedly, and I drop my hand. Too late. Matthew has already seen.

I quickly lose all sympathy for Abe when he proceeds to knock down two perfect shots off the break. I keep my hands to myself for the remainder of the game.

Matthew and Abe bond from the outset, united by a shared bloodthirst for my head. Matthew is easy to love, so I'm not surprised when he has Abe laughing within minutes. I am, however, surprised by how quickly Abe manages to ingratiate himself in return. He asks countless questions about

Matt's work at the hospital—a surefire way to his heart—and follows up with several insightful comments.

"Enough about me," Matt eventually declares. "What do you do, Abe?"

The answer comes quick, sliding off Abe's tongue like liquid mercury. "I've been working odd jobs lately, contracting for different things here and there." He shrugs, keeping it deliberately vague. "I'm between positions at the moment."

"If you're looking for something steady, I could put you in touch with people at the hospital," Matt offers. He bends over to take a shot and drops yet another ball. Beside me, Bobby winces.

Abe hesitates. "I don't know if the medical field is right for me."

Matthew shakes his head. "There's a lot more work to be had at the hospital than medicine. That's a common misconception. What are you interested in? Business? Maintenance? Administration? Security?"

"Security could be interesting," Abe ventures. His eyes briefly meet mine before landing back on Matt. "I have some prior experience there."

"Swell, I'll put you in touch. I'll give Kat the info and...and she can get it to you?" He looks to me for confirmation.

I nod faintly, shocked by this turn of the conversation.

"Thank you, Matt," Abe replies. He seems a bit discomfited by the offer of an inside track. It's certainly not something Abe is used to.

"Consider it done."

Bobby and Mellie excuse themselves after the first game—massacre—leaving me to navigate my way through the most awkward threesome of my life. We chat and shoot aimlessly, passing the pool stick back and forth. Our shots become more and more outlandish the longer we play.

"You're unbelievable," Abe says after Matt sinks a ricocheting trick shot.

"Please, Abe, his ego needs no inflating." I laugh as Matthew slings an arm around my shoulders. He turns his head for a kiss, and I oblige, putting everything I have into it. Fathomless depths of unsaid meaning. Because

I'm so grateful to him tonight, for his maturity and grace. He has absolutely taken my breath away.

As we part, Matt smiles, and my gut seizes with the certainty he knows exactly what I was trying to say. When I look at Abe next, there's no recrimination in his eyes. In fact, he's grinning. Then he announces he's going to take his leave.

"This was a real gas." His sincerity is apparent. "Thanks for letting me join you tonight. It was great to meet you, Matt."

"Likewise. We'll have to do it again sometime. We'll grab a drink, shall we?"

Over my dead body.

I walk Abe to the door alone, pausing to lean against the frame. After a quick glance to ensure Matthew is far from earshot, I turn to Abe. "What was that all about?"

"All what?" He checks his wristwatch, very nonchalant.

"You and Matthew were certainly...chummy."

"Yeah, he's a good guy. If I had to be here spying on you, I wasn't going to lurk in the corner alone. That's no fun at all."

"Why were you working him about the hospital?" I ask, suspicious.

"I wasn't working him. If he does give you the contact info, I want it."

"Why?"

"This life we lead, Kat...surely you realize it can't be permanent? It's not forever, and it would be good to have something stable to fall back on."

"Paul isn't going to like you taking a day job," I say. "Whoever will he send to spy on me in your stead?"

"Paul doesn't own me, Kat."

I tilt my head, considering the Abe standing before me. It's certainly a different version than I'm used to.

"Does he own you?" he asks, raising an eyebrow.

"No."

"I didn't think so. Not anymore at least." His gaze flicks briefly to Matthew. "All right, Kitty-Kat, I'm going to leave now so you can say goodnight to your beau in private. Neither of us will tell Master Paul I didn't stay all the way to the bitter end, keeping my eye on you."

I laugh, gratified. "Goodnight, Abe."

The billiard room is nearly empty now. Taking a fortifying breath, I return to Matthew.

"So..." I bite my lip. "Shall we go someplace we can talk?"

"Absolutely. You want a drink?" When he smiles, I know what he's suggesting.

"Sure, but we'll have to sneak out."

Turns out Matt isn't half bad at sneaking, if a little sunshine-y and giggly while doing it. The poor man has no idea what's coming.

After we slip into his mother's office, I'm the one to pull out the whiskey and tumblers. I pour Matthew a liberal drink. Very liberal. I keep going until the glass is two-thirds full.

"Uh-oh." He accepts the hefty pour, frown lines appearing. "Am I really going to need all of this?"

I want to smile and laugh so much. Because he's sweet and perfect...so very sweet and perfect. But I'm neither, nor is what I plan to confide tonight.

"You might." I pour myself a generous drink as well, then take a fortifying pull. "I'm going to tell you some things you might not like...things you definitely won't like, I reckon."

"All right." He's nervous, but he takes another sip and waits.

"I'm not really even sure where to begin."

Matthew leans back against the desk. "Perhaps the beginning?"

That will never do; we'd be here all night.

I tighten my grip on my drink. "You know there's a fella in the picture, from back home?"

"Yes. Is that fella Abe?" he asks, steady.

I love him for the fact that there's no accusation in his eyes, no judgment or reproach when he asks it.

"Yes and no."

"Yes and no?"

"No, because no, it's not really Abe. There's someone else." I blink and press my fingers to my closed eyes for a moment. "Someone who's quite important to me. But yes, because, in the past, Abe and I...Abe has been that guy for me. I've been with Abe before."

"Been with him in what capacity, exactly?" He puts his drink on the desk.

"In...every capacity."

Matthew falls silent.

"I'm not...I don't know what you have or haven't assumed about me, but I'm not a virgin."

He exhales slowly. "I didn't think you were. So...with Abe?"

"Yeah. Sometimes."

"When was the last 'sometime?'"

This, I don't want to answer. I really, really don't. But he stares me down with those trusting ice-blue eyes, and I make my decision. If I'm going down tonight, I'm going to do it in a blaze of truthful glory.

"My birthday," I confess. "But...but just as friends. It doesn't mean what you think it does. Honest."

"Christ, Kat, that was only three weeks ago! That's what you do with your *friends*?"

He closes his eyes, and I know I've hurt him. He picks up his whiskey and takes a big, gulping swallow.

I'm not sure how to make him understand. Not without going back to the beginning, like he originally asked.

So I do. The story pours out of me in a desperate cascade.

"Matthew, I've known Abe since I was six years old. I met him the day I found my mom dead on the floor of the Catacombs." The words come in a rush, tripping over one another in the haste to purge. "I lost the only family I'd known, but I built myself a new one. With Abe and someone else." I omit Tony because I'm afraid to admit there's four of us, worried he'll figure me out.

Three men and one woman...from the Catacombs...the four wolves...

"The three of us did everything together. We had to learn how to survive, and we kept each other alive. We were just kids, but we had no one. We became each other's everything. And we made it through every day together. Abe and the other boy, they took care of me." I fight to keep my voice steady. "They made sure I was fed every day...and when it was cold at night, they held me and kept me warm and made me believe tomorrow would come. That we would be fine."

Matthew stays quiet, listening. His expression is grieved.

"We were closer to each other than most blood-related families can ever claim to be. They were—and still are—my everything. They're my *family*, Matt. And as we got older and those cold nights came around, we started doing...other things to stay warm." My cheeks turn red.

"All *three* of you? Together?" He's wide-eyed now, a crack finally showing in his veneer.

"Yes." I throw the admission out as bravely as I can.

He only misses half a beat before giving a shaky laugh. "Well...at least I understand now why pecks on the lips didn't do nearly enough for you."

"You don't have to do that, Matt. You don't have to pretend to be comfortable. I know you're not. This *is* uncomfortable, but I want to be honest with you. I want to do it in a way that maybe, possibly, you can understand. I'm not some fast and loose vamp. I've only ever slept with two people, and they're the two people I love the most in this world."

Matthew nods slowly. "I don't think you're a vamp, Kat. I think you had a very difficult life. You had difficult choices, and you did your best with them. I don't know what it feels like to love people outside your immediate blood family the way you do, so I'm hardly in a position to judge how you navigate it."

"Abe and I really are just friends—family—at the end of the day. I swear. We're friends who happen to have chemistry, and sometimes, we end up on the make. As just another way to express how we feel about each other, how much we love each other. I care about Abe immensely, but not the way I care about you. It's not the same type of love, if that makes sense?"

"I think it might," he says cautiously.

"I'm not going to be with him again. Not that way, not anymore. You have my word."

"But what about the other guy?" Matthew says, the question soft. "He's the real problem, isn't he? You haven't said much about him. It's because he's more than just a friend to you, isn't he?"

"He is," I admit. "We've been together since I was thirteen. I've known him since before I can remember."

"Are you still seeing him?"

"I do still see him. Though much less often than I see you."

"Small consolation."

I don't say anything more. I've put as many cards on the table as I can, have laid myself bare and exposed for him. The vulnerability is awful. I look up at him, but only for a quick minute. I don't have the courage to read his eyes. I'm afraid of what I'll see there.

"So having said all that," I choke out, "I understand if you don't want me to spend New Year's with you and your family. I'm not really who you thought I was."

He sighs. "Of course I still want you there, Kat."

"Really?" I raise my gaze to him in surprise.

"You were more honest with me tonight than I expected, about things that are really hard to discuss. Things I don't know if I could say if our roles were reversed. You're exactly who I thought you were. You're brave and passionate, and when you love, you do it with your whole heart. And I'm not sure if we"—he gestures between us—"will ever get there, but I want to try. To be loved by you, Kat...it's a privilege. I hope he knows that, whoever he is. Because I do. And for tonight, that's enough."

"It is?"

"It is. For tonight."

I shake my head in disbelief. "I don't know how you've managed to keep your composure and integrity after the massive pill I just forced you to swallow, but I admire you for it."

"I just tried to swallow it with as much integrity as you showed by sharing with me." He reaches for my hands. "So is that everything, Kat? No more secrets?"

Don't let him catch you, don't let him see, my mother whispers in my ear. The hairs on the back of my neck rise, spooked.

"It's mostly everything," I answer.

"*Mostly* everything?"

"It's everything I'm able to share right now. I'm not going to lie to you and say it's my entire story. Because then later..." My vision starts to blur with tears. He rises from the desk. "Later, you'll say I lied to you. And then you'll leave for sure."

"Kat." He wraps his arms around me. "You know what? It's okay. I said it's enough, and I meant it. When you're ready to share more, I'll be here. I'm not going anywhere, okay?"

"Okay." I give a tiny sniffle into his shirt.

I let him kiss me then, a tiny kiss on my cheek to swallow the single tear I let slip. But that one kiss turns into two, and two turns into three.

Sweet butterfly kisses to soothe something that, deep inside me, is positively aching.

There has always been so much darkness in me, so many holes. But standing here with him, he lends me his light. And he shines it into every corner until I know I'm safe.

CHAPTER NINETEEN

AT OUR FIRST MAGPIE stakeout, I discreetly pass along an early Christmas gift for Abe—a neatly folded slip of paper with the name and contact information for the head of security at the hospital. There's also a line from Matthew saying he recommended Abe for an open position.

"You don't have to do this for him," I told Matthew when he handed me the note.

"Kat, I don't hold anything against Abe. He showed up to meet me head-on, like a gentleman, marching himself straight into the lion's den to do it. And he didn't so much as bat an eyelash when I kissed or touched you throughout the night. He's a stand-up fella. He respects you. Your history with Abe doesn't bother me."

I ignored his insinuation. That Paul—who hasn't shown his face—is neither a gentleman nor a stand-up guy.

"Even still," I replied, "this...setting up a job for him, this goes above and beyond."

He shrugged. "You go to bat for the people you love, Kat. I've watched my father do it time and time again for my mother. Even when it's hard for him. This is nothing. Abe is important to you, so if I can help him, of course I will."

Simple as that.

When I give the paper to Abe, he nods appreciatively and pockets it before Paul or Tony notice.

The Royals and I proceed to spend the misty December night outside, casing the Magpies' riverfront den on the outskirts of the bayou. How they came to be in possession of a dilapidated clipper ship on the Savannah docks is beyond me, but they've held the vessel for three years, sleeping below deck in their maritime clubhouse and stashing loot in the ship's underbelly. They post round-the-clock guards at the base of the gangplank, with the remainder of the crew safely ensconced inside the vessel.

We're about two hours into our initial recon, the scrapings of a rudimentary plan forming, when Paul makes a surprisingly rash announcement. He wants to hit the ship next week, on New Year's Eve. He says that date will make for a perfect "object lesson."

This is a bad idea for multiple reasons, the *least* of which being I've just made New Year's plans with Matthew. Taking a deep breath to steel myself, I tell Paul I won't be able to run a job that night.

"Why the hell not?" He whirls on me. "And so help me god, Kat, if your little boyfriend's name comes out of your mouth anywhere in your explanation, I'm going to lose it."

I stay silent. Stonily so. My eyes burn into his with frustration.

"We're going to talk about this later." I hear the threat in his tone.

"Oh, leave her alone, Paul," Abe says.

"Stay out of this, Abe."

"What's our Plan B?" Tony asks, blowing on his hands for warmth. "We push it back a few days?"

"No, we go ahead with the plan *as is*." Paul crosses his arms. "We don't need Kat for every job. Abe can do her part."

Tony and Abe can't hide their shock. I don't like his answer either, and I really don't like the thought of the boys going three wolves against eight or more Magpies, especially considering Abe's ribs are barely healed.

"You're a fool if you mean that," I tell Paul. "It's suicide to try this without me."

"Well, Kat, you don't really have a say in this," he snaps back. "If you aren't going to show up for us, you don't get to have an opinion."

And that clams me up good. Tony looks at the ground, uncomfortable.

Tears of frustration well in my eyes, but I hold them in because I refuse to give Paul the satisfaction. Instead, I wiggle my foot in my boot until I feel the tip of my dagger press my skin. I concentrate on the reassuring pressure until an hour later when I beg off early for the night. I reject Paul's, then Abe's, offer to accompany me back to the Academy.

The following evening, I turn up at Paul's downtown apartment to celebrate Christmas Eve together, same as every year. Unfortunately, we're not destined for a happy holiday.

We have it out almost immediately, beginning when he asks why I'm skipping out on the Magpie job. When I tell him about the overnight with Matthew on Jekyll Island, he loses it. Absolutely loses it. The fight continues for hours. We spiral.

"This has got to stop, Kat," he finally declares. "I can't have this argument anymore. It stops now. Jekyll Island Club or not, you're not going away with him."

"Why are you being difficult about this? *You* told me to get to know him, that he could be *valuable*." I throw his words back at him. "That Jekyll Island and those blasted DaMolin rubies are the ultimate prize!"

"That was before—"

"Before what?" I wait, but Paul doesn't reply. I release a bitter laugh and shake my head. "I guess that's just another point to chalk up on the long list of things you can't tell me, huh? Screw you, Paul. Trust is a two-way street. I'm going with him."

Paul's face darkens. "No. You're not."

"You don't get to tell me who I can and can't see." I narrow my eyes. "You've never minded sharing me with Abe."

"Christ, Kat! That's different. It's *Abe*."

"How is this different?"

"Well, for one thing, I don't imagine Sir Matthew DaMolin is interested in sharing *you* with *me*. Does he even know about me? Or Abe?"

"He does, actually. He knows about you *both*. And he handled the conversation with a lot more maturity and grace than you are."

A flicker of uncertainty flashes across Paul's face, but he covers it with another attack. "I'm sorry to disappoint you, Miss Katarina Quinn. I'm sorry I'm not living up to your newly raised standards."

"That's not what I said. Don't twist my words. *You* set my standard. You always have. It's him who has to worry about competing with *you*. Why don't you see that? I'm trying so desperately to choose you. Why can't you let me? I'm looking for a reason, Paul. *Any* reason. Just give me one."

Ask me. I look at him, beseeching. *Tell me it's me, only me, for you. Always.*

He stares straight back, unyielding, stubborn as the day is long.

When he finally speaks, it's not what I want to hear. "What have you told him about us? Have you compromised us for him?"

I'm struck dumb, so hurt by the question, I can't immediately answer.

"You know the motto," Paul breathes. Ice fills my veins. "Fool me once, Katarina..."

"I'm not fooling you. I would *never* risk you, or Abe, or Tony," I plead, tears rising. "It's a shame I can't say the same about you."

"What?"

"You're clearly willing to risk them by pushing ahead with this revenge scheme of yours. And your behavior tonight shows you're willing to risk losing me too."

With that, I rise from my chair, grab my coat, and run out of the apartment.

This love we have is all-consuming. Volatile, combustible.

But on nights like this, I truly wonder if both of us will make it out alive.

THERE'S NO THINKING. No hesitation. I go straight to the bayou house.

Abe and Tony are bumming around in the kitchen when I torpedo through the door. I stand in the entryway, shaking with both anger and cold. I never put on my coat; it's still bunched up in my fist.

Abe takes in my red-rimmed eyes and devastated face. "Oh, Kat."

I let out a tiny, pitiful wail before hurtling into his arms.

Tony walks around the table and hugs me from behind. "Mmm, it's a gringa sandwich," he mumbles into my shoulder. "It tastes so good."

He does his job well. I sniffle out a laugh.

"You shouldn't let him upset you like this," Abe tells me. "He's an idiot."

"He is, isn't he?" I agree with another sniffle.

"He is."

"You see, I know that." I pull back a little, enough to look at Abe. "Logically, I know it..."

"But?" Abe prompts.

"But why does it hurt so much?" I bury my face back in his chest. "He's *hurting* me, Abe. I don't want to feel like this anymore. And I don't know how to fix it. It just feels broken."

They stay with me in the kitchen for an hour, letting me get it all out. They listen, and they're there. When I'm finally all cried out, I do something I've never done before. I walk into Abe's room, forsaking the master bedroom, with him and Tony. And all three of us curl up on his bed and go to sleep.

It's another gringa sandwich. And it feels so good.

PAUL DOESN'T COME OVER on Christmas morning. Or afternoon. Or evening.

By the time night falls, the three of us are locked in a heated card game. When I'm laughing and playing with the guys, I can almost forget what a miserable Christmas this has been. But then Abe excuses himself for the bathroom, and I sigh, slipping back into a morose state. Absentmindedly, my eyes follow his back as he disappears.

"It's okay to love them both, Kat," Tony tells me softly, putting down his cards. "I do too. A little differently than you, I think, but still. It doesn't make you a bad person. El corazón quiere lo que quiere."

I look at him, surprised. He's referring to Paul and Abe, which means he only has two-thirds of the story.

"What about three?" I ask. "Does loving all three make me a bad person?"

"The *doctor*? Really?"

"Maybe." I take a deep breath as I try to explain. "Abe is my rock. Paul is my lifeline. And Matthew...when I'm with him, Tony...sometimes, it feels like Matthew is becoming my everything."

"That sounds rather serious." Tony sits back. "Paul knows?"

"He suspects. And he doesn't like it."

"Of course he doesn't like it, Kat. You're doing to him what you do to Abe—making him watch something that hurts."

"It's not like that with Abe. He doesn't mind. We've talked about it. A lot."

"He tells you he doesn't mind, Kat. That doesn't make it true. We have a saying back in Cuba, amor y celos, hermanos gemelos. Do you know what that means, gringa?"

"No."

"Love and jealousy, twin siblings." He crosses two fingers to demonstrate. "And you, Kat...I love you, but you've perfected this act. Abe was a dress rehearsal. The doctor's the real deal."

I'm saved from having to reply when Abe returns from the bathroom, but guilt taints my fingers and heart as we return to our game. There's no saving my mood this time, and the night quickly tilts to its inevitable conclusion.

We're packing the cards away when Paul stumbles through the door, completely and wildly drunk.

"Katarina," he slurs. He hangs off the door in the entry hall. "I knew you'd be here."

Tony scoots closer to me on the couch. Abe rises from his chair.

"Katarina." Paul tries to come closer, but he trips over the rug and crashes into the table.

Abe walks over to steady Paul by his shoulders. "Let's get you to bed. You can talk to Kat in the morning, okay?"

"You." He looks at Abe, storm clouds brewing on his face. "You have some balls, Abe." Paul gives him a shove backward. Right in the chest. It's not hard, but Abe isn't amused.

Tony gets off the couch. Wary.

"Where were you last night, Abe?" Paul asks. "Were you balls deep in my girl?"

"Paul!" I cry out.

Abe takes a deep breath. It sounds deadly, even from across the room. "I was right here, asshole. So was Tony. Where *you* should have been. With her."

Tony splits the two apart. "Yes, but not balls deep," he elucidates, putting a hand on Paul's heaving chest. "No one was balls deep anywhere last night. Come on, hermano, let's get you to bed."

Paul lets Tony tug him forward, but before they get to his bedroom, he turns back for me. "Kat?"

I wait, my arms and legs crossed, wound tighter than a pretzel.

"I'm really sorry," he finally says.

I blink twice, disarmed. Paul disappears into his bedroom.

I decide to sleep in Abe's room again. Tony doesn't follow us though, and without the buffer of his presence, I'm not sure how to behave. I turn on my side, away from Abe as he sinks onto the bed. The springs feel rigged to blow, like even the barest of wrong breaths may light the fuse.

"Don't worry, Kat," Abe says. He sounds exhausted. "I'm not going to touch you."

"Sorry." I roll back over toward him, shamefaced.

"It's okay. It doesn't mean I don't love you."

"I love you too, Abe," I whisper as he closes his eyes.

We're quiet for a few moments, but I need to say something before he falls asleep. I need to close this door. "Hey, Abe?"

"Yeah?" His lids crack open.

"Tony said something earlier."

"Tony's an idiot," Abe replies swiftly, punching his pillow before settling back in. "Whatever he said, you shouldn't listen."

"It was about you and me. And Paul. He said sometimes...it hurts you. What we do."

Abe takes a slow, deep breath. I wait, reading every flicker crossing his face.

"There was a time when it did," he admits, "but we're older now, Kat, and I've finally realized something. I used to think physical expression of love was the ultimate. I thought it was how you showed someone you love them completely. But it's not. The love I feel for you, it doesn't need to be physical to validate it. I don't think we're built to last that way."

"What happened for my birthday...that was the last time, Abe."

"I know it was. I saw you with the doctor last week, remember? I know where this is headed, and it's nothing I want to be a part of. You can trust me when I say I'm okay with it. I will always love you, but the bank is closed now. For good."

I laugh.

"You ready to fall asleep now, Kat? You feel better?"

"I do. Goodnight, Abe."

"Goodnight, little wolf."

We fall asleep beside each other, not touching. But he's there, and he lets me stay, even though I'm offering nothing more than my tired, plaintive self. It's a kindness, and I realize, suddenly, that's how Abe has always shown he loves me—with kindness. It's quiet sometimes, but that doesn't make it any less real.

I burrow down in my blankets and close my eyes. It's a very good night of sleep, the restorative kind. No dreams, no nightmares, just the endless, warm arms of rest. I wish it could go on forever.

"Get out."

I jolt awake to Paul's voice. He's standing over the bed, rustling Abe's foot. Daylight streams into the room.

"*Out.*"

If Abe is annoyed at being kicked out of his own bed—and I'm sure he is—he doesn't show it. He silently gets up and strides from the room, closing the door behind him. "Don't screw on my bed," he hollers through the wood, an afterthought.

I almost laugh, and Paul nearly does too. It's the icebreaker we so badly need, the familiarity we've lost. Paul sinks down on Abe's mattress with a heavy sigh.

"Is this your room now?" I hear sadness, not accusation, in his tone.

"No, Paul, but you really tied one on last night. You were corked."

"I know. I'm sorry. I was upset. You're my blind spot, Kat. I don't always see or think clearly where you're concerned. In fact, I don't think I'm making clearheaded decisions at all lately." He rubs his face. "You're right. We'll wait on the Magpie job. There's no rush. But there's something else...I need you to be honest right now. What else do you need from me?"

"I need you to treat me like a real partner, Paul. That means when you have a problem with me, you communicate calmly and rationally. Like an adult. And I don't want any cheap shots taken at Matthew in the process. He doesn't take them at you, so stop taking them at him."

Paul opens his mouth to interject, but I raise a finger because I'm not done.

"And I need you to let me figure things out on my own for a while. Even if it hurts you. I'm sorry about that, but you gave your permission. You told me to do this. I didn't intend for it to happen, but emotions got involved. I like him. And I'm done feeling guilty for something you instigated."

Paul focuses on his lap. "You're saying I made my bed, and now I have to lie in it?"

"Essentially."

He nods slowly. "How would you feel if I spent New Year's Eve with someone else, Kat?" he says, raising his eyes to mine. "If I kissed someone else at midnight? Whispered New Year's promises to another woman?"

This is what I wanted to hear from him last night, honesty and vulnerability, but it's come twenty-four hours too late. There's no way to know if these are true feelings, or just after-the-fact rationality. More manipulation.

"I wouldn't like it," I answer, "but I also wouldn't be allowed to care. You've made me no promises, Paul. Don't think I'm not aware of it. I'm still not entirely sure what's more hurt—your pride or your actual feelings."

It's nearly imperceptible, but Paul's mouth tightens. "Okay."

"I'll see you when I get back from the holiday. While I'm gone, I want you to know I'll miss you. Because I always miss you when we aren't together, Paul. It's not a zero-sum game. When he gains, you don't lose. So stop worrying about what I'm doing with him and just concentrate on showing me why it's been you and me all these years. I'm starting to forget."

Paul's fingers flex. His jaw ticks. "I know, I'm sorry. I want you to go. I want you to have fun. If you want to screw him while you're gone, then I even want you to do that. Because when this is all over, when we end up together, I don't want you to have any doubts." He pins his gaze to mine, the old smolder burning low. "I didn't make you promises because I didn't think I needed to. It's always been us, Kat. It always will be."

CHAPTER TWENTY

"AND THEN, WHEN THEY finally plucked up and asked, my father told them," J.P.—Jack—Morgan Jr. cackles, "'If you have to consider the cost, then you have no business buying a yacht!'"

I toss my head back and let out a pealing laugh, resting my fingers on Constance Pulitzer's arm. We giggle like schoolgirls and share a smile. Matthew, on my right, grins into his champagne glass.

"Oh, indeed," Constance trills. "And tell me, did you bring the *Corsair* down this year, like usual?"

"But of course." He gives a sharp puff of his Cuban cigar, and I inhale, sucking the spiced smoke into my nostrils with a suppressed, gleeful shiver. High on proximity.

"Tradition is what tradition does, eh?" Ethan chimes in.

Jack puffs again. "Now isn't that the truth? S'good to be back for another season." He gazes fondly around the Victorian clubhouse.

It's an hour to midnight on December 31, 1919, and the Jekyll Island Club is abuzz with festivity. Despite its looming mid-January deadline, not a trace of the Volstead Act and Prohibition threatens these hallowed walls. Tonight, waiters in full livery circulate with gleaming silver trays, endlessly replenishing champagne and cigars. Two romantically dimmed crystal chandeliers glisten overhead, casting long, twinkling shadows from wall-to-wall. Eight towering Christmas trees with Swarovski ornaments and platinum garland flank the room. And the guests...well, the guests shine brightest of all. Dressed to the nines—white tails, evening gowns, pocket watches, and diamonds.

Every inch of this exclusive soirée drips with old money. I can taste it in the back of my throat, fizzing swallows of crisp vintage champagne. Burning like tendrils of smoke from Morgan's Cuban cigar. Money lit on fire.

The night began with endless rounds of introductions and small talk, with subtly raised brows and scrutinizing eyes. A room full of lions thinking perhaps I, the newcomer in their ranks, am a sheep.

But blood, not money, drips in the back of my throat. I am a predator disguised as prey.

And in that role, I dazzle.

Perhaps it was my entrance on Matthew DaMolin's arm, his gifted diamonds sparkling in my ears. Perhaps it was when Constance Pulitzer declared herself so enamored with my gown—Coco Chanel, white, couture—that she simply *had* to introduce me to her friends. Perhaps it was the moment I sliced the neck off the Pol Roger Vintage champagne with the Marquess of Queensberry's saber, causing an uproariously glorious cascade of nectar to slosh over thrust-forward flutes.

A newcomer to the scene, they whisper behind my back, *but perhaps one to watch.*

Perhaps, perhaps, perhaps...

Perhaps I am a wolf.

Perhaps I play this game to *win*.

And with an hour to midnight, winning I am. Matthew's bright, happy eyes, oozing with near reverent worship, tell me nothing less. Tonight—together—we are invincible.

"I'm usually a wallflower at these parties," he murmurs in my ear, his nose brushing my temple. "You've never been a wallflower a day in your life, have you?"

I chuckle and turn to him, boldly lacing my fingers behind his neck. Invincible indeed.

"I refuse to believe you've ever been a wallflower, Matt."

At a quarter to midnight, the guests trickle outside for the culminating pièce de résistance—a spectacular fireworks extravaganza. There's a bottleneck at the double doors to the veranda, where ladies' arms are looped through gentlemen's, all stuttering footsteps and hesitating limbs as an elaborate dance of inebriated, door-holding chivalry plays out.

Matthew and I hover behind to allow Ethan, who's fallen in step, laughing with Harry Astor, to pass ahead of us in the crowd. I wrinkle my nose, certain the shared joke is something biting and faintly off-color. The only setback in our evening thus far was a short but rather unpleasant discourse with Harry at the start of the night.

He took one look at the diamonds in my ears and the comfortable drape of Matthew's arm around my waist before delivering his most unwelcome two cents. "How long has this been going on, Matt?" he asked, pointing to me.

"Um…" Matthew glanced at me with a small smile. "I don't know. A few months?"

"I thought you were just messing her around at Academy events. I never imagined it was serious," Harry continued, his tone disparaging.

Matthew was unperturbed. "I don't think it's your business either way, Harry."

"I only wonder where you see this headed. With her history, she's hardly a suitable match for a DaMolin."

Matthew's eyes narrowed at that comment, but I squeezed his arm, silencing him. We took our leave posthaste, and Constance Pulitzer, social butterfly she is, appeared and swept us away to greener pastures.

Blankets are distributed amongst the crowd outdoors as we await the impending display. Matthew and I stake out a secluded spot on the fringes of the manicured front lawn. We angle ourselves toward the river, where the fireworks will be launched. I can just make out the shadowy skeleton of a barge in the distance.

"Is your champagne empty?" Matthew asks. He's already wiggling his shoulders out from under our shared blanket to get a refill.

"It's fine. I don't want you to miss midnight."

"I'm out too." He raises his glass. "I want us to toast the New Year together. I'll be back in two minutes."

Reluctantly, I hold still while he drapes a pleasantly scratchy, cashmere-disguised-as-tweed shrug around my shoulders. Then he lopes toward the veranda in search of another round.

"Are you having a nice evening, Katarina?" Lady Genevieve materializes beside me. Her silver skirts rustle quietly, almost ghostlike, as she draws to a stop on the lawn.

"Oh, yes." I smile hesitantly, oddly nervous. "Thank you for inviting me as a guest of your family. It's been an evening I'll never forget, one of the best of my life."

"That's kind of you to say. I'm so glad you're enjoying yourself."

"I am. I've never been to a party like this. I mean, before the Academy, before Matthew...my life was very different."

She considers her words before she speaks. "Katarina, I remember you well from your interview. Girls like you don't come around often, but they are why I love what I do. I wonder, do you remember the interview?"

"Of course, bits and pieces."

"I remember bits and pieces too, some parts better than others. What I remember most is the moment one of the board members asked you to tell us why you believed you should be given one of the prized seats at the Academy over a better prepared girl from a nice upper-class family. Do you remember what you said?"

"No," I admit.

"He asked why you should be given a spot over another girl, and your response was, 'Why shouldn't I be? She's no more deserving than I am.' And you had this glint in your eye when you said it, Kat, like you were just daring him to disagree. And then you said, 'And frankly, I'm a far better investment than any of those other girls, because I understand hard work, and I will work interminably hard to be here.'"

I nod, remembering as she recounts the story. It was one of the few moments, possibly the only moment, when my wolf broke free. Biting and clawing the way she's done since I was six years old.

"I knew we had to have you, Kat," Lady Genevieve continues. "Your story is not unlike my own. I come from the wrong side of town myself, but I've never let it stop me. You just have to be a little bit faster, a little bit smarter, a little bit luckier. I gave you a bit of luck the day I accepted you to Telfair, but the rest you've done on your own. You've more than proven yourself worth the investment."

Much of what she says is true, but then I think of Tony, whose Latin accent, and Abe, whose dark skin, mean doors forever slammed in their faces. Doors no amount of luck or determination will open. What kind of place could our world be if there were more Genevieves and Matthews out there, opening access to institutions like Telfair and respectable jobs to *everyone*?

I swallow hard. "It means a lot to hear you say that. Thank you."

I catch sight of Matthew in the distance, fresh bottle of Pol Roger and flutes in hand. He salutes me with the bottle and smiles so wide, it socks me in the gut from all the way across the lawn.

Lady Genevieve observes us for a moment, then turns back to me. "It's been a pleasure to have you here with us tonight, Katarina. You make my son very happy, it's plain to see. And no matter what your other accomplishments or history may be, that's all a mother really cares about."

"He makes me very happy too," I reply quietly.

"Coming from different worlds...it doesn't matter so much at the end of the day. As long as you understand what makes you similar—that will always be far more important than what makes you different. After will always be more important than before."

I stay silent, uncertain.

"And as a mother," she continues, taking a deep breath, "I don't care where you've been before, Kat. I only care about where you're going and what you plan to do when you get there. What you plan to do with my son's heart once he's given it to you."

I continue looking at her. My palms start to sweat.

"Because he will give it to you. He already has, whether he realizes it or not. And all the rest"—she waves her hand at the glamour surrounding us—"is immaterial."

Immaterial? Is it though?

"I..."

"It's okay." She stops me, reaching out with a gentle hand. "You don't have to say anything. I just hope you know that if you want it, this can be your family too. You have a place with us, and there's no rush. It'll be right here waiting, if and when you're ready."

As Matthew comes to my side, his mother gives his cheek a soft pat. "Happy New Year, darling." She disappears into the crowd.

"Dare I ask?" Matthew hands me a fresh glass.

I laugh as I fib, a half lie, half truth slipping from my lips. "Just girl talk. I quite like your mother, Matt. She's progressive."

"You're two of a kind," he murmurs, pouring champagne. "There are about sixty seconds left in 1919, Katarina. What should we toast to?"

I raise my glass, clinking the edge to his. The crystal *ding* is ringing and pure.

"To the 1920s," I decide. "And to us."

"To us *in* the 1920s. Together," Matthew amends. His eyebrows lift, his silent question hanging in the air. The crowd is counting down the seconds around us, but I'm locked on him. Their voices fade to a dull roar.

"To us in the 1920s," I repeat slowly, tasting the words. "Together."

I toss back the drink. Matthew's eyes flicker, then hold on me. He takes his own tiny sip, then a slow breath. "Katarina, I—"

An explosion rockets into the air, and my gaze snaps away from his face. Gold erupts in a fiery blast overhead as the crowd screeches, *"Happy New Year!"*

Breathless, I turn back to Matthew. The burnished glow of the fast-fading opening salvo illuminates his face. Wordlessly, his right hand wends behind my neck and into my hair. He presses his lips to mine as the next firework launches. The explosion is both in me and around me, overhead and underfoot.

"Happy New Year, Kat," he murmurs against my lips.

My heart explodes into the sky.

<hr />

MATTHEW DEPOSITS ME AT the door to my room in Cherokee Cottage shortly after the fireworks display concludes.

"Is this goodnight then?" I whisper, checking up and down the hallway for an audience. I sense the ghost of Ethan's presence, just one crass joke or lewd insinuation away.

"It is." Matthew squeezes my hand. "Gentlemanly best behavior, remember? Those were the terms of the deal."

I crack my door. Raise a suggestive brow. "Perhaps I'd like to renegotiate."

"Don't tempt me, Katarina," he rumbles, moving a few inches closer.

"I can be pretty persuasive." I'm whispering again, even though the hallway is most certainly empty.

"And I'm a pushover," he replies. "We've been here before."

I latch my fingers into his lapels and yank. "I seem to remember *winning*."

Matthew stumbles into me. One hand moves, magnetized and possessed, to my hip. But the other stubbornly grips my doorframe, stopping our backward momentum.

He grits his teeth, exhaling barely an inch from my lips. "Not this time, Kat."

I pout and peer up through long lashes, giving him my very best nonverbal plea.

He laughs before kissing me, and somehow, it's deliciously sweet and terribly, terribly sinful all at once. Full of things promised but not given. When he pulls back, I'm left wanting.

"Matthew DaMolin, I do declare," I breathe, eyes searching. "I think you were the most unexpected twist of 1919."

He chuckles again. "That's high praise, coming from you. And you know what? I like knowing I'm both your last kiss of 1919 and the first of 1920. I like when you belong only to me, Kat."

I jolt, surprised to realize it's the first time I've thought of Paul all night. It's strangely damning, that realization. I run from it.

"Is being my first *kiss* of 1920 all you want, Matthew?"

"I'm not sure, but I'm not going to stay long enough to find out. Goodnight, Kat."

I'm disappointed when he moves away, but I step back over the threshold to my room nonetheless. "Goodnight, Matt."

When the door clicks shut between us, I sigh and slump forward against it, then close my eyes, thinking and breathing.

Paul, invited in by Matthew, slinks to the forefront of my mind. Looming. Prowling. The specter of countless New Year's kisses flits across my lips. I squeeze my eyes against the guilt.

Guilt, but not regret.

I breathe in and out, reliving the night in my mind. The feel of Matthew's tuxedoed arm beneath my fingers, the bright white of the bow tie against his neck. The luxurious taste of champagne gliding down my throat. The live wire of laughter buzzing from Constance Pulitzer's lips to my ear. The persistent glitter in the periphery of my vision, the glitter of priceless gemstones flashing about the room.

And me, walking through the wealthiest sea of people on the planet, somehow *belonging* there. Belonging in this place, where poets and vagabonds go to die. Where I used to think only the soulless live, people worth stealing from because they, in their ivory towers, deserve it. And maybe some—most—of them do.

But Matthew is here. And when I'm with him...

When I'm with him, everything I thought I knew and believed about the world has an annoying tendency to go sideways.

I don't like these thoughts. Don't like them one bit. I peel myself off the door and go to the mirror instead. I stare at my reflection, and God help me, I like what I see. This woman in a white gown, who can hold her own at parties on Matthew DaMolin's arm and breathe the same cigar-tainted air as Jack Morgan...I *like* her.

I *am* her, aren't I?

The swirling, blurring lines of the con and the truth choke me. I've told Matthew so few lies and so many truths, yet an ocean of things unsaid still swells between us. And I wonder what would happen if I simply...let him see everything? Am I really so bad for wanting to have it all?

I shiver, chastised by the thought.

He would leave, you silly girl, I tell myself. *If he knew the whole truth, he would be gone in a heartbeat. Expect nothing less.*

You aren't meant to be seen, Katarina. My mother's haunting voice. *If he can't see you, he'll never catch you, will never leave you.*

I spin away from the mirror in a swirl of skirts. These are dangerous thoughts, and I don't want to be alone with them tonight. I simply can't stand it.

In three strides, I'm back at my door, slipping soundlessly into the hallway. It's pitch dark, but Matthew's bedroom is just a few paces away. My heart rate ratchets up as the familiar thrill of evading detection rises. I slink down the hall, pausing outside his door. There's a faint, flickering glow, a lit candle perhaps. I don't knock, don't think; I just wrap my fingers around the knob and turn.

I blink twice as I slip inside, adjusting to the candlelight.

Then twice more as I take in the jarring sight before me.

Two bodies twined in each other. Two tuxedo jackets haphazardly tossed, abandoned, on the bed. Two joined silhouettes in dim light—one standing, head tipped back, mouth slackened, the other kneeling, head pressed to waist. A pair of pants around a set of ankles, thick black socks stretching over calves. Calves transitioning into powerful thighs, a bare waist, broad shoulders, a familiar jawline, dark hair...

Not Matthew's room, I realize. Ethan's.

Ethan with shocked eyes and mouth agape, his gaze whipping toward me. Harry Astor, falling back on kneeling haunches in horrified surprise.

"Fuck," I gasp. "Holy fuck." I slam a hand over my eyes and scuttle backward through the door. "I'm sorry...I didn't...I'm sorry!"

I slam Ethan's door in a fluster and fly down the hallway to my own room. With trembling fingers, I thrust open the door, then shut it behind me.

Holy. Fuck.

Ethan and Harry Astor? I rub my hands over my face, trying to scrub away what I just witnessed.

I've seen all types in the Catacombs. Men loving men is not foreign to me, doesn't shock me the way it might some. Christ, I've seen Tony swing both ways.

But *Ethan*? Womanizing, incorrigible Ethan? Heir to the DaMolin empire—that Ethan?

It doesn't add up. It plain and simply doesn't make sense.

Except...except I *saw* Ethan at Harry's house, all those months ago, in the dead of night. When we were casing Astor Manor. I watched them share a cigarette before disappearing inside together.

A quiet knock sounds at my door.

Fuck. "Come in," I murmur. I swallow hard as—a mercifully fully-clothed—Ethan slips inside.

"To avoid future confusion," he begins, clearing his throat, "Matt's room is the last door at the end of the hall. Mine is second to last."

My cheeks burn. "Ah. Got it."

We're both quiet, staring at the other. The secret hanging between us chokes the air from the room.

"Kat, about what you saw—"

I raise a hand to stop him. "I didn't see anything."

"Kat—"

"Honestly, Ethan," I say. "I saw nothing. I'll say nothing. I stayed in my room all night, slept the best sleep of my life here at Cherokee. That's all anyone will ever hear from me."

"Thank you." He sighs, stepping deeper into the room. He leans on the wall and closes his eyes. "It's nothing anyway. Harry made that very clear before he departed. We won't see each other again."

"I–I'm really sorry," I stammer. "I didn't mean to—"

"It's not your fault, Kat," he mumbles. "Harry and I were reckless. We're usually faultlessly careful—as military men, as *gentlemen*, we have to be—but it's New Year's, and we're both a bit corked. We were asking for trouble. But as I told you, it won't happen again. It's best we all just forget it. Move on."

"What you do in your own room of your own house isn't anybody's business but your own," I insist.

He smiles sadly at me. "It's not my house yet, Kat. It may never be."

"Well, that would be an absolute travesty. One I would never forgive your parents for."

Ethan looks at me then, *really* looks. His gaze sweeps me from head to toe, assessing, burning a trail across my skin. He pushes himself off the wall and comes closer, a slight frown on his face as his hand reaches for my head. My instinct is to pull away, but I freeze.

"You really *aren't* like the others, are you?" he murmurs. His fingers come to rest on my ear. He tweaks gently at Matthew's gifted earrings. "Or *are* you? These are real diamonds. Where the hell did you get these, Catacomb girl?"

My cheeks bleed pink again. "They're from your brother."

"From *Matthew*?" He drops his hand, incredulous. "Just how serious are you about my brother, Kat?"

"Um." I lick my lips.

"What I mean is, he's not just a meal ticket?"

"No!" Everything in me clenches against the accusation. I look at him with hard eyes, ready to rip his throat out for even suggesting it.

Ethan watches me, meeting my fire head-on. After a moment, he blinks in surprise and steps back. "Oh. Wow."

"Wow, what?" My stomach turns over, wondering which part of me has been found out—the side playing Matthew or the one falling in love with him. I don't know which I'm more afraid of.

Ethan has moved all the way back to my door. His fingers close blindly around the knob, and suddenly, teasing cocksure Ethan is back. A devilish smile blooms. "A secret for a secret, right? I won't tell if you won't, Katarina."

"Tell what?" My brows are sharp.

"Exactly." He winks. "I shouldn't be here. This has the makings of a terrible scandal. Goodnight, Katarina. See you around. And...take care of Matthew, okay?"

The barest hint of softening flashes in his eyes before he departs. Vulnerability. There and gone in an instant.

I'm not entirely sure how a moment that was supposed to be about Ethan's hidden love turned into one about my own, but darned if that man didn't manage it.

A secret for a secret, I muse. What a dangerous little game.

CHAPTER TWENTY-ONE

A FEW DAYS AFTER returning from Jekyll Island, I go to the bayou loft to meet the Royals. We're conducting another night of surveillance at the Magpies' riverfront hideout.

"How was your trip?" Paul asks.

Tony and Abe pull their shoes on by the door, listening.

"It was good." I offer nothing more.

A little tentatively, Paul leans in to hug me. "I missed you."

"I missed you too." I sink into him, and his muscles relax.

He doesn't ask anything more—nothing about the Jekyll Island Club or Matthew or his family. And I don't volunteer a word. My relationship with Matthew is no longer up for discussion.

Under the cover of darkness, we hover at the docks near the Magpie clipper ship all night, inspecting the people coming and going.

"This is going to be a hard task," I observe, watching Magpies carry crates of supplies up and down the gangplank. I point to the churning river, then the smooth wooden hull of the bobbing ship. "I can't climb that. We'll have to fight our way in."

"You don't need to sneak in, you just need to be able to get out," Paul says, eyeing the ship's rigging.

I study the complicated web of interconnected ropes, assess the distance of a swing from deck to shore. I gnaw on my cheek, mulling it over before nodding. "I can extract quickly. But I have to get *in* first." I gesture to the armed guards sitting dockside. "And they have guns."

We've seen eight people man the ship during our stakeouts, always three standing watch outside while the rest cluster aboard. It's a tall order but not impossible. The guns make me very nervous.

"I'm not sure about this, Paul." I turn to face him. "Is it really necessary? We took out nearly half the gang at Farley's, isn't that enough? They're crippled."

"I don't want them crippled. We made that mistake once before with Damien. This time, I want them *gone*. Their guns too."

I nod, drumming my nails on my leg. Still worried.

Paul takes my hand to stop my fingers. He leans in and softly kisses me. "I won't let anything happen to you, Kitty-Kat."

"It's not only me I'm worried about."

"It's a good plan, Kat. One we've used to great effect before."

"For much smaller jobs, with far fewer guns," I point out. "No guns, really."

"We'll disable the guns first. Abe will have your bag, and we'll get you inside. The rest will be quick."

"Okay." I let him convince me.

"We'll run the job next week," Paul says. "In the meantime, Abe, pick someone to tail during the day. Start tomorrow. A different person each day. I want a better idea of what they're doing and what they're moving. I don't want to run into any surprises when Kat gets onto the ship."

"I can't do it tomorrow," Abe says, "but I'll start the day after."

All three of us turn to stare at him.

"I'm working tomorrow," he explains carefully. "I picked up a job."

"A job?" Tony asks. "Doing what?"

"It's a security position downtown. Just for extra cash."

"If you need scratch," Paul says, "you got it. You don't need to take a job, Abe. There's plenty to go around."

"It's okay. I'm actually interested in the position. It's a good opportunity. I'll learn a lot."

Paul is puzzled, but he doesn't argue further. "Fine. Tony, you're up tomorrow. Take your pick."

"Tubby." He points at a large lump of a man on watch now. He's propped on a barrel with his head tilted back, half asleep on the job.

"Good choice." Abe laughs. "He looks like a real go-getter."

When we pack it in for the night, Paul walks to the streetcar with me. To my surprise, he rides back to the Academy, then walks me all the way to my window.

"Wow, full door-to-door service tonight," I tease.

"If I could crawl up there and fall asleep with you, I would do that too."

"Mellie would have a conniption."

He smiles at me, and it's achingly familiar, his crooked and shifty little grin.

"I've missed you so much, Kat," he tells me again, stepping closer. He slides his arms around my back and tucks me into his chest. He breathes me in for a moment, and I do the same with him. Faded smoke and cedarwood, crisp air. Pure Paul.

When he reaches for my chin, I give it to him. I let him tip my face up. When he does, I identify something unfamiliar in his eyes: uncertainty.

Paul is never uncertain.

I freeze, wondering—not for the first time—if something has broken between us. Something potentially irreparable.

He sighs and leans his forehead against mine. We stand together, just like that, for a while, neither of us saying anything. Just breathing. Without any prompting, our breaths gradually get heavier, a little faster. We sneak peeks at each other and slowly, my heart comes alive. Paul licks his lips and looks at mine.

"You don't have to ask," I whisper.

His eyes grow molten, and when our lips meet, he pours himself into me. He presses me to the brick wall and kisses me with everything he's got. Over and over again. And oh, can that boy kiss. He kisses me silly. Until I'm blue in the face and not sure what my first name is.

"Kat," he whispers against my lips.

That's right. I'm Kat. And this is...

"Paul," I whisper back.

He pulls away. "It's been a long time since you blue balled me, but tonight, I'm gonna let it slide and say goodnight."

I laugh lightly. "Okay. Goodnight, Paul."

"Goodnight, doll." He reaches for my waist and lifts me onto the wall, lightly swatting my behind as I scamper up. I swing through the window and turn to wave, but he's already melted into the darkness. I laugh again and, hoping Mellie won't stir, release the tiniest, quietest of howls out the window. I hold my breath and wait.

He doesn't disappoint. Hardly a moment later, I hear him, a playful yip from somewhere down the dark street. I don't need to see him to feel his eyes on me. With Paul, I always know.

CHAPTER TWENTY-TWO

"Matthew DaMolin?" I inquire. Per usual, the mere mention of his name proves the golden ticket.

"Oh, Doc Matt?" The security guard at the hospital door gives me a second look. "He hasn't left yet, and without an impetus, he likely never will." He checks with his partner for affirmation.

"Why don't you take her inside, James? Light a fire under the good doctor," the second guard says. "I'll be fine here."

"Where do you think he is?"

"Where he always is." The guard chuckles. "The pit."

James jerks his head for me to follow. I trail behind him, down several twisting, sterile hallways, past countless sets of double doors, up a derelict back stairwell. The guard pushes through a set of marked doors, and I step into a new world.

"The pit." The guard nods. "We've got a few small, dedicated medical and surgical wards, but you're lucky to get one of those beds. This is where most end up. Overflow."

"I see," I manage, finding my voice.

The pit is cavernous, a ballroom filled with none of the usual old-world trappings save high ceilings and wide windows. It's stuffed wall-to-wall with beds, four rows down its length. Some separated by freestanding screens, almost all filled with people. Grimacing people, coughing people, sleeping people. People with sallow skin and bruised eyes. Tired people.

Sick people.

I realize I'm holding my breath and release it in a rush, but I hesitate to take another. The air tastes different here. Sour. Infected. I, who make a living walking on highwires and sliding down drainpipes, feel nearly overcome in this sickroom.

"I'll help you find him," the guard kindly offers.

"Thank you," I murmur, faint with relief.

I follow him into the depths of the pit. We walk down aisles, passing beds. Endless beds.

"I hear him." I'd know his voice anywhere. He's just beyond the next screen, talking to a patient. Unable to help myself, I peek around the boundary.

A white-coat-clad Matthew leans over the bed with his stethoscope, listening and nodding as the man in the bed recounts something. Matt's fingers move over the man's abdomen, pressing while he asks questions. He flicks his hair out of his eyes to meet the patient's gaze as he speaks. He's fully absorbed.

The deftness to his fingers and unassuming confidence of his bedside stance tug my heart clear into my throat. I retreat, hiding behind the screen to sort out the immense feeling of love washing over me. It surprises me—not the fact it's there, rather that this is the time and place it chose to fully and unapologetically rear its head. Not at a fancy, exclusive party or under a firework-lit sky, but *here*. In a place surrounded by the masses of humanity.

I close my eyes, heart thudding. Blood pounds in my ears.

That, I tell myself, is an incredible man right there. Right in front of me.

Abstractly, I've always known it. This isn't the first time he's shown me. He does it time and time again, in a million small ways. But right now, his care, concern, and kindness aren't directed at me. And it's watching him give himself away to a complete stranger that ultimately takes me out at the knees.

"Katarina?"

My eyes open and there he is. Right in front of me. All his care and concern and attention now mine.

I open my mouth, then close it.

"Kat?" He's confused. "What are you doing here? I'm sorry I'm late for our date. We're absolutely slammed." He nods to the line of full beds.

That's right, I remember distantly. I came because he was over an hour late for our date.

"It's okay," I whisper.

"How did you even get in?" His eyes silently laugh at me, at my obvious discomfort.

"Honestly, I'm not quite sure." I lower my lashes. Afraid if I meet his gaze for even one minute, he'll see it in my eyes. The love. And then he'll know. My voice speeds up. "I shouldn't be here...I don't know how I ended up here at all."

"Kat." He reaches for my arm. "Kat, it's okay. Don't worry. It's fine."

"I'm so sorry. I'm not trying to rush you."

"I know you're not. I'm almost done. I just need to throw some stitches in bed seven and order an x-ray for this fella." He jerks his head over his shoulder. "Then I can leave."

"Okay."

"I don't want you to wait. I'll be maybe twenty or thirty minutes here, but in the meantime, take these and go to my apartment." He fishes in his pocket to pull out a set of keys. "It's 1052 Jones Street."

I accept the keyring from him, the room tilting beneath my feet.

"This key," he says, pressing a silver one into my hand, "will get you into the building. I'm on the top floor, the sixth. 1052 Jones, sixth floor. You'll need this key again at the top of the elevator. You got that?"

"1052 Jones," I repeat feebly.

He frowns and pulls a pen from his pocket. He grabs my hand and inks 1052 on the side of my thumb. "There. So you don't forget. I'll be there as soon as I can. Make yourself at home."

With a final, quick nod, he strides away.

A little dumbfounded, I retrace my steps, following the guard to the hospital entrance.

"Nice to know the doc has a life on the outside," he says, holding open the door to the street for me. "Have a good night, Miss...?"

"Quinn," I answer. "Katarina Quinn. Thank you for your help, James."

"Anytime. A friend of the doc's is a friend of ours. You take care now."

Bundling my hands into my pockets against the cold night air, I set off for Jones Street.

CHAPTER TWENTY-THREE

He would live in the bloody penthouse. Naturally.

I wander slowly from room to room in Matt's apartment. It's a large place for one person. Bigger than Paul's city flat. The ceilings are high, loft-style, the walls decorated with graphic geometric prints. Some of the wallpaper is brushed with light metallic accents, wealth glinting in the periphery. It's tasteful, if not entirely subtle.

I pass through several rooms before finding Matt's pool table, and I smile, running a finger along the thick mahogany edge. There's a credenza in the corner, topped with a glittering array of bottles and decanters. Remotely, I peruse the labels. There are some good ones here. Expensive.

Not that I'm surprised.

I sink down on a velvet couch, staring at the pool table. My eyes trace the craftsmanship as I think about Matthew, about him trusting me to come here for the first time, unsupervised. I think about his bedroom, a few paces down the hall. I imagine his bed, him *in* his bed...

I swallow a shiver. Love and desire make good bedfellows.

Finally, I think about Matthew at the hospital. The quick, self-assured movement of his hands. The casual flick of his hair. The concern and attention in his blue eyes.

Love rises, rushing in. Deep and unrelenting. An undertow I can no longer fight.

I make a decision.

I cross to the pool table to rack up the balls. I grab a crystal decanter of whiskey and put my lips directly to the mouth, sucking it down. Then, whiskey still in hand, I steal into the back hallway. I drag my free fingers along the patterned wall, tracing gold, until I reach his bedroom.

A large, four-poster bed dominates the space...or perhaps just my attention. There's a discarded white undershirt on top of the sheets, likely one Matthew slept in. With a solid *thunk*, I place the decanter on the bedside table, then pull the undershirt over my dress.

I cross to the closet and slip two button-up shirts from hangers. I put them both on. Then a jacket on top. I repeat the layering technique on my bottom half. Finally, I select a discarded fedora to complete my look. Grabbing the decanter and taking another sip, I return to the room with the pool table and chalk up the stick. There's a phonograph on an end table in the corner, so I aimlessly select a record and set the needle to spin. As the notes of a classical requiem fill the air, I settle in to wait.

The distant rattle of the front door announces his arrival. I hold my position, leaning on the table.

"Kat?" he calls.

"Back here."

His footsteps echo from room to room, searching for me. When he reaches the doorway, he pauses. His white physician's coat is slung over one arm, the buttons of his shirt undone at the collar. "Kat? What...what are you wearing?" He squints and walks closer, tossing his coat over the arm of the velvet love seat.

"I want to play pool."

"Okay...are we playing in the arctic?" He gestures to my getup and laughs.

"No." I give him a small smile. "But we're going to play my way tonight. It's a little different from our usual game." I hold his gaze, trying to make the suggestion clear in my eyes.

"Oh really?" Intrigue flashes. "And what way, pray tell, is that?"

I cock my head. "The way that gets me exactly what I want. One piece of clothing at a time."

A long silence. Nothing but eye contact, promise, and unfathomable desire between us. Swelling with every breath, with every pining note from the phonograph.

"That sounds like a dangerous game, Katarina."

"I certainly hope so."

"All right." He licks his lips. "Let me layer myself up, and we'll get started."

"No." I grab his suspenders, stopping him. "You don't get to put on another stitch of clothing. This is the only way it's fair."

"It doesn't seem fair." He bats the brim of the fedora for emphasis. "Though I do have home-field advantage. My table, my balls."

I reach down and boldly place my hand over his crotch. "*My* balls tonight, I think."

He kisses me. Fiercely. So fiercely, I almost abandon the game entirely and yank him onto the table here and now.

"I'll break," he whispers, pulling away to pick up the pool cue. He spots the crystal decanter of whiskey on the edge of the table. Sees my lipstick marks on the mouth. He keeps his eyes on mine as he swallows his own big sip. Then he bends over the table and fires off a smattering break. A solid ball rolls into a side pocket in the scattering. Matt leans on the table. Expectant.

"Don't get too excited." With a laugh, I swipe off the fedora and flick it at him. He catches it midair, then tosses it to the ground.

"I'm only just getting started, Katarina. I have a lot of ground to cover." Briefly, he eyes my ridiculous layers, then turns his attention to the table. He takes aim at another solid and drops it into a nearby pocket.

I bend over obediently and unbuckle one of my T-strap heels. A moment later, the remaining shoe is discarded as well, and I up my strategy. On stocking feet, I walk behind him as he lines up his fourth attempt. I wrap my arms around his middle, my hands teasing the waist of his pants.

"Kat," he warns. "That's against the rules."

"My game, my rules," I murmur and press my lips to his earlobe. I gently nip him as he takes the shot, firing just a hair wide. I let him go, and he snorts, no longer amused.

I score my first stripe in the side pocket, and Matthew wordlessly unhooks his suspenders. His pants drop tantalizingly low on his hips as I bend over again and focus. Every turn is valuable. I have the option of another easy shot, and I knock it down. He pulls off a shoe and tosses it aside.

I peruse the table. My choices are harder now. I sigh and fire off a long pass at the corner pocket, but the ball hits the edge and bounces away. A little reluctantly, I hand the cue to Matthew.

I lose three more articles of clothing in quick succession as he drops solids four, five, and six. I shrug, and his jacket comes off, followed by the long pants under my dress, and finally, the first of his button-up shirts.

On my next turn, I take Matt's second shoe. Unfortunately, when I bend again to aim, he comes behind me and uses my own trick against me. Predictably, I miss.

I turn to mock glare at Matt.

"I don't have much left." He gestures to his shirt and trousers. "I need to play good defense."

He only has one solid on the table, and the ebony eight ball sits right outside a corner pocket, just begging to be dropped. His gaze darts, calculating angles.

"Looks like a tough shot," I comment, flippant.

"You're undervaluing both my skill and motivation." He walks around the table until he's satisfied. "I've been waiting for this moment since the words 'strip pool' first slipped from your beautiful mouth."

"Your patience astounds me."

"It shouldn't. I'm so jealous of those other fellas, I could snap their necks."

"I thought you liked Abe," I tease.

"He will never play this game with you again. From now on, it's *mine*."

He fires off his shot. The cue ball whips across the felt, rebounds on a wall, and taps his target. The solid rolls slowly, teetering on the edge before dropping into the pocket.

I exhale in disbelief and slowly unbutton the last shirt. I'm standing before him in only my dress and his white undershirt now.

The eight ball looms.

Matthew shakes his head, smiling. "Eight ball. Corner pocket."

He knocks it down seconds later, and just like that, the first match is over. I hesitate, making sure his eyes are on me when I reach below my dress. I pull off the pair of his swim shorts I'd concealed underneath.

He curses under his breath. "Are you hiding my entire closet in there?"

I laugh. "As much as I could fit."

While Matt reracks, I take a fortifying sip of whiskey. I pass the bottle to him as I break. I'm hoping for a good, clean shot that will drop a ball, but I'm disappointed. Handing over the pool stick feels like signing my own death certificate.

Matthew eyes the table, assessing the layout of the balls. He selects a solid in the corner, a close-range shot, and taps it in with ease. Sighing, I pull off his undershirt. I'm officially down to basics now. The dress will have to go next.

He points to my one remaining article of clothing. "That's a beautiful sight, Katarina."

I'm forced to rely on my fallback, scooting behind him again. I slip my hands under his shirt and trace my fingers over his bare stomach and chest.

"It's not going to work this time," he tells me, shaking his head. "I want it off. All of it."

"We'll see." I tug the top of his shirt aside and plant a kiss on his shoulder, then move up his neck.

He inhales, exhales. When I pause to check the table, he fires. The solid ball drops into the pocket.

Matt turns around to lean against the table. His blue eyes meet mine, fully open with his desire.

"Strip."

The music from the phonograph swells in my ears. My stomach turns over.

Slowly, I reach for my hemline. I hold his gaze until the dress lifts over my head. As it flutters to the floor, I enjoy every second of shock on his face.

"Is...is that a pair of my drawers?" he finally asks, a muscle jumping in his jaw.

"It is." I stand in front of him, smiling devilishly. I let him enjoy the view as I pose in my black brassiere, stockings, and his underwear.

He swallows. "Anything else under there?"

"Don't know." I shrug. "Guess you'll have to find out. It's still your turn."

He glances back at the table. There's a long shot down the right side. I take a different tack this time and drape myself over the pocket. I put my elbows on the table and lean in, giving him an eyeful.

To my complete delight, he misses the shot. The ball hits the corner and bounces from rim to rim twice before rolling out.

I smile, victorious. "Ready to lose your shirt?" I ask, taking the stick.

"I'm not holding my breath. You haven't gotten anywhere so far."

But I have all my options on the board, and he's placed the cue ball perfectly outside the corner pocket. I grin and bend over, making sure to stick my ass out a little extra. He gets a good look at his own drawers as I gently tap my stick to nudge a stripe into the pocket.

He unbuttons his shirt and tosses it aside, revealing a sleeveless undershirt. The rounded swell of his bare shoulders is tantalizing.

"I'm about to go on a roll," I warn.

I aim for the opposite corner and drop another ball. Matthew gives me a tiny, adorable smile before reaching back with one arm to tug off his undershirt from behind.

I take a moment to appreciate the sight, drinking him in. Two broad shoulders, the smooth planes and hard ridges of his chest, a smattering of dark blond hair trailing down, down, down...all the way down until it disappears under the waistline of his pants.

"Your trousers are mine," I say, a little breathless. "And I'm *really* going to enjoy taking them."

There's another across-the-table shot available, this time a side pocket. I don't have the best angle, but the ball is right on the edge. The lightest tap will likely see it over.

I bend down and concentrate. Shirtless Matthew is highly distracting, but pantless Matthew would be even better.

I taste victory the minute I release the shot, grinning before the ball tumbles. I walk around the table to Matthew as his hands, obediently, go to his waist. I put my fingers over his, halting him.

"I won them," I whisper. "They're mine."

I slowly unbutton his trousers, holding his gaze as I do. I brush my fingers against him far more than necessary before letting the pants drop to the ground. He steps back to kick them aside, and my heart stutters.

He moves his lips to the shell of my ear. "Can you finish?" he asks dangerously. "Or should I?"

"You're mine." I take a deep breath and try my hand at a ricocheting shot, a trick he could probably pull off. I miss.

He takes the pool cue without a word and lines up his next strike. Just before he releases, he flicks his eyes to mine. He holds there and slowly smiles. It's heady, that smile. So heady, I hardly notice when he knocks down a ball.

Unceremoniously, I drop his drawers to the floor and step out, revealing silk French knickers. Matthew's gaze traces over me. Hungry. Reverent. Head to toe, then back again. Everywhere his eyes linger, I feel the burn. Burning and burning and burning until I'm aflame all over. You'd think I was wearing the laciest and skimpiest of lingerie from the way he's looking.

It's still his turn, but he leans the stick against the table and slowly walks over to me, stopping scarcely an inch away.

"It's your shot," I murmur. "What's wrong—afraid you won't be able to finish after all, Matt?"

"I'm finishing the way I want to," he growls. "Myself."

His hand starts at my hip. He slides a finger beneath the waistband of my knickers and drags it softly across my stomach. My groin clenches, begging him to go lower. He teases his touch up my side. Tingles and shivers overtake me, raising gooseflesh on my skin.

When he gives me his lips, I'm starving for them, starving for him. My tongue crashes into his. He lifts me up, slamming my butt onto the rim of the pool table. Chills ripple down my spine as he works the hooks of the brassiere. When I shrug it off, his hands go straight to my chest.

Matthew groans into my mouth and lowers me across the table. With fumbling fingers, we clear the stray balls. Once I'm on my back, he bends my knee and unrolls my stockings, one leg at a time. Dragging his fingers over my bare skin, pressing kisses to my inner thigh. My knee. My ankle. His eyes are raw, his lips fervent. Ravaging me.

I whimper as he works his way back up, moving toward my center. The wanting, the way I hunger for him, is ruinous.

He pulls my knickers down and slips two deft fingers inside me. My back arches as I cry out.

"God, you're so wet." His voice is gruff, rough with longing. He kisses me hard, swallowing my cries as he curls his fingers. First two. Three. He doesn't let up until I'm screaming his name, over and over. Until I lose myself entirely, exploding into incoherence.

When my eyes finally open, I take a shuddering breath. Matt is there, waiting, gazing down at me with so much abject love in his eyes, it hurts. It sucks the breath straight out of my lungs, that look. Rearranges the gravity in the room. Something new blooms in my heart. Matthew's love is sunlight, water, and air.

The look on his face, pure reverence.

What a heady way to be loved.

In the corner of the room, the phonograph skips. I lick my lips, then part them. Not entirely sure what I'm going to say, but breathless with conviction. Before I find words, his fingers start to move again.

"Matt..." My vision spins. I reach for him, and he grabs my hand. Bringing the inside of my wrist to his lips, he presses an open-mouth kiss to the tender skin.

"I want you screaming my name again," he tells me, pressing a second kiss to my palm, tongue flicking. "Over and over. Exactly the way you just did."

And in a matter of minutes, I am. Again. And again and again.

And only when my voice is hoarse, my breath ragged, my mind thoroughly obliterated, does he slide his hand out of my silk shorts. He locks my shaking legs around his waist and lifts. His lips move over mine as he carries me to his bedroom—building, crashing, falling.

Matthew kicks the door open, and we fall onto his bed. He pins me, securing my wrists above my head. He kisses his way down my chest. I wrap my legs around his waist and lift my hips, pressing against the hardness in his groin.

We roll, lips devouring, hands searching.

I straddle him low, closer than close, yet not close enough. I press down, the softest part of me against the hardest of him.

His answering moan is pure sin. Sheer longing.

I move my lips over his shoulder and pecs, trailing kisses across his chest and abdomen. I slide his drawers down and take him in my hand. He's dripping wet. I don't want to wait much longer, but there's one last thing I desperately want to give him, this man who is always hell-bent on giving to others.

I open my mouth and pull him in. Deep. All the way to the back. I stay there for a minute, exploring pressure points with my tongue, listening to his response. He's a new experiment, one I plan to figure out quickly. I sit back on my heels and take a breath. "How long can you hold out?"

"Not...long..." he pants.

I laugh and suck him down again, letting the vibrations from my throat taper out on him. He's surprisingly vocal about what he likes, and he's right. It doesn't take long.

"Kat." His tone is telling, and I see the question in his eyes. The need.

"Yes," I tell him. "Yes. Now."

He pushes me down, settling me between his legs. I lift my hips as he slides my pants off. He kisses me, full and deep.

"Matt, I need you inside of me," I beg. "Now."

He reaches to his bedside table for a condom. I snatch it from him and roll it on, his eyes drinking me in.

When he pushes inside me, it's slow. It's agonizing.

It's *everything*.

My head falls back on the feathery pillow, and I whimper with relief. With a guttural groan, he fills me completely. Buried to the hilt.

"Kat?" he rasps. He can't even lift his head; he has it buried in my hair, lips pressed to my ear.

"I'm fine. Please, Matt."

He starts to move, and I lose all sense of myself. Everything fades except him. There is only the sound of his panting breath. Only the tangle of his fingers in my hair, the heat of his lips on my neck. Only the feel of him, deep within me. Turning me inside out.

He pulls back and moves a guiding hand to my hips, changing the pace, pushing in deeper. I cry out, trying to absorb each strike. I'm hovering so close to the edge.

"Matt. Oh god, Matt."

"You. Are. So. Beautiful. Kat." He punctuates each word with a plunge.

I cling to him and move with him. Allow him to have me exactly how he wants me, as many times and in as many ways. Because in this moment, I finally know what it feels like to be his. I realize what being his truly means.

Absolutely everything.

I am his, and he is mine.

And I can't remember ever wanting to be anything else.

WE SLIP HAZILY INTO the after. Languid, shifting in the bed as one. Whispering, showering soft kisses on each other.

"I wondered if you were going to take these off one at a time out there," Matthew murmurs. He's holding my hand, slipping his fingers in and out of mine, brushing over my rings.

I shake my head and smile. "I almost never take off my rings."

"I'm glad you didn't. We would have been out there all night." His fingers move to Paul's chunky, silver band, and I stiffen. My tattoo pulses beneath it, a dangerous secret.

My reaction gives him pause. "What's this one mean?" he asks, kissing the finger.

I take a deep breath. "That one is a story for another day, one I do intend to tell you," I say, surprising myself. "I have to figure out how first. It's going to take a little more time."

"Hmm." He considers me, still tracing, but he's moved to another finger, another ring. Another kiss. I wiggle around, taking his hands in mine.

"I was watching you earlier," I admit. "At the hospital, before you saw me."

"Oh yeah?"

"I was watching your hands move. How comfortable you were."

"And?"

"And I know you love it, Matthew, but what I don't understand is *why*? Why do you love it? Why did you choose it? There were a million other professions you could have chosen. A million easier jobs that would have given you more money and more time and more freedom. With far less responsibility. Why this?"

He shifts in the bed, watching as I run my nose, then my tongue, up the length of his index finger.

"I mean, don't get me wrong, I loved seeing you there." I laugh softly as I continue. "Watching your hands move, these hands"—I kiss them—"and your brain working. You're so smart, Matthew, and I can't imagine you doing anything else. But I want to understand how you got there. How you came to be this way."

"It's just...my hands are mine, you know?" he says. "A few years ago, I had to decide what kind of difference I wanted to make with them and sitting behind a desk like my father, choosing headlines...it didn't feel right. I wanted to touch people, make a real difference."

"Doesn't it scare you sometimes? What you do?" It scared me just being there, just standing in that cavernous room of overwhelming need.

"It did, at first." His expression changes as he ponders, trying to explain. "The first time someone's heart stopped in front of me...that's not something you forget. That feeling of terror, of not knowing what to do. I remember looking around for someone older than me—another physician, anyone—but all eyes were on me. And you don't get to run. It's hard, but when the world falls apart around you, you learn how to stay."

"What happened to that person?"

"He died." Matthew looks straight ahead. "But there have been many since him who didn't. People I've been able to save."

I think of myself. How I take lives while he saves them, because it's quicker, easier. Feels necessary even, to protect what's mine. How what he does is so much harder, infinitely so, looking into someone's eyes and committing yourself to giving rather than taking.

Taking is easy. I would know.

Slowly, I kiss his hand again, right in the center of his palm. "You are an incredible person, Matthew," I tell him. "To give so much of yourself and ask for so little in return."

He sighs and looks away. "There are plenty of men out there who have given just as much, Kat. More, even. Men who have made the ultimate sacrifice for God and country. What I do now, it's a pittance of penance for what I failed to do years ago."

I roll onto my side, awareness heightened by the tension entering his body. "What on earth do you mean? Are you speaking of the war? There are more ways than one to serve your country, Matt. You've accomplished just as much good here as you could have done by enlisting in medical school."

He takes a slow, deep breath. "I didn't just turn down the offer at Vanderbilt, Kat." He closes his eyes, and my heart stutters.

"What do you mean?"

His lids remain tightly shuttered. "When the Selective Service Act passed, I allowed my family to buy my name out of the draft...through unsavory channels. Ethan was already deployed on the Western Front, and my father didn't want to risk losing a second son. He offered to buy my name out, and I accepted."

"I see." My gaze roves across the taut lines of his face.

Conscription began in 1917 and cast a shadowy pall across the entire nation. It was unprecedented, summoning men to war by lottery. I remember the day Abe went to Savannah City Hall to register, the dread brewing in my stomach. Tony is an immigrant, and Paul has been hidden since he was a child, erased by a "missing, presumed dead" tag filed by the orphanage years after his disappearance. Only Abe was at risk of the draft, and it was perhaps the biggest break of his life that his name wasn't pulled. Many men, many *families*, weren't so lucky.

I reach a gentle finger toward Matthew's face, trying to smooth the lines burrowed there. "One selfish decision in a wholly unselfish life does not the measure of a man make, Matthew. Not in my eyes. You value life, including your own. There's no shame in that."

"There's great shame, Kat." His eyes spring open, blazing blue. "Shame I carry every day. That I must carry, for all the men who answered the call and didn't return. Men whose lives, perhaps, I could have been there to save."

I lay my head on his chest, pressing my cheek to his bare skin. "Your friend from Vanderbilt—I've forgotten his name, the one with whom you exchanged letters. Did he come home?"

"William?"

"Yes, William. Did he make it home?"

"No."

It's only one word, one single word, but the pain it represents is so great, a solitary tear falls from my eye to his skin.

"Hit by a stray shell." His words rumble in his chest beneath my cheek. "While he was triaging wounded on the field."

I allow the words to sink in. I breathe in slowly, then out. I wanted to know how Matthew became this way, and here it is. It wasn't his first answer, but this is the one that matters. There will always be the story we tell the world and the story we live. It's in the intersection of the two where the greatest truth lies.

"He was very selfless and very brave," I murmur, turning to press a kiss into Matthew's chest, right on the damp spot where my tear landed. "And so are you."

CHAPTER TWENTY-FOUR

THE SECOND THE FRONT door shuts, he's on me. His fingers unbutton my coat, and his lips ravage mine. My hands shoot to his hair. He drops my jacket to the floor of the foyer. I tear at his shirt, ripping it up and over his head.

We are animals. We are ferocious.

And we don't make it far. Matthew makes love to me on the wood floor of his foyer, just out of reach of the front door. Later, we make it to his bedroom, but only by stumbling and fumbling the entire way. It's been like this between us for the last week. A comet set on fire, streaking across the sky at a thousand miles per hour. Consumed by each other in every moment we can find.

When dusk falls, the cocoon breaks. It's time for us to emerge into the real world. Matt is working at the hospital overnight, and unbeknownst to him, I have my own job with the Royals.

Ironically, the first time Matt notices my carefully selected lingerie is when I'm strapping myself back into it.

"This is nice," he says, tracing the cups of the lace brassiere. "How did I miss this?"

"You were otherwise preoccupied," I say with a laugh. "And to think, I picked it out special for you this morning."

"I'm looking now."

Once we're presentable, we leave his apartment, hand in hand. Matt walks me to the streetcar stop, even though it's in the opposite direction of his route to work.

"Which way are you boarding?" he asks. It seems an innocent question, but the Academy is one direction and the bayou another.

I hesitate.

"You're not going home, are you?"

He's being clever with his words, but I know what he's really after. He wants to know where I'm going this late at night.

So I tell him. Kind of. "No, not home. I'm meeting Abe in the bayou."

"And...someone else too?"

I nod. "Yes. Someone else too."

I can tell from the frustration in his eyes he wants to say more, but he bites his tongue. I also catch the tiniest flash of pain across his face. It's enough to stab my heart.

"Be safe then," he finally says.

"I will." The lie tastes bitter, so I chase it with a shot of truth. "Hey, Matt?"

"Yeah?" His lips part softly. The streetcar rumbles in the distance.

I unbutton my coat and tweak the lace strap of my lingerie. "I wore this for *you* today. No one else. You understand?"

His sweet, sunshine smile breaks through the clouds on his face. He's easy, so very easy, to make happy. I wish I could stay here with him all night, to keep doing exactly that.

But the streetcar waits for no one, least of all me. Before I climb aboard, Matt hooks his pinky with mine, stretching for one last point of contact. When he looks at me like this, standing there with the light of the sun shining through his earnest blue eyes, it's on the tip of my tongue to blurt out three very dangerous words. I vacillate, wondering what would happen if I said them. If I was brave.

I've always thought of myself as brave. Wolves are brave, aren't they? I always thought so.

But in this moment, I'm not brave at all. I'm a coward. Once I say those words, there's no taking them back. And there'll be no going back either. I free my pinky and wordlessly climb aboard the streetcar, waving to Matt as we pull away.

I get off at the familiar bayou stop and go straight to the loft. With some dismay, I note the night turning foggy, the air damp. The deteriorating weather feels foreboding, especially since I won't be in my usual black suit tonight. Not for this job.

In the privacy of the master bedroom, I braid my hair and wind the plaits around my head. I secure a red wig on top before shedding my clothes. I step into a pair of jodhpurs, and over them, I pull on a long skirt.

I'm busy selecting a matching bodice from the closet, upper half clad only in lingerie, when Paul walks in. Ordinarily, this wouldn't warrant a reaction, but today, it sends my heart careening guiltily through my chest. Paul sees the lace before I can cover it.

He drags out a low whistle. "You wearing that little number for the benefit of the doctor? Because judging by your reaction right now, it sure as hell isn't for me."

"Maybe I'm wearing it for myself," I answer, beginning to remove my rings.

"Yeah right, Kat. At least have the decency to shoot me straight. I'm not an idiot. And I told you it was okay. You can do whatever—and whoever—you want."

I don't answer and keep removing the rings, saving his for last. When I turn, he hands me my gloves. Elbow-length and white for the job tonight.

I pull on the left one, but before I can do the same with the right, he snatches my hand and kisses my finger. Right over my red tattoo.

"You never have to hide this from me. Can you say the same about him?"

"Paul, don't do this. You promised you wouldn't."

"I won't." He steps back. "We need to go. But he's never gonna know your whole story, Kat. He's never gonna know you like I do. And he's sure as hell not going to be able to give you what you need. Not forever. I just wonder what your grand plan is. You think you can tell him everything and then live happily ever after?"

"No." I yank my hand back and pull on the glove. "You don't think I know that, Paul? God."

He's quiet for a minute, watching me closely. I can never hide from Paul, and the longer he stares, the more convinced I am he can see straight through me.

"Please, Kat." His eyes are sad. "Please don't fall in love with someone else. Not while I'm watching from the sidelines."

I don't answer, can't answer. Instead, I gaze into the mirror and hurriedly brush light makeup over my face.

"You ready?" Paul asks.

I continue staring into the mirror, uncertain. The woman gazing back at me with long scarlet hair...she looks suspiciously like my mother. I swallow, tilting my head this way and that, watching her move. It's eerie. I consider changing the wig but decide against it.

Ghosts only have the power we give them.

"Yes, I'm ready," I finally answer, breaking eye contact with the woman in the mirror.

"M'lady." Paul extends his arm and sweeps me from the loft with Tony and Abe on our heels. He's holding his posture so foolishly erect, I laugh.

"Gentlemen don't really walk like that, you know," I tell him.

"Well, it's like I always tell you, Kat—it's a damn good thing I'm not a gentleman then."

Paul and I stroll the streets of the riverfront district arm-in-arm, playacting a wealthy couple out for a late-night stroll. Tony and Abe keep to the shadows, slinking behind us. When we're directly around the corner from the Magpie's dock, we halt, checking for onlookers in the darkness.

There are none.

Abe has my satchel slung over his right shoulder. Paul pulls off his gentleman's coat, revealing working-class clothes underneath. Before he drops the jacket, he pulls two glass beer bottles from the oversized pockets. Tony holds two more.

"Is everyone ready?" Paul is focused only on me.

I nod, not trusting my voice.

"Kat, I won't let anything bad happen. I promise." He takes my white-gloved hand and kisses it, then bends over to brush my lips.

"You got your knives?" Abe asks me.

"Yes. I'm ready."

"Off you go then, Kitty-Kat," Paul whispers.

I take a deep breath, step around the corner, and let out a bloodcurdling scream.

CHAPTER TWENTY-FIVE

When I pause for air, Paul smashes his beer bottles against the wall. The shattering of glass rings into the night.

I scream again and start running, pounding my heels on cobblestone streets, then the wooden planks of the wharf. I let out a third scream as I rocket toward the Magpie dock like a bullet. I'm pretty close before I'm able to locate the three guards through the fog.

"Please!" I shriek and hurtle myself into the arms of the nearest man. "You have to help me."

"Oof." He lets out a grunt as I sock into his gut.

"Please..." I grab the lapels of his coat. "Someone's after me. There's a man out there."

Another shatter of glass sounds from the corner as Tony breaks his bottles. The dense fog renders everything beyond a ten-foot radius invisible.

"There's definitely someone out there, Ben," one of the men says. His hand twitches for his gun.

I pant in distress and lock onto my target's eyes, summoning a crazed fervor within my own. "I've been running for blocks and blocks. I need help...you'll help me, won't you?"

The third guard sidles over, interested. He takes in my eveningwear and prim white gloves with a smile.

"Looks like we got ourselves a lady, fellas. A pretty one at that."

"If she's such a lady, what the hell is she doing in this part of town so late at night?" Ben's lips are downturned. He tries to shake my grip from his lapels, but I won't budge. "What's your name, lass?"

"Wendy, my name is Wendy." The name initiates a ten-second warning code for the Royals. I begin to fake cry on cue, sagging into Ben. Instinctively, he supports my weight.

Target acquired.

"Ugh, help me with her, will ya?" He turns to his friends. "We'll take her inside. I'm sure the boys won't mind having a little fun tonight."

A second guard comes over—the one with the itchy trigger finger—and that's when I make my move. I collapse fully into Ben's arms, going limp. As though I've fainted.

"Christ!" he cries out.

It's the last thing he ever says. From my slumped position, I slip out one of the knives strapped to my waist and slide the blade through his lung with the quickest, quietest of pops.

Target eliminated.

I whirl on the second guard, stabbing him in the gut as the three other wolves descend from the shadows.

The third Magpie, unfortunately, is out of my reach. He fires a warning shot with his gun and opens his mouth to scream. "Wolves! Wolves!"

Paul silences him with a single cut from his knife. Abe grabs my arm and drags me toward the gangplank. He pushes me to my knees, and I crawl into the tiny space under the wooden ramp. My feet dangle over open air at the edge of the pier. A lick of water laps at me, wetting the hem of my skirt.

"Here, Kat." Abe shoves the satchel into my outstretched hands.

Footsteps rumble aboard the ship. Magpie men appear overhead. Gunshots fire into the night. They target Paul and Tony, the two most visible attackers, as they scamper down the gangplank. Abe emerges from his crouch with a roar, rushing the first Magpie to step dockside.

While the remaining Magpies descend, I shoulder the satchel and begin to climb the underside of the gangplank. My skirt flutters over open air as my fingertips latch onto the edge of the ramp. Our enemies' feet stampede down, rattling the wood beneath my grip, but I'm undeterred. Legs swinging and fingers creeping, I glide upward. By the time I've reached the top, all the Magpies are at the bottom, none the wiser.

I swing my legs up and over, ready to slink aboard the ship when the gunshot fires. It whizzes so close to my temple, my red hair blows forward, sucked briefly into its wake. The bullet lodges in the wooden hull.

When I glance back, Abe pounces on my attacker. His hand grapples for the gun, and it fires again, a bullet piercing through the wooden pier. Twisting, Abe wrests the weapon away and tosses it into the water with a splash.

"Go, Kat!" he yells.

And even though my gut tells me not to leave them, I do.

The ship lurches as I dart aboard, moving with the tide.

As I fight for my footing, a body slams me from behind. We fall to the ground, rolling and tussling. I scramble my way on top and deliver a wicked throat punch to my attacker's neck. He gasps, hands flying to his crushed trachea. His face pales as he tries to suck in air, panicking when he realizes he can't. Soon enough, he'll be blue.

My thoughts errantly fly to Matthew. What would he do if this man presented before him in the hospital? His response would be so inherently different from mine; Matthew would move to save. Instead, I pull out my knife to end the suffering.

When it's over, I rise and yank off my ridiculous skirt, tossing it into the Savannah River. In just my bodice, jodhpurs, and heels, I pace the deck to search for hidden Magpies, but I'm alone.

Shouts ring and fists *thud* down on the dock, but there's no time to worry. Like always, I have to trust the boys to do their job. Same as they trust me to do mine.

I stride back to the gangplank and kick until it dislodges from the ship, falling into the water with a resounding splash. No one is ever coming up or getting off this ship that way again.

I wrench open the door to the hull and descend. In the belly of the ship, I rip open my bag and pull out a tankard of gasoline, splashing it across the wooden floor. I sprint around the hull to drizzle the accelerant all over, dragging it up and down walls, over piles of cash and crates of supplies. I freeze when I come across dozens of white blocks on a table.

Cocaine powder.

I grimace and dump gasoline directly on the dangerous cache. There are opium bottles and marijuana hash nearby as well. I pluck a freshly rolled joint from the bunch, clutching it in my free hand while I hurry onward.

When I reach the back of the hull, I catalog a few kegs of gunpowder and give them a very wide berth. When my gasoline runs out, I race up the steep stairs to the deck. At the top, I pull out Paul's silver cigarette lighter and start thumbing it.

Once the joint is lit, I toss the smoking stick into the hull. Flames erupt. I don't linger to watch.

A breath of cool wind kisses my cheeks as I cross the deck. I whip a knife from my waistline and cut a long, thick strand of rope free of the rigging.

Down below, Abe, Tony, and Paul are all on their feet, ducking and swinging punches. One Magpie is down, three still standing.

Rope lanced free, I swing one leg over the ship's rail. As I'm dangling myself overboard, preparing to dismount, I see it happen. Two of the Magpies jump Tony. He plunges a knife deep into the chest of one attacker while Paul grabs the other by the collar to hurl him back. The Magpie tumbles and rolls away, then fumbles for something silver at his waist.

The gun goes off a second later. Before I can even open my mouth.

"Paul!" I scream. I push off the deck, swinging wildly into the night. Flames erupt behind me. My feet touch the ground just as the second gunshot fires.

I'm behind the guilty Magpie in a flash, and I snap his neck. Tony is on his knees, his hands checking Paul's stomach, his *bloody* stomach. My vision swirls as Tony yanks the shirt off his own back and presses it tight, slowing the flow of red.

I stumble to them as Abe puts down the final Magpie, running him through with a knife. He takes one glance at Paul on the ground and starts giving orders. "Pick him up! Kat, hold the shirt."

I maintain pressure while Abe and Tony lift. My white gloves stain red immediately.

"I know a place, shut down for Prohibition," Tony says.

"How far?"

"Three blocks into the city."

We go, staggering through side streets as quickly and quietly as we can. Tony swings open the door to an abandoned tavern. It's small. There's a shanty entryway with coat pegs. We drag Paul into the pub and sling him onto a long table. Tony bends over, panting. I keep my hands pressed tight against Paul's stomach.

"Paul?" I call out. "Paul?"

"Hey, Kitty-Kat," he groans. His eyes are closed, face stretched tight in a grimace.

My mind races. We have very little time and even fewer options. There's nothing for it.

Matthew. I need Matthew.

I look between Abe and Tony's anxious faces, trying to make a decision. As much as I want Abe here with me, I have to send him. He's the fastest runner. And Matthew knows him.

"Abe." I swallow hard. "Go to the hospital and ask for Matthew DaMolin. Tell him...tell him I need him. Right now."

"Motherfucker," Paul hisses on the table.

"Kat, I'm not sure—"

"Go!" I bellow. My voice is shrill and unlike my own. *"Go!"*

Abe takes off without another word.

"Tony." I turn to him. "How far from the hospital are we?"

"Maybe ten blocks?"

Abe can do that in five minutes. I glance down at Paul's stomach. I want to look, but I'm afraid to lift the shirt.

"How many times did he get hit?"

"I'm not sure. I think twice."

"It hurts like a motherfucker," Paul groans.

"I know. I'm sorry, Paul. I'm so sorry." I can't help it, I start to cry. Slow, fat tears cascade down my cheeks.

I try to be brave. Because wolves are brave, right? *Right?*

I brace myself and lift Tony's balled-up shirt. It's not as bad as I feared. Maybe. There's no rush of bright red blood, not like there was initially.

I cover it with the shirt again. My white gloves are disgustingly blood-soaked, but I leave them on. "Tony, when Matthew gets here, he'll need to be able to...to do his thing. We need to get Paul's shirt off."

Tony pulls out a knife and cuts through the front of Paul's top, around the sleeves and the neck. Then he lifts him—Paul cries out in pain—while I yank the shirt from underneath. I toss it on the ground, the fabric landing with a wet, bloody *slop*. I reach up and rip off my red wig as well, throwing it next to the shirt. I undo the pins securing the braids around my skull, letting them drop.

That's better.

I take a deep breath, already feeling lighter and more clearheaded. I resume holding pressure on Paul's bare abdomen while Tony goes to the window.

"Stay awake, Paul," I order. "Keep your eyes open."

"Okay," he answers, but his eyes stay closed.

"Paul. Look at me. Open."

He sighs but forces his lids up.

"I love you," I tell him, trying to hold his gaze. "You are going to keep your beautiful eyes open and stare at me until Matthew gets here to help you. Do you understand?"

"Yes," he whispers. His eyes are dazed, but I see him try. "Love you too, doll."

We lapse into silence. Every now and then, I call out Paul's name or press his stomach a little harder to startle him awake.

"Kat." Tony turns from his perch at the window. "I see them."

Abe and Matthew rush into the room seconds later. Abe stumbles and yanks out a chair from a neighboring table. He collapses into it, panting and exhausted.

"Kat?" Matthew looks at me, frightened. "What's going on?" His eyes widen as he takes in the sight of me standing over Paul, my bloodstained gloves pressing into his stomach.

"Matthew, I need your help." I scrunch my face against the tears. "I'm so sorry, but I need you."

He walks over. There's a bulky bag strapped over his shoulder. He drops it to the ground and reaches to move my hands. "Let me see."

I step back. No longer able to stand Paul's blood on my hands, I peel away the gloves, tossing them to the floor beside the red wig. Matthew's eyes follow their flight. He sees the wig, then looks at me again, at the incongruous pairing of my bodice and jodhpurs. He looks at Paul on the table. Paul, whose wolf tattoo is visible, climbing over his neck and shoulder. Then to the shirtless Tony across the room, paw tracks inked across his side and ribs.

It's all micromovements—Matthew's flickering gaze—but I see him putting two and two together, the way I've always feared he would. His eyes flash to mine, and I know. With Matthew, I've been dancing too close, far too close. Matthew is the sun, and I'm about to get burned.

Exhaustion hits, hard and sudden. I collapse into a chair beside Paul. I take his right hand in mine and when I do, Matthew's eyes latch onto the final piece of damning evidence, zeroing in on our matching tattoos—the king and queen of diamonds.

"Oh my god..." he whispers.

"Matt, this is Paul," I whisper back. "I am asking you, asking you with everything I have, to save him."

"Anytime would be good, doc," Paul grunts from the table.

Matthew shakes his head in disbelief. "What happened? Kat, we were together a few hours ago. *What the hell happened?*"

"He...he got shot. Twice. On his right side."

Matthew takes a deep breath and lifts Tony's blood-soaked shirt. He looks for a few seconds, then bends to check Paul's side.

"Shit," he hisses. He drops the shirt back down and squeezes his eyes tight, thinking.

Abe skulks over as Matthew opens his eyes.

"Did you notice any holes in his back?" Matt asks.

"No," I respond. "No, it's only on the front."

"That means the bullets are still inside him. They didn't go through."

"Can you fix it?" I'm breathless. Desperate.

"I'm a physician, Kat. Not a surgeon."

"Is that a no?"

"I mean, I can try to dig the bullets out, but it's not going to be pretty."

Paul lifts his head. "I never...cared much...about being pretty," he manages. "Alive is...far more important."

"It could get infected." Matthew looks around the dirty tavern. "Easily."

"Just do your best." Paul drops his head. "And try not to kill me, even though you probably want to."

"I'm not going to kill you," Matthew answers, reaching to open his bag. "But those bullets might. Especially that one." He points to the upper hole.

"Why that one?" I ask.

"Because it's damn close to his liver."

"What if we leave them in there?" Tony asks. "The bullets. And you just close him up?"

Matthew shakes his head. "Then it will definitely get infected, and he'll be dead in a week."

Paul lets out a small chuckle, wincing. "So I'm either dead tonight or dead in a week? You're a bundle of joy, doc."

"Paul, just...just clam up for a minute," I tell him.

"Okay, doll."

Matthew digs through his bag, pulling out supplies one by one.

"If we can help," I say, "just ask."

"Oh, you're going to help. I'll need it. Get up, Kat."

I spring to my feet, and he kicks my chair aside, dragging a nearby table over. He starts assembling supplies across the surface. He tosses me an alcohol-soaked cotton pad.

"Clean his arm. Over his biceps."

I take the wipe and dutifully scrub Paul's arm. I have no idea how thoroughly I need to do it, so I just keep swiping. Matthew does the same on Paul's stomach, cleaning the area around the two holes by pouring a harsh, ethanol-smelling solution directly over it.

"*Motherfucker.*" Paul graces us with his new favorite word.

Matthew doesn't apologize, just keeps moving. He snaps open a small case filled with drug vials. He draws something up with a tiny needle, flicking the glass syringe twice.

"What's that?" I bite my lip.

"It's phenobarbital—a tranquilizer and hypnotic. It'll help with the pain and, hopefully, some of the memories, because trust me, he won't want to remember what's about to happen." He looks at Paul. "I'm giving you a dose big enough to take down a fucking horse, but I'm probably going to start digging before it hits. It's going to hurt like a *real* motherfucker."

Paul smiles slightly at Matthew's use of his word.

"You might pass out," Matthew adds.

"Just do it," Paul grits through tight teeth. "Kat? If you want to tell me you love me one more time, sounds like now's the last chance."

"I love you," I tell him. If it bothers Matthew—and I'm sure it does—he doesn't show it.

"Love you too," Paul murmurs, eyes falling shut.

"All right. Stick." Matthew plunges the needle into Paul's biceps without fanfare, emptying the drug out.

Paul's face doesn't even register the prick.

"It'll get better in about five or ten minutes." Matthew pulls on a pair of white gloves and picks up a scalpel, tweezers, and gauze. "Kat, put on a pair of gloves, then don't touch anything else in the room—they're sterile. Keep them by your face, but don't cough or breathe on them. And when you're done, don't throw out the packaging. Drop it over his chest for me. Fully open, like a napkin."

I do as I'm told, trying my best to follow his rapid instructions.

"Abe, get up here and hold his head and shoulders. And you"—he jerks his head at Tony—"get his feet."

When everyone is in position, the entire room takes a collective inhale.

"All right. Paul?" Matthew says. "You're going to feel me touching you. Light at first, and then...bad."

"Got it." Paul braces himself, taking a deep breath as Matthew begins.

I knew it would be bad—Matthew just said so—but even still, I'm unprepared for just how bad it really is. Matthew cuts in with the scalpel at the lower bullet hole first, enlarging the area. Paul does okay with that part; he tenses and groans, but he manages. When Matt goes deeper with a smaller knife, that's when it really gets rough. Paul starts shouting and kicking. Tony blankets himself over his legs, and Abe does the same on Paul's arms and shoulders.

"Kat, roll up some gauze from the table. Lengthwise. Four pieces," Matthew says, not looking away from Paul's stomach.

"Done."

"Good, now stick it in his mouth."

"Are you serious?"

"Dead serious. Give him something to bite down on."

"Paul, open your mouth," I say, but he's well beyond listening. I wait for his next scream, then shove the gauze roll in, right between his teeth.

"Good. Now change your gloves," Matthew directs.

Moments later, Paul's fight starts to die down. His eyes gradually drift shut.

"Is it the medicine?" Tony asks, hopeful.

"Maybe," Matthew mutters. "Or he passed out. Probably both."

It's quiet while he works. He frequently asks me for gauze; Paul is bleeding again.

"I see the first bullet," Matthew eventually says. "I think I can get it."

A minute later, the metal bullet drops to the table, atop the bloody gauze.

Matthew stands and cracks his neck.

"You...you did it. You got it!" I'm shocked.

"The first one, yes. The second is going to be harder." He shoves some fresh gauze into the oozing first hole before turning his attention to the second.

The process begins anew. Cutting in with the scalpel to enlarge the hole, then slowly working his way deeper with smaller tools as he searches for the bullet. He's right, it takes longer this time, and he's more cautious with his digging. He curses under his breath, then stands to stretch his neck and back again.

"This one's a tricky bastard," he mumbles before he goes back to digging, using a tiny scalpel this time. He makes a few more cautious, exploratory cuts.

An indeterminable number of heartbeats later, Matt asks me to hand him tweezers. I hold my breath as he works, jiggling and concentrating. Eventually, he pulls back and drops the second bullet on the pile.

"Mother. Fucker." He steps away from the table and wipes his face, exhaling loudly.

"Did you...did you do it?"

He nods. "I have to close him up, but the bullets are out. I can't believe it. He's got a lucky horseshoe up his ass."

Abe chokes out a relieved laugh while Matthew dumps more antiseptic over the bullet holes, an entire bottle. Then he picks up the sutures.

I'm more relaxed now, relaxed enough to notice the details, the steady finesse behind Matthew's movement. How he weaves the needle in and out. How he ties off threads with a complicated series of twisting knots. Over and over, working deep to superficial. I watch as the holes slowly knit together, layer by layer. It's like magic.

No, not magic. *Matthew.*

He sighs mightily when he cuts the final thread. He smothers the wounds with ointment and dresses them. At long last, he rips off his gloves and falls into a nearby chair. Hands trembling, exhausted. His eyes flick to mine. "It's done."

I look at Paul, somehow sleeping quietly and peacefully through it all. Completely unaware Matthew DaMolin has hopefully-possibly-probably saved his goddamn life.

CHAPTER TWENTY-SIX

THIRTY MINUTES PASS. WE all sit and watch Paul breathe. We don't speak. I barely move my gaze from the rise and fall of his chest.

Eventually, Matthew stands to clean up his supplies.

"What about...for the pain?" I ask, nodding at Paul. "When he wakes."

"I can inject him with morphine before I go. That'll cover him for a few hours."

"What about when that wears off?" Abe speaks up. "Is there anything we can do for him?"

"Do you guys have access to, say...off-market painkillers?" Matthew asks, sinking into his chair.

"We don't move drugs," I tell him, more harshly than I probably need to.

"Kat, I'm not here to judge. This is about your friend. I can come back in a few days with some painkillers, but I already risked a lot by skimming these narcotics tonight. If they catch me, I could lose my job."

I lower my eyes. Sufficiently scolded and embarrassed.

"So do you have anything? A joint even?"

"A joint?" Abe's ears perk. "I can get him that. Easily."

"Then do it. It'll help."

Tony rubs his hands on his pants. "We really can't thank you enough. For everything you did for him."

"Just watch him closely," Matthew advises. "For fevers especially. He may have one for a few hours tomorrow morning, and that's fine, but beyond then, it could signal an infection. If that happens, Kat knows how to find me."

Abe walks over to shake his hand. "You're a good man."

Matthew nods faintly and bites his lip. He looks down at Paul, his gaze lingering on the wolf tattoo.

"Matt?" I force myself to speak. "Can we go outside to talk?"

We walk out together, side by side but not touching. I feel stiff. Like I've been beaten and whipped. I brace for what lies ahead.

When the tavern door closes, Matthew turns on me.

"Christ, Kat." He runs his fingers through his hair. "How many different times and ways are you going to gut me? Again and again."

I'm silent because I deserve it. That and a thousand more, so I don't say one single word.

"Have I proved it to you yet, Kat?" he continues. "That there's nothing I wouldn't do for you? No piece of me I wouldn't give? That I would *sell my soul* for you? Because I think I just did."

"I'm so sorry I asked that of you. I'm so sorry," I whisper.

"Kat, I am in love with you. And you...you're in love with someone else. Someone who is my opposite in just about every way."

"It's not as black and white as that. I've been wanting to tell you for months. I've *never* lied to you about this...I just haven't been able to tell the full truth."

"And what is the truth, Kat? What was I to you...a mark? A simp?"

"No." I shake my head, desperate for him to understand. "You're not a simp, Matt. I'm not playing you. My feelings for you are real."

Too real.

His jaw is tight, set. "You can see why it's difficult to believe you, right? How am I ever supposed to believe another word that comes out of your mouth?" His eyes scan my face, looking closely. So closely, I could cry. "*You* are the Cat Burglar? The femme fatale of the Wolfpack?"

"Get it?" I smile softly, sadly, and share our inside joke with him. "*Kat* Burglar?"

It costs me everything to say it. I know this—this right here—is where the sidewalk ends.

"Hilarious," he whispers, tone hollow. He reaches for my left wrist, turning it over. Rubbing his thumb over blank skin.

"You won't find anything there," I tell him. He's searching for the mark, the one his family's newspapers made infamous. I raise my right hand instead and show him my real tattoo. The one he saw when we were inside with Paul.

The queen of diamonds.

"This is it. My mark."

He takes my hand and looks closely, breathing in and out. "This is the finger where you wear that ring, the big silver one. The one I asked you about."

"Yes."

"Is it his ring?" He nods toward the pub, toward Paul.

"It is."

"And you're in love with him?"

"I am...I was." I grope for words.

"Those are two different things," he says, watching me.

I stay silent.

"Are you in love with me too?" he finally asks.

And I want to say the words. They're right there, right on the tip of my tongue, but something holds me back.

Because I've never truly believed I deserve Matthew, that I get to keep him forever. Not really.

"Kat." Matthew takes my trembling hands, gearing up for one last try. "I want you to listen very carefully. I'm not running from this. I don't care about who you were before me. I don't care about what you did. Who you slept with. If you've...hurt people. I don't care about any of it. All I care about is what you do from this moment forward. We're at a crossroads. Right now. No more lies, no more *bullshit*."

I nod numbly.

"I'm asking you, here and now, to consider another way. Another life. One with me, away from...all of this." He gestures at the dark night around us, back toward the pub, where Paul sleeps, unaware.

All of this.

The words sting. My kaleidoscope of a world, my entire *life*, wrapped in a neat little package with three small words. By someone like him.

I take a slow, deep breath. "You think I need saving, don't you? Like one of your patients? I don't. Matthew, *all of this* is who I am." I spread my arms. "I'm not ashamed of it. I'm not. Those are my best friends in there. We were underdogs, the biggest out there, and we beat the odds together. Did I set out to hurt people? No. But if someone threatens one of them, I won't hesitate. I protect what's mine. And they do the same for me. They're my *family*, and I won't leave them behind just because a better offer comes along. I can't."

He doesn't miss a beat. "If that's your choice, so be it. I won't ask you to compromise, but you can't expect me to either. I won't play second fiddle, and I cannot condone hurting people. I can't be a part of that. I folded on my morals once before and have regretted it every day since. I won't bend here, not again. Not even for you."

"So this is it." I hug myself, preparing for the fracture. Bracing for it. "An insurmountable impasse."

"It wasn't insurmountable, Kat." He shakes his head. "It's very simple. You're either mine or you're his. Tonight, you made your choice."

And he walks away. Away from me. Away and away, straight-backed and strong, until he disappears in the foggy depths of the Savannah night.

For the first time in a long time, there's no one to catch me when I fall.

CHAPTER TWENTY-SEVEN

THE PAIN IS LIKE nothing I could have imagined. Like a knife stuck in my chest, the blade scratching, slicing—endlessly—through the outermost layers of my black heart. I'm still alive, but with every beat of my pumping, wounded heart, a new gash appears, each mark gouging deeper than the last.

It's death by a thousand cuts. Over and over. And through it all, the same haunting memory—Matthew walking away, head held high. Higher than me. Always.

"Goddamn him!" I scream the words into my tear-soaked pillow. I punch the feathery fluff, stuff my bruised knuckles against my teeth, biting down.

My mother's voice comes next. *You aren't meant to be seen, Katarina. Why, oh why, did you let him see?*

"I don't know," I mumble, burying the words in the pillow. I imagine myself dancing with the sun. The warmth rushing in, then sputtering out. Plunging me into frigid darkness. It's so cold now. A starving man knows hunger all the better for having feasted. I wish I never had. I wish—

"Kat?"

The door creaks open, light streaking in. I roll away from it.

"Kat?" Mellie is poking my back. "I brought a plate of dinner for you. Meatloaf and potatoes. You should eat."

"I'm not hungry. Leave me alone, Mellie."

There's a gentle *thump* as porcelain hits the wood of my desk. Then, to my abject horror, the foot of my bed sinks, lowering under Mellie's weight.

"Get out, Mellie." I try for my usual fierceness, the tenor that always makes her capitulate, but her butt remains firmly planted on my bed. Her body warms the bundle of blankets around my feet.

"Kat, it's been three days."

Three days? I blink stupidly, the action painful in my swollen, sandpaper eyes.

"I can't cover for you much longer. Headmistress Helena is sending for a doctor in the morning."

I grunt, unmoved.

"Kat." Her hand lands on my ankle, her fingers curling around it with worry. "What happened?"

I want to kick her away. I want her to stop talking. I want her to leave me alone.

"I'm not moving from your bed until you talk to me." She wiggles backward, all the way back, until her spine rests comfortably against the wall. Legs stretched out, she settles in for the long haul.

I pull my bedraggled head off the pillow to stare at her, aghast.

"Golly." Her gaze roves over my splotchy face and tangled hair. "Things are worse than I thought."

"What are you doing?" I croak, summoning a weak glare. "Get off my bed and leave me alone."

"I won't." There's a stubborn tilt to her chin.

"Why not?"

"Because you're my friend and you're hurting. I don't know why, but—"

"We're not friends." I'm shocked by her assertion.

"Of course we are."

"No. We're not." I drop my head back to the pillow, exhausted. Certain now I've won, and she'll leave me in peace.

But Mellie does something wholly unexpected. She punches the blankets hard, right beside my feet. "You better hope we're friends, Katarina." The bedsprings creak as she shifts her weight. She's climbing up the bed, right on top of me. "You better hope we're friends," she repeats, her body pinning me, her head mere inches from mine. "Because you do not want me as your enemy."

I sputter. Her hands press my shoulders into the mattress. Her bony little fingers form claws, digging into pressure points at my clavicle.

"Please don't make me do something that isn't ladylike, Katarina."

"Like what?" I cock my head because I'm almost curious. A tiny flare of light, of engagement with the world, blooms in my belly.

Mellie's eyes are pure fire. "Like slap the shit outta you," she cries, voice squeaking. "Slap some goddamn sense into you!" She shoves hard, pressing me into the mattress. We both bounce lightly on the rebound before she shoves herself off, sliding onto the bed beside me. She slips her legs, rather audaciously, under the sheets alongside mine. "Would that make you listen to me? We *are* friends, goddammit. And friends *tell*."

My mouth opens, then closes. I blink furiously, trying to stave off the floodgates.

"Oh, Kat." She reaches for me, brushes a tangled strand of hair away from my face. "What happened? Is it Matthew...or your beau from back home? Please tell me. We can fix this. Whatever it is, I know we can fix it."

And it's her kindness that undoes me, her gentle patience, when I simply don't deserve it. I begin to wail, words rushing out so fast and jumbled, I wonder if she'll be able to make any sense of them. "I've ruined everything, Mellie. I've gone and ruined it all..."

The whole sordid tale spills out with very few omissions. I don't tell her about the Wolfpack, but I tell her about getting into trouble in the bayou, about Paul getting shot, about sending for Matthew. About our conversation at the end of the night, the one that ended with Matthew leaving me, walking away as I crumpled in the street. I pull very few punches.

Mellie's eyes grow wider and wider as the story progresses.

"I wish it had never happened, Mellie," I cry, blinking through tears. "I wish I'd never met him." Because the pain of this—this *leaving*—cuts so deep. Especially after I tried, tried so hard, to be worth sticking around for.

"You don't mean that. You love him."

"I don't *want* to love him," I roar, flinging back the covers. "I don't want to feel this way at all."

"But you do." Her voice is small. "You do, and you need to tell him. You should have already told him."

"I can't tell him, Mellie. I need to let him walk away clean. He deserves it, after all I've put him through."

"He wants to know." Her chin juts out again. "He asked you outright, and you lied. Again."

"Perchance I didn't lie," I stipulate. "I simply held my tongue."

"*Perchance* that's bullshit, Kat. And you know it."

A tiny laugh slips out, the absolute tiniest, but it breaks the dam. I cover my face with my hands, laughing and crying all at once.

"Sometimes, Katarina," Mellie says, a small chuckle betraying her own lips, "you can be a real simpleton. And a harlot, to boot, juggling all these men. I told you this wouldn't end well, straddling two worlds, but you didn't listen to your *friend*, now did you?"

I laugh a little harder now, simply because it feels good. Mellie yanks me to a sitting position. She swipes a hairbrush from my dresser and begins running it through the rat's nest atop my head.

"This is a horror," she murmurs, ripping the brush through snarls. Not gently. "An absolute horror. And we'll need teabags for your eyes, for the swelling. You must promise me something right now, Kat. Swear?"

"Swear what?"

"Swear you will never give a man this kind of power over you again. Not Matthew. Not your fella from the Catacombs. No man is worth your dignity, and no man should accept you without it. If he does, he doesn't have your best interest at heart."

I consider this. I buried my dignity so very long ago, locked it inside a chest alongside my heart and handed it to Paul. Deep in the Catacombs.

"You're a lady now," Mellie continues, running the brush through, again and again. "So swear it to me."

"I swear."

<hr/>

IT'S NOT NEARLY AS simple as Mellie believes, digging myself out of this hole. Weighing my dignity against Matthew and Paul. I know perfectly well what Mellie believes I should do. The fairytale has written itself, and all that remains, in her mind, is to declare my love and allow the prince to sweep me away. Because no one ever roots for Paul.

No one, that is, except me.

Even still, with Mellie's encouragement, I send a letter to Matthew at the hospital. It's brief, borderline impersonal, but I tell him where I'm going to be and when. I make no promises, no sweeping statements, because I have none. I'm wrung plumb dry.

It matters not. He meets me at the streetcar stop in the late afternoon.

I'm not sure how to greet him, but Matthew makes things quite simple when he leans in and kisses me on the temple as we wait for the streetcar to arrive.

Then we stand in roaring silence, the kind that punishes your eardrums. After we board the streetcar, Matthew speaks. "How's he doing?"

"Fine. He's doing well." A note from Abe two days past said as much. "It's...it's nice of you to check on him with me."

"I said I would."

When the train pulls up to the bayou stop, I grab his hand. Together, we weave through the streets until we reach the loft. I keep ahold of him as I unlock the door. He gazes with interest at the riot of color in our den. The draped silks and tapestries. Persian rugs. Well-worn furniture and eclectic—stolen—knickknacks scattered on tables.

"It's very...you," he pronounces.

"Really?" I look around, a bit surprised.

"Bohemian," he observes. He lifts our joined hands. "Like your rings."

"I suppose."

We go to Paul's back bedroom, and I steel myself before giving a sharp knock on the door. Just one, then I push it open and walk inside with Matthew. Our entrance sucks all the air from the room. Tony lets out a stream of Spanish curses, more colorful and lengthier than I've heard from him before.

"What the hell is he doing here, Kat?" Paul immediately tries to sit up.

"He's here to check your stitches, idiot."

Tony paces, still muttering curses. Abe is dumbstruck, paling at the sight of a newcomer to our sacred loft.

Paul shakes his head. "Kat, why on earth would you bring him here?"

"He's not going to say anything, Paul. We can trust him."

"I don't trust him any further than I can throw him. Which, right now, isn't very far." He glances down at his abdomen.

"Ha ha," I mock laugh. "You're hysterical. Just let him take a look, would ya?"

Stony silence. All around the room.

"Phew." Tony exhales, breaking the tension. He glances from Abe to Paul to Matthew, all of whom are glowering. "Mierda. I want no parts of this."

He shoulders past me to escape. Abe moves too, settling himself in the doorway like a guard dog.

"I guess it's a good thing we moved out of the Catacombs a few years ago." Paul watches Matthew, assessing. "You'd probably piss yourself if you had to go down there for a house call."

"It wouldn't be the first time," Matthew answers steadily, leaning over Paul to pull off his dressings.

"What?" I ask, unable to help myself.

Matthew glances at me before answering. "Not every trauma makes it through the doors of the hospital, Kat. I go where I'm needed. It's part of the new emergency protocols the hospital is trialing, the ones I told you about. You know where there's a lot of trauma? The Catacombs."

"Well, aren't you a saint?" Paul practically gags.

"Not quite," Matthew replies, giving a strong yank of the dressing tape. Paul grunts.

Abe snorts in the doorway.

Once the dressings are off, I lean forward. The area around the stitches is light pink and a little puffy.

"How painful is it?" Matthew asks.

"What? Sitting here with you?" Paul retorts. "About a nine outta ten."

"Your stomach, smartass. Though I have to say, it's nice to finally learn where Kat gets her sharp tongue." He tosses a grin at me.

"It's fine when I'm not moving around," Paul says, watching us with shrewd eyes. "But trying to get up is a real bitch. Like a seven outta ten."

"That'll get better as the muscles heal. When your obliques and rectus muscles knit back together, it won't be as painful. Give it a week or two. And increase your activity gradually. Sitting, then standing, then walking.

Nothing strenuous for at least four weeks—no running, no lifting, no sex...nothing."

"What was that last one, doc?"

"No sex. For four weeks. In your case, make it four months. I think Kat will survive."

Paul snorts and turns to me. "I can see why you like him. He's a riot."

"We're not having sex anyway, Paul," I snap. "We haven't for weeks, so what does it matter?"

Abe chortles again.

"I know, I know. You're sticking it to the doctor now. I'm in the doghouse. I get it."

"Paul..." I sigh crossly, closing my eyes in frustration. When I open them, I turn to Matt. He's quietly gathered his things, ready to go.

"I guess this is where we part ways then?" Paul observes.

"Reckon so," Matthew replies. "Unless there's an issue, you shouldn't need me again."

"Kat, hand me my billfold," Paul says. He fidgets in the bed to look directly at Matthew. "Tell me, what's the going rate for a doctor's soul these days?"

"That's really not necessary." Matthew puts out a hand to stop him.

"No. It is." Paul's tone is deadly. "I don't wanna owe you *jack*."

"I don't do what I do for money."

"Oh god." Paul collapses back. "You truly are sickeningly sweet, aren't you? It's hard to stomach."

"Just take good care of Kat," Matthew says, "and we'll call it even."

Paul laughs. "You see, that's how I know she's never gonna choose you. *Nobody* takes care of Kat. She's more than capable of looking out for herself. You don't know the first thing about her."

"He knows more than you think," I tell Paul as Matt heads for the door. "He would know it all if I was willing to tell him. So next time you want to take a shot at him, don't. Matthew has done nothing wrong. He's never shown me anything but the utmost respect, and he did the same for you when he *saved your life*, Paul."

"For you, Kat. He saved my life for *you*, not out of the goodness of his saintly heart."

I shake my head. "You don't know anything, Paul. What's worse is you don't *want* to know. He's here again today, solely to make sure you—renegade leader of the Wolfpack—are doing okay. And you don't even have the courtesy to thank him."

Matthew hovers in the doorway beside Abe, waiting for me.

"You know what?" I rise from Paul's bedside. "If you could muster up the humility to manage even a tenth of the grace he has"—I point at Matthew—"maybe I could stomach staying here with you. I love you, Paul, but you have never made it easy for me. There's not enough room in your life for both me and your ego."

Before I step back from the bedside, I do something either very crazy or very brave. Something long overdue. I lean over to kiss Paul's forehead, then stand up straight. I pull his silver ring off my finger and plunk it down on the nightstand.

"I love you," I repeat, "and I'm so happy you're alive. I never want to lose you. I hope you'll always be in my life in some capacity, but not like this, not anymore."

When I walk out of the room, Abe's eyes are wide and, I think, a little proud. But my heart is pounding in my ears, and the only person I really want to see or talk to is Matthew. So I take his hand and lead him out of the bayou loft and onto the street.

"Thank you," I tell him. "For what you did in there."

"I'm just doing my job."

"No, you're not. You're doing way more than that. Paul isn't easy, especially when his pride is damaged. More days than not, he thinks the sun comes up just to hear him crow. I'm sorry this is how you met him, because there's a lot of good in him you'll likely never get to see. But I'm eternally grateful to you, and you continually impress me, just by being yourself."

He waits silently, knowing more is coming.

"I just can't believe how much grace and compassion you have," I finally manage. "How big your heart is...that you can always find room in it, no matter who the person is."

"It doesn't matter who they are. Everyone deserves the same, Kat. When someone is dying in my hospital, when a family member is crying in the hall, when someone is *hurting*—like you—or him," he says, pointing back to the bayou house, "only kindness matters."

He meets my glistening eyes and reaches out to wipe the corner with his thumb.

"Kindness matters, Kat," Matthew repeats. "Love always leads with kindness."

And in his simple, Matthew way, he absolutely floors me.

I think of Abe, how he loves me. With kindness. And what it means to me.

It's how Matthew loves me too, I realize. With kindness and forgiveness and understanding. Even if he doesn't really understand and may not want to forgive, not everything. I mean, how could he? Like Paul always reminds me, there are some things you have to live through to fully understand. Even still, Matthew always tries, and he never, ever runs.

I remember what Lady Genevieve told me on New Year's Eve. It's not about what happened before him, it's only about what happens after. The differences don't matter if you don't let them.

And finally, Ray. *I want you to be able to say you chose your life, you didn't settle for it.*

For so long, I've been afraid there was this dark part of me Matthew could never possibly understand, that fundamentally, we're different. That the glitz of Matthew's world was a temporary, seductive escape from my own. That Paul, ultimately, was right—Matthew could never fully give me what I need.

But what do I need, truly?

He's standing right here. Right in front of me. Staying when anyone else would run.

Matthew. With his kindness and his wit and his courage and his grace. His eyes piercing through me, always seeing, always trying to understand. Figuring me out, one puzzle piece at a time, never looking away from the dark parts. Sharing his light with me, helping me find my own.

Of course I choose Matthew. How had I ever thought it could be anyone else? Because Matthew is the sun. Yes, I've always seen that, but it's by standing in his light now that I can finally see everything else.

"Do you know the moment I fell in love with you?" I ask quietly.

He shakes his head.

"When I saw you in the hospital, treating a perfect stranger with the same attention and care and love you show to your own family. And to me. That's when I knew I loved you beyond saving, beyond return. I'm sorry I didn't tell you, and I'm sorry for keeping secrets. You deserve far better, but you make me want to *be* better. You told me the other night you weren't running. Did you mean it?"

"Of course I meant it, Kat."

"Then I want to be very clear about something. I'm not some princess in an ivory tower or a lost girl in a bad situation. I'm not looking to be *saved*, Matthew. I love my life. I wouldn't change a thing about the path that led me here. Not one single thing. If I leave this life for you, it will be a *sacrifice*."

He nods.

"The reason I want to be clear about that is so you understand just how totally and completely in love with you I am. You aren't just an option to me, like you offered the other night. I'm not looking for options. But if you'll have me, I would very much like to be yours. There's nothing in this world I wouldn't give to be yours."

"Mine?" His gaze latches onto me, searing through with so much hope and love, I'm blinded.

"Yours and yours alone," I confirm.

I smile as he reaches for me. And when he kisses me—a blue blood boy and a bayou girl, in the middle of the cobblestone streets of Savannah—he grins against my lips and starts laughing. Whether with relief or happiness or God only knows what...either way, it's Matthew.

I smile and laugh back. Because I'm his.

CHAPTER TWENTY-EIGHT

I'M WORKING ON A functional modification to Cleopatra's cobra ring—one deemed necessary after recent events—when Ray calls from the storeroom. I drop the piece. It's near completion, near perfection.

"Can ya give me a hand, kid?" Ray grunts as he moves a few boxes around.

I move to help him. "What are you doing?"

"Just a little black-market inventory. Which reminds me..." He reaches into his pocket and pulls out one of his white envelopes. "Can you pass this along to Paul?"

I take it and peek inside. More cash. A lot. Way more than there should be, considering we aren't getting Magpie tribute anymore.

I shake my head. "What are you moving for him, Ray? Where is this scratch coming from?"

He rubs the back of his neck. "Just give him the money, Kat. Questions aren't a part of the deal."

"Is it drugs? Guns? Something worse?"

"Kat." He looks at me hard. "I'm just the bagman. You want answers? Go to the supplier."

I sigh and walk away, tucking the envelope into my jacket. I won't get anywhere with Paul. Especially not now. I should have tried to fuck it out of him months ago, when I had the chance.

Even still, I make a run to the bayou loft that evening to drop off the cash. I'm surprised but pleased to find Paul up and moving around the kitchen.

"Hey, how're you doing?" I ask, dropping my bag at the table. "You look good."

"I've been up for a few days, Kat. I even went outside with Tony yesterday. Which you'd know if you'd been around."

"Sorry." I drop my gaze to the table. "I wasn't sure how I'd be received if I just stopped by. But I come bearing gifts." I dig through my pockets and pull out the envelope.

"Thanks." He swipes the cash and heads for the bedroom.

I cautiously follow him. The bed is unmade, and I automatically start fixing it, tucking in sheets and fanning out the duvet. He watches me with amusement before heading to the safe in his closet. I wander around the room, absentmindedly tidying. My gaze lands on his bedside table, his signet ring still atop it.

When Paul emerges from the closet, he sighs. "Yeah, it's still there. Right where you left it. In case you ever decide to pick it back up."

"I don't think it's a good idea, Paul. We were ripping each other apart. I have questions you refuse to answer, and Matthew makes me happy. I'm sorry for how it happened, but you were right. I'm in love with him."

"You're in love with me too," Paul replies. "You're just choosing the easier life. The prettier one."

"I'm not. It's not that simple, Paul. The way you and I love each other...it's not a healthy kind of love. It's consuming and captivating, but it's not built to last. One way or another, it will end in flames. Whether it's like this—with me walking away—or with you bleeding out from another bullet in the street...I don't know how exactly, but this way is for the best. We're dangerous together."

"Maybe," he says, "but if I don't get to have you, I don't want him to have you either."

I laugh. "That's probably the most honest thing you've said to me in months. But the time to say it has come and gone. You should put the ring away, Paul, and we can lay this to rest."

He sighs but doesn't budge. "What are the new rules? Are you even allowed to be here? Does he know?"

"Not yet. But I'll tell him, and he won't mind. He's good like that."

"He's really willing to look the other way?" Paul scoffs. "We'll see how long that lasts."

"Stop." I put out a hand. "Stop right now. We're not going down this road, not ever again. Do you hear me? You don't know anything about Matthew, and you don't know anything about my relationship with him. You can either shut your mouth and be respectful so we can continue being friends, or you can keep talking, and I'll walk out that door and never return. I mean it, Paul. I'll leave, and I won't look back."

"I can keep my mouth shut," Paul mumbles.

"Really?"

He chews his lip, then sighs. "Yes."

"Okay, then let's play a few hands of poker. I'm in the mood to kick your ass."

———◦———

It's about two weeks later, near the end of January, that I finally crack the case of Paul, Ray, and the cash envelopes.

It starts out as just another Tuesday. Breakfast, classes, lunch with Mellie, off to Ray's for the afternoon. When I let myself in through the back door, I call out a greeting but don't get a response. I assume Ray is on the floor, so I head to my desk to deposit my things. Once I do, though, I notice a familiar satchel on the corner of my desk.

"Paul?" I call.

"Back here, Kat," he says from the storage room. "I'll be out in a sec."

"Okay." I go about setting up my things, bending over my desk, getting out my tools. I'm laying out my soldering equipment when it happens.

"Hey, Kitty-Kat," Paul says. He must have snuck up behind me, and his unexpected squeeze to my shoulder catches me off guard.

"Oh my god!" I cry, startled. I jump and accidentally knock his bag to the floor, scattering its contents. "Paul, you gave me a fright."

I bend over to help clean up the mess. He's very quick to sweep everything back in the bag, but not before I've seen something.

Something I know I wasn't supposed to.

"What's that?" My eyes burn with accusation. I yank the satchel from him and rip out the bag of powder.

"Kat..." He says my name like it's a warning, and I explode.

"What the hell is this?" I demand. "I told Matthew we don't move drugs. Are you making a liar out of me? Is this something we do now?"

"Kat," he tries again, but I take him out at the knees.

"We don't move drugs, Paul. That's *always* been our deal. We don't mess with this shit." I shake the tiny bag at him, madder than a wet hen. "We've never supported this part of the black market. It's twisted and it's dark and it ruins lives. So tell me—why do you have this? I'd think very carefully before answering if I were you."

"Come on, Kat. Don't be so damn naive. If I don't move 'em, someone else will." His eyes are hard. "And we can't have that. It's my bayou. I control it all."

"Not this," I hiss. "We don't control this. How long has it been going on?"

Paul is silent.

I nod, biting my cheek. "That long, huh?" I throw the bag at his feet. "All the extra cash that's been coming in from Ray—it's been for *this*? All year?"

"Yes," he finally answers.

"Who else knows?"

"Why does it matter?"

"I want to know if Abe knows."

"Oh, you mean boy toy number two? Or is he number three now? It's hard for me to keep them straight. Maybe you should ask him yourself."

"I will. And you're going to stop doing this. It cannot continue. This is so dangerous, Paul. So incredibly dangerous. Thefts and heists are one thing, this is a different beast entirely. One we can't control."

"Unfortunately, Kat, you're not my girl anymore. You don't get to tell me what I can and can't do."

"I'm just trying to look out for you. This won't lead to anything good." I can't believe how short his memory has proven to be. Mine is as indelible as ever. My mother...face down in the Catacombs...

"You're overreacting, doll."

"I don't think I am. You know who else was moving drugs?" I ask. "The Magpies. I saw it in their storeroom. The night you got shot."

"They were," he confirms.

I bite my cheek again as pieces fall into place. I'm so angry I could reach out and choke him. "I imagine you didn't like that, them encroaching on your turf?"

"No. I didn't like it at all. And I didn't like the guns either. They were getting very dangerous. And they hurt you. And Abe. And Farley. They deserved what happened."

"And you? Did you deserve to get shot? Was that the price you were willing to pay?"

"Better me than you or one of the other guys."

"So gallant," I mock.

"We've always had a code of honor, Kat. It's what makes us different from the other gangs. We look out for each other, no matter what. I'd take another bullet for any one of you. I'd take three, one each, if I had to."

I sigh, frustrated he can't see what I see. It's so simple. "Nobody has to take bullets for anyone anymore. Why don't you get that? We've made our money, enough for a lifetime. Enough for *two* lifetimes. We've done what we set out to do—made the splash we wanted, received the respect we were after. Now it's time to get out. There's nowhere to go from the top except down."

"We don't have to go anywhere. We can stay where we are. I'm handling it."

"Do you know how you win at gambling, Paul? By knowing when it's time to walk away."

He stares at me.

I wish I could get through to him, but I don't know how. I don't know how to reel him in this time. I look at the drugs on the floor between us and sigh again.

"I think you should stop this. I think this is a mistake," I whisper. "I'm asking you to stop."

He swallows as he considers me.

"Why do you feel like you need this?" I ask, searching deep in his dark eyes.

"Because, Kat, if I don't have this, what do I have? Not you, not anymore. What's been the point of all these years if I let it go now, with nothing to show for it?"

"You have plenty to show for it. And you still have me and Abe and Tony."

"I don't have you the way I want you."

I have no answer for that, so I bend over and scoop up the drugs. I put them in my pocket and pull my jacket on. Slowly. "You got any more drugs in that bag?"

"No."

"Let me see." I take it from him. "Fool me once Paul, shame on you. Fool me twice..."

I pull out a second bag and dangle it in front of him. He smiles at my use of his catchphrase.

"Nobody fools me, right? I'm taking these. You're not selling them."

He shrugs as I pocket the second bag. When I'm confident there's no more, I hand his satchel back.

"Satisfied, commandant?" He arches an eyebrow.

"For now. Will you at least think about what I said? Thefts and heists are one thing, Paul, but the drug trade is a dog fight. Don't drag your wolves into it."

"I'll think about it."

———◆———

I RUN ON ANGER and adrenaline all the way to the streetcar. When I sit down, however, I slowly deflate. By the time I'm unlocking the door to the loft, I'm exhausted. I emptied the drugs down a sewer drain before going up, and I feel like I aged ten years.

"Abe?" I call out.

"Yeah?" His voice sounds from his bedroom.

I rap my knuckles on the doorframe before entering.

"Hey, Kat." He picks up a joint from his desk, thumbing his lighter.

"Put that down and do not light it," I tell him firmly.

"Why?"

"I need to talk to you. And don't you work at the hospital tomorrow? You need to be careful with that shit."

"It's just hash, Kat. Geez." But he puts the joint down and collapses on the bed. "What's going on?"

I walk over and sit next to him. "I just ran into Paul at Ray's."

"And?"

"Did you know he's been moving drugs?" I watch Abe closely. He won't lie to me. When he sighs, I know.

"Not at first," he admits, "but yeah, I've known for a while. I figured you did too, after Farley's."

"What about Farley's?" My head snaps to attention.

"You heard Farley ask us to get the powder out. He wasn't comfortable with it. You heard me tell Paul."

"I thought he was talking about *gunpowder*. Are you saying Paul had drugs stashed at Farley's?" I'm aghast.

"Yeah." Abe shrugs. "Not a lot, but some."

I slap him on the forearm. "Why didn't you stop him?"

"Why didn't I? Why didn't *you*?"

"Because I didn't know! Not until now."

"You're the only one he listens to, Kat. All that stupid king and queen shit. Don't bullshit me and say you didn't know. You're a smart gal. You know one plus one doesn't equal five."

"All right, fair point, but Paul wouldn't tell me what he was doing. And you didn't tell me either."

"You were happy to look the other way and distract yourself with Matthew." He shakes his head. "Which only made it worse."

"Don't lecture me."

He throws his hands up. "What do you want me to say?"

"I want you to tell me how to fix this, Abe!"

"We *don't* fix this, Kat. This is broken. It's been heading this way for a long time, slowly picking up speed. That's why I took a job at the hospital. It's time for an extraction plan. I've been working on mine for a while. I hope you have a good one up your sleeve too. You're going to need it."

"This is such a mess," I moan.

Abe is silent. He glances at his joint with longing.

I roll my eyes. "Oh, just go ahead and light up if you want it that bad."

"No, I'll wait until you're feeling better."

"You'll be waiting forever then."

"Maybe you should take the first few puffs," Abe says. "It'll help."

I laugh and fall back on the bed. "Tempting, but no. I'm meeting Matthew tonight, and I don't want to show up half-baked."

"Why show up half-baked when you could be fully baked?"

"Abe!"

"Lighten up, Kat." He chuckles. "I'm teasing."

I manage a small smile, then sigh. "So what's your plan? For...extraction, did you call it?"

"There's the job, for one, and I'm getting a place of my own downtown. I toured a spot I like this morning, actually. I may sign the papers this weekend, just in case. Then there's my relationship with you, but I think we're going to be fine."

"We will be," I whisper.

"I've been talking to Tony too. Trying to nudge him in the same direction, because the implosion is coming. It's only a matter of time."

"I don't want things to change."

"Things were always gonna change, Kat. We just thought it would be a different kind of change. That you'd come back here to us after you finished at the Academy, screwing Paul every other night so we'd have to buy earplugs. That kind of change."

"I really made a mess of things, huh?"

"No, you didn't. You made the best choice you could for yourself. I told you before Christmas this life wasn't built to last. It's been great, a real rush, but you and I can't be climbing up buildings and sliding down drainpipes forever."

"I probably have a few more years left in me, if I want to," I observe.

"Maybe, maybe not. But you don't *have* to. Whether you realize it or not, you've been working on an extraction plan too. Matthew is a good man. He'll treat you right. Better than Paul, in the long run."

"Paul always treated me fine." I feel oddly defensive.

"You really think so? You think sharing you with me when he was feeling adventurous equates to taking care of you? Matthew's not interested in sharing, right? He wants all of you."

"That's not fair," I say, frowning. "Paul was only willing to share me with *you*. It was an exception, not the rule."

"And lying to you about moving drugs? Using you for jobs when it was convenient for him? Without listening to your concerns when you didn't feel good about it—like the Magpie hit? You think that equates to taking care of you?"

"There were problems, of course, but I still care about him. He's not a bad person, so don't vilify him."

"I'm not. Paul is one of my best mates, but he never fully appreciated what he had with you. Now it's time to face the music. Remember the bedtime adventure story we used to read when we were kids, *Peter and Wendy*?" He looks at me, and I nod. "How does it end, Kat?"

I'm silent.

"Peter loses Wendy."

The words fill me with terrible sadness, but Abe isn't wrong.

"I'm not one of Peter's Lost Boys any longer," he continues. "I'm not going down with this ship when it sinks. I hope you don't plan to either."

"Believe me, I don't."

"Did you have a good day, darling?" I ask as Matthew steps into his kitchen after a shift that evening.

"I did." Amusement flickers in the lift of his brow. "Are you cooking?"

"I am. I'm trying my hand at domesticity." I step back from the stove and cock my hip. I'm wearing a horrifically frilly apron I found shoved away in one of his cupboards. "What do you think?"

"I think it's the culmination of every fantasy I've ever had about you." He laughs. "Although, if I truly had my druthers, you'd be wearing the apron and nothing else."

I laugh and return to the stove, stirring in the pot, around and around, as Matthew trots over.

"So what's for supper, my darling domestic Katarina?"

"Buttered noodles."

"Dilly. Super domestic. They teach you that at the Academy?"

"I dropped out of home ec before we got to the really fun parts," I admit, pulling a joking face. "I could call Florence though, and she could probably put together a roast."

He laughs again. "Noodles will be fine."

"Good." I grab a bowl and dish out a hulking portion for him. He takes it to the table and starts inhaling it.

"How was your day?" he asks between bites.

"It was good. I ran into Paul at Ray's shop this afternoon..." I trail off, the drugs looming large. So dangerous.

"What was he doing there?"

"Oh, Ray runs a black market out of the back of his shop a few evenings a week," I say offhandedly. "Paul uses him to move some of our stuff. It's how I got my position there."

"What?" He looks up from his bowl, surprised.

"You said yourself that Ray's is a prestigious place to intern. Well, he'd never apprenticed an Academy girl before. He only took me on because he had a very specific and vested interest."

"Huh." Matt slurps his last noodle. "Ray is pretty old these days, isn't he?"

"Pushing past sixty, I gather."

"Is he going to retire soon?"

"I don't know. I've never really thought about it. He's like one of those ancient tortoises, you know? The ones that live forever, just plodding along, spending their days in the same sunspot for all eternity. I can't imagine him going anywhere or doing anything else."

Matthew laughs. "I was only wondering because you seem ideally placed to take over for him someday. If you want."

I put my fork down. "You think I could run Ray's?"

"Why not? I'm sure you could. He doesn't have kids, so whenever he calls it quits, he'll have to close up shop."

"I don't particularly enjoy front-of-house sales though. Ray keeps me in the back, making pieces, both real and forgeries. It's what I'm good at."

"So you hire someone to run the floor. It wouldn't be challenging. Hold on...did you say forgeries?"

"Yeah, black market out of the back room, remember? And jewel thief?" I point to myself. "It's not exactly an honest operation all the time over there. I'm good at what I do, trust me. Ray trained me himself."

"Christ, Kat, I don't doubt it. I just...there's this whole other world out there I didn't even know existed before I met you. Sometimes, it feels like a sinkhole, getting bigger and bigger and sucking everything into it. You duel in gunfights by night, make forgeries by day, scale walls to break into my friends' houses in your free time...it's far from needlepoint, that's for sure."

"Most of those things are Paul's idea of fun. Paul's plans."

"That *you* execute."

"Yes."

"He couldn't do anything worthwhile without you," Matthew says. "He's not going to let you walk away, Kat."

I don't have a response. Because per usual, I'm worried Matthew is exactly right.

CHAPTER TWENTY-NINE

THINGS GO FROM BAD to worse at the end of the week. I'm walking through the Academy halls between lessons when a sight ahead freezes my blood.

Paul. In the hallway. Wearing a three-piece suit and shaking hands with Lady Genevieve.

Paul. *Here.* Inside the Academy. With *Matthew's mother*.

Paul has undoubtedly seen me; he can sniff me out from a mile away. As the halls empty, I make eye contact and jerk my head. He follows me down a side corridor, into an unsecured maintenance closet. It's not ideal, but it's private.

"Are. You. Insane?" I hiss, clicking the lock on the door.

"Maybe." He gives me a shifty grin. The kind that used to drive me wild with excitement, made me wonder what adventure he was dreaming up next.

Now I just feel sick.

"Why are you here?"

"You're looking at the Academy's newest top tier donor," he announces proudly.

"You didn't..." My eyes widen. "*Why* would you do that?"

"Why shouldn't I?" He shrugs. "I'm a charitable man, Kat, and I have more money than I can count. Besides, I've seen firsthand the doors this place opens for young women." His voice is dripping with smarm by the end of his little speech.

"How noble." I fold my arms across my chest. "Now tell me the real reason."

"Come on, Kat. You've been around these people long enough to know how they operate. They can smell money from a mile away. The only thing better than hoarding wealth for themselves is leveraging it amongst their crowd. After I wrote Genevieve a hefty check for the Academy, she very kindly extended an invitation to one Jekyll Island for the annual Ides of March ball. Said philanthropic opportunities would abound at the event, and she would simply *love* to introduce me to her many charitable friends."

"You're after Jekyll Island," I say, understanding. "Still? After all this time?"

"It's a prize like no other, Katarina. But I haven't even gotten to the best part. Have you heard what the theme of this year's ball is?"

I don't like the gleam in his eye. "No."

"*Bejeweled* Ides of March. The theme this year is *jewels*, Kat. As many as the upper crust can stuff on their fingers and around their necks. There will be priceless pieces at that party, family heirlooms and new money extravagances alike. Think of the opportunities."

"You want to come to the ball," I say, nodding, "because of the jewelry."

"One piece of jewelry, Katarina. A necklace that, word on the street, is going to come out of the DaMolin vault for the first time in nearly a quarter of a century, making a special appearance at a special event. How can I possibly pass up an opportunity like that?"

"What?" I gasp, feeling his interest shift from professional to personal. "You want to steal the DaMolin rubies?"

"Of course I do."

I breathe deeply, in and out. Fight to keep my panic at bay.

Matthew and I talked about the rubies the very first day we met. The piece is renowned in the jewel world, a reclusive legacy item, passed down in the family for generations. Paul has never hidden his lust for the jewels, but somehow—perhaps naively—I assumed things were different now, that he would never ask this of me.

"Why?" I finally ask. "You just admitted you have more money than you can count. You don't need this. This is Matthew's *family* you're talking about, Paul. This isn't a heist, it's revenge. You're too close to this con to see clearly. You're going to bring the entire house of cards crashing down around us."

"I assure you, Katarina, my mind is crystal clear. I know exactly what I'm doing. We'll talk more about it later at Ray's. I'll wait there for you this afternoon."

"And if I don't show up?"

"You will. You could never resist a jewel heist. It's your specialty, and this one's a doozy. Besides, I thought you'd be happy. You're the one who told me I should get out of the drug game and go back to our usual gigs."

"I did say that, didn't I?" I narrow my eyes.

"I'm just trying to give you what you wanted, doll."

———◆———

TRUE TO HIS WORD, Paul is waiting with the shopkeeper in the back room of Raymond's when I arrive. I'm still heated from our encounter at the Academy, but I'm also frightened. The thought of stealing from Matthew and his family makes me sick.

"Nice of you to show up, Kitty-Kat." Paul checks his watch. "Running a few minutes late, aren't you?"

"Be thankful I'm here at all, Paul."

"Come on, I know your fingers are twitching, same as mine. This is an heirloom piece, Kat. One of the biggest in the jewel industry."

Ray stands by, listening, but at this statement, he offers a small nod.

"My fingers aren't twitching. This is a big ask. This is dangerous."

"It's no more dangerous than the job at Astor Manor," Paul counters. "Actually, I'd argue this is *less* dangerous. It's a simple bait and switch. You'll make a forgery, and the night of the ball, we'll pull the swap. We've done it a million times. No one will even bat an eye."

I stare at him, thinking. Looking for a way out that won't bring Paul's notorious wrath down on me. Or worse, on Matthew.

"You know you and I can easily do this together," he says.

He's right; I do know it. That's exactly the problem.

"This is the necklace, Kat." Ray passes me a society newspaper clipping with a photograph, and I give it a cursory glance. It's a picture of Matthew's parents dancing at their wedding. The necklace is massive, a traditional loop of diamonds interspersed with five ovular rubies. Vertical spokes drop off each blood-red gem, more diamonds alternating with two more rubies. Per spoke. Times five.

"There are *fifteen* rubies on this necklace. It's massive. I need a lot more information than this photograph to pull off a forgery for a piece like this. I need specs and reports and a million more photos..." I lift my hand to my forehead, overwhelmed.

"Well, lucky for you, I have the specs," Ray replies.

"Horsefeathers." I snort. "It's impossible—that piece is on its third generation."

"My grandfather was commissioned for that necklace in England, Kat. It was one of the biggest pieces he ever made, and it put him—and our family name—on the map. The rubies came from Queen Victoria's collection. I have all the original reports in my files. You'll have everything you need."

"See?" Paul slaps his hand on his thigh. "I told you we can do this."

"There are going to be dozens of security guards and a hundred people at that ball, Paul. How on earth are we going to steal that necklace?"

"Oh, I don't think it'll be challenging at all."

"Really?" My tone turns biting. "You think you'll just waltz out the front door with it?"

"Yes." He sticks his hands in his pocket and peers at me.

"How can you possibly believe it will be so easy?"

"Because someone at that ball is going to be wearing the necklace, Kat. And I'm fairly confident your little boyfriend will make sure it's hanging around *your* pretty neck."

Matthew.

"And if it's not?" My voice is deadly soft now.

Paul shrugs. "You'll find a way to make sure it is. I know you, Kat. It won't even be hard. You can charm the dew right off a honeysuckle."

I raise an eyebrow. "If I refuse?"

"Ray, would you give Kat and me a minute?" Paul says, glancing at the jeweler.

Ray shifts his weight, uneasy.

"I just want to talk to her privately." Paul raises his hands.

"You okay, kid?" Ray checks with me.

I cross my arms. "I'm fine. Go."

"Katarina." Paul sighs once Ray departs. "Why is everything such a struggle lately?"

I shake my head. "I want out, Paul. We used to take controlled risks because we needed to. Then we upped the stakes because we wanted to. But it's not fun anymore, and it's far from necessary. I don't want any part of this."

"If it wasn't the DaMolin family," Paul says, glaring at me, "you'd be singing a different tune. You accused me of being too close to this, but the truth is, *you* are. You're blind to this opportunity because of your feelings.

That's a rookie mistake, Kat. The oldest in the book. You're too skilled for me to stand by and watch you make it."

I drop the newspaper clipping on my desk. "A forgery like this will take inordinate time and resources. And for what? Say we get the necklace, what then? Those rubies would be too hot to even consider moving. How would you ever find a buyer?"

"I found one for *The Dancer* faster than you could blink. It's not about the money, Kat. We don't *need* this, but I *want* it."

"For what? Some kind of trophy?"

He shrugs. "If it was the old days, you wouldn't even have to ask. We'd steal the necklace together, you'd put it on in my bedroom, and you'd let me make love to you wearing it. All night long."

"Well, *that* is certainly not going to happen, so if that's the end game, I'm afraid you're going to be sadly disappointed."

We're quiet for a moment, staring at each other.

"You really want out?" Paul finally asks.

My heartbeat picks up. "I really do."

"Fine. Do this job with me, then you're free. I'll cut you loose, and I won't ask for anything again. If it's truly what you want."

I lick my lips. Tempted.

"I'm serious. You wanna escape scot-free with your nine lives? This is it, Kitty-Kat. The last job. We should go out with a bang, shouldn't we?"

"Can we pick another job?" I ask weakly.

"No." He shakes his head. "This is it—the ultimate heist. If you're going to have a last, this should be it."

I think for a few minutes, but I still feel absolutely sick about it. I could say yes, appease him, but then what? If I steal from Matthew's family, he'll know who did it. And he'll never forgive me. I could try to make a fake so perfect, they'd never know...but even if I succeeded and the necklace went back in the vault for another twenty-five years, there would always be a festering secret between us.

No more secrets.

Paul must realize I'm still not convinced, because he pulls his trump card. "Okay, I'll sweeten the deal, Kitty-Kat...or sour it, depending on your view."

"How?" I frown.

Paul leans in close. His breath is hot on my cheek as he whispers, "I know where your saintly little boyfriend lives. I know where he works. How and when he goes back and forth. I know where his family lives. Where you like to go out together. I know it all. Need I go on?"

I inhale sharply. The walls close in.

"You're at my mercy, Kat. I think I'd take the deal if I were you. Before the terms change."

"Fine." There's no other option.

He leans back. "Smart girl."

"But this is it. After this, you leave Matthew and me alone. I want your word."

"You have it," he promises. "You know I'm good for it. Part of the code."

"Then let's quit piddlin' and get Ray back in here. This is going to take weeks, so I need to start straight away. The ball is in March."

"Done." Before he walks away, he gives me one final look. "Don't try to get cute with this job, doll. I want that necklace, and you're going to get it for me."

CHAPTER THIRTY

THE WORK ON THE DaMolin rubies is all-consuming, a massive undertaking that monopolizes all my free time. I tell Matthew that Paul has his sights on a new con, but it'll be the last one. It's my ticket out. When he asks for details, I'm vague.

"There's a job in a few weeks," I tell him. "A heist. Paul has me working on something for it, that's why I'm pulling such long hours at Ray's. But it'll be over by mid-March, and this is his price—one final job and I get to walk. For good."

Matthew's jaw ticks, the pieces clicking into place. He knows the Ides of March ball is in a few weeks; he's already invited me to be his date. I don't know if he connects the dots all the way to his own family, but I've given him enough for now.

Over the course of the month, the necklace is pieced together before my eyes. Additional photographs and reports reveal the main strand of the necklace is three rows of tiny diamonds, each cut to the same exacting microscopic specifications. It's a replication nightmare in the sense of tediousness, but the real challenge comes with the rubies. Duplicating the cut, color, and clarity of those elliptical gems is a large-scale challenge. Not to mention attempting to account for each tiny inclusion and flaw. While I work, my mind is constantly churning, trying to figure out if I'm really going to go through with this.

If I don't, what options do I have?

Paul stops by every week to check my progress, and his overbearing presence reminds me just how trapped I am. I've taken to wearing Cleopatra's completed cobra ring while I work. The engraved cartouche of her name on the underside of the deadly serpent's belly brings intangible comfort.

I'm working late at the shop near the end of February when an epiphany hits. I'm focused on my fingers, carefully prepping and securing tiny diamond after tiny diamond in the fifth spoke. I pull back to examine my work, impressed against my own will at what I see. When I zero back in, staring at my nails working the tiny gems, my vision starts to blur. I blink, trying to clear it, but my mind is elsewhere.

I think about Matthew, about his hands. How he told me they were so important to him. How he talked about choosing what work we do with our hands, choosing the kind of difference we make. I look into the emerald eyes of Cleopatra's cobra—at my own nimble fingers, which are slowly and carefully bringing the counterfeit ruby necklace to life—and I wonder what kind of difference I'm going to make with this.

Not a good one.

My hands are mine, he told me. *I decide what kind of difference they make.*

I put the necklace down. I look at my fingers, now trembling, and I start to rethink.

Recalculate. Recalibrate. Replan.

I decide. *I* choose.

And I don't choose this. Not anymore.

My hands are mine and so is my brain. And those are two things Paul doesn't own, doesn't control. Not anymore.

I can make a different kind of difference. I only hope I have enough time to do it.

Nearly a week later, the daily routine endures. Once my morning lessons at the Academy conclude, I hurry to Ray's, mechanically pull out the DaMolin rubies, and immerse myself. Hours pass. My eyes are so tired.

"Looking good, Kat," Ray proclaims over my shoulder. I jump and drop the tiny diamond in my tweezers.

"Ray! You startled me." I hunt for the fallen stone.

"You need to take a break, kid," Ray says, reaching out to still my fumbling hands. "You're going cross-eyed."

I sit back and drop the tweezers, blinking rapidly.

Ray plunks his drafting book on the corner of my workstation. He's been sketching. Engagement rings. I reach for the book, intrigued.

"They're for next season's line," he mutters as I flip through his work. "What do you think?"

He has five pages of designs, three rings apiece. The third and fourth pages display my favorites.

"These ones." I trace my finger over the charcoal rings. "These are really special. Very new."

"I've decided the oval is the shape for next season."

"It's beautiful...and the star halo here?" I point. "Absolutely divine. You're a virtuoso, Ray."

He tears a piece of paper from the back of the book and drops it in front of me. "There's room in the line for three more. I want you to design them."

"What?"

"You're graduating in two months. You're not going to be an apprentice much longer. I can't very well keep you hidden back here forever, tinkering away on whatever my latest fantasy is."

"I don't even know where to begin."

"Sure you do. You're full of ideas, good ones. And you've more than paid your dues." He nods at the mess on my desk, indicating my latest project. The one that has me headed for a straitjacket.

"Speaking of, would you like to take a look?" I stand to offer him my seat. "I could use a fresh set of eyes."

I hold my breath as he pulls out his loupe. He cranks up the light overhead, and his face descends into squinty-eyed concentration. He examines every gem on the necklace, assesses every millimeter. When he removes his loupe, he lifts the piece on one finger, checking for balance and weight.

"It's not quite done," I remind him.

"Pretty darn near, Kat." He dims the light and looks closely at me. "How did you do this? This is incredible work—it's near perfect. I can barely tell the difference, and I've been at this a long time. Plus, I know what I'm looking for."

I exhale, relieved. "Just...you know, working hard."

"I've always known you had an eye, kid, but this...this is next level."

"Thanks," I murmur.

"Now tell me what your plan is."

"My...my plan?"

"Yeah. Are you really gonna fork over the real necklace to Paul? Or is something else at play?"

I reach for the back of the chair, seeking support. I don't reply.

"You're a smart girl, Kat," he tells me, rising. "I'm very interested to see what you do here. Whatever Paul comes back with that weekend, I'll look at it closely."

"And what will you say if it's not what you expect?"

"I'm not sure. Should I expect any surprises?"

I shake my head.

"Regardless, I hope you know I'll still expect you for work that Monday. No longer as an apprentice. A partner, with real jobs from here on out. This is excellent," he says, gesturing to the rubies, "but it's a waste of your talent."

"Make it Tuesday," I bargain. "I think I've earned a day off."

"Tuesday it is, but I want those ring sketches two days from now. Welcome to the big leagues, kid."

"Ray?" I call out as he lumbers away.

"Yeah?"

"I'll be wanting a raise." I smile. "From my usual cut."

His eyes twinkle. "You got it, girl."

CHAPTER THIRTY-ONE

THE MONTH OF MARCH roars in like a lion, all bluster and humid rain-storms. The azalea bushes throughout the city bloom in full force.

Unfortunately, I'm scarcely outside to appreciate them. I stop seeing Matthew regularly, rarely finishing my work at Ray's before midnight. Mellie leaves the window open for me every evening, but she can hardly hide her concern in the morning. The shadows under my eyes become permanently etched.

We're one week into the month when she stages an intervention.

"Kat, are you on drugs?" Mellie asks, genuine concern in her tone.

I laugh her off, insist I'm fine. Or I will be soon.

One more week, I promise both Mellie and myself. I throw her a gilded bone—I've secured an invitation for her to the Ides of March ball. As Captain Ethan DaMolin's date, no less.

Mellie's ear-piercing shriek of excitement could crack glass. I manage a smile as she twirls away, floating on clouds straight to my closet where she begins pulling out gowns. Wondering what on earth she'll wear—from my collection, evidently—to the party of the year on Jekyll Island.

Five days out from the ball, I stop sleeping. Three days out is when I go off food. In the final twenty-four hours, my hands develop a tremor that won't go away.

I'm wide-awake, lying in my Academy bed, when the hallowed morning of Saturday, March fifteenth dawns. I rise with the sun, pull on a dress, and out the window I go. Matthew is due to pick Mellie and me up at noon to travel to Jekyll Island, and I need to go to Ray's this morning.

The shop is still dark when I arrive. I flick on the lights in the workroom and head straight to my desk. I unlock the drawer with the DaMolin rubies. I place them on the table and give everything a thorough once-over with my loupe. Then another. And another. Checking for perfection. My heart pounds with each scan, praying no eleventh-hour problem materializes.

When I'm satisfied, I dig out a polishing cloth and start buffing. Over and over and over, compulsively. Over and over and over again.

Today...this necklace...everything needs to go perfectly. No room for error.

Today, several millennia ago on the Ides of March, a lover of Cleopatra was felled by a blade. A dictator. Julius Caesar.

Tonight, I'm aiming to take down a despot of my own.

———◆———

WHEN MATTHEW, MELLIE, AND I arrive at the Jekyll Island Club, there's a croquet game on the great lawn. The participants are all dressed in white, whacking away at a set of pastel balls.

"It's all very prim and proper, isn't it?" I point to the game with a chuckle. "Like an advertisement in a magazine."

"Indeed," Matthew concedes. "Aside from the fact they've likely put ridiculous wagers on the outcome. Family fortunes don't spend themselves, you know."

My chuckle turns into a full-fledged laugh.

"Oh look, Ethan is on the veranda." Matthew points, then taps the back of the front seat to catch the driver's attention. "Excuse me, could you let us out here?"

Mellie perks up, scanning the porch for her escort.

"What?" My laughter dies instantly. "Matt, no. What about our things, our bags?"

"He'll deliver them to Cherokee Cottage," Matt replies, nodding at the driver. "Don't fret."

"But...but...my dress..." I say weakly. It's not the dress I'm concerned about. It's the DaMolin rubies. The forgery is burning a hole in my luggage; I don't want to let it out of my sight.

Matt smiles indulgently. "Your gown will be fine, Katarina. Let's introduce Mellie and have a lemonade with Ethan. There are hours to kill until the ball. We'll walk to Cherokee to get ready later this afternoon."

He doesn't wait for my response; he's already opening his car door, walking around to mine. Reluctantly, I follow him into the sunshine.

After introductions are complete, we sip lemonade on the porch with Ethan for the next hour, chatting and making outlandish projections as we observe the croquet match. I notice Harry Astor among the players. I haven't spoken to him since New Year's Eve, since the night I walked in on him and Ethan together. I casually point him out, but Ethan gives no reaction. Mellie, naturally, is blissfully unaware, all pink cheeks and puckered lips as she sucks down her second glass of lemonade with contented vigor.

"Yes, I believe Harry has been on the island this whole week," Matthew says, looking to his brother for confirmation. "Have you seen much of him, Ethan?"

"Hardly," Ethan replies, smooth. "I've been locked up in Cherokee going over accounts with Dad. I believe Harry has been quite busy though. His cousins are visiting for the ball." He points to two white-clad gentlemen beside Harry.

Less than a half hour later, the game breaks up. Most of the players slip past us to enter the clubhouse, but the Astors remain on the lawn. Harry shades his face to gaze at us. His eyes glide over Ethan with practiced ignorance, but they land on me with distaste. His posture coils tight.

Matt and Ethan lean over the porch railing as they chat, oblivious to the fast-approaching storm cloud that is Harry. His footsteps *thud* up the veranda steps. Mellie puts her empty glass of lemonade on the railing and moves to my side.

"Matt?" I reach for his arm, a bit anxious. "Perhaps we should—"

"Still slumming it, Matthew?" Harry asks. He flicks his eyes over me as he peels off white leisure gloves. "Is your little Catacomb toy really that good a fuck?"

I blink twice, shocked by the unprovoked vitriol. His aggression slices through the humid air.

Matthew rises and steps forward. I reach to stop him, but it's Ethan who gets there first, firmly pressing a hand to his brother's chest, halting him. His gaze slides over to Harry with confusion.

"Is that what you like, Matt?" Harry continues, prowling forward. "Paying a slut to get you off? How much does she charge per fuck? I hope you're getting a deal." He slides a hand in his pocket, produces a flask, and takes a long swig.

Ah, well, that explains it. I eye the alcohol warily, understanding all too well what fuel like that does to a smoldering fire.

Heat flames Matthew's cheeks. "If you utter one more vile word against her," he growls, glowering, "I'll—"

"Yes, that's quite enough, Harry," Ethan jumps in, keeping the restraining hand on his brother's chest. "How much have you had to drink?"

"Stay out of this, E," Harry drawls. "I'm talking to your brother, not you. It's not your fault he has piss-poor taste."

"He can't help it," one of Harry's cousins says. "It's in his blood. His mother was a courtesan, after all."

"That's right." Harry's eyes light up. "Guess the apple doesn't fall far from the tree, huh, Matthew? Like father, like son. The DaMolin men sure love their trash."

As soon as the comment about their father is uttered, Ethan drops his arm from Matthew's chest. Both men rush forward, and neither Mellie nor I try to stop them.

Matthew collides with Harry. Ethan targets the Astor cousin who spoke. I stare for a moment, astonished, as fists fly. It's not that I'm unaccustomed to a good scuffle—far from it—but it's hardly something I was prepared for today. This isn't a back alley of the bayou, for Christ's sake. It's the Jekyll Island Club.

Matthew delivers a sharp blow to Harry's left eyebrow before being hauled off by an Astor cousin. Ethan takes two blows to his side before getting a hit in edgewise.

I crack the knuckles on my right hand as I observe and consider. It's three versus two, which simply won't do. Mellie flounders and gasps beside me, a wind-up toy running circles at full steam. Ineffective.

"For the record," I announce, "I want it stated…I didn't start this fight, but I'm not above finishing it."

No one is listening. Fine. They will be in a minute. After ascertaining there are no bystanders in the vicinity, I throw myself into the fray.

I grab the man's shoulder who has Ethan in a lock and yank him back. I snatch his wrist and give a sharp flick, flipping him forward onto the floor. I turn my attention to Harry as he lands a glancing blow off the corner of Matthew's jaw.

Target: Harry Astor.

"Enough." I rip him away by the biceps while delivering a swift kick to the back of his knees. He drops like a sack of flour, but I'm not done with him. I yank backward, wrenching his arm in a way designed to *zing* in its socket. I shove his spine into the wall of the clubhouse with the full, explosive power of my anger. I raise my arm to lock him in across the neck. Behind me, Matthew and Ethan stand over the Astor cousins, victorious.

Mellie shakes out her fist as though she's thrown a delicate punch of her own, a secret smile of satisfaction playing on her lips.

"God, Kat you are such a bitch." Harry spits out the insult as though he expects it to hurt.

Adorable.

"You're right," I say. "I am. With one key distinction—I'm the special kind of bitch they only breed in the Catacombs."

I pull back and sink my fist into his gut, doubling him over, followed by a swift knee to the balls as he drops, just for good measure.

Paul would call it an object lesson. And I know to make sure it hurts.

———————◆———————

IT TAKES A LITTLE explaining on the walk home to Cherokee before Ethan is willing to let it go.

"You just decked him...absolutely leveled him. How did you do that?"

I shrug. "Ethan, don't worry about it. I've always been able to take care of myself."

"I'll say."

The four of us promenade along the walking path that loops the property, linking the cottages and clubhouse together. Spanish moss cascades romantically from the ageless oak trees. A few strolling couples mill about; the nearest pair holds a parasol to block the midday sun. In the corner of my vision, I notice Matthew's mouth is bleeding. I pass him a cocktail napkin to dab away the evidence.

"Well, you're officially in now, Kat. Just in case there was any doubt before," Ethan continues.

"In what?" I ask absentmindedly, distracted by Matthew spitting blood into the grass. I slap his arm and point to an approaching passerby. He straightens quickly, chastised.

"You're one of us," Ethan clarifies. "You're a DaMolin. One hundred percent."

I pause, snapping my eyes to him as I remember the last time someone said something like that to me. Abe, when I was six years old, declaring I was a wolf, just like him. A Royal.

Ethan watches the burst of emotion flash over my face. "If he doesn't marry you," he continues, jerking his head toward his brother, "I will. I want you on our team."

"You most certainly do," Mellie purrs her assent.

I nod and blink quickly, trying to bury the emotion stirring deep inside me. The feeling of belonging to something. To a whole greater than the sum of its parts. What that means to me.

"I'm going to marry her, dick." Matthew spits into the napkin this time. It's only passably more subtle.

"Matthew?" I turn to him, forcibly ignoring the flutter in my stomach at his unexpected but casual mention of marriage. "Do you need ice when we get to the house? Would that help?"

"No, I'm fine. It'll stop bleeding soon. The mouth is a highly vascular area of the body, like the rest of the head. It will clot imminently—the intrinsic cascade takes a few minutes to kick in before establishing a decent platelet plug."

"At ease, doc," Ethan mutters.

The parasol-toting couple is less than ten feet away now.

"Shall we?" I formally slide my arm back into Matthew's.

To my surprise, Ethan takes my other arm, anchoring me between them. Mellie is tucked securely to his opposite side, chin up and hat tilted to keep the sun out of her eyes. The men walk slowly, genteel grins pasted to their faces. Not a hair out of place. No one would ever suspect the four of us were just involved in a brawl. Instead, we drift along the walking path like a respectable unit. A quad of con artists in their own right, no one the wiser.

It's not the unit I'm used to, certainly, but as I chance a glance to my left at Ethan and Mellie, another to my right for Matthew, I decide something.

It's not a bad trade-off. Not a bad trade-off at all.

CHAPTER THIRTY-TWO

MY LIPS BLEED GARNET red. Green eyes lined with black coal. My dark hair is pulled back in a sleek twist, swept away from my face and neck.

My fingers are—for once—wholly bare, save a thick, decorative silver band I crafted in Ray's shop to cover my tattoo.

My evening gown is black and drop-waisted with ornate obsidian beadwork shimmering down its barrel length. A low, scooped neckline graces the front, plunging deeper than deep across my back, bare skin cleverly muted by a trailing sheer cape cascading from my shoulders to brush a quarter-inch on the floor. It whispers behind my heels, sensual and mysterious, as I walk. The cut of the gown is just loose enough to conceal two deep, silk-lined pockets at my waist.

It's within those pockets I place my plunder—the forged DaMolin rubies. Hundreds of hours of impossibly hard work dropped unceremoniously into the lining of a skirt. It's irreverent.

"Come in," I call when a knock sounds at the door.

Matthew leans on the doorframe, arms crossed, open appreciation filling his blue eyes. "Kat, you are stunning. So beautiful."

So is he. His blond hair is swept back and tamed, flipping out in adorable curls over his collar. His white bow tie and dark evening tailcoat are crisp and sharp, black patent shoes shining on his feet. And his smile is, as always, radiant.

I cross the room to join him. "Shall we proceed downstairs to meet your family?"

He shakes his head. "Not yet. I have something to give you. Something for you to wear tonight." He takes my hand to lead me from the room, going deeper into the second floor of Cherokee Cottage. My heart accelerates—anxiety, trepidation, and excitement rolled into one.

Matthew pauses at an innocuous door at the end of the hallway. "This is the vault. Ethan locked me in here once during a game of hide-and-seek when I was four. I screamed for hours, but it's soundproof. Mom was livid when she finally found me."

"I bet," I reply, breathless, as he slides a brass key into the lock.

The vault is brightly lit, as luminous as the front room of Ray's shop. Full length mirrors dominate an entire wall; a row of white drawers and compartments stands opposite. Glass cases are stacked in a back corner, and I squint, tempted to behold the treasures therein. Matthew distracts me when, with a flourish, he opens a long, flat drawer to our right.

I'm dazzled by the gemstones hidden within. Necklaces, rings, earrings, bracelets...glittering in every color of the rainbow and all tucked snugly into black velvet.

I laugh. "Matt, I'm not certain I should be in here."

"Believe me, I know. Keep your sticky fingers to yourself," he teases as he slides the drawer shut. I fold my hands before me, prim. He laughs.

"You know diamonds are my Achilles' heel," I point out. "And there are an awful lot of them in this room."

"There are," he agrees. "You'll be wearing some tonight."

My heart hammers as he crouches down. He produces another key to open a low drawer. When it slides open, I finally see them. In the flesh.

The DaMolin rubies.

I blink and hold my breath as Matthew lifts them out.

"Turn around," he tells me.

I do. In the reflection of the mirror, I watch a very intentional, sure-fingered Matthew DaMolin slide the ruby necklace around the throat of a wide-eyed woman. Only their weight grounds me in the moment, the unexpected coolness of the gems resting heavily against my décolletage.

Matthew and I lock eyes in the mirror, blue meeting green.

"No one has worn this necklace for more than twenty-five years, not since my mother on her wedding day. Do you know what it is?"

"I do," I admit.

"Then you know what it means. And you know there's no one else in the world I'd want wearing this tonight."

"Are you certain?" My tone is slow, measured. "You really want to put these rubies around the neck of a jewel thief?"

"I'm certain. Besides, it's what you need from me, right?" He looks meaningfully at me. Once again, he has me all figured out.

"Paul is going to be here tonight," I whisper.

"I assumed."

I release his eyes in the mirror to look down at the dangling jewels.

"He wants me to put these around your neck. He's expecting it," Matthew says. "And he's right. I am. These rubies mean something intangible to my family, Kat, and tonight, I'm giving them to you. I trust you to keep them safe."

He steps back, and I continue staring in the mirror. The weight of the forged gems throbs in my skirt pocket.

"You look beautiful, Kat," he murmurs. "You wear them well."

And then I watch in the mirror as he drops to one knee behind me. My jaw slackens, my eyes wide with astonishment. His own stay locked on me.

"Turn around," he whispers.

As I do, he pops open a ring box.

"Kat, I love you. Completely, irrevocably. I haven't been able to stay away since the minute we met. I want to spend the rest of my life being surprised by you. Loving you in new ways every single day. I'd sell my soul over and over again, sell it for all it's worth, to be worthy of your heart. Katarina Quinn, will you marry me?"

My legs go weak. It's a life-altering moment, seeing this tuxedoed man on bended knee before me, the weight of the world around my neck. A life-altering question. A question with only one answer.

"Yes."

And he smiles. Oh, how that man smiles! He smiles so big and so dazzling and so full of light, it hits me square in the face. Like gazing into the sun, I'm blinded. Heated and captivated all at once.

My left hand is trembling when I hold it out to him. He slides the ring onto my finger.

I blink rapidly, wholly unprepared.

"Do you like it?" Matt asks.

"I...I can't even see it," I admit with a laugh. I look up at the ceiling and continue blinking to clear my swimming vision. The lights are bright, so I close my eyes. When I finally recover, Matthew is still on the ground, still smiling, pushing my hand up so I can see.

I swallow, recognition dawning. "It's one of Ray's, from the new line...this hasn't even been produced yet. How on earth did you get it?"

"It's never going to be produced, Kat." He stands up. "Ray pulled it from the line. It's called the Katarina, and this is the only one that will ever be made. It's yours."

"Oh my god." I study the ring, recalling its charcoal-sketched predecessor. The stone is a colossal, ovular diamond surrounded by a double star halo, jutting out like rays of sunshine. It's a work of art.

"Do you like it?"

"I love it. You chose perfectly."

"Well, I had a little help. Ray designed half the new line with you in mind, so I couldn't go wrong."

"What?" I recall the day the shopkeeper trundled to my desk, sharing ring sketches, seeking my opinion...

"Yes, he made sure I had plenty of options. We both agreed—only the absolute best for you." Matthew steps closer and turns me back to the mirror. I take in my flushed, happy face. Bright eyes. He traces his fingers around my neck, dancing over the rubies. "That is why you're wearing this tonight," he says. "Not for Paul. For me. Because I love you, and you are the next Mrs. DaMolin."

I nod.

"I'm assuming, of course, you have a plan?"

"I do."

"Do you need me?"

"I just needed you to put these around my neck. Which you, very graciously, have. And then some." I glance down at the engagement ring before reluctantly twisting it off my finger. "But, Matthew? I'm not sure tonight is the best time to announce this news."

"I understand. I came prepared." He reaches inside the lining of his jacket and pulls out a pair of black silk, elbow-length gloves. "I know how you like to hide your secrets, Kat."

I smile, pleasantly surprised. I take the gloves and pull them on. The lump of the ring protrudes slightly, but unless someone's looking, they'll never notice.

"You look positively grand, darling." He twirls me for emphasis. "Now let's go celebrate the Ides of March. I want to show off my devastatingly gorgeous, clandestine fiancée."

CHAPTER THIRTY-THREE

THE PARTY HAS ALREADY begun when Matthew and I arrive. I glide into the clubhouse on his arm—on my *fiancé's* arm—like we own the joint. I'm convinced there's a bullseye on my left hand beneath the glove, but nobody glances at it twice. All attention is focused on the DaMolin rubies dripping from my neck.

I'm immensely popular with the guests at the ball. Everyone wants to see the reclusive rubies, drool over them, dance with them. I'm separated from Matthew again and again to take to the outdoor dance floor with donors, friends, and strangers alike, but I always drift back to his side as soon as I'm free, a pair of magnets snapping together.

"Is it finally my turn for a dance?" he asks after our fifth separation.

Not that I'm counting. Not that I'm counting every minute I spend apart from him tonight. That doesn't sound like me at all.

I move with Matthew to the beat of the band. They've set up an outdoor stage in the central courtyard of the club. Bejeweled partygoers step and twirl beneath lamplight and low-swooping moths while friends cluster both around and above, leaning over porch railings, smoking cigars, swapping gossip, and sipping endless refills of whiskey and gin.

As expected, the Jekyll Island Club would never be so gauche as to fall victim to a matter as commonplace as Prohibition. In a rather impressive display of audaciousness at the start of the evening, Johnnie Rockefeller and his new bride poured out Pol Roger, bottle after bottle, over two towering pyramids of crystal glassware, creating twin champagne fountains at the edge of the dance floor. High color graced the new Mrs. Rockefeller's cheeks, and a raucous giggle erupted from her lips as the foam overflowed with abandon.

Merriment abounds in every corner of the club, and Matthew spins and dips me across the floor until I'm laughing and dizzy. The stars swirl and blur overhead with every twirl, sweeping me into the infinite expanse of the universe, which has never felt nearer than tonight. One song fades into a second. Matthew pulls me close; I tuck my head on his shoulder and sway. My gaze lazily peruses the party, noting the discreet presence of several well-dressed security officials interwoven through the crowd. They sip clear drinks—an old trick, likely tonic water and lime—as they try to blend in, but their stiff posture and surveying eyes don't fool me. I'm surprised there are so few, perhaps only three or four. Their presence seems more cursory than truly threatening.

Paul was right, I begrudgingly admit. This party is carte blanche.

Matthew and I complete another slow revolution. Harry Astor appears on the veranda, elbows propped on the railing as he chats with a petite redhead. I snort lightly when I notice a bruise above his eye, right where Matthew hit him. I look around for a few more minutes, but I don't see Florence or Daniel anywhere, though I'm certain they're here together. Florence is chasing her own engagement ring, and according to Matthew, she'll be taking her bounty within the month. I do locate a Mellie-free Ethan, hovering at the bottom of the porch stairs. He waves cheerfully, sloshing whiskey over the rim of a tumbler.

"Your brother is watching us." I point him out to Matthew.

"Let him watch. It's good for him to be on the sidelines. Healthy." He bends down and kisses me.

When I pull back, I spot something over Matthew's shoulder that wipes the relaxed smile from my face. I stiffen as I meet Paul's eyes across the party.

He raises an eyebrow, then returns his attention to the statuesque woman he's conversing with. My hand flies to my neck as I realize I haven't been to the bathroom yet. I lost track of time.

"Matthew, would you excuse me? I need to visit the ladies' room."

"Certainly." He moves to escort me, but I shrug him off, weaving through the crowd with single-minded determination. Ethan waylays me at the base of the stairs.

"Katarina." He slips his arm through mine and glides up to the veranda with me. "How are you? Having a pleasant evening?"

"I'm exceedingly well, Ethan," I reply. "Whereabouts is Melinda? You haven't lost her, have you?"

"Quite the opposite." Ethan nods to the dance floor where Mellie prances and spins happily in the arms of a tuxedoed gentleman. "She's quite the dame, your farmgirl friend," Ethan teases. "Her dance card is full."

"You don't say?" My eyebrows raise.

"Indeed, arriving on a DaMolin arm will do that for a lady. Speaking of, you and Matthew make quite the pair," he says. "A matching set, perhaps? The grapevine is positively abuzz with speculation, and it got me thinking...what are your plans when you depart from Telfair?"

"My plans?" I repeat, steering Ethan into the club. "I'm not certain what you mean."

"Please." He reaches for my gloved hand. My left hand. "Don't insult me, Kat. I'm no simp."

I glance down at my ring finger, then do a quick scan of our surroundings. There are too many people around, so I grab his arm and pull him into an empty sitting room.

"Relax, Mrs. DaMolin. I'm not going to spill the beans," Ethan assures me. "But it wasn't hard to figure out. My brother's been grinning like an idiot all night. I'm happy for you both. Does anyone know?"

"No. He only asked a few hours ago."

He smiles. "I knew he would. Everyone else here should know too, honestly. The DaMolin rubies don't come out of the vault very often. And they're only worn by the women we choose."

"What if it's not a woman you want to choose," I whisper, eyes full of significance.

A flicker of pain crosses Ethan's face, and I reach for him.

"Ethan," I begin, "about earlier today...with Harry—"

"Don't, Kat." He pulls back. "Whatever you think you've seen, whatever you think you understand, I'm asking you to forget. Because you can't possibly even *begin* to understand. Not ever. I am the firstborn son of the DaMolin publishing dynasty. There are rules."

"Hang the rules! You don't have to stay here, Ethan, in a world that keeps you locked in a rigid little box. There are places you can go, out there, where you can be anonymous and live your own life. Any kind of life you choose."

He shakes his head. "There's no way I would abandon my family, Katarina. I'm going to do the job I was raised to do, and I'm going to do it damn well. It will have to be enough."

"And if it's not?" I tilt my head. "If it's not enough, Ethan?"

"It will be. My family writes headlines, we don't feature in them. I don't plan on repeating history."

"It just doesn't seem fair—"

"Life isn't fair, Kat," Ethan replies. "Don't let your miraculous ascent from the Catacombs allow you to forget that. It's one of the things I like best about you. Please don't lose that when you marry into this family, into this world. Be my ally, my *friend*, from the inside. God knows, we can use some forward thinkers in here to freshen up the place."

I nod, my heart tight in my throat.

"I'm glad you're here, Kat. I'm glad Matthew found you. He's lucky in a way not all of us can even dream to be. Now if you'll excuse me, I need another drink." He tips his empty glass. "A stiff one."

With that, he takes his leave. I shake the conversation from my mind and push deeper into the club until I arrive at the powder room.

I slip inside and twist the lock. Then I reach behind my neck to work the clasp on the DaMolin rubies. I sigh quietly with relief when it gives, releasing the weight from my neck. I drop the necklace into my right pocket, exchanging it for the forgery.

As I secure the Trojan horse around my neck, I gaze into the gilded mirror. A doe-eyed beauty with flushed cheeks in a black gown stares back at me. I look closely, trying to find the girl from the Catacombs who Ethan just referenced, but I'm not sure I can. She's there and gone in mere heartbeats. There in a flash of resolve in my eyes as I straighten my spine, gone when a genteel smile rises on my lips. There in the steadiness of my fingers as I fan out the counterfeit necklace, gone when I reach for the door.

When I rejoin Matthew on the dance floor, my face is smooth, demeanor unruffled. As we revolve and spin, my eyes flick around the room, this way and that until I spot him. He's leaning sideways, casual and comfortable, in a doorway to the clubhouse. His eyes are locked on me, watching as I dance in Matthew's arms beneath the stars.

When Paul sees me looking, he reaches into his jacket and pulls out his silver cigarette lighter. He thumbs it twice, then drops it back into his pocket. I give him the barest of nods, recognizing the signal, but I don't rush; I linger with Matthew for another song. Only when the band pauses for a break do I extricate myself.

"I told Constance Pulitzer I would make a few rounds with her. Do you mind?"

"Really?" Matt steps back and scans the room, presumably looking for her. "Shall I join you?"

"No, of course not. It'll be shoptalk with the other gals. You'd be terribly bored. I'm sure I won't be long, just five or ten minutes."

"Okay." He looks quizzically at me but gets distracted when he spies a small cluster of gentlemen, Daniel included, waving him to the sidelines of the dance floor.

"Go on." I shove him toward his friends. "I'll be right back, and I'll come find you."

When I'm confident he's sufficiently sidetracked, I look back to the doorway where I saw Paul. As soon as our eyes meet, he fades backward into the club, melting away. I take a deep breath and follow, moving at a leisurely stroll. When I reach the entrance to the clubhouse, I do a quick sweep for nearby security officials but find none. Paul chose his moment well.

Once inside, my stride lengthens. The crowd is thin here, but there are still bystanders. I know Paul well enough to know exactly where he'll go to avoid them. I move deeper into the labyrinth of the clubhouse, down a heavily paneled corridor with rows of closed doors. At the end of the hall, I turn left and pass through an open doorway, giving a cursory glance over my shoulder to ensure I wasn't followed. My cape slithers on the marble floor behind me.

The hallway dead-ends in a sitting room. There are bookshelves and a fireplace along one wall. Silhouetted against the windows at the opposite end stands Paul. I walk toward him, stepping through rays of moonbeams. It's dark in here, but I can still see his sharp eyes. His arms are crossed tightly, muscles on edge.

I wait for him to speak, coming to a stop a few feet away.

Target acquired.

"I see congratulations are in order," Paul rumbles, jerking his head toward my gloved left hand. His eyes glitter with anger and pain.

"What?" I knew I shouldn't have worn the blasted ring. "How did you—"

"Come on, Kat. I could see the lump of that rock from all the way across the room. I'm the one person in the world who knows you only wear gloves when you're hiding something. You don't think I deserve even the courtesy of a heads-up?"

You're no longer the only person to know that, Paul, I think stubbornly. Even now, he can't give Matthew a single ounce of credit. I do feel bad about blindsiding him with the engagement though.

"He only asked tonight, Paul," I whisper. "I'm sorry. Of course I would have told you."

"And you said yes."

It's a statement, not a question, and I don't contradict him. I feel his anger building beneath the surface, brewing into quiet fury. I brace myself.

"I just can't believe this. I really can't. I cannot believe you want to run off to play housewife for the DaMolin family. For *him*. I can't believe you would sell out like that. I didn't think you had it in you."

"It's not like that. I'm not selling out."

"No, you are. Off to greener pastures the minute something better came along. That's exactly what happened, Katarina. Don't fool yourself or me. I don't have the patience for it."

"If that's how you need to remember so it hurts less, fine," I say. "I don't care."

"Don't psychoanalyze me, Kat. I should have tied you to our bed in the bayou loft and burned the whole place down with you inside months ago, the minute you dug in your heels and refused to stop seeing him."

It's a sucker punch, those cruel words. "You don't mean that."

He tilts his head and licks his lips. "Forget it. I'm done. Just give me the necklace. Now."

I hesitate. "I don't want to do this, Paul. Please don't make me."

"Katarina, I don't give a fuck what you do or don't want. Take it off."

I unfasten the clasp of the forged necklace and hand it over. He immediately pockets it. I remove the original from my pocket and slip it around my neck. I fight to keep from heaving as I secure it.

"You're right, Paul. We're done. For good. Piss off, would ya? And try not to get caught waltzing out the front door."

"You know what? I don't think so." Paul extends a hand, seeming to make a decision. His eyes glint dangerously. "We're done when *I* say we're done. Give me the one around your neck too, Katarina."

"What the fuck, Paul? That's not the plan," I hiss at him. "If you take both, I'll have no cover. They'll know the necklace has been stolen. Immediately. And the first person they'll suspect is me."

"Not my problem." He pulls the first necklace from his pocket and jerks it in his hand. "I need insurance, doll. You're the only one who knows which is the real necklace. And unfortunately, the minute you slipped that sparkling ring on your finger, I decided I couldn't trust you anymore. Your allegiance has changed."

"You can trust me," I try weakly.

"I don't think so." He's not buying it. "Fool me once, Katarina, remember? *Nobody* fools me. Not even you. Take it off. Now."

I turn away from him in frustration, showing him my back. He moves forward to unclasp the necklace himself.

"Don't fucking touch me, Paul," I say, my voice sharp over my shoulder. "I can do it myself. I don't want you touching me ever again."

I feel, rather than see, Paul's smirk at the fluster in my tone. He lets me undo the necklace before speaking again. "Good, now hand it over to me, Katarina. Like a good girl."

I do, my pulse racing as I slowly turn right to face him, passing the necklace off with my left hand.

"That's good." He pockets both necklaces, satisfied.

"You realize you're throwing me to the wolves out there. What, pray tell, am I supposed to do?"

"Oh, you're a bright girl. I'm sure you'll figure something out." He backs away from me.

"We're done, Paul," I repeat. "For good."

"We are," he confirms. "I'll let you have your happily ever after. Starting now." He gives me a sanctimonious smile, looking at my bare neck.

"You better run," I tell him. "The minute I walk out there, they're going to lock this whole place down. I'm not feeling very generous to give you much time."

"I'll be gone before you even blink, doll. Remember, if I go down tonight, so do you. I'm always watching."

"Don't contact me again. Not until you've grown up, Peter Pan."

"Don't be bitter, little wolf. You know this is how it has to be."

"No, Paul." I tilt my chin to hold his gaze. "It really isn't."

He takes a final step back, half-hidden in the shadow of the dark hallway. "You know the rules. Fool me once, Katarina..."

"Nobody fools me," I mutter, finishing the adage as he disappears.

Alone in the empty room, my heart flails and my mind races as I consider my options. I need to return to the ball. Matthew will be looking for me, among others. Hopefully not security, not yet. Without the rubies around my neck, the club will descend into chaos. I do want to give Paul time to get out; I'm not going down tonight. Hopefully, he isn't stupid or egotistical enough to linger to see my next move...but he just might be. Which means I need to play this very carefully. And I'll likely need Matthew's help.

I make a decision. I lift my chin and walk back down the long corridor. The chatter of the party rises to a crescendo as I near the doors to the courtyard. Once outside, I make a beeline for Matthew. He's not far, just over by the empty stage. Matthew's eyes widen as soon as he sees me, and he excuses himself from his conversation.

"Katarina, what's going on? Where's the necklace?"

"Listen to me very carefully," I murmur. "Paul is here, and I need your help."

"Where's the necklace, Kat?" he repeats, whispering. A few people stare already, noticing my bare neck. We both feel it. We have only minutes.

"We need a distraction," I tell him. "I need you to trust me right now, in case Paul is still around. I promise you can trust me, but I need you to help me think of something."

He hesitates for a moment, deliberating. Then he takes a deep breath and meets my gaze head-on.

"Take off your glove."

"What?"

"The glove. On your left hand. Take it off." He nods at my finger. "If you want me to trust you, I will. You want a distraction? Watch what happens when you pull that off. And when I do what I'm about to do."

I swallow hard.

"I trust you. Do you trust me?" he challenges.

There's nothing for it. I push all my chips in and pull off the glove.

Matthew smiles reassuringly, then climbs to the small stage behind us, where the band is still on break. He grabs the freestanding silver microphone and taps it twice, gathering the attention of the room.

"Good evening, everyone," he says. His voice is smooth, like dripping hot butter over the microphone. "It's an absolutely swell night to celebrate the Ides of March here on Jekyll Island, is it not?"

The crowd applauds obediently.

A wildly corked Ethan cups his hands around his mouth and shouts, "Maaattttt! Speech, speech!"

Onstage, Matthew chuckles. "Thanks for the introduction, Ethan. For anyone who doesn't know me, my name is Matthew DaMolin. My family has been members of the club for years." He gestures at Lady Genevieve from across the way. "My mother throws the most legendary Hallows' Eve parties this island has ever seen."

The crowd hoots appreciatively, stomping their feet. I'm awestruck as I look around; the entire peerage rests, riveted, in the palm of Matthew's very capable and charming hand. My stomach clenches with a tiny surge of pride.

"But that's not the reason I'm standing up here now—though, of course, you are all invited next October." He winks, and the crowd laughs. "The real reason I'm up here is because the beautiful Katarina down there—the one so many of you noticed tonight because she's been wearing the DaMolin rubies—has just agreed to marry me."

There's a loud whoop from the corner of the courtyard, and I know without looking it came from Ethan. An excited ripple torpedoes through the crowd.

"We couldn't think of a better moment to announce our engagement than right here, right now, with so many friends in the room. Katarina, will you join me?" He looks earnestly at me and offers his hand.

I would never leave him hanging, not ever. He has me eating from the palm of his hand, just like the rest of the guests. I smile, heart still hammering, and let him pull me onstage. The crowd screams as he does, and I laugh. Bubbling with something that, incredibly, feels like undiluted happiness.

"This is my *fiancée*," he continues. "The one and only and very beautiful Katarina. The theme of tonight's party is Bejeweled Ides of March, and for the rest of this beautiful March evening, she will be wearing the only jewel that matters. The one I gave her. The one here on her finger."

The crowd descends into cheers of madness as Matthew lifts my left hand. He has them completely spellbound. I look at him in wonder, marveling at his quick thinking, at his ability to provide this spin at the drop of a hat. For me.

"I've never loved you more than I do right now," I murmur to him, sliding my arms around his neck. He dips me low and pauses, letting the crowd have their moment as they think they're sharing in ours.

"You're not going to let me down, right?" he whispers, a glint of nerves barely visible in his eyes.

"I'll never let you down. Now kiss me like you mean it. For them and for me."

He beams, giving me a full dose of Matthew DaMolin dazzle. It lights me up from the inside out.

When the crowd screeches this time, I barely hear it. It's the intensity and purity of Matthew's happy kiss that's roaring in my ears instead.

CHAPTER THIRTY-FOUR

THE REMAINDER OF THE night is a whirlwind. A hundred different hugs and congratulations. A hundred different faces. Champagne glass after champagne glass. One brief encounter with a security official inquiring after the necklace, which Matthew quickly puts to rest.

"I have the necklace—*my family's* necklace—in my pocket. But thank you for your overactive concern," he tells them.

Hours pass before it's socially acceptable for us to slink away. So many hugs offered, so many best wishes given and inquiries about the wedding made.

The wedding.

Suddenly, somehow, I'm planning a wedding. To Matthew DaMolin. A luminescent Mellie, cheeks flushed with excitement, has already reminded me of the fact no less than eight times.

When Matthew finally drags me out the front door of the club, I'm nearly dead on my feet. Silence hangs between us, heavy as the Spanish moss overhead. Revelations too dangerous to share dance in the moonlit shadows, secrets crunching unassumingly like the gravel beneath our feet.

Matthew's hand is wound tightly in mine as he leads me into his family's house. He pulls me up the ivory staircase and down the hallway. I pause, a little uncertain, but propriety be damned, Matt swings open the door to his room and tugs me inside. He closes and locks it behind us, then presses me back into the wood.

"All right, out with it you little minx. What the hell happened tonight?"

"What do you think happened?" A smirk plays on my lips.

"I have no clue, but you better have that necklace hidden on you somewhere. Shall I strip search you to find it?"

"I do have it."

He drags his gaze up and down my body. He reaches and dives his hands into both my pockets.

Empty.

I laugh at him. "I swapped the necklaces in the ladies' room," I explain. "I put the real one in my pocket and the fake around my neck."

"But it's not in your pocket anymore," he points out.

"No. Because when I met up with Paul, he deviated from the plan. Thankfully, it was nothing I wasn't prepared for."

"How so?"

"I gave him the fake necklace and put the real one back on. But being Paul, he couldn't resist trying to royally ruin me. He told me to give him both necklaces, just in case I was trying to trick him...I suppose I can't exactly blame him, since I was."

"And?"

"And I gave him a second necklace, like he wanted. But still not the one he was after. I made two counterfeits. It was nearly impossible in the short timeframe, but I did it. As my own insurance policy."

"He took *two* fakes?"

"Sure did," I report, grinning. "He walked out of here with two fakes in his pocket and a smile on his face, thinking he got me. Meanwhile..." I trail off and reach two fingers beneath my gown's bustline, plunging them into the ironclad depths of my corset. Slowly, I pull them out, a glittering chain of diamonds and rubies trailing behind. The jewels swing innocently in front of Matthew's shocked face. He doesn't say anything, but I provide the answer.

"I used the oldest trick in the book—sleight of hand. I spun around and unclipped the real necklace, letting it drop. Then, as I turned to the right, I slipped the second fake from my left pocket and handed it to him. It's almost poetic in a way—Paul is the one who taught me those tricks when I was six years old."

"Well, I do declare, Miss Katarina." Matthew's eyes sparkle. "Color me impressed."

"You should be," I whisper. I raise my left hand and show him his watch, the watch I slipped off his wrist while I was talking.

He bursts out laughing and snatches it back from me. "You're a menace."

"I am." I grin.

"And a handful."

"Your handful."

"Yes. Mine." He takes the necklace from me, flattening it across my chest. He secures the clasp around my neck again. "There, back where it belongs."

"You're very sweet. And very trusting."

"I'm only a little sweet, Kat. Turn around."

I obey. He presses his lips to the side of my neck, grazing his nose and breath along the shell of my ear. His fingers move to the buttons at my back, working until the beaded gown drops to the floor. The laces of my corset loosen next, then release and tumble away. I turn to face him, but he stops me.

"Don't turn around."

He presses my palms flat on the door and kisses my neck again. His hands glide down my bare sides, unhooking my garters, sending my underwear to the floor with a quick flick of his wrist. He slides his fingers back up, skimming the sides of my breasts.

"Get on the bed," he rumbles.

I move, his eyes drinking in my every step.

"I'm only a little sweet, Katarina," Matthew tells me again, reaching for me. His lips brush softly over mine. "Because I'm going to fuck you now, right here in my parents' house, while you wear only this necklace. And I don't care who hears us or tries to interrupt. You are *mine*."

"Yours," I agree, my pulse quickening with excitement.

He's as good as his word. Better in fact, because for the next hour, he shows me how incredible it is to belong to him. To think only of him. To be only with him. To feel only him, call out for only him.

To be consumed by him.

To be loved by him.

Him and only him.

CHAPTER THIRTY-FIVE

EVEN THOUGH HE TECHNICALLY gave me Monday off, my feet still lead me to Ray's. I take to the streets of Savannah like a butterfly emerging from a cocoon—ebulliently chasing air and sunlight. As I stroll down the brick sidewalk, I tell myself I'm headed nowhere in particular, but five minutes later, I'm on the streetcar. Ten minutes more, I'm outside the shop.

Ray is inside, sitting at the counter, paging through his little black registry book. He glances up as I push through the door, thinking he has a customer. His eyes spark when he recognizes me.

"Kat, fancy seeing you here. On your day off," he teases. "The one you bargained so hard for."

"I simply can't stay away." I raise my hands in a playful shrug.

"Heavens to Betsy, what is that *rock* on your finger? I'm blind!"

"Oh, this?" I lift my left hand, then place it flat on the counter between us. "Just a token from my fiancé. I believe you know him. Would you care to see?"

"I certainly would." He lifts my hand for inspection, checking it from every angle. "Perfect balance, colorless, organically unique...whoever designed this is wildly talented."

"I have to agree."

Ray releases my hand and smiles. "The lad picked well. Couldn't have chosen better myself. It suits you."

"It suits him too," I muse. "It reminds me of the sun, with the pointed halos. And Matthew is...he's like my own personal sun, pulling me into his orbit." I look up at Ray and wince. "Sappy, I know. Sorry."

"You don't have to apologize. I hear all sorts when people come in here shopping for rings. I'm happy for you. He's a good kid, like you. Smart as a whip—also like you." He looks meaningfully at me, the slightest lift gracing his eyebrow. Perhaps the tiniest trace of a knowing smile playing on his wrinkled features.

"So..." I swallow, knowing the answer before I ask. "Has Paul stopped by?"

"He has." Ray is grinning in earnest now.

"And did he...bring you something?"

"Two somethings, actually."

"And?"

"And I gave him one to go home with, and I kept one for myself as a souvenir. It's in the back, if you want to see it."

"You...you *what*?"

He looks carefully at me. "Kat, this isn't a hill to die on. Not for me. I told Paul exactly what he wanted to hear. He doesn't plan to sell, so what does it matter? He was only after the trophy. So I gave it to him."

"You didn't have to do that." I shake my head. "If he ever finds out—"

"How will he find out? The only two people in the world who know about this are you and me. And maybe that new fiancé of yours. I'm certainly not going to breathe a word, are you?"

"No."

He nods. "This is how it ends, Kat. It's for the best. No one burns this way. Life goes on."

My eyes fill with tears. Relief and gratitude.

"You're a good kid, Kat. A good young lady, actually, and you made the right choice. I don't know how you managed to pull it off, but you did.

I've never been more proud of you. I examined those necklaces for damn near twenty minutes before I figured it out. And when I did, my choice was easy."

I look up at him, unable to manage words.

"Go home and be happy, Katarina. It's over."

"Go home and be happy," I repeat, tasting the phrase. I look down at my engagement ring in disbelief. "Just like that?"

"Just like that."

Before I leave Ray's shop, I'm seized with the irresistible urge to go to my desk to retrieve Cleopatra's showpiece collar and ring, as integral a symbol to my victory today as anything else. I'm single-minded when I push into the back room, so focused I've pulled both pieces out to admire before I notice the note. It's my name scrawled across the top that finally alerts me, written in Paul's shaky yet meticulous hand.

> *Katarina,*
>
> *It seems you've held onto something of mine. Something quite precious and coveted. In return, I've stolen something of yours. If you'd like him back alive, meet me in the place where everything began.*
>
> *An eye for an eye, little wolf. You know the rules. Fool me once...*
>
> *Yours,*
> *Paul*

The room spins around me.

Matthew, Matthew, Matthew...

His name echoes with every *thump* of my heart. I reread the note, the parchment crisp beneath my trembling fingers. As I do, shock and fear harden into ironclad resolve. My hand clenches into a tight fist, crumpling the offending message within.

Paul wants me to be frightened, to rush to the Catacombs—the place where everything began—in a blind panic, but I won't give him the satisfaction. No one steals from me, certainly not Paul. He's taken enough.

Deadly calm now, I reach for my battle armor. I pick up Cleopatra's collar necklace and secure the heavy weight around my throat. I slide on the cobra ring, directly over my red queen of diamonds tattoo. Before I depart, I pause to admire the deadly glint of those serpentine emerald eyes. The blade of the ever-present dagger in my boot throbs with my first step.

Paul thinks I'll come crawling back to his den like the old days, playing marionette to his puppeteer. But in his descent into madness, he's somehow overlooked the most important thing. The very *first* thing.

I am a wolf.

———◆———

I'VE FORGOTTEN THE DANK, omnipresent darkness of the Catacombs. The heaviness and static tension. There's a cloying quality to the air down here, an almost alkaline, sulfuric dampness that leaches into my nostrils, burrowing its way into my brain and lungs. Part distant memory, part ubiquitous reality.

My footfalls are quiet on the limestone floor. I move with prudence, knowing even the smallest of sounds can echo resoundingly throughout these subterranean tunnels. My eyes are wide, unblinking, as I scan the dim passageway. I pause before every offshoot, listening, peeking, finally—carefully—moving.

As I near Paul's hideout, just beyond the final bend, I come across a stray drunkard—spine leaning on the limestone wall, head tipped back in a lolling snore. Hardly unusual and not necessarily threatening, but an unacceptable variable on this most macabre of missions. I sink to my haunches and slide the dagger from my boot. I press the tip into the soft flesh of his neck, just below his chin, increasing pressure until his eyes startle open.

"Scram," I hiss. "If you value your life, make haste."

His stuporous eyes alight on my glittering obsidian and emerald collar, greed piercing through the dullness of slumber. But one unwritten law in the Catacombs trumps all others: the one wielding the blade makes the rules. The man scampers to his feet without protest and staggers away as fast as his liquor-laden legs can carry him. He isn't quiet, so I wait calmly until the echoes of his retreat fade to nothingness. Until the quiet drip of a stray seepage nearby is all I hear. Only then do I look to the ceiling. It's nigh impossible to see, but experience knows there's a fissure up there, slanted and treacherous. Just large enough for a pack of child-thieves to crawl through day after day. Coming home.

Home to the place where everything began.

<hr />

As I SLIP INSIDE Paul's den, my gaze darts—instinctive and automatic—to my corner.

Empty.

I check Paul's corner next, and there he is, waiting for me. He's seated on the floor with his legs bent, fingers steepled beneath his chin. Several days of dark stubble coats Paul's chin, and his left eye blooms black and blue. Diagonally across, in Abe's corner, is Matthew, also seated but half-doubled over, his hands and feet bound together. Near hog-tied and quite effectively neutralized. I start for him, taking in his rumpled hair and bloodied face.

The *click* of a revolver halts me in my tracks.

"Kat." Matthew is the first to speak. "Get outta here! Go—"

"I shoulda gagged you when I had the chance," Paul interrupts.

I turn to face him, slowly. He's risen to his feet and crossed half the space with his characteristic silent tread. The barrel of his revolver is trained on my face.

"Hello, darling." I offer a saccharine smile, and Paul snorts. "Playing with guns now, are we? Fascinating."

"Nice of you to join us, Lady Katarina." He tosses me a lopsided, maniacal smile of his own.

"Pleasure." I tilt my chin up. "Bringing a revolver to a swordfight, Paul? I'd like to say I'm surprised, but how does the saying go? Lie down with dogs..."

"And what did you bring, little wolf? Perhaps something laden with diamonds and rubies—*legitimate* ones, I sincerely hope."

"I already gave you the necklace, Paul."

"You gave me a *fake*." He spits, moving one stride closer. Instinctively, I take a step back, maintaining the distance between us. In my eagerness to help Matthew, I've committed a cardinal sin; Paul now stands between me and the exit.

"Why do you believe that?"

"Because Ray's not nearly as smooth as he thinks he is," Paul says, shaking the gun in my face. "He *lied* to me. For *you*. You've turned everyone against me. First it was Abe, my best friend. You took him from me, flashed your smile and split your legs to win his loyalty, like a dog. Then it was my mark." He swings the gun toward Matthew, gesticulating wildly. "Same story there—a sweet smile, a few whispered promises, and you swept him out from underfoot. And now at the eleventh hour, even my goddamn bagman—the man who should worship at the altar of my payment—has thrown his lot in with you. He'll have to be dealt with. All because you're a goddamn snake charmer, a viper. I should have put you down like a mutt ages ago."

The gun is trained back on me, and Matthew starts shouting. I can't make out his words, the thunderous pounding of blood in my ears is far too loud.

"Paul." I raise a hand between us. "Stop. You don't know what you're saying."

"Are you going to beg for your life, Katarina?" Paul asks, another demented smile rising. "Go ahead, sweetheart. *Beg.* If you do it just right, maybe I'll listen."

"You know me well enough to know I don't beg. I *take* what I want. You taught me that."

"I seem to remember you begging quite nicely on two particular occasions, bargaining for my life. Once to stop the bullet, the second to save me afterward."

"You think that gives you power, don't you?" I move closer. One step, two. All the way until the revolver presses against my forehead. "You think your life brings me to my knees? It doesn't. Not anymore."

"You're a liar." He steps back and sticks the barrel of the gun to his own chin. His eyes are desperate, his finger on the trigger. *"You love me."*

My breath catches in my throat, every nerve ending in my body fighting the urge to wrest the gun away. To stop him from pointing it at himself. In this battle of wills, I don't move a muscle.

"You love me," he says again, whispering now.

"Love isn't power, Paul," I breathe. "You can't weaponize my feelings and expect them to remain true. You can't make me say it, you can't make me feel it, and I can't make you believe it. Not anymore."

In one smooth motion, Paul swings the gun away from his chin and points it at Matthew.

There's zero thinking, zero rationality. I move.

"Don't take another goddamn step, Katarina," Paul thunders. "I'll shoot him dead where he sits, make you watch the life leave his eyes. Tell me, is *he* the one you'll beg for now? The one you'll die on your knees for? Prove it. Drop."

I was never very good at following directions. I don't drop. I charge. Socking into Paul's gut and batting the gun away as it fires. The bullet slams into the ceiling, raining dust and limestone upon us.

We struggle, tussling back and forth. The gun goes off twice more into the ceiling before I manage to release Paul's grip. It falls to the floor with a clatter. I kick it to a far corner.

I'm going for the knife in my boot when two hands, Paul's hands—once loving, now enraged—encircle my throat. He grabs me by Cleopatra's collar and lifts, raising me off my feet, slamming my back into the wall. My head rings with the impact, air choked from my windpipe. The bite of the golden collar digs in, cutting off circulation and air.

Paul's face is inches from my own, his breath hot on my cheek as he chokes the life out of me. The boy I knew and loved is well and truly gone, completely over the edge. This man is going to kill me. There's not a doubt in my mind.

My fingers scramble hopelessly against Paul's, prying for purchase, but it's useless. Even now, my vision swims, beginning to tunnel. I have only seconds, and the dagger in my boot is out of reach. I stretch my fingers for Paul's face, my right hand falling short to brush his neck. It's almost loving, this caress...

But then I thumb Cleopatra's serpentine ring. Right over my queen of diamonds tattoo. I thumb twice until the cobra head flips open. A tiny blade pops out of its mouth, right between the fangs.

My hand is there, curling into a tight fist alongside the smooth curve of his neck. Matthew told me once the carotid artery lies less than two inches beneath the skin.

I stab, deep and true. Twice, for good measure. The second strike spurts bright red blood. Arterial.

Paul releases me, and I fall to the ground, sputtering and clutching my throat. It's wet with blood where my necklace sliced through skin. Within seconds, Paul collapses to the stone floor beside me. His exsanguination is quick and merciless. I don't want—can't bear—to watch, so I turn away.

"Kat!" Matthew cries in my periphery. He's wiggling like an inchworm toward me. "Kat, untie me. Cut me free."

"He's beyond saving, Matthew," I rasp, but I pull the dagger from my boot and cut him loose. Matthew doesn't move toward Paul. He wraps his body around me, pressing his thundering heart directly to mine.

"You're safe," he murmurs.

"*We're* safe," I answer, pulling back and running my hands down the length of his arms. "It's over, and we're safe."

Bittersweet is the only way to describe the taste of the words as they leave my lips. Born of my own blood, sweat, and undoubtedly soon to come, tears. Tinged with sorrow, relief, hope...all of it and more.

———————◦◦———————

MATTHEW AND I ARRIVE at the bayou loft together, but I leave him on a bench outside to wait. This is something I have to do alone.

My footsteps fall heavily on the stairs, each one echoing like the toll of a funeral bell. Louder and louder. I knock twice on the door, not trusting my voice, before swinging it open. Tony sits at the table and looks up from two wristwatches in his hand. Five more timepieces tick away on the surface in front of him.

I meet his eyes and open my mouth, but all that comes out is a hoarse squeak.

How will I ever find the words to tell them?

"Mierda, Kat!" Tony flies out of his seat, taking in the sight of my bloodstained hands and bruised neck. "Santo Dios! Abe? Abe, get out here."

I fold myself into Tony's arms as my legs give out. We sink into a puddle on the floor. Abe walks in as Tony's hands trace over me, up and down. Spanish curses and exclamations fly from his lips in rapid succession.

"Kat?" Abe drops to the ground beside us, his eyes drawn to my injured neck. "What happened?"

And it's the hardest tale I've ever had to tell—all harsh truth, no coddling lies—but somehow, I'm brave. I find the words. One sentence at a time.

When I reach the conclusion of the story, the horrible moment when Paul's hands throttled my neck, that's when my gravelly voice falters. I turn away from Abe and Tony. I can't look them in the eyes for this. For this admission that the boy I loved my entire life turned on me. That he hurt me. And then...

And then I hurt him. Irreparably.

I feel violated and victimized, but also horribly, horribly ashamed. I rip the cobra ring from my bloody finger and throw it across the floor.

"I should have done more," I rasp. "I don't know how I could have stopped him...it all happened so fast. But I should have—"

"No, Kat. None of this is your fault." Abe is there first, gripping my hand. His forgiveness, his love, comes quickly.

My eyes move, hesitantly, to Tony. He sinks back on his haunches, grief in his tear-filled eyes. Silence falls. I bite my lip, waiting for his pronouncement. His judgment.

"He's gone?" Tony finally asks.

I swallow, sandpaper on sandpaper rubbing my throat raw. "He is. I...I'm so sorry."

When Tony's face crumples, when his hands move to cover his eyes, Abe and I are there to encircle him in our arms. Without any hesitation, Tony embraces me in return. He pulls me to his chest without recrimination, and I nearly cry out with relief.

There's grief, yes. Terrible grief. But there's also love, so much love, with simply no place to go. He pours it into me, molten and raw. Into the marrow of my bones. It settles in the fault lines of my shattered heart, and I shudder. The weight is so very heavy, but with all three of us shouldering it together, we manage. One breath at a time.

The sun will set over Savannah this evening, and it will rise again at dawn. The streetcars will trundle over cobblestone lanes, and the hanging moss will blow silently in the breeze. The world will continue to turn as always, marching ever forward without pause.

And tonight, three wolves will howl at the moon, their fourth forever lost.

EPILOGUE

Six months later

THE DRESS IS WHITE. And long. And lace.

The flowers are white, cascading and soft.

The drapery is white, flowing and billowing on the wings of the wind.

Matthew's bow tie is white. His smile is blinding. I see it, there at the end of the aisle.

White and light and bright.

Yes. The color of the day is once again *white*.

It's a blazing September day, just one week after Matthew's birthday, a year to the day after we met, when I walk up the aisle to marry him.

His family is here and a few close friends. Ray stands by, near the top of the aisle, with our wedding bands. Florence Vanderbilt has a seat on the aisle, a ring on her finger and Daniel Dufour on her arm. Mellie is here too, positively bursting with excitement. And there's Harry Astor skulking in the back, because it simply wouldn't do to separate the trifecta in the waning hours of their prime.

But all I really see is Matthew, straight ahead. Next to the altar, which drips with Spanish moss and white blooms. He's smiling, beaming. Pulling me toward him on an invisible string. The light is shining from both the sun above and his gorgeous face. When it hits me, I am radiant.

"This is it, Kitty-Kat."

I turn to look at Abe as we reach the top of the aisle.

"Who would've thought you'd have a white wedding?" he whispers, leaning in to give me a hug. "And that I'd be here with you to see it? To give you away."

"Not me," I admit.

Matthew moves forward, and I give him my hand. Abe steps back, settling into a seat in the front row beside Tony and Ethan.

Matthew's bright blue eyes latch onto mine. "Beautiful dress."

"Thank you. It's new." Parisian House of Worth couture, pearls and lace, drop waist, and—of course—antique white. Smiling, I listen as the minister speaks. He uses many words, pretty words. Flowery words.

Yours. Mine. Ours. Forever.

Matthew slips a wedding band on my finger, and finally, I get to slide a ring on his. One that marks him as mine.

Yours. Mine. Ours. Forever.

"Ladies and gentlemen," the minister proclaims, "for the very first time as husband and wife, I present to you...Dr. and Mrs. Matthew DaMolin. You may now kiss your bride."

Wife.

Not wolf. Not Royal.

Not Paul's. Not Abe's.

Matthew's. Matthew's *wife*.

He dips me back and gives me the sweetest, simplest, most perfect kiss. I let him take my hand and raise it high. Everyone cheers as we run down the aisle together.

A new adrenaline rush fills me, the one I associate with being his.

It's a different kind of rush, certainly, but it's one we discovered together. *From* each other, which makes it the only kind I'll ever need.

And if my well-conditioned sticky fingers just so happen to dart in and out of a few pockets during the receiving line or swipe a diamond hairpin from a certain blonde Academy socialite's head on the dance floor...well.

Maybe you saw me, maybe you didn't.

Old habits and all that.

Author's Note

I'm going to tell you a secret—

I am an accidental historical romance writer.

Somewhere hidden away on my hard drive is the original version of this manuscript, a fantasy heist novel set in a secondary world. I was inspired to rewrite the story into Prohibition era Savannah after traveling to the city and to the neighboring Jekyll Island with my husband. I walked around the Jekyll Island Club amidst curtains of Spanish moss, gazing into the shadow of history. Confronted with such unfathomable wealth and privilege, my author brain kept whispering, "What if someone had tried to rob it? What if *Kat* tried to rob it?"

When I came home from Savannah, I reopened my old heist manuscript, and I started editing. In the end, I had a story I loved more deeply than ever before. All this to say…I did not set out to write a historical romance. I had certainly never written one before, and unlike most historical novelists, I didn't start down this path by immersing myself in research. My research came in the middle of the process, and it was all triggered when I discovered Jekyll Island.

The Jekyll Island Club first opened its doors in January of 1888. A members-only association with a steep admittance fee, the island and club-house became a private retreat off the coast of Georgia, a place for the wealthiest families of Progressive America to spend their winters. Mansion escapes, termed "cottages," were built on the grounds surrounding the central clubhouse. Famous families such as the Rockefellers, Morgans, Vanderbilts, and Pulitzers all owned real estate on Jekyll Island.

The cottage names that appear in this book were pulled directly from historical record. The Rockefeller family did, in fact, own a cottage on Jekyll Island named Indian Mound. Moss Cottage was owned by the Macy family, and—as Florence (arrogantly) narrates in the book—it was the first on the island to be wired for electricity. Matthew DaMolin and his family, however, are products of my own imagination. I chose to situate them at Cherokee Cottage, a beautiful, Italian Renaissance-inspired riverfront estate originally owned by the Shrady family. George Frederick Shrady Sr. was an American physician of great esteem, which felt like a noteworthy connection to Matthew and his passion for medicine. Cherokee is also my personal favorite of all the Jekyll Island cottages, so I took the creative liberty of fictionally "gifting" the property to the DaMolins.

The turn of the century through approximately 1930 marked the zenith of the Jekyll Island Club. At its height, one-sixth of the world's total wealth wintered there. It was nicknamed "The Millionaires' Club." In 1904, Munsey Magazine called it "the richest, most exclusive, most inaccessible club in the world." Several groundbreaking historical events happened on the property, most notably perhaps was the drafting of legislation to form the Federal Reserve in 1910, the foundation of the modern currency system used in the United States. The club exemplifies an inescapable, unflattering truth—where wealth goes, power flows.

As an epicenter of clout and privilege, the Jekyll Island Club proved fertile ground for storytelling. To best maintain the integrity of Kat's story, I did take a few creative liberties with the club and the history of some of its members. Technically speaking, the island was accessible only by boat until the 1950s. Yachts, like J.P. Morgan's *Corsair* as briefly mentioned in the text, were the primary method of arrival for the wealthy members. I certainly could have had Kat arriving on the island via ferry, then motorcar from the docks to the club, but in order to best streamline the narrative, I placed her in a motorcar from start to finish.

Another sticking point in my research was the timing of generational changeovers. The descendants of many of the original Jekyll Island owners were not reaching maturation around 1920. John and Blanchette Rockefeller, for example, did not wed until 1932 (therefore no stag party occurred in the year 1919 on Jekyll Island, at least to my knowledge). Because of this, I created my own full cast of secondary characters, some of which were loosely inspired (in name only) by descendants of famous families. Florence Vanderbilt, name derived from real-life socialite Flora Vanderbilt, is a prime example. Harry Astor and Daniel Dufour are also complete fabrications, imagined relatives of John Jacob Astor and J.P. Morgan.

Astor Manor, the site of the Wolfpack's first on-page heist, is a bit of historical sleight of hand as well. Although the Astor family had extensive real estate holdings up and down the east coast, they did not, to my knowledge, own property in Savannah. However, eagle-eyed readers might note the address given in the story, 447 Bull Street, is a real one. This is the location of the Armstrong-Kessler Mansion, built in the early twentieth century and nestled in the heart of the Savannah Historic District adjacent to Forsyth Park. Much of the Wolfpack's reconnaissance of this property was drawn from historical record of this very manor, including the sunken classical neo-Roman gardens, the twenty-six thousand square feet of living space, marble-glazed brick exterior, and the attached carriage house. I must admit, however, I was not able to find out precisely how many fireplaces exist within. I trust Kat and Paul did their fictional due diligence though.

This story is my love letter to the city of Savannah, one of the most vibrant and enthralling places I've ever visited. From the dripping Spanish moss to the brick sidewalks, the hydrangeas and azaleas decorating the city squares, the hint of haunting on the air, and even the tropical humidity...I fell in love when I walked the downtown streets. I chose to title Kat's fictional collegiate finishing school Telfair Academy because the Telfair name is near synonymous with Savannah—it graces several historic landmark buildings and public works downtown, including a wonderful art museum and a hospital. The Telfair family was one of the most prominent and philanthropic in Savannah history dating back to the eighteenth century, and it's not hard to imagine they might have been involved in an educational institution for the young ladies of the American South.

Although it is not widely known, there are catacomb tunnels running underneath the city of Savannah. These tunnels have a dark history, somewhat a blend of fact and lore. They most certainly exist, there are records of their construction as well as several sealed entrances still scattered throughout the city. However, as any good Savannah ghost tour will admit, there are more rumors than historical facts detailing what these subterranean labyrinths were used for. Popular stories in circulation suggest the channels near the riverfront were once frequented by sailors and pirates. There are confirmed tunnels running underneath the city hospital, built during and after the yellow fever epidemics of the late nineteenth century. These passages were used to transport the dead. There are also many whispers surrounding the Savannah slave trade, an inescapable horror of US history. There are more rumors than concrete answers where the catacombs are concerned, and this was one of the few setting details of my original fantasy manuscript that did not need to be significantly altered—the Wolfpack always got their start underground. The Savannah catacombs were pure serendipity.

When I pulled together all the whispered stories about the catacombs, the emerging common thread was that they were used as a place to hide the disenfranchised, be they pirates, the dead, or enslaved persons. We live in a world that likes to look away from the hard things, the ugly things. But looking away or moving a "problem" underground is not a resolution.

It's an illusion. With Kat's character, I hoped to give a voice—a loud, passionate, and beautiful one—to some of these groups.

In many ways, Kat stands for everything Jekyll Island does not. She doesn't come from inherited generational wealth; she is self-made (whether you agree with her methods or not), and she pushes back against privilege and prejudice whenever possible. Though she does marry the blue blood boy in the end, she doesn't choose him for his wealth. In some ways, she chooses him in spite of it. I like to think Kat will go on to do exactly as Ethan says near the book's conclusion, "Be my ally, my *friend*, from the inside. God knows, we could use some forward thinkers in here to freshen up the place."

Despite her strength and tenacity, Kat is far from a perfect character. For much of the novel, she is blinded by love, sliding down the slippery and insidious slope that hallmarks many unhealthy relationships. Abuse can take many forms, be they mental, emotional, or physical, and it often begins not with a shout, but with a whisper. If you or someone you know needs help navigating a love that has twisted into something unrecognizable, please call 1-800-799-SAFE (7233) to speak with someone who can help. Love should always be a safe space.

Despite not setting out to write a historical novel, write one I did! I went down the rabbit hole of internet and travel-guided research to the best of my ability. Any errors contained within are my own. It is a true challenge to blend history and fiction, and I hope this author's note has illuminated how I navigated my decisions. While I tried to stay true to the setting and historical time period, I made a few deliberate anachronistic choices to create a world twenty-first century readers would want to inhabit.

Kat is a heroine some might call "ahead of her time," but women like her have always been out there. They just aren't the ones the history books often remember. History is written by the victors, the ones with yachts to access private islands and craft legislation that steers our nation. I took great pleasure in watching an underdog like Katarina Quinn infiltrate such an elite group and take it by storm. She had more than a few things to say, and it was an absolute delight to hear her voice in my head during the evolution of this manuscript. Kat has been mine for so many years, and now, dear reader, her story is yours.

Acknowledgements

This has not been a journey of weeks or months. Not of a single year or even two. This story, these acknowledgments, they are the stuff of quiet dreams built over a decade.

I have to start with Paulette Kennedy, brilliant mentor turned treasured friend. Paulette, you were the first to pull this book out of a slush pile. The first to tell me I had something special—a voice. Thank you for teaching me how to use it, both on and off the page. You are my touchstone in the wild world of publishing. When I grow up, you are who I hope to be.

To Jess Armstrong, who took my hand early on and showed me the way. Who wrote the most stunning blurb for this book, a blurb that belonged nowhere but the front cover. Thank you for your beautiful words, Jess. I hope we continue destroying one another's TBR piles for years to come.

Erin Langston, shall I count the ways? You are a powerful force for good in the indie romance community, a real-life fairy godmother. When I first told you I might go rogue like Nate (aka indie), you were my champion supporter. Thank you for talking me off the ledge on the hardest days and being so generous with your wisdom. Your words on the page inspire me. Your friendship off the page uplifts me.

Christie Curry and Katrin Dreessen-Engler...I will not cry. I will *not*. The two of you have been on the ground floor of this operation for years. You've seen every twist and turn, and you never lost faith, even on the days I lost it in myself. You've read every word of this book (more than once), and your fingerprints are all over this story. I couldn't ask for a better pair of critique partners, and I don't know how I got through my days before our group chat. Or without your screaming words of encouragement in the margins of my drafting docs. Never leave me!

This story has existed in many iterations, and it would never have crossed the finish line without the keen insights of my beta readers—Kimberly Lynn Hanson, Maren Jenner, Celine Oliver, Briana Newstead, Demri Redmon, and Rhiannon Bloss. A huge thank you to Hannah Sharpe as well, who read this story as a beta for a publisher and convinced them immediately this book *had* to be on shelves. And to the SF 2.0 and Write-Hive Mentee Discords—the big wide world is full of so many talented and passionate writers, it is a privilege to share space with you all.

My endless gratitude to my editor, Rachel Shipp, who polished my words to a shine and keyed seamlessly into Kat's voice, gifting the world one of my favorite cheeky lines in the whole book, "A Kat-arina if you will." My immense thanks as well to my sharpshooter of a proofreader, Rachel Fitzjames. Nothing escapes you and thank goodness for that! You are the reason I was able to sleep (albeit fitfully) in the weeks leading up to release.

For creating the book cover of my dreams—Austin Drake. It never felt more real than the moment you pinged me with your initial sketch. It is a dream to have Kat and Matt (and our shared love, Savannah) drawn by your hand on my cover.

To my closest friends—Alexandra, Brooke, Erica, and Johanna. All of whom, when I low-key casual dropped the "oh by the way...I wrote a book" bombshell, didn't bat a single eye. Just replied with a (relatively) unsurprised, "Well, of course you did. And I bet it's fantastic." You all believed in the dream before I even had it. Likewise for my anesthesia girlies, Trisha and Kelsey. A little more shocked, sure, but absolutely relentless with your love and support.

For *my* Royals, Anna, Ashley, Meghan, and Natalie...turns out I wasn't only studying in those dorm rooms we shared! Now the rest of the world knows our college secret: a pack of wolves call themselves Royals.

For my family. Full stop.

My mother, for taking me to the library multiple times a month, lugging heavy bags *stuffed* with books to feed my impossibly voracious reading appetite. Somewhere amidst all those trips, a lifelong love of storytelling was born.

My father, for telling me when he looks at our living room couch, he still sees me there—twelve years old, Christmas morning, devouring my favorite gift under the tree...a book.

My brother, for going first and paving the way. Teaching me one of the most important lessons in this very book: love always leads with kindness.

Bear, for making me close the laptop, step away from the manuscript, and go for a walk.

And finally, for my husband. The man who has held my heart in his hands since we were eighteen years old. Now I truly am going to cry...

Scott, if I know anything at all about love, it is only so because of you. If I love romance novels the most (and I do), it is only because they remind me, endlessly, of you. I am the shadow, and you are the light. The two can't be separated; one cannot exist without the other. I believe in myself because you believe in me. And this dream, the biggest one...you believed from the very start.

"Very, very rarely is our first love our final love. Or even our truest love."
But if it is...
Scott, darling, it looks like us.

Looking for more of your favorite characters...?

Sign up for Lindsay's newsletter and receive a free Savannah Royals
BONUS EPILOGUE, told from Matthew's point of view.

https://www.lindsaybarrettbooks.com/newsletter

ALSO BY LINDSAY BARRETT

THE DRAVENHEARST BRIDES

ABOUT THE AUTHOR

Lindsay Barrett is a Maggie and RWA award-winning author who crafts dark stories with lots of kissing. An avid world traveler, most of Lindsay's writing inspiration comes from perpetual wanderlust. When she isn't snowshoeing atop glaciers in Alaska, drinking bourbon in Kentucky, or binge eating tapas in Spain, she can be found in her home state of Maryland, where she lives with her husband and their tiny titan (read: prince) of a rescue dog.